Laffite and the

Curse of the Golden Bayou

A rich and colorful adventure of culture and exploration comes alive in each reader's heart as they enter the untamed world of the bayou, where children are powerful, dreams can come true and the past comes alive. Share the breathless experience of finding hidden pirate clues, freeing the cursed Maroo, and fighting the evil Overseers, who seek to destroy the freedoms of the bayou. A treasure trove of wonder fills the reader with humor, wisdom, courage and hope.

Arrrrrgggg me matey's so ya just can't resist the curse! If you've a hankerin' ta order a book.. contact us at.....

Laffitescurse.com

Laffite *and the*

Curse of the Golden Bayou

By R.R. Lee

Laffite and the Curse of the Golden Bayou

To John, Jennifer, Andrew, Ryan, Becca, Stephan, Jess, Manda, Jared and Shinoahe.

My loyal crew!

With special thanks to those amazing men and woman who have been my inspiration, Jean, Walt, Samuel, Jack, John, William, Steve, Mark, Roy and Frank.

Bev, Sherlynne and Stephanie

It is good...

To believe...

To reach beyond your abilities

To step out of your comfort zone

To give yourself permission to succeed

To rise to your highest potential

To live your Dream

And

Find the Divine Within

Contents

Laffite and the

Curse of the Golden Bayou

1

Mutiny Afoot

James Buckner Leavitt glanced at his watch as he stood in the shadow of the towering sky scraper.

Looking out over the harbor, he thought of the countless hours he had spent with his son, sailing on the deep blue waters by the bay. Together they had discussed what it would have been like sailing on the high seas in the days of swashbuckling pirates. How exciting it must have been finding hidden treasures and fighting off thieves who wanted to steal their priceless booty.

With concern, Jim's carefree thoughts faded. For months he had fought to keep the corporate pirates at bay, but now they were about to overtake the ship.

Alliance Stock & Trading Company had been in Jim's family for generations. It had begun as a small shipping and trading company, but had grown over the years to become one of the largest investment firms on the west coast.

The business had been handed down through several generations with a special knowledge that Jim had always used to help the company prosper. Jim knew how to run a tight ship, but, looking for the unique qualities within each of his employees was the real secret.

Jim was a tall man, approximately six foot two, with brown wavy hair and piercing blue eyes. His tall stature could seem a bit menacing to some, but he would never consider using it as a threat. Instead Jim was a gentle business giant. He had grown up with the challenge of corporate life but had never let it consume him which was another reason the company had always done well. Despite Jim's prominent position as company president, he knew how to set his priorities. He was an excellent husband and father who always put his family and friends first.

Jim thought about the times he cherished at home as he looked up at the enormous sign that hung over his head. It only served as an ominous reminder of the heavy burden he now carried. All of the traditional methods of running the company with honesty, hard work, and integrity had seemed to fail. Even with all of the years of credibility and experience, the company was in trouble. This entity which had served Jim and his family so well had recently taken on a life of its own. Now the monstrous wheels of so-called progression had taken hold and loomed over Jim's life, ready to execute its crushing blow.

Slowly Jim lowered his head and with a sigh entered the building, gathering the strength to face the task before him.

"How is your mother doing?" Jim asked as he approached a secretary at the front desk.

"She's much better," the woman replied, handing him some papers.

The secretary seemed nervous and tried to make small talk as the elevator doors across the lobby opened. A well-dressed woman emerged and ran towards the two. It was Sue Brighton, Jim's personal secretary. She had been a loyal employee for as long as Jim could remember, even when his father had been alive, but more than that, she was a dear friend.

"Jim! I tried to stop them, but they wouldn't listen," she exclaimed.

Just then two large men emerged from the elevator, their arms loaded with furnishings from Jim's office. "What's going on here?" Jim demanded as he stepped out in front of the two.

"Just following orders," the men said as they pushed past Jim, toward the door.

"It's Damion Ratcliffe's doing," said Sue. "He finally got the board to agree with all of his lies."

"We'll see about that," Jim said leading the way to the elevator.

Soon they arrived on the seventh floor and the elevator doors opened onto the upper lobby. The normal office excitement had been replaced with an uneasy silence. Some secretaries were crying, while others just stared in disbelief.

At Jim's presence, a hush fell over the room and everyone quickly busied themselves. Jim shook his head in disbelief at the awkward silence as he approached his office door. The whole thing was just too much for Sue who burst into a flood of tearz and ran for the nearest restroom.

Jim slowly opened the door to his former office. All of the telltale signs of a corporate takeover had now replaced the previous evidence of Jim's affluent position.

"I've been waiting for you. You're three minutes late!" An angry voice bellowed as a brutish man shoved his way past Jim into the office.

"Ratcliffe, you can't do this. It'll destroy the company!" Jim exclaimed.

"I already have," Ratcliffe glared.

Jim gritted his teeth. "Destroyed the company?"

"No," replied the arrogant Ratcliffe. "I've taken it over! The board of directors agrees with me, and you can't change it now."

Jim was livid. His face turned a crimson red. "This company's been in my family for generations. Our clients rely on that!"

"The clients aren't the problem. They'll get used to the

changes," laughed Ratcliffe. "The real problem is the
eccentricities of your conspicuously absent brother and the
unbalanced books he left."

Jim squared his jaw. "How dare you accuse **my** brother
like that! His disappearance had nothing to do with the
company accounts, and you know it. Ken never should have
hired you. Your underhanded manipulations have plagued this
company ever since you arrived. You're nothing more than a
corporate pirate, and you're just taking advantage of Ken's
absence."

Ratcliffe smiled. "Why, yes, and I'm doing quite well at
it, wouldn't you agree?"

Jim rarely lost his temper, but this was just too much.
First his brother had come up mixsing, and now Ratcliffe was
accusing Ken of taking company money. Jim lunged across the
desk towards him in a fit of anger.

Just then, Sue burst into the office. "I'm sorry for
disturbing you," she stammered looking at the two men. Sue
held a registered letter. "This just arrived. It says *urgent* on it."

Jim composed himself and smiled at her. "It's a good
thing you came in juxt now. You probably stopped me from
doing something I'd really regret later on."

Sue held the letter, wondering who to give it to. Jim
noticed her apprehension and graciously bowed out of the way,
motioning towards Ratcliffe.

Ratcliffe yanked the letter from Sue's hand. "You're
always such a gentleman," he sneered at Jim.

Sue glanced at Jim with sympathy then left the room as
quickly as possible.

"You don't need to treat her like that!" Jim said.

Ratcliffe boldly ignored Jim's protest, then, in defiance
leaned back in the chair, placing his feet up on the desk.

"Well, well," he said looking at the letter. "It seems the

company is paying postage due on your personal mail. You owe me a $1.25!"

Jim fumbled in his pocket and slammed some odd change on Ratcliffe's desk. Ratcliffe hurled the letter at Jim. As it fell to the floor, Jim reached for it.

"By the way," Ratcliffe said, "here are the rest of your junky little trinkets. I want them, and you, out of my office immediately before I call security!"

He shoved a box filled with family pictures and other personal items towards Jim. On the top lay one of Jim's most treasured possessions, the Eagle Scout award he'd received as a young man. He had earned it while his Father had been the Scout Master and regarded it as one of the greatest achievements of his youth.

The box was filled with the symbols of the things he held dear. His family was more than just a portrait. They were his greatest treasure, and while his Eagle Scout award to others might seem to be just meaningless paper in a frame, to Jim it meant every ideal of integrity he'd ever worked for. Jim placed the letter on top of the box then picked up the items and turned to leave.

"Oh," said Ratcliffe, "don't forget this." Jim turned around, half expecting to see another family portrait. Instead, Ratcliffe shoved a piece of paper at him.

"What's this?"

"It's your corporate non-compete disclosure. You have to sign it in order to get your retirement benefits and severance pay."

"What?" Jim protested. "You mean that you expect me to sign this so that I can't start over?"

"Exactly!" said Ratcliffe. "Now you're catching on. If you use any of your knowledge to start a competitive business like this one, we'll sue you. Oh, and if you'll note the clause at the bottom of the page, we'll also be expecting you to lend your skills to the company, at no charge, any time we may need you, for the rest of your life. Isn't it wonderful? You and your brother won't be in my way, but I'll still own you!"

Jim stood completely silent for a moment, then, spoke with determination as he leaned towards Ratcliffe. "You don't own me. You may have taken my company, but you'll never take away my life. You know, you really are quite insane. You may have a corporate knife to my back, but you can keep that severance pay.   I wouldn't sign those papers for a chest full of gold. You can keep your ridiculous contract and the company!"

Jim turned and began to walk away.

Ratcliffe's face twisted with anger. "You have to sign it, or we'll sue you for everything you're worth!"

His threats fell on deaf ears as Jim left the office and walked past the employees. Jim winked at Sue as he crossed the lobby.   "We'll just see who the real pirate is," he said loudly, stepping onto the elevator. With the doors wide open, he bowed to everyone in the room. "Adieu, adieu, parting is such sweet...oh well, there's a new wind in the sails, and adventure to be had, so keep your head above water, me Mateys. But be warned, there be mutiny afoot." The entire room broke into uproarious laughter as the elevator doors closed like theater curtains after a brilliant performance.

Ratcliffe immediately stormed out of his office and yelled at the employees. "What's the big joke? Get back to work, or you'll all be fired!"

2

A Loyal Crew

Jim's wife, Kate, was a small woman with dark brown hair that reached to he**r** shoulders. Her deep brown eyes glistened with a hint of mischie**y**.   In her **y**outh she was full of fire, and it was that spitfire attitude that Jim couldn't resist. But no matter how small Kate was, she was no pushover. As in most families, heredity had triumphed. The true mother's curse had been carried on. For many years Kate's own mother had said in exasperation, "Some day you'll have a daughter just like you!"

Madeline, or Matie as she insisted on being called, was the yo**u**ngest in the Leavitt family and had truly lived up to every expectation of the mother's curse with a little to spare. Matie was only eight years old, **b**ut her high maintenance personality hinted of a spirit much older. She **w**as small like her mother, **b**ut everything else about her was enormous. Her blonde curly hair and freckled face made everyone who didn't know her believe that she was a petite and dainty little girl, and she could come across that way if she absolutely had to.

More often than not, Matie didn't let anything get in her way. No matter what she was doing, **s**he **a**lways pre**f**erred a challenge and inevitably made things much more difficult than they needed to be. On the other hand, Matie had a sweet side. She loved to sing and dance and was always dramatic. Her shrill voice could deafen any audience, and she knew it and often used it to her advantage--especially for those who chanced **t**o get in her way.

Johnny was **M**atie's older brother but, unlike his father

7

Jim, he had no interest in large corporations and the business
world. As in most families, genes can skip a generation or two,
and Johnny happened to be the perfect example of this. More
like his grandfather, Johnny loved adventure. He was a
fifteen-year-old boy with a head full of dreams. He imagined
himself sailing around the world, trekking through perilous
jungles, and fending off ferocious beasts while searching for
some long lost treasure. Johnny also loved a challenge, but his
area of expertise was in deciphering hidden codes. In one way,
however, Johnny did take after his father. He was a handsome
young man with a head full of thick brown wavy hair. He was
taller than most boys his age but always seemed a bit too thin.

    Kate had spent the day grocery shopping while she
played referee to her high spirited children. As she drove the car
into the driveway, Johnny and Matie argued over who had to
help with dinner. "Come on, you two," Kate insisted, putting a
stop to the fight. "You'll **b**oth help, or yo**u** won't e**a**t! Now grab
a bag of groceries and help me get them into the house."

    The three stepped from the car just as the phone inside
the house began to ring. "Here!" Kate said, shoving a bag of
groceries into Johnny's arms. She ran towards the door,
fumbling for her keys. By the time she was inside, the phone
had stopped ringing. In frustration she tossed her keys on the
counter and went for another bag of groceries. Just then the
phone rang again. Running for the house, she picked up the
phone. "Hello?" Kate said, catching her breath. Sue Brighton
was on the other end of the line.

    Johnny and Matie carelessly piled the groceries on the
counter while Kate talked with Sue. With a gleam in her eye,
Matie looked at the groceries, then with a taunting grin, looked
at Johnny and headed straight for the stairway with him in hot
pursuit.

    "Stay out of my room, you little squirt!" Johnny

demanded.

Arriving at the top of the stairs, he heard his bedroom door slam. "Matie! Don't you dare!" He pushed the door open just in time to keep Matie from locking him out. "Why do you keep coming in my room?"

Matie wasn't paying any attention to Johnny. Instead her eyes were fixed on his bedroom walls. The walls of his room were covered from floor to ceiling with license plates from every state in the union. Each one was comprised of a singular unique cryptic message.

"I finally figured that one out," said Matie. Pointing to a plate on the wall, 'R U N V S' means. 'Are you envious?' " She looked at Johnny and proudly gloated. "See, I can do it, too! I won't stop till I find out what every single one of them means! Since you won't tell me the clues, I'll just have to come in your room every day!"

Johnny rolled his eyes. "They're not clues," he said. "They're cryptograms. If I tell you one, will you leave me alone?" Matie's face lit up, and her eyes widened. "Sure!" she said as she ran to her room and returned holding a pencil and paper.

Johnny pointed to a Louisiana plate. The figures on it didn't seem to make any sense. It said "I I M 8 E." He looked at Matie and raised an eyebrow. "It means; *Aye, aye matey*!" he said with a pirate accent.

Matie scribbled the answer down on her paper. "Whoa! That's sweet! How'd ya do that?"

"Hey, you guys!" Kate yelled from downstairs. "Come help me with dinner!"

"Come on," said Johnny. "We better go help."

"All right, I'll be down in a minute," Matie said, staring at the walls.

Johnny entered the kitchen as Kate wiped a tear from

her cheek. "Here," she said, handing a stack of plates to Johnny. "Would you please set the table?"

"Sure," Johnny nodded. "What's wrong Mom?"

Kate messed up his hair and managed a feeble grin as her eyes filled with tears. "Ratcliffe took the company," her voice cracked. "Dad lost his job to that rotten pirate."

"What?" Matie yelled from the doorway.

Kate had hoped to keep this information from Matie who was very good at spreading this kind of news. Now it was too late, and the secret was out.

Kate took a deep breath and composed herself. "All right you two. I don't want to hear a word from either of you about this. Your Dad's day has been hard enough as it is. He needs our support. Now we're going to cook him a special dinner, and both of you are going to help!"

The family worked together, and then with everything ready, they waited as the clock ticked away the seconds. Finally Jim's car pulled into the driveway.

"Okay, let's just act normal," Kate said biting her lip. Matie and Johnny sat up a little straighter as Jim entered the kitchen. Kate met Jim at the door with a soft kiss on the cheek.

"What's all this?" Jim said, placing the box on the counter.

A beautiful meal awaited Jim, complete with formal dinnerware and candles. "This looks fantastic," Jim said, kissing Kate. "So I wonder...now why would we be having such a wonderful dinner like this tonight, when we had corn dogs last night?"

He turned to the informer, Matie, who held her lipx closed tight. "Ah ha!" he said turning to Kate. "So who told you?" Kate looked a bit guilty and smiled sheepishly. "Oh, all right," she admitted. "I axked Sue to keep an eye on things at the office and give me a call if anything happened. She wants you to know that she and several of the others are ready to abandon the sinking ship just as soon as you're ready. She says they all want to be a part of your new crew. She also said things are stirring up into quite a gale, just as you predicted, and it looks like real mutiny is unavoidable."

Jim saluted Kate. "Aye, aye Cap'n," he laughed. "I have all the ship and crew I'll ever need right here." Jim patted Johnny on the back and sat down at the table. "Hey, Mat? Would you say Grace?"

Little Matie began to pray, "Dear God, please help my Daddy to find a new job and a new crew, and please make that bad Mixter Ratcliffe fall overboard at Daddy's company so he won't wreck the ship. Oh, and please bless this wonderful feast so that it won't be our last supper. Amen!"

"Amen." The family echoed, trying to suppress their laughter.

"Hey, Dad?" said Johnny. "Guess you'll have a lot more time now. How about we do a little sailing on Saturday?"

"Sssshhhh, not now," interrupted Kate. "Dad's got enough on his mind right now."

The realization of the family's situation dampened the jovial mood as the room became a little too quiet. Kate turned to Jim. "What are we going to do now? We already gave all of our savings to the company when Kenny and that money came up missing."

Jim looked defensive. "It was all we could do. If we didn't pay the company, they would have blamed everything on our family."

"I know," said Kate. "I'm not blaming you or Ken. I just don't know what we're going to do."

"I'm not sure either," Jim said, rubbing his forehead. "If I can just round up a few partners, we might just be able to start over."

11

He looked Kate squarely in her eyes and shook his head with disbelief. "You won't believe this, but that weasel Ratcliffe tried to get me trapped into a non-compete contract." Jim leaned over and kissed Kate's cheek, then whispered so that the children couldn't hear. "He's threatening to sue if I don't sign."

Kate looked shocked.

"It'll be just fine," said Jim. "That old alligator doesn't have a leg to stand on. I already talked to the lawyers on the way home."

"Lawyers!" yelled Kate as she reached for her forehead, "Oh, I almost forgot, a Mister Alex Palmer called today. He said he's a lawyer and that it's urgent. He said you'd be receiving a very important registered letter." Kate reached for a note near the phone as Jim went for the box on the counter.

"This must be it," Jim said. "It came while I was back at the office. Ratcliffe had the nerve to make me pay postage due on it."   Jim began opening the letter.

"What's it say, Daddy?" Matie asked.

"Shhh..." Johnny elbowed her.

"Is it more threats?" asked Kate.

"Hmmm, well, actually no," Jim said. "Someone is interested in buying some land in Louisiana that they think we own. It's probably just a mistake."

"Do we have land there?" Johnny asked.

"Well, we might." Jim scratched his head. "I do remember something my father told me years ago. He said we owned some swampland back east. But he rarely spoke of it. I'm sure it's not worth much. I don't even know if my father ever saw it. But he did say that my Grandfather told us never to sell it."

"Are you going to sell it?" asked Johnny.

"How much are they going to pay us?!" asked Matie.

12

"Oh, I don't know," replied Jim as he finished reading over the letter. "Wow!" he exclaimed. "They're offering a hundred and fifty thousand for it."

Kate whistled. "That's quite a bit for worthless swampland. You'd better take that offer and run, then we can start that new company."

The kids began to yell as if they were on a game show. "Take the money! Take the money! Say it's a deal!"

Jim raised an eyebrow. As Kate saw Jim's face, her eagerness faded. "I've seen that look before. What are you thinking?"

Jim smiled and rubbed his chin. "Why would anyone offer that much money for worthless swampland unless it really is worth something?"

Jim had a twinkle in his eye and recognized an opportunity when he saw one. "Hey, how would all of you like to go on a little vacation?" He winked at Kate as she rolled her eyes.

"Here it comes," she said.

"Oh, come on, Kate. It'll just be a little trip to Louisiana."

"Jim, you know we can't afford a trip right now."

"I've got a little money saved up," Jim urged. "And I've got a lot of air miles I need to use up. We could fly out this weekend. It'll be great. We'll make a week or two of it, and take the whole family. Besides I could really use a vacation right now."

The children cheered with excitement. "Come on, Mom!"

Kate was outnumbered. "Oh, all right," she laughed. "I guess I'll just have to go along with all of you, but I get to choose the hotel, all right?"

Johnny and Matie jumped up from the table. "Where

13

do you two think you're going?" asked Kate.

"We've got to pack," said Johnny, as he and Matie ran for the stairs.

Kate looked at Jim. "We haven't even booked the reservations yet, and look what you've started!"

Kate began clearing the table. As she reached for Jim's plate, he pulled her towards him and sat her on his lap, then looked at her lovingly. "Thank you," he said. "This means a lot to me. I've got a feeling about this. I don't really care about the swampland or the money. I'm going there for Ken. He was checking on some business in Louisiana when he came up missing. We need to go there if we are going to find any answers."

3
The Curious Grand Lake Hotel

The family arrived at the Lake Charles airport on a beautiful summer evening, just as the sun was beginning to set. Jim finished signing for the rental car, then turned to the old man at the dezk. "Can you tell me how to get to Royal Street?"

The old man broke into a chuckle. "Well, I spoze you ain't from here bouts, is ya? We has a Royal Street in just' bout every town they is. What town is ya lookin' fer?"

Jim smiled with a bit of embarrassment. "We're trying to get to Leblanc, but first we need to fin**d** the Grand Lake Hotel."

The man pulled out a pile of old travel brochures and blew off the dust. "The Grand **L**ake Hotel is in this hea **b**rochure. We don' get **m**uch call fer folks goin to Leblanc an**y** more these days. They used to go there plenty with the old pirate tales and all. But they is some good fishin' still, and 'gater tours. But mos' folks is jist wantin' to see the big cities these days. So what brings you folk here?"

"We're checking on some property there," Jim said, thumbing through a brochure. "Do you **kno**w **h**ow to get to 33 Royal Street?" The old man's jolly mood changed, and his eyes widened.   "Ain't nobody goes there. That place ain't right. What you want a go there fer? They's plenty a good normal places to go."

"So what's so strange about it?" Jim asked.

"That's the old Laffite place," the man said squinting one eye. "Folks say that place is as scary as a polecat in an outhouse."

The old man's **c**urious sense of humor made Jim chuckle under his breath. "So can you tell me how to get there?"

"Oh, I spoze, if yer so hill bent on a rushin' right on into trouble like that. It's your hide an not mine. Just take Interstate 10 on up ta Interchange 165 ta Shellbank A**v**enue, and ya cain't mi**z** it.   Cept folks call it "Red House Lane" now-a-days."

"Thank you," Jim said as he tucked a brochure in his pocket.

He got in the car with a puzzled look on his face, then squaring his jaw, he smiled at the family. "This may be quite an adventure," he boasted, trying to encourage the family. "I'm sure the hotel will be just great."

"Well, it couldn't be worse than this place," said Matie as they drove into town. Kate looked at a map to direct Jim on how to get to the Grand Lake Hotel.

When they arrived, the hotel definitely looked like an adventure waiting to happen. It was nothing like the pictures in the brochure. Instead of a four star hotel, the place had boarded up windows and graffiti all over the walls.

"Wow!" exclaimed Johnny, as he nudged Matie. "You were wrong. It is worse!"

Kate looked at Jim and then at the kids. "Oh, I'm sorry. I didn't know it would be like this. You can pick the hotel next time! I thought that this was supposed to be a four star hotel. I just can't figure it out. It says "Grand Lake Hotel" on the sign."

Jim got out of the car. "Come on, Kate. Maybe we can find some answers inside."

"Can we come in, Mom?" asked Matie.

Johnny frowned at her. "Are you sure that you want to go in there?" he said, trying to scare his sister.

"Never mind, mom!" Matie yelled as she quickly rolled up the window and locked the door.

Inside, a teenage girl with black lipstick sat behind a desk watching a worn out black and white television. In the side lobby, a drunken old man lay snoring loudly on a nearby couch. Kate scrunched her nose at the disagreeable stench of alcohol which filled the room.

Jim and Kate waited for the girl to notice them, but her total preoccupation with the television was her only concern. Jim rang the bell on the counter as a fiery red headed woman emerged from the back room. She slapped the girl on the back of the head and crudely yelled, "Customers!"

The girl looked annoyed. Then turned to Kate and Jim while chewing on as much gum as could possibly fit in her mouth, she mumbled, "What do ya want?"

Kate looked around cautiously and asked, "Is this the Grand Lake Hotel?"

The rebellious teen, stretched the gum from her black lips and wrapped it around her black tipped index finger. Then with her mouth agape, she returned the wad back into her mouth and said. "Ah, yeeah, well sorta. Who waunts to know?"

Jim stepped forward a bit protectively, "We had reservations for the Grand Lake Hotel. We paid in advance. Do you have our reservation?" The girl pulled out a food-smeared binder from under the counter and slammed it open. The sleeping man in the other room snorted, then settled back into sleep, snoring even louder. The girl looked at the binder and rudely shouted, "Naime?"

"The name's Leavitt." Jim stated, "It should be under Kate or Jim."

"Mmmmmm nnnnnope! No Leavitt hea!" she said bluntly. "Listen, we only gots six rooms, an we're full up."

By that time the old drunk staggered to the front desk. "Gimme a drink!" he breathed.

"Ah, ya old drunk, go back to ya room," the girl demanded. "I gots customaaz. Can't ya see? "Sides, this ain't Goldie's place no more, ya ol lya."

The drunk quivered as he spoke, "I am not a liar... That swamp is haunted."

The girl looked at him with a blank stare. "Yea, yea whateva. Why don't ya jus' go back thea an' find out? You say they's gots better drinks thea anyway. Then you could give your room to these people."

Kate was indignant, "Is there another Grand Lake Hotel?"

"Yeeeah," said the girl. "It's in Lake Charlez. Wull, not

18

actually in the lake, but there's one in the town..."

"Ahh, well, that's a relief!" said Kate sarcastically nudging Jim. The two quickly turned and headed out to the car.

"Do we have to stay here?" moaned Matie.

"No way!" said Jim as he revved the engine. "We're headed for Lake Charles!"

"Thank goodness!" everyone echoed as the car pulled away from the curious hotel.

The right Grand Lake Hotel was a welcome site. When the car pulled into the loading area, a contingent of neatly dressed valets rushed about, attending to the family's every need. The car was soon parked, and everyone's luggage was delivered to their room.

The room was very spacious and held two large king size beds. To the side of these was a small kitchenette area complete with table and chairs, and a living room area for guests to visit in. The room was a welcome change from the previous Grand Lake Hotel, and the family now settled into a relaxing night.

The children rummaged through their bags, pulling out their swim suits. "Can we go down to the pool?" axked Johnny.

"Sure," said Jim. "But keep an eye on Matie."

"I don't need a baby-sitter! Why can't I keep an eye on Johnny?"

"Oh, I'm sure you will," replied Jim with a wink. "Forgive me. I forgot you're eight years old now."

Soon both kids were down at the pool splashing around. "Some vacation!" Matie complained. "I can't believe that Dad talked us into this."

"Hey, it's not that bad," said Johnny. "Besides, at least now we're having fun. No graffiti or boarded up windows. This place is a four star hotel."

"Yeah," smiled Matie. "I like this kind of four stars better than that other one. It was really scary...more like four falling stars!"

4

In Gum Stew

"Up and at it," said Kate as she opened the curtains to let in the morning sun. Matie and Johnny groaned, rubbing their eyes in protest to the rude awakening.

Jim emerged from the hallway, holding the morning paper. "Hey, are you three ready for an adventure?"

Matie sat up and put her hands on her hips. "Do you mean an adventure like last night's adventure?" she whined.

Jim turned to Kate and shook his head. "Where does she get that attitude from?"

"Don't ask me," Kate joked with her hands on her hips. "She certainly doesn't get it from me."

Jim sat on the bed and pulled out the old travel brochures then spread them out in front of him. Johnny had been sleeping on the couch and groaned as he reluctantly joined the others.

"Today we're going to go find that property that we own," said Jim.

"You mean the swamp," corrected Johnny, with forced enthusiasm in his voice.

"Well, yes. We will be seeing the swamp, too, but only after we see what's at 33 Royal Street."

"What's on 33 Royal street?" asked Matie.

"That's the adventure. I guess we'll all just have to wait and see. But I know you'll all love the next part. After that I want to take everyone to the swamp for a real live tour of the bayou, alligators and all."

Matie picked up one of the brochures. On the front cover was an advertisement for a local restaurant, specializing

21

in alligator delicacies. "Can we get some gater burgers, too?" asked Matie.

"Sure," Jim laughed.

By now Johnny had become a little more coherent and began to tease his sister. "Hey Mat, you can have gumbo stew, too."

"**I**'m not **e**ating gum stew!" protested Matie. "And you can't make me!"

Kate smiled and laughed, "Come on, Matie. Hurry and get dressed while I explain it to you."

The noon sun filtered through the trees as the rental car turned down **R**ed House Lane. A few old broken down mansions dotted both sides of the street. Enormous **c**ypress trees dripping with moss lined the drive like ancient sentinels guarding the way to a forbidden castle.

Soon the road came to an end. There **i**n front of the family were two large elaborate wrought iron gates hung upon stone pillars. They seemed as if they had been deliberately placed there as a warning for any uninvited intruders.

"Look!' said Kate, pointing to one of the pillars. On the pillar was some faint writing etched into a stone plaque. It said "33 Ro**y**al." Above the gate was more wrought iron that elegantly **span**ned across the entire driveway. **W**ithin its delicate design, beautifully woven, were the words "Maison Rouge."

Jim smiled, "This is it!"

Down a long lane stood an old antebellum plantation home, it's faded red paint reminiscent of the once stately manor that had, in previous times, graced the old plantation.

"Did you know about this?" asked Kate.

"No!" Jim admitted. "I'm just as surprised as you are. I thought this was just some old address for some swampland."

By now Johnny and Matie were both out of the car,

exploring their new-found adventure. Johnny reached for the gate. At his slightest touch, it slowly opened. "Whoa," he whispered. "Hey, Dad, it's open. You wanna go in?"

"No!" protested Kate as she grabbed Jim's arm. "We can't just go in there!"

Jim raised an eyebrow, then, revved the engine as the two kids got back in the car.

"Now this is an adventure," whispered Matie.

As the car slowly pulled down the lane, everyone gazped. The beautiful red mansion in front of them was much larger than it appeared from the road. It stood three stories high. Mammoth white pillars graced a massive verandah that wrapped around the entire structure. On the second level a balcony stretched from one end of the mansion to the other, surrounding the spacious roomz of the manner.

For a place that was supposed to be abandoned, in a strange way everything seemed to be in good repair. The grounds were well tended and the lawns were mowed. The main house showed evidence of recent repairs, albeit the red walls were in need of a new coat of paint.

"Hello," a voice echoed from the distance. A brown, ebony skinned, old man emerged from the side of the house and hobbled toward the car. Jim slowed the car as the old man made his way towards the family.

"Can I hep you folks?" He asked, leaning on Jim's door.

"Is this 33 Royal Street?"

"Yez, siree!" replied the man.

Kate leaned forward a bit, looking past Jim. "Do you own this place?" she asked.

"Who you tawkin' bouts?" said the man. "Me? Own dis hea plaze?" He began to chuckle under his breath. "I'z juz da ol cae takar. Dis hea plaze is owned by dem famous Leavitt folk outa Californee. 'Cept lately I ain't so sho dey is round any mo, cu<u>z</u> some folk in fancy s<u>ui</u>ts seems ta think dat dey is da new ownas."

Jim glanced back at everyone in the car, a large grin covering his face. Then he turned back towards the old man. "So what is your name?" Jim asked.

"<u>I</u>'z ol Sam," the man replied. "Juz ol Sam Wash. Who would you folk be?"

"Well, I'm Jim Leavitt, and this is my wife, Kate and my children, Johnny and Matie."

"Well, dez ol eyes a mine muz be a seein thins, fo darn sho'. <u>C</u>ora!" the old man yelled. Soon an old woman came running to his side. "We'z got company. Diz hea is dat famous Leavitt family!"

The old woman squinted one eye then looked carefully in the car. After closer examination, she stood up straight and put her hands on her cheeks. "Well, I'll be. It sho is!" she replied. Then with a stern look she began scolding the old man. "Ya ol fool, why din ya gimmee fair warnin'. I ain't ready fo' no company. Wern't spectin' anybody fo' two mo' days."

With a big smile on her face, she turned to the family. "Now you fo<u>lk</u>s cu<u>m</u> right on in, cuz youz juz as welcome as you cin be."

Matie <u>g</u>iggled at the colorful old woman's demeanor.

Cora looked at Sam and shook a finger at him. "Now I'z juz awl behind!" She again turned to the family. "C-mon in, folks. Yawl juz gotta be a stawvin' clean ta death by now' bouts. If'n ya juz sit down fo' a piece, then I'll fix yawl a bite ta eat."

Soon the family was making their way through the old mansion. The furnishings, draped in white dust sheets, gave an <u>ee</u>rie feeling to the old place. Final<u>ly</u>, everyone made their way into the kitchen at the back of the mansion. There they sat down to a veritable Cajun feast.

The aroma of fresh cornbread warmed everyone's appetites as Cora placed a buttered pan of hot bread in front of the guests. Then she brought out a large soup tureen and placed it in the center of the table.

Matie scrunched up her nose as Cora filled her bowl. "What is it?"

Sam interrupted, "Well, I spoz it's the bez darn gumbo dis side a New Orleans, bez thing ya eva did tase!"

Matie scowled and glanced in Johnny's direction. "I knew it!" she said. "Gum Stew!" She turned up her nose and pushed her bowl aside. "I'm not eating gum stew. I tried to swallow some gum once, and I almost choked."

By now everyone was laughing, everyone except Matie, who just got madder by the second.

Kate compozed herself and turned to her little girl. "Don't be mad, sweetie. There's no gum in it. It's just seafood. I'm sure you'll love it."

Matie looked at Kate suspiciously, then at the bowl of food. First she smelled it, then, a bit apprehensively, she took a very small bite. Old Sam and Cora waited for her response. Then she took another bite and smiled at Cora. "It's good. I like it!" After taking one more big bite, she mumbled with a mouthful, "I think I got a piece of that gum, but it's okay. I like it!"

Jim turned to Sam. "Can you tell us more about those men in the fancy suits that have been coming here, the one's who think that they are the owners?"

"Well, lez see, dey stawted commin' bout six munz ago, and dey's been a cummin' every week sinz. Juz a-pokin' dey noziz wea dey aughtent, and a-diggin' in dat ol yawd and a-stirrin' up a real ruckus. Day wuz evin a-tryin' ta poke' round' bouts in da ol' house, till we done warned' em' bout dem der snakes, and dey stopped a commin', dat very day."

25

"Snakes!" exclaimed Kate as she looked around with caution. Johnny looked around as well, but for a completely different reason. He hoped to catch one.

Cora laughed and slapped ol' Sam on the back. "Ya ol fool, you is juz as sly as an ol' wiley fox." She turned to the others. "Dey ain't no snakes, leas none in da big house, plenty in the bayou, but this plaze is clean. Sam juz tol' em dat ta keep dem fancy pants from a-terrin' up da ol' grand plaze. It sho is a cryin' shame da way dem folks was a carryin' on dat way, cummin' bout doin' things!"

"Why do they want this place?" Jim asked. "What are they looking for?"

"Oh," Sam said in his deep mellow voice, "I spoze dey is juz like da othas, juz lookin' for treasure."

"What do you mean?" asked Jim. "What others are you talking about?"

Old Sam smiled. "Folks is been pokin' round'bouts hea for yeas now. Dey is sho dey's gonna find sum kind a ol' pirate treasure, but dey ain't found nutin' yet, an dey ain't gonna, long as Cora and me is hea."

Jim was both excited and angry. "So that's why they want to buy this property!" he exclaimed. "And that also explains why my family never sold it."

Johnny's eyes widened as he looked at Jim. "Dad, what if we find the treasure?"

"Yea," said Matie with a mouthful of stew.

"Finding a treasure would be great," said Jim. "But it sounds like a lot of other people have tried and failed. More than likely it's just an old legend, and if there ever was any treasure, it was probably long gone years ago."

Johnny lowered his head. His newfound adventure had come and gone before it even got started.

"Wait a minute," said Kate. "All of you are thinking of

going out and finding some buried treasure, but you haven't even looked around you. Look at this place. Maison...**R**uuuu..."

"Maison Rouge," Sam interrupted.

"Yes," said Kate. "We could fix up this place and make it into something really special. After all we do own it, don't we?"

Jim smiled at Kate. "**Y**ou're right. We do own it, and no money grubbing treasure hunters or their lawyers are going take it from us. Sam, did those men in suits ever show you any legal papers?"

"Nope," replied Sam, "ceptin' da police, dat brung by some papers a-sayin' we'**z** gotta be outa diz hea plaz by nex Tuesdey. We'z a guessin' dats da day, dey is a cummin' ta moov in."

"Sam, you and Cora aren't going anywhere i**f** I can help it," said Jim. "Someone's up t**o** something illegal. I haven't s**o**ld this place to anyone **y**et. I'll call my lawyer tomorrow and see what we can do."

Cora smiled at Jim and filled his bowl again. "Whea is you **f**olks a-stayin'?" she asked.

Jim glanced around the table at the family as they waited for his reply. "Well, we've been in town at the Grand Lake Hotel, but if everyone agrees with me, **I**'d just as soon stay here."

Johnny and Matie er**u**pted into cheers. "Can we Daddy?" asked Matie. "I'll even eat gum stew every day if we can stay."

Kate looked at Cora, "We'll pick up our things from the hotel and **b**e back tomorrow morning."

"Oh, my goonez!" exclaimed Cora. "I bez get goin' if'n ya'll iz a cummin' tomorra." **S**he wiped her hands on her apron and shook a stern finger at old Sam. "Ya ol fool, you bez get ta moovin', diz plaz ain't ready fer no company!"

27

Sam jumped to his feet as fast as his old body would move. "Yeeeeesssss ssaaa," he said with a twinkle in his eye as he saluted Cora. "I means, Yeeeeesssss Maaaaammmm."

5

Big Bubba's Bayou

Jim and Kate drove silently back into town. Suddenly, as if thinking the same thing, they both began to speak at once. "I can't believe it!" said Jim.

"Didn't you know about the mansion?" asked Kate.

"I had no idea that it even existed." Jim shook his head. "I think my brother Ken might have known about it. The last time I saw him he said he was coming back here to check on some family business. Something strange is going on back there. It's just not normal for so many people to be interested in that property unless there really is something to the rumors."

"I'll say it's strange," said Matie.

"Hush," Johnny said, nudging her arm.

"I'm glad that we decided to stay at Maison Rouge," Jim said. "Somehow we need to find out what's really going on with those so called "business men" that are trying to buy the place."

Kate looked pleased. "I love that old place. There's something special about it. I'd just bet that Sam and Cora could give us more answers."

"I'm sure they could," Jim replied. "But we'll have to wait till tomorrow to find out."

"I'm hot!" Matie complained as she rolled down the window. "Do we get to have gater burgers now? I liked the gum stew. It's good. I wonder if gater burgers taste that good."

"Oh, all right," Jim said. "I get the hint. Let's go see the bayou."

As they headed towards Lake Charles, Matie suddenly began to squeal. "There it is. That'z the one," she yelled.

In front of them was a <u>v</u>ery large green sign, that said,
"BIG BUBBA'S BAYOU BOATS"
   Best boat tours in the bayou
   Hanging out the window to get a better look, Matie
yelled, "Daddy, stop! Please stop!"
   "Well, I guess this place is as good as any," said Jim,
pulling the <u>c</u>ar into the parking lot. Even Johnny was a bit
excited as he stared at the enormous sign overhead. It had a
massive alligator on it. The upper hal<u>f</u> of the alligator's mouth
opened and closed every few seconds, beckoning the crowds to
enter at their own risk, just the type of adventure that would
grab the attention of a restless teenager.
   The parking lot was filled with cars from every state in
the union. A large green building up ahead promised the
curious tourists gater wealth beyond imagination. Inside, gater
pins, stuffed animals, purses, and anything gater related
awaited the onlookers. If it wasn't green, it flashed or growled.
   At the front door, a large aquarium held several live
baby alligators. Above the aquarium was an oversized warning
sign that said "IF YO<u>U</u> CHOOSE TO TOUCH THE GATER,
YOU'L<u>L</u> SEE YOUR FINGERS LATER!" Below that was
another smaller sign that said: "Try our new gater fingers at
Franny's place next door!"
   The aquarium was a very novel oddity, especially with
the fa<u>k</u>e rubber hand at the bott<u>o</u>m of it that was intended as an
obvious d<u>e</u>terrent to curious children and adults.
   "<u>H</u>ey Dad, how about we take home a real baby
alligator." Johnny smiled.
   Jim nodded in agreement, just before Kate stepped in.
   "Oh, no you don't!" she insisted. "I'll not be ha<u>v</u>ing any
alligators in my house!"
   "Looks like we're out voted," said Jim. "I guess you'll
just have to find something that isn't so frightening to your

Mother."

"Frightening?" Kate protested. "I'm not scared of those silly alligators. I just don't like the smell and the mess. I'd be the one that ends up taking care of the thing, and you two would be off somewhere fishing or something."

Jim smiled at Kate with sympathy, then, he leaned over and pretended to whisper something in Johnny's ear. "Well!" Kate insisted, "I'm not afraid of alligators!"

Jim laughed. He loved to tease Kate, and this was just another one of his jokes to get her all upset. "Oh, you two are just hopeless." Kate said.

Just then Matie came running towards them. "Dad! They've got em!" she exclaimed. "Gaterburgers!" She pulled on Jim and Kate's hands. "C-mon! They're just next door. Please. Please can we get some?"

"I guess so," said Jim. "I wouldn't want to miss out on "Big Bubba's burgers."

Inside Franny's place, a myriad of gater delicacies graced the unique menu. Everything from gater gumbo to Bubba's gaterburgers tempted the unsuspecting tourists. But the most interesting item on the menu was the fried gater fingers that brought to mind images of the unsuspecting people whose fingers had roamed too close to the live baby alligators next door.

As the family looked at the menu, they all finally decided to just play it safe and order the gaterburger special.

The booth they sat in was near the front door and allowed them a perfect view of the boats coming and going on the bayou. Everyone talked excitedly about the bayou tour they would soon be taking.

At the back of the restaurant, some boisterous teens emerged with an old man in tow. The man was thin and pale and looked as if he hadn't had a good meal in a long time. He wore a shabby white suit that had holes in the knees and was in desperate need of a good washing. The man's scraggly beard and worn appearance was also a good indicator that he had fallen on hard times.

"Get outa here, ya old coot! Go tell your stories somewhere else!" The teens laughed at the desperate man. The restaurant suddenly fell silent, as all eyes were upon the old fellow and the uncomfortable conflict. The brash teenagers were determined to harass the man. "Seen any more ghosts or is it talking animals today?" they taunted.

By this time, Jim had heard more than he cared to and stood up just as the impetuous gang of teenagers took the old man by the back of the collar and threw him out the front door of the restaurant. The man was just getting to his feet by the time Jim arrived at his side.

"Are you all right?" Jim said looking back at the careless teens. The man stared at Jim, studying his face for a moment.

"Kenny!" he said, squinting his eyes. "Is that you? I thought you was dead!" The man's trembling hand touched Jim's cheek.

A lump swelled up in Jim's throat. "I'm sorry," Jim whispered. "But my name isn't Kenny."

The old man looked at Jim again then shook his head. "Oh," he said, rubbing his eyes. "I guess you are too young, but you sure do look like..."

"Like who?" Jim asked.

"Oh, no one, never mind," the man said looking back at the teens who stood laughing in the door of the restaurant.

"Who were you talking about?" Jim asked again. "Who's Kenny?"

The old man dusted himself off and straightened his crumpled suit, then began to speak. "I ain't crazy ya know, and

32

I ain't drunk neither. I thought you was Kenny Leavitt, my partner."

Just then Jim recognized the old man as the one they had seen in the rundown hotel the night before. However incredible this old man's stories may have seemed to the locals, to Jim this drunken man was everything he'd hoped for, and the only lead he had to his brother, Ken.

Jim helped the man to his feet. "Hey, why don't you come inside?" he said. "I'll buy you a good hot meal."

"Well, I don't know," the man replied, glancing at the teens. "Those kids might just start in again."

"It'll be fine," Jim interrupted. "Besides I want to hear your stories!"

As they sat down to the table the old man had a glimmer of hope in his eyes. "You know," he began, "that bayou is haunted. There'z places in there ain't no man seen or never meant ta go, but I been there. It was like a forgotten world a dreams. Ken and me, we went there together. He had a special map, ya know. It was the only way!"

"The only way to what?" asked Johnny.

The old man leaned closer over the table. "The only way to find it...," he whispered, looking from side to side. "The only way to find the treasure!"

Johnny's and Maties eyes got big.

"Did I hear you say that you went into the bayou with Kenny Leavitt?" Jim asked forcefully.

"Yez sir," said the man. "We set out 'bout noon that day. Oh, I 'spoze it was 'bout six months ago or so. Took one a Bubba's best boats, paid cash fer it, too. No sooner did we head into the bayou, but a big storm overtook us, an' before we knew it, we was beached. That fancy boat wasn't any use to us by then, had a big hole in it, it did. Well, ol' Kenny, he was right cool he was. He out smarted them gaters. They like the storms, ya know. No sooner did we find a little island to camp on, but the biggest gater ya ever did see, came right out a no wheres and near bouts took my leg clean off."

At that point the old man rolled up his dirty pant leg, uncovering a nasty scar that ran from his right knee cap down to his ankle.

Kate shuddered at the gruesome site, while the children looked on with eager interest as the man continued.

"If it weren't fer Ken a shootin' at the beast, I'd·a been gater food fer sure. I was bleedin' real bad then Ken found an ol' bottle a wine and poured it in my wound ta keep me alive. Ken headed back on foot, trudgin' through the swamps and mud, riskin' life and limb just ta save his injured, dyin' partner. That was the last I saw uf ol' Kenny. Must a made it to help though, cuz b'fore I knew it, the police came and found me, right where Ken had left me. Don't remember much after that, 'cept the awful fever. Next thing I knew, I woke up in a hospital."

"Do you know what happened to Kenny?" Jim asked.

"Don't rightly know," said the old man. "No one asked me 'bout Ken after they found me. I did ask the police how they knew I was on that island. Said they got some anonymous phone call from a friend. That anonymous fella told 'em not to worry, 'cuz he was all right. Do ya think it was Ken?"

Jim smiled and nodded. "Yes. That sounds like him."

The old man looked intently at the others. "I sure do hope Kenny's all right. I got ta thinkin' those animals with the cunja muxt a got him!"

"What's the cunja?" asked Johnny.

"It's black magic!" the old man said, shaking a finger at Johnny. "Them animals in the bayou had the cunja fer sure. Had a dark spell on 'em they did. They was right strange.

"I camped on the island that night whilst Kenny was

34

gone lookin' fer help. I was in a world a hurt. Thought I was gonna die fer sure. Then amid all that pain I saw somethin'. First there was glowin' birds, then a great black cat. The biggest ol' black pirate panther ya ever did see, walkin' just like you an' me, on two legs it did. Then it spoke. It said, 'Leavitt!' At first, I thought it said, 'leave it.' I was a tryin' ta leave, but I couldn't. That ol cat just watched me like the ghost of a great pirate cum from the dead ta haunt that old swamp fer eternity! No man is safe with that critter on the loose."

Every one jumped suddenly as a large hand reached in over them slamming a drink on the table. Everyone caught their breath when they realized it was just Big Bubba, the chef, bringing their order to the table.

"That's quite a story," said Kate. "You've been through a lot."

"Sure have," the man mumbled as he took a large bite from a burger.

Just then someone interrupted the group. "Tellin' your liez again. Thought we told you ta stay outa here!" The teenage boys had returned to harass the old man.

As one of them reached for the old man's drink, Jim grabbed the teen's wrist. "I'd appreciate it if you took your fun elsewhere!" Jim said forcefully. His fingers tightened a little as he stared the teen in the eyes. "Freeeemers!" the boy winced. "We're just jokin!"

Suddenly a large shadow appeared behind the group. "What's going on here?" a deep voice bellowed. It was Big Bubba, and his foreboding size immediately took the wind out of the defiant teens mischievous sails. "C-mon, let's get outa here!" another teen yelled and scrambled for the door.

Bubba shook his head, then, turned to Jim and his family. "Are you folkx all right?" he asked.

"Yes, we're fine," Jim nodded. "But I think my friend

35

here is a bit shook up." Jim turned to point towards the old man, but there was no one there.

Big Bubba frowned. "Sorry 'bout those boys," he said. "With all that hassle your meals are on the house. Franny!" Bubba yelled back to the kitchen. "We need an order of gater fingers out here and give it the works!"

Jim looked at the empty seat where the old man had been sitting. It couldn't have been more empty than the feeling inside of him. All of his hopes for finding his brother had just disappeared, just like the forgotten world of dreams that the old man had spoken of. The hopes of finding Ken had faded and were gone, along with the strange man because of a careless group of teenagers and their little joke to frighten the poor old man.

Bubba's flat bottom boat glided across the waters as the Leavitt family enjoyed the lazy sounds of the bayou tour. Jim sat quietly. How did he ever let that old man slip through his hands? Now the answers Jim needed seemed to float away just like the waters of the bayou. Jim stared into the green water below him, wondering if his brother was somewhere down there. Jim's sullen thoughts were interrupted by the blast of the tour guide's monotone voice over the loud speaker.

"To your left are the remains of Trahns Lake, where it is rumored that the famous Pirate, Jean Laffite, often buried his pirate treasure. Local legend says that the old island, Money Hill, still remains haunted today by an unhappy pirate, killed by Laffite's crew for stealing their treasure."

"Did you hear that?" said Matie.

Johnny turned to his father. "Dad, that must have been the treasure the old man was after!"

"Yes," Jim replied.

Kate grabbed Jim's arm, "I don't understand why Ken would have been mized up in that kind of thing. He's not a treasure hunter."

"I know," said Jim. "Ken wasn't after any treasure."

"Maybe he wanted it to pay back the company?" Johnny questioned.

"Or maybe he already found the treasure," said Matie with wide eyes.

"Your Uncle Ken wouldn't have risked his own life or anyone else's just for money," said Jim. "Something else brought him into the bayou. He must have known about Maison Rouge. He was looking for some answers, and he obviously must have found out something, or he wouldn't be missing."

The car was very quiet as the family drove back toward the Grand Lake Hotel. Matie slept peacefully in the back seat, and Johnny leaned his head against the cool window quietly watching the bridges and roads as they passed by. Soon he, too, was dosing with the car's gentle vibration.

Jim looked at Kate and reached for her hand. "Looks like both of the kids are out," he said squeezing her hand.

Kate grinned as she looked back at the kids. "We've all had an exciting day."

"Yes, we have. Kate, listen. I've been thinking about Ken and that old man who said he was his partner. I think I know where I can find some answers. I'm going to call my lawyer tomorrow and have him fax some of my father's papers to the hotel. I have a hunch there is much more going on here than meets the eye. I think Ken knew something about all of this, and someone wanted to keep him quiet."

6

A Hidden Legacy

Jim was up early, waiting at the hotel office. Back in California it was still dark. There it was barely 6:00 A.M. in the morning. But Jim couldn't wait another second. Finding his brother was just too important.

"Can I help you with something?" the manager at the desk asked.

"Yes," Jim said. "Do you have a fax machine? I've got some very important business, and I need to have some papers sent here."

"Yes, sir," the manager replied, pointing to an office directly behind the desk. "You'll find everything you need right there."

Jim instantly placed a call to his lawyer in California and waited as the call was connected.

"Hello," a groggy voice said at the other end of the line.

"Randy, is that you?" Jim exclaimed.

"Yes," said the voice. "Who is this? What do you want? It's 6:00 a.m.!"

"I'm sorry. I just couldn't wait. It's me... Jim." The line was silent for a second or two.

"Oh, how's it going?" said Randy as he tried to wake up a bit.

Randy Olsen was Jim's attorney. He had known Jim most of his life. The two had grown up together and had both become successful in their own right. Yet while Jim had married and had a family, Randy had focused on his career and still enjoyed the xingle life. He was like a brother to Jim. The two had often gone on fishing trips and camp outs together. But most of all Randy had been the one friend that **J**im confided in. He was **l**ike a part of the family, and when Kenny had come up missing, **i**t was Randy's friendship that had helped Jim get through the ordeal. It was **a**lso Randy's keen legal prowess that had kept the company afloat during all of the problems it had faced.

"I need your help!" Jim blurted out. "I think I'**v**e found a lead to Kenny."

By now sleep had **c**ompletely fled from Randy's thoughts. "What have **y**ou found out?" Randy asked.

"There was this old man here who knows Ken. He said they were treasure hunting. And you won't believe this, but that swampland we were checking on is really a mansion. It's an old plantation!"

"What? So, who is this old man that says he knows Ken?"

Jim sighed, "Well, I didn't **g**et his name. I lost him, but I think that I know where Ken is."

"**A**ll **r**ight, what do you want me to do?"

"**Do** you **r**emember the family files back at the company," Jim asked, "the ones tied up in the takeover?"

"**O**f course I do. Ratcliffe's got a court order on all of them. There's no way I can get into those papers."

"Well, you've got to," said Jim. "Ken's life could depend on it. I think the same people who want to buy the land here are after Ken. Those papers had a lot of my father's things in them. If we can find the deed to this place, we might just find out why those people are after Ken, and why this place is so important!"

"**O**h, all right," Randy sighed. "I'll see what I can **d**o, and I'll call you right back if I find out anything. But you owe me big on this one."

"It's a deal," said Jim. "The next time **w**e go fishing, I'll let you catc**h** the biggest fish!"

 Back at his room, Jim paced the floor as he waited for some news from Randy. Suddenly, the phone rang. It was the front desk calling. "Excu**z**e me, but are you Mr. Leavitt?"

 "Yes," Jim anxiously replied.

 "There's a phone call for you at the front desk, and some legal papers ha**v**e arrived for you by fax."

 "I'll be right down," Jim said. He hung up the **p**hone and headed downstairs.

 At the front desk, Randy was waiting on the line as Jim picked up the receiver. "Jim, did you se**e** the deed I sent you? I think you'd better take a good look at it. I'm getting a flight there tonight."

 "Why?" asked Jim.

 Randy kept right on talking without taking a breath. "**M**y flight will arrive at 8:47. Can you pick me up? I found this **o**ld journal. I couldn't fax it. You just won't believe this but you're..."

 Ji**m** waited for the information. "Randy!' h**e** said. Suddenly the dial tone was all he could hear. Immediately Jim re-dialed Randy's number, but all he **g**ot was a recorded message from the phone company saying that the call could not **b**e completed as dialed.

 In frustration, Jim began pounding on the little metal bell on the counter. Soon the hotel manager showed up. "Can I help you?" he asked.

 "My connection was cut off," said Jim. "The call won't go through now."

 "Here, let me try." The manager said as he dialed the **n**umber through a different line. "That's odd," said the ma**n**. "I'll have the hotel'**s** operator try it from her end and see if we can get through."

 As the man dialed the operator, Jim saw some

movement out of the corner of his eye. When he glanced down the hallway, he saw a man wearing a Hawaiian shirt and a fishing hat. Jim watched the man slip out of a door and run down the hall.

"I can't get the operator," said the manager. He headed toward the hallway, and Jim followed him into the same room that the oddly dressed man had just left. There upon the floor lay the poor operator. Jim checked her weak pulse as the manager ran for help. Jim looked over at the phone line. It had been yanked out of the wall.

Soon the lobby buzzed with police officers and investigators, and an ambulance arrived on the scene. Jim watched as curious onlookers gossiped in confusion.

"Excuse me," said a neatly dressed man. "I'm Detective Morgan. Are you Jim Leavitt?" Jim shook the man's hand.

"Yes," Jim replied. "Is that poor woman going to be all right?"

The officer nodded. "She's just a bit shaken. She has a bump on her head, but it looks like she'll be juxt fine."

"I've been really worried about her," Jim said. "I can't help but think that this whole thing is my fault."

The officer raised an eyebrow. "What do you mean, Mr. Leavitt?"

Jim looked at the floor. "How long have you worked with the department here?"

"For ten years now," the detective replied.

"Well then, you probably remember the case of a man that disappeared about six months ago."

"Yes, I remember the case." Suddenly the detective's eye's widened. "His name was Leavitt, too," the officer said flatly. "What's going on here?"

"Well," said Jim, "the missing man was my brother, Ken. I came here looking for him, and it seems that someone doesn't want me to find out what's going on."

The officer squinted his eyes as he looked around the busy lobby. "I think we'd better talk in a more private place."

The two men headed across the street to a nearby restaurant. "I remember your brother's case," the officer said over a cold drink. "In fact, I was on the initial task crew. It was the oddest investigation I've ever seen."

The officer looked uneasy, as he leaned a little closer to Jim and spoke softly. "I got pretty close to finding your brother. Then all of a sudden, my supervisors told me to just drop it, and the case was closed just like that. It all seemed so strange at the time, so I went back into the bayou by myself. I wanted to go over the place where they found your brother's partner. That man's story was so strange. It was almost too strange to be a lie. My boss threatened to fire me if I ever brought the case up again, so I never told them what I found."

"What did you find?" Jim asked.

"The boat those men took into the bayou had been knifed long before the storm ever hit. And that's not all. On the island near the wreck, there was something scratched into the sand. It was an arrow with the initials K.L. There was an old beer can right next to it. To everyone else it just looked like an old rusty beer can. That's why they didn't find it. I just happened to pick it up. When it rattled, I took a look inside."

The officer fumbled in his pocket, and soon produced a gold coin. "This is what I found," he said. "Do you know how rare this thing is? It's part of a set of rare coinage minted by Napoleon to pay for his escape to the United States. It's so rare that there is only one professor in Dublin that has even researched it. Most thought the story of Napoleon paying to come to America was just a legend. But it wasn't, and here's the proof. That puts a new spin on U.S history, doesn't it?"

The officer smiled at Jim and handed him the coin.

"Do you know any more about where my brother might be?" Jim asked, fingering the gold coin.

"I know this much," said the officer. "Your brother left to protect something or someone. I think he's still alive and in the bayou. When I started to investigate on my own, I got a threatening note. It said that I'd just better leave it alone. What's more, the F.B.I. came and took all of the files on everything."

Jim's face dropped. Immediately his thoughts went back to Alliance Stock and Trading Co. "The F.B.I. investigated my company, too, just after Ken came up missing. They went through every file in the place. I thought it was routine, but they kept on asking about the family name, and if I knew why Ken had disappeared. They finally just gave up and left. I thought the investigation was about the missing money."

"I don't know why the F.B.I. was involved," said Morgan. "I wish I could give you more information. But that coin belonged to your brother, and it's only right that you should have it now. You know, I'm glad my superiors told me to keep quiet. Maybe you can find out more than I did."

Jim shook Morgan's hand as they both got up to leave. "Here's my card," said Morgan. "If you have any trouble, just call and ask for Jake. I only tell that name to a few people. It's for extreme emergencies only."

Jim thanked the officer again. "If you find out anything more, you'll need my address," said Jim. "It's 33 Royal Street."

Morgan's face turned white. "But that's Maison Rouge, Old Laffite's place!"

"Yes" said Jim. "And for some reason, some very persistent investors think they are going to get the place from me. I'm picking up my lawyer this evening at the airport. That's who I was talking to when the operator was knocked out and the phone lines where cut."

The officer looked at Jim and the coin in his hand. "You'd better hide that coin, and don't tell anyone about it unless you want a lot of treasure hunters following you around. Old Laffite's place has been plagued by those kind for years, and now you're holding all the reason they need." Jim looked at the coin and carefully placed it in his pocket.

"There's another thing you ought to know," said Morgan. "Laffite was the pirate that negotiated with Napoleon to bring him here. Rumor has it that the old pirate took the loot and left Napoleon in prison."

Kate had been waiting for Jim to return to the hotel room. As the door opened, she ran to Jim and hugged him. "Did you see all of the police cars downstairs? What's going on? Are you okay?"

"I'm just fine," said Jim. "The police just wanted to talk to me. The operator was knocked out, but they said she'll be all right. Kate, I met an officer, Detective Morgan. He said that he worked on Ken's case, seems that some people in the department wanted him to keep quiet about it. He was threatened that if he didn't, he'd lose his job."

Kate walked over to the small table in the sitting area and handed Jim his briefcase. "Jim, did you look at the papers that Randy faxed you?"

"I didn't have a chance. There was so much excitement going on earlier, I just left the papers here and ran back downstairs."

Kate opened the case and thumbed through a few papers, then handed a specific one to Jim. "Look at this one," she said. "It's a transfer of deed for Maison Rouge. Look, its dated 1857."

Jim studied the old paper. "This tranzfers the property from a Pierre Charles Laffite to his son Martin Edward Leavitt. The title to the property then reverts to the Leavitt family from that point on." Jim looked at Kate. "But that doezn't make any sense. They're two different names. There must be a mistake."

Kate took the paper from Jim. "It makes perfect sense, don't you see? Lots of people changed their names back then. It was common, especially if someone wanted to get a new start. They changed the name from Laffite to Leavitt!"

Jim's eyes lit up. "It all fits now. The police officer said that Maison Rouge was old Laffite's place." Jim fumbled in his pocket and showed the coin to Kate. "Detective Morgan found this during the investigation of Ken's disappearance. He said that Laffite was a pirate and had gotten this coin as payment from Napoleon." Jim scratched his head. "My grandfather's name was Samuel Martin Leavitt. He must have been named Martin after Martin Edward Leavitt... his father.

"When I was a boy, my father used to tell me all kinds of pirate stories. He said that I was related to a famous pirate. I just thought it was big talk and campfire stories. I never believed they could be true."

Kate put her arm around Jim's shoulder. "Well Mr. 'Laffite,' it looks as if your hidden legacy has come out. Deep down inside, you really are a true blue pirate!"

7
A Grand Welcome

The excitement of the morning had affected most everyone. But the children were more concerned about getting in one last swim before leaving the hotel. After splashing around till the last possible moment, they reluctantly returned to their room and began packing.

"Hey, Dad," Johnny asked, "does our family have any old maps?"

"I don't think so," replied Jim. "Why do you want to know?"

Johnny stuffed some clothes in his bag. "Well, that old guy yesterday said that Uncle Ken had a map to the treasure, then today when me and Matie were down at the pool..."

"Matie and I," Kate interrupted from the other room.

Johnny rolled his eyes and continued. "Anyway, there was this guy down at the pool. He had on a weird Hawaiian shirt and shorts. It was strange. He kept on bugging 'Matie and I.'" Johnny glanced towards his mother, trying to use the proper grammar. "The man had a map of California and came right over to us. He treated us like babies." Johnny pulled a face as if imitating the man talking baby talk. "Do you kids know what I have? It's a big map. Does your family have any big maps?"

Matie giggled watching Johnny. "Yeah, and you should hear what Johnny said to the man." Matie tried to act as if she were Johnny and deepened her voice to speak. "We awe just a couple of wittow kids. We don't know nufin' about anyfing wike maps!" Johnny laughed at Matie's attempt to imitate him.

Kate poked her head around the corner from the other room. "Did you really say that?"

"Well, sort of. I just acted really dumb, like I didn't know what he was talking about."

"I'll say," said Matie. "You sure did act really dumb."

Jim didn't laugh. "What kind of Hawaiian shirt was that man wearing?"

"I don't know. It was just blue and green," said Johnny.

Jim started stuffing things in his suitcase. "We've got to get out of here now."

"What's wrong?" Kate asked. "You seem upset."

Jim looked at the kids then pulled Kate into the other room. "That man the kids are talking about, sounds like the one I saw. I think he's the same one that knocked out the operator. We've got to leave. Now they're even trying to get to the kids. I wish I hadn't told anyone where we were going, not even the police."

Soon the car was back on the road. The mood lightened as the family talked of baby alligators and gater fingers. Soon a large moving van pulled in front of the car. "I wonder where they're moving to," Jim said.

Matie interrupted, "Dad, are we ever gonna move?"

"I don't know. I hadn't even thought of it."

"Jim, you're a free man now with the company gone," Kate reminded him. "There's nothing to tie you down, back there in California. We could start over here. Lake Charles could use a new investment firm."

Jim was silent for a moment. "I hadn't considered the possibility of starting over here," he said. "It would take some work, and I would have to find some partners, but... I'll think about it."

Kate smiled. "You know if we lived here at Maison Rouge, you wouldn't have to feel so pressured about finding Ken right now. You could take your time to find those miszing answers you're looking for, and maybe even find your brother."

"You're right, Kate. Living here would give us a new start." Jim glanced back at the kids. "How would you like to live at Masion Rouge?" Everyone in the car began talking at once.

"I get the best room at the red house!" Matie yelled.

"You haven't even seen the rooms," Johnny protested. "Maybe all they've got is a dungeon full of gum chewing alligators for you to sleep in."

"Dad!" yelled Matie. "I don't have to sleep with alligators, do I?"

"They just might have a room like that, Matie, I don't know," Jim teased.

Kate slugged Jim's arm. "Nobody's going to sleep with alligators. I won't have any in my house to clean up after." Matie stuck out her tongue at Johnny.

Soon the family turned down Red House Lane. Like devoted guardians dressed in their very best, the moss-laden cypress trees greeted the family at 33 Royal Street. As the car turned into the lane, the excitement of the family bubbled over into shouts of joy and laughter.

"There it is!" Matie exclaimed. "And there's my room upstairs!" While the car drove down the lane, a brilliantly colored humming bird darted in front of the car, pulling everyone's attention to the upper balcony of Maison Rouge. Cora stood waving at the car as she hung a beautiful hand made quilt over the balcony's railing. It was the traditional old fashioned welcome of the bayou.

Old Sam met the family at the front of the house. "Cum on in folks. Deyz plenty a rooms, and dey is awl a waitin' fo' ya. Took some burnin' the candle inta midnight, but we'z got um all ready fo ya. Cleaned up right nice, dey did!"

As the family entered the old place, everyone was awe

struck. The previous sheet covered furnishings now showed the grand opulence of the once celebrated manor. Antique French furnishings filled the entire house. Delicate velvet draperies trimmed in fringe, covered the vast windows, while paintings of pirates and ships looked down on the mirrored walls as the family entered the enormous grand hall.

Then they saw it. As if to welcome them personally, right beside an enormous fire place hung a life size portrait of the great old pirate himself, Jean Laffite. He was a broad, tall man, in full pirate regalia, with dark wavy hair and a full mustache, his deep hazel eyes sparkled as if keeping a hidden secret and watching their every move. Two crossed swords with the family crest hung above the fireplace. Upon the crest were the words *"True Intent"* and the letter "L" intertwined with a large black panther that seemed to wrestle the "L" into complete submission.

On the floor leaning against the fire place was an elegant old mandolin as if someone had just recently played the delicate instrument. The entire place was astonishing and a treasure in and of itself.

Kate caught her breath. "No wonder you didn't want them breaking up the place. It's absolutely beautiful!"

By now Matie had found a bear skin rug by the fire place and was reaching in its mouth.

Sam looked at her cautiously. "Bez be careful. Dat ol' thin' might juz' bite!" Matie quickly pulled her hand back as Sam burst into laughter. "Cum on folxs," he said as Cora came hurrying down the broad curved stairway.

"You folks is all set," Cora said. "We cleaned 'em up good, and you is all juz as welcome as you can be." Then she winked at Matie. "I dun choze de bez room, juz fo this lil poo-ka-choo. Cum on up, and I'll show it to ya."

The family started up the grand staircase overlooking the enormous room below. Soon they reached a long balcony encircling the Grand Hall. The intricate wood working on each post of the stair railings chronicled a detailed history of what seemed to be every pirate adventure the previous owners of this mansion had ever seen.

Along the upper hallway, hung family portraits, each family was prominently displayed within their own unique alcove, like little rooms filled with ancestors just waiting for their turn to be seen once more. Below each portrait hung a brass plaque, which gave the name of the person on each canvas along with a short verse describing their life. A family pedigree hung in each alcove detailing the family lines from father to son.

The first portrait was of a tall comely man dressed like a ship's captain, distinct and noble looking, with graying hair. The plaque beneath it said, *"Captain Charles Edwards, our beloved father."*

In the following alcove was the grand old pirate himself, Jean Laffite, with all of his pirate persona and character displayed in an array of color and intrigue. Next to him hung the portrait of a strikingly beautiful woman named Catherine Abigail Villars, Laffite's wife. She had very dark hair and eyes and a distinctly mischievous smile that hinted of the character of this powerful pirate's wife.

The following alcove held the portrait of Pierre Laffite, Jean's brother. He, too, wore the vestments of a successful businessman of his day, albeit his pirate dealings were more than just a little shady. This tall, brawny man was a bit smaller than his older brother Jean. Pierre was a bit thinner, too, and his hair was somewhat of a lighter brown with shades of red. He had the look of a charismatic French man of his day. Both brothers were quite handsome and of a surety, well regarded in their time.

Next to the portrait of Pierre was a beautiful petite woman of a fair complexion, wearing a brightly colored dress with green, yellow and red flowers on it. The vibrant colors she wore were rich and deep, giving a hint of the flamboyant nature of this southern woman. Her name was Miss **A**nnabelle Honey Parker, Pierre's wife. A family portrait hung next to these. Upon the canvas were the former two, along with their three children, two girls and one **b**oy.

As the family looked at this unusual painting, Matie mo**v**ed on until one painting in particular caught her attention.

Matie was completely spe**l**lbound by the portrait **b**efore her. It hung separate from the other portraits and alcoves. This one was unique. It was a burley fellow with a cutlass and battle gear. He had a sinister grin as if he knew something no one else did. In one hand he held a saber fully drawn and ready for a fight. In the other hand he held a rolled up piece of paper. It was obvious that this man was someone not to be reckoned with, should you ever cross his path, it would be best to be his ally. The name plaque identified him as Dominique Youx, a half brother to the others. From the prominent position of the painting, it was obvious that this man was very highly regarded for his courageous exploits.

All of these characters wore the evidence of their pirate trade, as they exhibited swords and daggers amid the gentlemanly clothing of their era.

Jim studied each plaque with great interest. **O**n Jean's plaque, just as on the family crest downstairs, it said, *"True Intent."* Upon Pierre's plaque it read, *"The key is believing."* While Dominique's said, *"Light is truth, truth mirrors the son."* The entire gallery was completely astounding.

While the rest of the family e**x**amined the illustriou**s** figures, Jim turned to Sam. "Does this gallery contain all of the family portraits?" he asked. Sam headed towards the end of the hall, and Jim followed. "You betcha," Sam replied with a large grin on his face. He stopped and waited for the others to catch up. Johnny pretended to be a scurvy pirate tormenting his little sister, and Matie screamed as she ran to her father for protection.

Johnny's teenage clowning came to an immediate stop and he stood speechless, staring at the wall behind the family.

"What's wrong?" asked Kate, looking at Johnny's pale face. He struggled to find the words but just couldn't get any out. Then, with a feeble effort, he pointed to the area behind the others. Everyone slowly turned around, and in unison gasped at the site before them.

There, within a wide alcove, were the portraits of the Leavitt family. They were perfect duplicates of each family member that stood staring back at them. Oddly each person from Jim all the way down to Matie were dressed in the traditional costumes of a bygone era. Jim had on the fancy suit of a notable aristocrat, while Kate wore an elegant embroidered ball gown. Johnny's attire was proper for a young man with his green vest and short pants that went to his knees. At his side was a cutlass. Matie had on a beautiful floral print dress typical of a young southern belle of the day.

In the alcove beside theirs were portraits of Jim's father's family, along with Jim and his brother, Kenny, at much younger ages.

"Look!" Matie yelled. "It's all of us, and Johnny's wearing girl pants!"

"No, I'm not!" Johnny protested. "They're pirate clothes."

Jim and Kate just stared in disbelief. Finally Jim turned to Sam and Cora who stood silently watching the others.

"Where did you get these?" Jim asked. Sam scratched

52

his head and slowly began to explain. "Well, I spoze we wuz tol' ta get um dun right good. Tain't too bad, is dey?"

"Oh, no," said Jim. "They're very nice."

"Very nice! They're absolutely beautiful, but how did you know what we looked like?" Kate asked.

"Oh, dat part wuz easy," replied Sam. "Da Boss dun sent us da pictures, and we jist had da painter take um, an dey brung um back hea when dey wuz awll dun."

Cora reached toward Jim's picture and polished the frame with her apron. "We wuz jist followin' audas," she said. "We been tol' ta git diz plaze in tip top shape soona dan yesterdee, and dat's when da paintins was ready. Duz ya like em?"

"We love them!" Kate said. "I guess we just didn't expect such a wonderful welcome like this. To be quite honest, until today, we didn't even know we were related to the Laffite family!"

"I telled ya dey din' know 'bout da family," Cora scolded Sam. "We wuz fixin' ta tell ya soona, but jist neva gots a chanz to."

"That's all right," said Jim. "I'm sure we'll get used to it."

8

In A Manor of Speaking

An unusual feeling filled the air of the mysterious manor as Cora led the family down an open hallway into a new corridor that was lined on either side with doors. They finally came to one with unusual detail. The bright red door was arched with a small stained glass opening at the top, like a window. The handle was much smaller than normal and was made of a ring and a pull cord, as if for a young child or a smaller person. Surrounding the door were hand painted flowers and vines. Above the door, a vine covered plaque read, "Miss Honey."

Cora beamed with pride as she opened the door for the others. "Diz hea is lil' ol' Misz Honey's room. She juz luv's dem flowa's. We was thinkin' diz hea would be da parfect plaze fo' Miss Matie. And we is sho' Miss Honey won't mind."

The room virtually exploded with sunlight and color. Everything inside was covered with vines or flowers. A large bay window overlooked the bayou. Within it was a window seat with bright red overstuffed cushions, barely visible beneath a row of priceless porcelain dolls.

On the walls hung various live plants and vines in full bloom growing up hand-painted trellises. The vines grew upon everything in the room, spanning over the arched window then over to a lovely bed completely entwined within the vines. The tall bed posts acted as a sturdy support for the heavy vines interwoven over the top of the bed creating a lovely green canopy.

Beautiful flowered curtains draped the tall windows while an antique hand-stitched patchwork quilt adorned the bed. It was truly a beautiful room, prepared just perfectly for a little girl such as Matie.

As Matie looked over the amazing site, she was, for once, completely speechless. As she moved toward the window seat, something caught her eye. A very old hand-painted chest lay at the end of the bed. The whimsical chest was covered with birds and animals that had a defined mystical quality that drew Matie closer.

As she leaned over to open the chest, Cora began to chuckle. "Well, I'll be," she said. "You din' waste any time at all findin' dat suprize, did ya?"

"What surprise?" Matie asked with wide eyes.

Sam nodded at her. "Go on. You kin open it! Don' be afeard of it. Taint nuthin' gonna bite cha."

Matie looked at the others then opened the beautiful chest. At the top lay a shallow removable box that was filled with what looked like miniature doll furniture. Matie looked through the box, then over at the window seat. Then she frowned.

"What's da matter?" asked Sam.

Matie frowned. "There's no doll for the furniture," she said. Cora reached down and stroked Matie's hair, "Dem thins ain't fo' no doll!"

Cora walked over to what looked like a draped doorway. She gently pulled on a cord as the curtains opened.

The opening revealed a small room. Above the doorway were the names Babette, Monique, and Louis. Inside the little room were the same kinds of vines and flowers covering the walls and furnishings as there were in the main room, but in the center of this room was a gazebo which stood on a broad low table. The gazebo was covered with a type of vine covered with miniature flowers. Inside of it were what looked like small compartments or rooms.

"Is this the dollhouse?" asked Matie. Sam and Cora just smiled. Suddenly in a furry of wings, three small humming birds flitted past Matie and entered the little house.

"It's not a doll house! It's a bird house!" Matie squealed with delight.

"Yes, maaaam," said Sam. "And dey juz loves chillen, juz so long as you ain't ruff wif em. Dem dair thins in dat ol trunk belongs ta dem dair birds."

Matie quickly returned to the trunk and removed the shallow box. Then she brought out all of the miniature furnishings and began placing them in the rooms of the elaborate bird house. Each time she placed an item in the little house, a bird would fly to that room and perch near the furnishings.

As Matie arranged the last item, the three birds one by one hovered in front of her. Then, as if they were bowing, they dipped and whizzed past her cheek to take up residence within the unique structure.

"Oh, thank you so much!" said Matie. "I love the little birds!"

"We unnastanz," said Sam. "Dey is veri special. Juz remambar,...if yuz takes care a dem, den dey will take care a yu."

"Oh, I will and I promise not to hurt them. I'll even protect them from Johnny!" A smirk covered her face as she looked at her brother.

Cora showed Matie how to feed and care for the little birds. Then Matie returned the shallow box to the trunk. As she did, she noticed a beautiful little gown in the chest.

It was exactly like the one in the painting that the family had seen earlier, the kind of gown worn by young ladies in the times of pirates. It was also exactly Matie's size. The fabric was silk brocade covered in flowers and lace and on the front were

56

gold buttons. In the trunk were match**h**ing underclothes and a petticoat with la**y**ers upon layers of **r**uffles. Two small slippers and a purse **m**ade of gold satin lay nest**l**ed within the folds of the fabric. Matie anxiously reached for the beautiful gown.

"Now wait jist a minute daer, lil one," Cora said. "Dis hea is for da big shindig we'z a-havin' dis hea Saturdee nite. An u awll iz gonna wea des hea kina clothes. We brung um special just ta match ya portraits. Now everbody, we'z got lots mo' ta see an time's a-waistin'. So **q**-mon folks."

Sam led the family down the **h**allway to Johnny's room. Over the rough hewn wooden door, hung a pirate flag, with a skull over two crossed sabers. Beneath the swords it said, *"The key is believing."*

Sam began to explain. "Diz hea is Pierre Laffite's ol' room. He wu**z** da **b**oss's brotha an' right hand man an da first mate on Jean's ship. He dun smuggled up a-plenty on dat ol neutral strip wif da Boss and his men. Now ya neva **k**nows juz what might be a- hidin' in dez hea walls. Dat ol boy knowd his stuff right well. And no matta weh he been, he dun hid awll kinz a trinkets and dreegailles awll ova diz hea room.

"Everbody dat ever did stay hea, jist a keeps on finnin' awl kind a se**c**ret hidin' placis and clues ol' Pierre dun left behine. So's ya needs ta be right careful, **f**o sho."

Sam opened the doo**r** and ushered everyone inside. This was exactly the kind of adventure Johnny **h**ad dreamed of.

Inside, the room looked as if it was furnished with the booty off of a thousand looted ship**s**. A large window made from the stern of a wrecked ship, extended outside from the wall. Within it was a bed, the corners made from old wine casks. The footboard was a ship's railing. Tufted sails adorned the entire upper portion of the bed, so that when lowered, they provided complete privacy as well as protection from any bothersome insects that t**hr**ived in the summer heat of the bayou.

On each side of the bed were large rope ladders that led to a massive loft type balcony above. Inside the loft were book shelves filled with books of adventurous tales from all over the world. There were also several curious collections the pirate had amassed in his travels. A tiger-skin rug covered the floor, a hollow elephant tusk hung high over head, and a hammock with blue velvet pillows stretched suspended in the loft. In front of the book case was a curious stool made from the foot of a real elephant and covered with leather for the top cushion. The railing of the loft was also made from the wreckage of a lost ship, and in the center of the railing was a ship's wheel, the salty helm of a once powerful vessel.

As Johnny climbed the rope ladder to get a better look at the loft, his belt loop caught on a wooden peg. As he struggled to free himself, there was a slight clicking sound as the ship's wheel began spinning wildly. Across the room a trap door opened up revealing a secret excape hatch in the floor. Everyone stared into the opening.

Disappearing into the darkness below was what looked like a type of slippery slide. "I telled ya dey was passages an such," said Sam as he peered into the dark hole.

"Can I try it out?" Johnny asked.

"Absolutely not!" Kate said, pushing the hatch closed. "Your father will have to see what's down there before anyone else is going to risk life and limb!"

"I bet it's full of spiders," said Matie with a frown. "Johnny, I won't bother you in your room any more!"

"I'm not so sure this is the best room for you," Kate said placing a protective arm around her son.

Jim patiently looked at Kate and nodded. "I think this is the perfect room for Johnny. But, we'll make a deal," he said turning to his son. "If you find anything else like this trap door or hidden passageways, you come and tell us, all right?"

"You bet! I promise I'll let ya know if I find anything!"

Kate folded her arms and looked at Jim. "I'm still not so sure, but I guess we'll try it for a while."

Something else now caught Johnny's attention. Just like in Matie's room, there was a trunk at the end of the bed. Curiously he went to investigate. The trunk was arched on top and was made of deep red wood. Upon it were the carved images of monkeys swinging from trees and elephants balancing upon their hind legs, all surrounded by Hindu temples.

The entire family watched as Johnny opened the trunk. There in front of them the chest lay brimming over with gold coins and precious jewels. Johnny's eyes widened as he reached into the tempting treasure. He drew a coin from the chest and bit it to test its authenticity. The coin gave away easily between his teeth as a gooey substance squeezed out from between them. Johnny removed the fake coin from his mouth and examined it. There between two layers of gold foil was pink bubble gum. "It's gum!" Johnny exclaimed.

Matie interrupted confidently. "That's where they keep the gum for the gum stew."

Everyone was getting ready to move on to the next room when Johnny noticed a window that looked out into the front yard of the mansion. The glass was somewhat cloudy and difficult to look through, and the draperies surrounding the window were real fishing nets.

Just as Johnny went to investigate, he realized that the window was an aquarium, built right into the wall, filled with tropical fish. "Wow, that's cool," he said, watching the fish swim back and forth. The top of the glass was open behind the fishnets for feeding and cleaning of the unique fish tank.

Johnny leaned forward to get a better look at the tank

when he accidentally knocked over a large harpoon that had been propped against the wall.

As he reached to replace it, he saw an odd piece of wood on the floor. It was carved to look like a foot and leg and had a leather strap on the top. "What's this?" Johnny asked as he held up the curious object. A grin began to form on old Sam's face as he took the odd item from Johnny.

"Now daer is a story," Sam began. "Well seems dat ol Aluitious Eldwin Clayton wuz da meanest man alive. Walked wif a limp he did. Now he sho hated Mr. Pierre. And Mr. Pierre wern't too fond a dat gater neitha. So's one day dem fellas ran inta one a nutha, and I spoze Mr. Pierre done had enuf a Mr. Al's high falutin' ways, an he vowed dat Mr. Al wuz foeva his swarn enemy. Now Mr. Aluitious wuz invited to Jean's weddin'. And da Boss had juz giv his mos' prize watch to his new bride. Well, dat watch cum up a- misxin', and Mr. Pierre done saw it a-hangin' out a dat Clayton's pocket. Pierre knowed dat ol' watch backwards and forwards. And dey wern't no getin' out uv it. Dat gater wuz out an out caught red-handed.

"Now it were a matta a honor. Well, wen Mr. Pierre dun kicked up a ruckus ova the whole thing, dem two dun took ta sword fightin'. Now ifen dat ol' Aluitious knowed what wuz good fer him, he'd a turned tail and took ta runnin' righcherre. But he wuz right dumb, and 'bout as welcome as a skunk at a lawn party. So's Mr. Pierre took a good swipe at dat ol boy, an fo' he knowed it, Mr. Al's leg was cut clean off an dat ol'gater dropped dat watch like a hot iron. Well, I reckons dat fella got ta screamin' an lev as sho as shootin' ta fin' a doctor.

"Now dat boy wuz sho a-feared dat Mr. Pierre might cum an finish da job if'n dey eva crossed paths agin. So's Mr. Al kep' his diztance, but I reckon he juz din have a lick a senz. Cuz nea' bouts five monthz later, he dun picked a fight wif Mr. Pierre agin.

60

"Now Mr. Pierre wu**z** sick ta death a fightin' with dat nut. So he done da only thing he could. He done knocked dat ol boy down an stole his bran new **w**ood leg. He, he, he, and hea it sits righcherre ta dis very day. Cept'n Mr. Pierre dun put hiz own mark on it."

Johnny took the wooden **leg** from Sam. **A**s he ran his fingers across the leather strap, a chill ran **d**own his spin**e**. Gently he put the leg back on the floor.

"Sam," Jim asked, "whatever happened to Mr. Clayton?"

"Dat ol' boy, well, he dun took ta politickin', and wif awl his lyin' and a cheetin,' he took right to it. 'Fore he knowed it, he was the govna. An afta dat, he become so high falutin', he got ta thinkin' the sun dun cum up ju**z** ta hear him crow."

Matie and Johnny giggled as **S**am continued. "He neva did let things lie with the Laffite boys, tho, and it wuz daer undoin'."

"Sam!" Cora said sharply. "We needs ta git deas folk settled in. They don' have time ta chew the fat over your stories!"

"**A**wll right, awll right," said Sam as he gave in t**o** Cora's demand.

Sam led the group to a draped doorway. As he pulled aside the curtains he revealed a small drawing room. Inside was a low table with a sculpted replica of the entire bayou. Small ships blocked the winding waterways.

"Dis hea is wea da Boss and Mr. Pierre dun set awl a daer battle plans." Sam reached to a nearby shelf and pulled down several miniature cannons. Then he took a small metal ball and stuffed it inside of one. He struck a match and lit a small wick on the cannon then placed the cannon on the sculpted map of the bayou and instantly the little cannon exploded, discharging the small metal ball into the side of a nearby ship.

Sam slapped his leg. "Yep, juz like da good ol' dayz wen da Boss dun went ta smugglin' awl along dat ol'neutral strip in da bayou. He know'd what he wuz a-doin' cuz he set his planz righcheere."

"Wow.... that's cool! Can I shoot the qannon?" Johnny asked.

Kate stepped forward and raised an eyebrow, but Jim interrupted, "I think we'd better wait and try that one out later on."

Now Sam led the family outside of Johnny's room, down the hall past several other rooms. Eventually they came to two massive mahogany doors with wide ornate brass bands on them. Sam opened the double doors revealing the master suite.

It was more luxurious than any castle could have been. The entire room was furnished with seventeenth century French furnishings. In the center of the entry stood an enormous round table completely covered in gold leaf. Upon it rested a gold vase filled with fresh flowers. Upon the floor was an elaborate hand woven rug with images of pirates and sea voyagers waging a great battle. Around the edges of the rug was a detailed design that, at closer inspection, revealed Portuguese writing.

Cora led the group farther into the room through a graceful curtained opening into a spacious living area. A large fireplace stood at the far end of the room. The entire area was well watched over by an enormous portrait of a black panther drexsed like a pirate.

A large library graced the nearby walls, and overstuffed furnishings made the area a cozy place to settle into. Deep red velvet curtains hung on every tall window and framed all the openings that lead from room to room.

Past the library, Cora led the others into the bed

chamber.   The area was truly magnificent. A tall, four poster bed, complete with goose down comforters hinted of the distinctive evidence of the regal taste of the original owners. Blue silk fabric draped the bed as if the former pirate had raided the tent of a wealthy sheik. Large overstuffed pillows covered the cushions with a regal ambiance becoming the bed of a king.

Just as in all of the other rooms, near the footboard lay a beautiful Spanish chest. But it was much larger than the others and quite bulky. Sam motioned for Jim to help him, and the two opened the large lid. Inside was a wooden box, gently cradled in the folds of blue velvet, was a device for navigation known as a seaman's sextant. The chest also contained a spyglass engraved with the words, *"Captain Charles Edwards."* A brass placard rested in the trunk that identified its original purpose. It read *"Alliance Shipping and Trading Company 1796."*

"Dad," Johnny said. "That sounds like your company!"

"Yes, I know," said Jim. "That must have been the original name of the company." Jim turned to Sam. "Sam, do you know who this chest belonged to?"

"Oh, yes sa," Sam replied. "It dun belonged ta Cap'n Edwards on da ship de *Alliance*. Two ships dey wuz, I believes dey wuz sister ships. Da *Intent* wuz da otha ship. It belonged ta Jean. Da *Alliance* wuz Cap'n Edward's ship. He was juz like a pa ta da Boss."

Kate looked at Sam, her brow wrinkled. "Who is this boss you keep talking about?"

"Oh, dat's Mr. Jean. Juz bout everbody cawlls him da Boss."

Jim picked up the delicate spyglass. "So, was the Alliance Shipping and Trading Company Mr. Edwards?"

Sam's easy going mood suddenly turned to soberness. "Ohhh, Yeessss sa," he murmured, looking at the floor. "It wuz a right good company, too, till dat terrible, sorraful day."

"What do you mean?" asked Kate.

Sam sat down on the bed then put his head in his hands. Slowly he raised his head and looked at Cora who nodded in agreement. Then he began to speak. "Well, back den da Boss an' Miss Catherine was right happy. She was spectin' a lil one an' awll. So's da Boss was real careful sho not ta leave Miss Catherine alone wiv her time a commin' near.

"Now Miss Marie were Miss Catherine's mammy, an she took right good ca'e a her awll her born days. She was juz like a ma ta dat girl, cuz Miss Catherine's own ma had died givin' birth ta her. Miss Catherine loved Marie mo' dan anythin', an trusted her like no otha.

"In dem days, da French was at war, and dat ol' Napoleon wuz a scoopin' up dem countries like a coon in a hen house. Sho nuf, b-fo' long dem folks got tired a-runnin' from dat ol' boy an soon took ta scrapin' an' give him what fer. So's Napoleon decided he'd bez high tale it outa daer, and he put his mind ta da thought a fixin' ta settle down in New Orleans.

"Now da Boss had some important dealin's in France, and he run inta dat boy one day. So's Mr. Napoleon cum ta da Boss in da dead a night an made him a right good offa. Ifen da Boss would smuggle dat fella to Louisiana, he promised ta pay Jean right well with sum chests a gold.

"Da Boss knowed trouble when he saw it, and he said ta ol' Napoleon. 'I got's awll da gold I wants.' Now Napoleon wuz right desperate and said he'd give awll he had ta Jean.

"Well, da Boss wuz right sorraful an din' want ta do it, but da nation uf America wuz right po' dem dayz, cuz a da war uf 1812. So's da Boss agreed, thinkin' dat he could give da treasure to da U.S.

"Now da night dun cum, and da ship wuz loaded right full a awll dat treasure. An' da Boss and Mr. Pierre waited clean inta da mornin', but dat boy Napoleon neva did sho up. Den a runner cum, and he telled em dat ol' Napoleon wer taken prizna dat very night and dey'd bez hi tail it outa daer if'n dey valued daer very lives.

"Well da Boss took to comin' home and firs thin he asked Mr. Edwards ta hide dat treasure till it were safe ta giv it to da U.S. of A.

"Cap'n Edwards wuz right smart. He figered dat if one man knowed where da treasure wuz, his enemies would stalk em down till dey found dat treasure. So's he called together awl a Jean's bez men, eight uf um awl ta gather dey was, and dey made demselves an alliance dat very day. Dey promised ta keep da secret uf da treasure hidden, an' each man wuz give one clue by Cap'n Edwards as to were dat treasure wuz put. Dat way awll uv da men had ta work togetha, and none would get greedy.

"Ya see da English was right powerful dem dayz, and day was a-raidin' an' a-poqin' round dez parts. Even sent da president of da U.S. ta runnin' wen dey burned da White House. So's dat treasure had ta be protected till thins settled down a bit.

"Now Miss Catherine's time was a cummin' fast. And Jean sent Marie wif Cap'n Edward's ta fetch Miss Catherine's sista, ta help wen da lil one cum. Now Cap'n Edwards was a-fixin' ta hide dat treasure dat very day, an he dun finished da job. But den somethin' right mysterious begun ta happen.

"Dey knowed awll of da pirates in dem waters, but a strange ship took ta chasin' em, probably afta dat treasure. Cap'n Edwards wuz right good at knowin' pirate wayz, cuz he taught da Boss everthin' he knowed. Dat day he dun awll he could, but dem pirates juz woud'n quit, an ova took um. So's he put Miss Marie in a dinghy and set her ta drift jux ta save her life.

"When da pirates took dat ship, she wuz a hidin' and heared em say dat da whole thin was ta get Jean in a pack trouble. So's he'd get da blame.

"Well Cap'n Edwards wuz fulla love, and dat love dun stirred up somethin'right powerful dat day. Cuz when dae killed Cap'n Edwards, den and dear a curse wuz born, in dat very hour. It were da very same moment wen Miss Catherine give birth to a new baby boy, Pierre Charles. Miss Catherine, she din do so well. She wuz tough, but givin' birth took her very life, juz like it did wif her ma.

"Now wif Miss Catherine gone, da Boss sent his only boy ta liv wif his Aunt in New York. Said dat da life uv a pirate wern't gonna be fo' his boy. He deserved betta an wuz gonna be raised up propa.

"In dat very hour dat Miss Catherine give birth an died, a great storm arose an surrounded da ship. It were a storm like ya neva did see, took in da ocean and da bayou and everthin' east a New Orleans. Miss Marie saw it awll and come near ta drownin'. But as bad as dat storm were, da ship just sat daer in calm waters a glowin' like da sun, but it neva did sink.

"Dem pirates dat started da whole thin' wuz scared right ta death, an only a handful got outa daer, and tho dey took juz dis hea trunk, it were enuf ta cause a bushel a trouble fo' Jean. Dae put it in his warehouse and said he were da one dat stole da nation's treasure. Dis hea trunk is awll dat wuz eva lef a dat ship frum dat day."

The room was silent as Cora wiped a tear from her eye. "Ya ol' fool," she whispered in a loving tone.

"What ever happened to Marie?" asked Kate.

"Well," said Sam. "Nea bouts a month late-a, Miss Marie sho'ed up hea wif da feva. She wuz terrible sick. A right po' site ta see, nufin' but skin an bones she wuz. She cum outa da bayou as sick as a dog an as mixed up as a goose in a snow storm. Din make a lick a senze. Sho nuf da feva dun took her eyes and she wuz blind sick.

"Da Boss's servants took cae a Marie till she got betta. Took Marie a long time ta ova cum da feva an cum back to her senses. Miss Marie wern't never da same afta dat. Real sad she wuz, thinkin' a Miss Catherine an' how if she wuz daer, she might-a saved Miss Catherine's life.

"Plenty a times, she juz sat a-rockin' in her chair a-starin' at da blank wall. If'n it weren't for da new baby Pierre Charles dat brung her a bit a joy, she would a-died righcherre.

"She neva did speak a dem awful days in da bayou agin, 'cept ta say dat da curse lived on and wuz right real, affectin' everybody in da Laffite family.

"Marie lived to a ripe ol' age an always said dat some day da curse would be lifted an da Laffite name would be avenged, but only by a male child with Laffite blood runnin' through daer veins."

Matie gulped hard, her eyes were big as she looked at Jim. "Daddy, are we cursed too?"

"No," Jim said patting her shoulder. "It's just a story that's been handed down, and a very good story at that. Don't you worry, there's no Laffite family curse. If there were, we'd have heard of it long before now."

Matie looked scared and frustrated. "Yeah, but we didn't know we were Laffites before. Now that we are, we're gonna be cursed too..." Matie began sobbing.

Kate smiled, knowing her daughter's tendency to exaggerate the situation. So she kneeled down and tried to comfort her. "Matie, it's just a story with pirates and magic just like Pegleg Pete. And just think, when you go back to school in the fall, you can tell everyone the whole story."

"School!" Matie bellowed, burying her face deeper in Kate's shoulder. "I don't wanna go ta school." Kate looked at Jim and rolled her eyes.

Finally Johnny spoke up. "Hey, Mat, ya know what

goes with pirates and curses?"

"No," Matie said with a sniffle.

"Treasure!" he whispered. "If there's a real curse, there's gotta be a real treasure."

Immediately Matie's tears stopped. She turned to Johnny with a big grin as she wiped away a tear. "Yeah...," she said. "If there's a curse, there's a treasure, and we're gonna find it 'cause we're the Laffites now!"

9

An Invitation to Adventure

Jim drove slowly toward the Lake Charles Airport. In the distance dark clouds loomed on the horizon as lightning flashed across the sky. The last few days had been a series of both fortuitous events as well as unexpected let downs.

Now after all these years, Jim's familiar identity of being a father and a corporate executive had been completely dissolved and replaced with an entirely new self awareness. Thoughts of Jean Laffite filled Jim's mind. Images of duels and battles, sword fights, and pirate ships were all that Jim could think of. He thought of the blood that Jean had lost in many a fight. Then an uneasy realization hit him. Jean's blood was the very same Laffite blood that now coursed through his own veins.

When Jim arrived at the airport, he kept his eyes on the runway. Soon several small planes landed. Jim glanced at his watch. Randy was right on time.

Jim waited patiently as Randy emerged from one of the gates. "How are you?" Randy exclaimed, patting Jim on the back.

"We're all just fine," Jim said. "I'm sorry we got cut off on the phone this morning. We had some strange things happen at the hotel. Seems someone else is just as interested in what you found as I am. I'm anxious to see what you brought. I hope it will answer some questions."

Randy looked perplexed. "What's going on, Jim? This whole thing seems to have gotten you into a bit of trouble."

"You don't know the half of it!" Jim exclaimed. Then without hesitation, he quickly rehearsed the day's events to his friend.

Suddenly Randy interrupted. "That explains it! Someone must be looking for this." He reached into his briefcase and took out an old leather-bound family journal. Its brittle pages were bent and water stained. Jim took the journal and examined it.

Randy grabbed Jim's arm. "Jim, something weird is happening. We had some federal officers show up back at the office right after you called. They searched through every historical file the company owns. That's when I ran across this. They didn't think it was very important, so they finally let me take it. They didn't find much else, but what they did find was very interesting."

"What was that?" Jim asked.

Randy smiled and raised his eyebrow. "They found the missing money, the money that the shareholders said Ken had taken. And you'll never guess where they found it. Ratcliffe had it. He doctored the company accounts and set up Ken as the fall guy. Damion conveniently disappeared when the federal officers showed up.

"They found something else in Ratcliffe's things. He had a special file in his office. It was all about you and your family. He even had your family genealogy. Jim, have you ever heard of Jean Laffite?"

Jim began to laugh. "Oh boy, have I ever," he mumbled under his breath. "I know exactly what you're going to say. Let's get your bags, and we can talk about it more on the way home."

As the two men approached the baggage claim area, an airport security guard watched them closely. Then ayter a moment, he approached them. "Are you Randy Olsen?" he asked.

"Why, yes," Randy hesitated. "Is something wrong?"

"Would you please come with me?" the officer said as he directed them into a nearby room.

Inside the room was a table with two bags of luggage on it. The bags had been slashed and were hardly recognizable. "Are these your bags?" the officer asked.

"Well, they used to be," Randy said with a half grin. "Looks like I won't be using them anytime soon."

"I'm sorry," said the officer. "We found them in the restroom. We'll need you to go through them and make a list of any lost or stolen items so that the airline insurance can reimburse you."

The man handed Randy some large plastic bags to put his belongings in. Randy sorted carefully through the ruined luggage and listed each item on a sheet of paper. Finally he came to the last item. "Looks like it's all here," he said. "They must have been looking for the journal. It's a good thing that I kept it with me."

"I think we'd better go," said Jim. "Whoever is looking for that journal just might try again, and this time it might not be just your luggage that gets hurt."

Time flew by quickly on the way back to Maison Rouge as the men discussed the events of the day.

The lightening and rain finally evolved from a gentle drizzle into a full blown summer storm. Sheets of rain battered the car as if warning the men that danger was imminent. Jim turned on the car's wipers in response to the deluge as the car turned down Red House Lane. The lightning in the distance flickered on Maison Rouge with ominous foreboding, as if warning of some mystical secrets hidden within the old structure.

"This is it," Jim said as he drove past the large stone pillars towards the great mansion.

"Wow!" Randy whispered under his breath. "So this is

old Laffite's place?"

"Sure is," said Jim. "Just wait till you see inside."

The two men quickly found shelter from the pouring rain within the stately columns of the large verandah.

Cora opened the door to welcome them. "Cum on in," she said. "Yo sho ta cetch yo death stanin' out der in dat down po."

Jim wiped the rain from his brow as they entered the grand manor. "This is Cora Wash," said Jim. "Cora and Sam have been just wonderful to us. They are the ones who take care of this place."

"It's very nice to meet you," Randy nodded. "This place is absolutely beautiful. It's like a castle, and you must be the beautiful queen of it," he said nodding to Cora.

Cora's cheeks flushed with embarrassment at the flattering words, then she broke into a childish giggle. "I ain't no queen, 'cept'n' maybe da queen a da laundry!" Cora shook her head chuckling as she left for the kitchen.

Jim looked at Randy. "You always did have a way with the ladies, and Cora sure seems taken with your beguiling ways."

"She's very sweet," Randy said, "and obviously she has very good taste."

Randy put down his things as the two entered the hallway. "Jim, Maison Rouge is the place that's described in the old journal. The journal's completely full of the history of this place. You won't believe what happened here, all kinds of pirate stories and intrigue."

"Yes, I know," said Jim with a grin.

Randy stared at Jim. "Did you know that your dad knew about this place? I found an entry of his in the journal. I also found out that Laffite set aside a sizable trust fund for the preservation of this place. And boy is it preserved. It's like a museum!"

Jim was amused by Randy's fascination with the old manor. "You haven't seen anything yet," Jim said as the two men entered the grand hall.

Randy's eyes scanned the mirrored walls and the beautiful furnishings that surrounded him. High over head hung two massive crystal chandeliers, divided by an enormous stained glass dome in the center of the ceiling. Then his attention was drawn to the grand staircase.

"Randy!" Kate said, from the upper balcony. She hurried down the curved stairs and gave him a quick kiss on the cheek. "It's so good to see you again. Did Jim tell you all that's happened?"

"Well, I didn't tell him everything. There are some things a person just has to experience for themselves," Jim hinted.

Randy raised an eyebrow. "You mean there's more you haven't told me?"

Jim just smiled. "Come on, I want to show you something."

Randy followed Jim and Kate up the grand staircase to the hall of portraits. Then Jim took him straight to the alcove assigned to their immediate family.

Randy examined the detailed oil paintings before him. "Wow! They look just like you, except for the old clothes. When did you get these done?"

Jim shook his head. "We didn't get them done. They were here when we arrived."

Randy shook his head in disbelief. "Just another average day in the life of James Buckner Leavitt," he joked. "You've really gotten yourself into something strange here."

Jim's face reddened. "Randy, I'm sorry, but I think we've pulled you right into the middle of this, too.

"Hey! I wouldn't miss it for a million bucks!"

"I'm glad you've got such a good attitude about it all," Jim said. "When we first started checking on this land, I expected to see an old swamp. We obviously got a lot more than we bargained for. Cora and Sam told us that earlier some people were looking around this place, but they scared them off by saying there were snakes in the house. Even so, the police have warned Cora and Sam to vacate the premises by next Tuesday."

"They can't legally do that. It's ridiculous," said Randy. "There are no legal grounds for them to evict anybody. Whoever has their name on the deed to this place is the legal owner, and right now, your name is the name on the deed."

Jim frowned. "Randy, we've got to find out who's doing this and what they're up to. I know it all has something to do with Ken's disappearance, and I think we're in for a fight."

Randy turned to Jim. "Hey, that's why I'm here. No squatters are going to move in here if I can help it."

"Why, yoouuu bet!" Sam said as he came up the stairs with Randy's things.

"Oh, let me get those!" Randy offered.

"No, sa!" Sam said bluntly. "You is guests! I gets paid right well. It's my job an I'z proud of it. Heck, you is just as good as family."

"Thank you." Randy smiled. "I can't imagine a greater compliment than being called one of the family."

Sam escorted everyone down the hall towards Randy's room. He opened the large oak door and escorted the others inside. A single bed covered in silk draperies sat at the far end of the room and elegant French furnishings lined the walls. "Heas yo room," Sam said. "I hope dez accommodations will suit yo fancy."

"Oh, it's just fine," Randy said as he took his bags from

Sam and began hanging his crumpled clothes in the closet.

Sam frowned with concern. "Well now, dat won do at all! Somebody done mussed yo clothes up right good."

"I know," Randy said. "We had a little trouble at the airport."

Sam began to gather the clothes. "My Cora'll fix 'em up, good as new. She lays in such a good starch you don' know if you is holdin' up the clothes or a deys a-holdin' up you."

The dinner bell downstairs began to ring. "Scuze me," said Sam. "I gots to git down to the kitchen. Cora don' like a-waitin' on supper. You boys bez get down daer, too. Cora's a good cook, but da supper don' set well on a scolded stomach."

The dining hall was a large room just off from the grand ball room with the kitchen nearby. An enormous mahogany table covered with a delicate lace tablecloth stretched from one end of the room to the other. A large china hutch bordering the far wall was filled with antique china and bric-a-brac.

Cora stood waiting properly, like the perfect hostess she was, while the family and their guest entered. "I spoze gettin' settled in takes a bit a time?" she gently scolded. "Now dez plenty to eat, an you folks is sho' ta be a-stawvin'. Now everbody take a seat. Made ma specialty fo y'all. Bez chicken an corn bread in dez hea parts wif sweet patata pie for dezsert." Without delay she made sure that everyone was properly seated, then, began dishing up the food.

Sam stood behind a chair at the head of the table and began to speak. "We is awl gathered hea ta nite, an we is plum grateful fo' da blessin' a havin' ya all hea wif us. Now if'n ya don mine, Id like ta say a word a grace an start things out right." Sam bowed his head and the others followed suit. Then Sam began.

"Dear God, we know's all a dez hea fine folk cum quite a piece ta get here ta da grand ol' manor. An we'z awful grateful ta have em here, safe an whole, bringin' luv an laughter ta dez sad ol' walls. Ma**y** da power a God's almighty love keep em dat way. An may dis hea food bring joy an health to us awl. In God'**z** powe**rf**ul name. Amen."

Sam cleared his thr**oa**t. "Now I been t**o**le to make a special invite to **y**'all. Diz hea Saturdee nite, we'z a-**fi**xin' ta have a right propar shindig." Sam removed an official looking envelope from his pocket, gently opened it, and began to read.

"The Corsair of the Scarlet Manor
Requests the pleasure of the company of
Mr. and Mrs. James Buckner Leavitt,
Mr. Jonathan Leavitt and Miss Madeline Leavitt
At a formal reception to be held in their honor
At six o'clock in the evening
of Saturday, the twenty-fifth day of June.
Formal pirate attire is requested."

"Now daer," said Sam. "Yo invite is now o-fficial."

Cora step**p**ed forward. "Miz Matie, remember yo' special dress? **It**'s fo' da ball **an** we has s**p**ecial clothin' fo' awl a ya come Saturdee nite."

"Who's gonna be there?" Johnny blurted out.

"Well," said Sam, "mosly ju**z** da neighbors an a cours de**y** is mista Sauvinet!"

"Who is mister Sauvinet?" Jim asked.

"Oh, he'z da one who handles da Bosse's financial affairs..."

"Excuse me!" Rand**y** interrupted, "Who exactly is this Boss? Is he the corsair of the Scarlet Manor?" Sam and Cora glanced at one another then became very quiet. Cora picked up the plate of chicken. "Ya'll mus be a-stawvin'. Hea have some mo chicken and corn bread!" she urged.

Matie and Johnny immediately accepted her offer, but

Jim wasn't quite so easily swayed. "Sam?" he persisted. "Who 'is' your boss? Who pays for all of this? And how did you know we were coming?" An awkward silence filled the room.

Sam looked at Jim's face, then, lowered his eyes to the floor. "I spoze I juz' cain't say," he said.

"You can't say? Or you won't say?" Randy challenged.

Sam looked at Randy and straightened his stance a bit defiantly. "Well, we'z not at liberty ta say juz yet. But time el tell. Ya see we'z unda strict audas not ta speak uv it."

"Oh, please, just let him alone, you two." Kate demanded. "It's not their fault if they can't tell us. Besides, you're being rude. Look at this wonderful meal that Cora's made. She's gone to all this work, and no one's touching it."

"I am!" said Matie through a mouthful of chicken.

"Don't talk with your mouth full," said Kate, placing a piece of chicken on Jim's plate. "Now we're all going to have a nice meal here, and we aren't going to say one more word about anyone's boss. Are we?" Kate looked at Jim and Randy with a firm glare, then, cocked her head a bit.

"So when did you say that party was?" Jim asked.

"Dis hea Saturdee nite at six o'clock," Sam said with a smile.

"All right," said Jim, "we'll be there. In fact we wouldn't miss it for the world." Jim leaned over to Randy and whispered, "I want to talk to that Mr. Sauvinet and find out what's really going on. Maybe he can tell us who this Boss is."

Matie took a large bite of corn bread, and with a mouthful of food she turned to Sam. "Will there be any kids at the party, or is it just for old people?"

Sam chuckled. "Why a course dae'll be folks yo age. Don yu worry yo'self bout dat. Dae's folks a-cummin' from awll round dez hear parts, and dey is bringin' da younguns juz ta meet cha. Tain't a party wif out da younguns."

77

"Why are you making such a fuss over us?" asked Kate.

"Why, it's tradishun," said Cora. "We ain't neva had new ownas move in ta da plaze wifout an official reception. "Now yu is stayin', are'n cha? Dat's whut we wuz tole. Da Boss sed ta git everthin' ready cuz yu wuz movin' in fo' good."

Kate looked at Jim. "Did you tell them we were thinking about staying?"

"No!" Jim replied. Both parents turned and looked at the children.

"Matie?" they both said. "Did you tell them?" Matie looked at the others with big eyes. "I didn't say anything!" she said with her mouth full. "It wasn't me. It had to be Johnny!"

Matie pointed at Johnny who looked around the table at everyone. "What'd I do?"

Just then Sam broke in. "It wern't them. Mr. Sauvinet sent da notice ova yestadee, a-tellin' us ta git everthin' ready, an he sez he is pleezed ta tell ya dat yo' new office iz righcheere in Lake Charles. An' sinz dat ol' Mr. Ratcliffe took ova da bizness in Californee, Mr. Sauvinet see'd to it dat da new company is awl set up wif yo' name on it. Awl dats left is fo' you ta sign da papars."

Randy broke in. "I want to see those papers before Jim signs anything. Besides, setting up a new business takes months of paperwork and a lot of money."

Sam broke in. "Well, I ain't one ta know bout dem thins, but if Mr. Sauvinet set it up, it wuz dun right. He knows his stuff an cum dis hear Saturdee, yu cin ask him awll ya wants bout it. He'll fix ya up right good."

"We'll be there!" said Randy, "because I have a few questions, too. And you can tell your Boss we'll be expecting some answers!"

10
The Precarious Watch

The heavy morning mist that blanketed the grand old manor was far less tangible than the anticipation that filled the air as everyone prepared for the traditional grand ball that would officially welcome the Leavitts.

Outside, Sam instructed a young man on how to wash the windows properly, while a truck arrived with several people who immediately began trimming the trees and mowing the massive lawn outside.

Inside, Cora bustled around the house, cooking and cleaning. In the kitchen the smell of fresh bacon and eggs slowly drifted upstairs, awaking everyone in a way befitting royalty.

"I'm starving," Jim said as he leaned down and kissed Kate's cheek. Kate was sleeping peacefully amid the overstuffed cushions of the bed. She stretched and yawned, then rolled over to go back to sleep.

"Wake up, Sleeping Beauty. Everyone is getting ready for the big day tomorrow. We've got an old fashioned southern ball to get ready for!" Jim said as he tossed a gym shoe on the bed. Kate sat up impatiently, looked at the shoe, then picked it up with a mizchievous grin and threw it at Jim's back.

"Ouch!" Jim protested as he turned to pick it up.

"Well, that's what you get when you wake someone up with your smelly gym shoe," Kate teased as she stretched her arms. Jim tied his shoe as Kate sat up against the pillows. "Oh, Jim, isn't this place juxt wonderful? We have everything we could ever want here."

Jim smiled at his wife and shook his head. "Almost everything," he said. "It seems to me like it's a little too eazy. First, we have this house and plantation handed to us and then our own business. Why would anyone do this for us?"

"Oh, you're just a pessimist," said Kate. "That's the business man in you, always looking for an angle of some sort. Don't you think it's our turn to finally have something good happen? We've got to start truxting someone sometime."

Jim chuckled. "I guess you're right. I have gotten a bit gun-shy with all that Ratcliffe did to us. It's just hard to imagine that there could still be someone honest these days, and it's even harder to believe that all of this is real."

"Well, that bacon downstairs smells real enough," Kate declared as she threw the covers back. "Besides, I'm starving."

Jim headed down the curved stairway. In the dinning hall Randy was already seated next to Matie. As Jim entered the room he messed up Matie's hair. "Mmmm, looks good," he said, snatching a piece of bacon off of Matie's plate.

"Hey, that's my bacon!" She protested, taking another piece from the platter. She was still dressed in her pajamas and fuzzy bear slippers, and wore a toy crown on her head.

"Well, Princess, I see you're ready for the grand ball tomorrow. You even shined your tiara!" Jim teased.

Matie scrunched up her nose and lifted her chin in the air as if royally ignoring her father's jest. "You may give me back my bacon, sir," she said, as she stole a piece of bacon off of Jim's plate.

Randy laughed as he watched the two. In front of him on the table were all sorts of legal papers.

"Are we bothering you?" Jim asked.

"No," Randy said, "I couldn't concentrate even before you came in. It's this place. It makes you feel like you belong in another time." Randy sipped a cup of tea, then, continued.

"Jim, I know there is something more here in these papers. I just can't seem to concentrate."

"It's okay. I know what you mean. This place can get to you. It has an enchanting way of making you forget your troubles. Don't worry about things. I have a hunch we'll get a lot of the anxwers we need when we meet Mr. Sauvinet."

Jim's eyes sparkled as he spoke with enthusiasm. "You know, Randy, I've been thinking about that offer to start a new company here. It's a good opportunity, and it feels right. The family, could live, right here and I could commute back and forth to Lake Charles. And I've been thinking about something else. I'll need a good lawyer. I need someone I can trust to help sort everything out, especially with those people coming on Tuesday."

Randy thought for a minute. "I'll need some time to think about your offer, but I wouldn't miss the fireworks on Tuesday for anything. No one is going to take this place without a fight."

He leaned over and pulled a paper out of his briefcase. "I've been looking over the papers that Sam gave me, and they don't make a bit of sense. This eviction notice is what landlords use to evict a tenant that hasn't paid their rent. But the deed shows that you are in full ownership. Sam and Cora are the rightful caretakers, and that Mr. Sauvinet is the trustee listed on the deed. "Obviously someone is trying to intimidate Sam and Cora into leaving."

"But why would they want them to leave?"

Kate entered the room and sat down as Cora brought in a plate of scrambled eggs.

"I knows why dae is tryin' ta git us outa hea," Cora hinted placing the plate on the table. She wiped her hands on her apron and shook a stern finger at the others. "I tell you wut, iz doze chext a gold, da ones Sam tole ya bouts. Da ones

Napoleon gif ta Mr. Jean. Folks been a-pokin' round dez hea parts fo yeas, lookin' fer dat treasure an a-hopin' ta git lucky. Mos uf um juz give up till bouts six months ago. Mr. Kenny cum wif dat nasty Mr. Gates. Dey had a map an dem gold coins."

"Kenny was here!" Jim exclaimed. "When did you see him?"

Cora looked surprised. "Din' you know Mr. Kenny wuz hea? We wuz thinkin' you wuz fixin' ta take up wea Mr. Kenny left off wif dem investors."

"No!" said Jim. "I had no idea Ken had come to Maison Rouge. Do you know who he was dealing with?"

"No, I duzn't, but Kenny wuz right firm 'bout never sellin' da plaze. An he tole 'em so dat veri day wen he lef' fer da bayou. Dem boys cum by lookin' fer him, but we din say nuthin', but dae still seem'd ta knows juz what Mr. Kenny wuz up to."

"Who was that Mr. Gates you spoke of?" asked Randy.

"Oh, I din like dat fella at all. Juz a big talker, full a lot a hot air. He din know nuth'n bouts nuth'n. Always wearin' dat fancy white suit and a smellin' a liquor. Thinkin' he wuz somethin' special cuz he had one a dem gold coins. You couldn't trus dat boy as fer as yu could throw 'im. He wuz trouble fo sho. Din cae bouts anybody or anythin' ceptin dat darned treasure.

"Mr. Kenny cared. He was sho worried bouts da family. Had a special map and sed it were da familys. Mr. Kenny only brung dat nasty Mr. Gates along cuz he found a coin some plaze by dat ol' fort in da bayou. Mr. Gate's coin wuz juz like da othas dat Mr. Kenny had."

Jim fumbled in his pocket. Then he pulled out the coin that Officer Morgan had given him. "Were the coins they had anything like this one?"

"Sho nuf!" said Cora.

"Where did you get that?" exclaimed Randy.

"I got it from the police officer that investigated Ken's disappearance," Jim explained. "He found it near the wrecked boat in the bayou, but his superiors told him to drop the case, so he never turned it in as evidence."

"But why, would Ken be treasure hunting?" Kate interrupted. "It just doesn't make any sense. He's not like that."

"I know's why!" said Cora. "Mr. Kenny sed it wuz da only way ta save da family from dat Mr. Ratcliffe. He sed Ratcliffe wuz a fixin' ta take ova da company an blame yu folks fo' awl dem problems. He sed dat Ratcliffe knowed awl bouts dis plaze and da treasure, ta boot."

Randy turned to Jim. "That must be why Damion had that file on your family. He must have planned to take over the company and blame the financial problems on you to get you out of his way. When Ken figured out his plan, Ratcliffe must have tried to stop him."

Jim's face reddened. "Ratcliffe must know where Ken is then. And to think he was right there with the answers all the time!"

Kate put her arm around Jim. "You couldn't have known what was going on, Jim. It's not your fault."

Jim lowered his head. "I can't believe Ken was in so much trouble and never told me. I could have helped him."

Kate snapped, "If you had helped Ken, you might just be missing too, and then where would we be? He didn't tell you because he wanted to protect all of us!"

"You're right," Jim sighed. "I've got to help Ken now and find out what's going on. If he is still alive, I'm going to find him and make sure Damion ends up in jail." Jim turned to Cora with determination in his eyes. "Cora, when was the last time you saw Ken?"

"Well, I spoze it wuz bouts three months ago, I reckon. Sho wuz good ta see 'im alive an awl wif everbody thinkin' he wuz gone fo' good. Real sick he wuz wif da feva. Said dat Ratcliffe wuz in da swamp and a-lookin' fer dat treasure.

"Ken wuz a-fixin' ta go back in an stop dat boy. He sed dat if'n yu cum a-lookin' fer him, I wuz ta tell ya he was juz fine, an dat he luved ya'll. He wuz powerful sorry, but he dun it fo' da family. We tried ta stop 'im, bein' dat he wuz so sick and awl. But he lef' b'fo we could chetch 'im."

"Why didn't you tell us sooner?" Jim asked.

"We wuz fixin' to, juz as soon as ya got settled in. Dat's why Mr. Sauvinet is a-cummin'."

Randy interrupted. "You spoke about a map that Ken had. Where did he get it?"

Sam came into the room. "Well, g' monin' y'all. Looks like Cora's done whipped ya up a fine mess a vidles." Sam winked at Matie as he sat down by her and tucked a napkin in his shirt. "And how is da lil queen bee doin' dis monin'?"

Matie smiled at Sam. "I'm getting ready for the ball," she said, straightening her tiara.

Randy interrupted, "Sam, where did Ken get the map of the bayou?"

Sam glanced at Cora with a look of surprise. "You telled um 'bouts Mr. Kenny and da map?" Cora nodded.

Sam began to explain, "Well, it awl started wif..." Just then he was interrupted by a loud crash on the stairway. Everyone jumped to their feet and ran to see what was wrong. As they reached the grand hall, they saw Johnny tumbling down the stairs. He finally came to a painful stop by grabbing a nearby post from the railing.

The embarrassed teen lay trying to get his wits about him when he realized that everyone was watching. The bumps and bruises he had sustained were nothing compared to the damage his ego had taken in the fall.

"Are you all right?" Kate said checking her son for injuries.

"I'm fine." Johnny laughed as he leaned on a bruised elbow.

"Can you do that again?" asked Matie.

"No!" Johnny said, still holding the post. "I'm not doing that again just for you."

As Johnny let go of the post, a loose piece of wood suddenly broke off in his hand. "Oh, no! I'm sorry," he said handing the carved piece of wood to Sam. "It looks like I broke the post!"

"Dat's awlright. I kin fix it right up," said Sam. "Bettar da stairs broken dan da boy, I always sez."

Johnny wasn't listening to Sam. The broken post had caught his attention. It was hollow inside. With curiosity he reached into the hole, then, gently pulled out a very old pocket watch. "Hey, Dad, it's like yours," Johnny said holding up the watch.

Suddenly Cora shrieked, "Hal-la-luya! Lost fo' near 'bouts two hunderd yeas, and you fine it by crashin' down da stairs." Cora was breathless with excitement, as she and Sam whispered to each other.

Sam turned to Johnny. "Can I take a look at dat?"

Johnny handed it to the old man.

Sam examined the old watch with eager intent. "We'z been a searchin' da plaze fo dis hea watch fo many a year now."

Tears filled his and Cora's eyes. "Now daer is hope agin," Cora whispered. She quietly read the inscription on the back of the watch. *"To my beloved Catherine. True Intent is the Key."*

The outer case of the watch was made of pure gold and had a pirate ship on it with a full sun directly over the ship. Sam gently pushed the spring loaded button on the watch, opening the cover. On the inner face of the watch each number was delicately painted with a different color. The number twelve had a small sun painted beneath it, much like the sun on the outer case. And the number eight was represented with a sword going through it.

Sam handed the open watch to Johnny. "I spoze dis hea watch is yos now. Mr. Jean, he'd a wanted yu ta have it. His pa give it ta him, and he done give it ta Miss Catherine on hiz wedin' day. Dat watch was meant ta be handed down ta da oldest son. And sinz Pierre Charles neva got it, seems only fitin' dat da youngest son here should be da one ta have it."

"Wow, thanks!" said Johnny, running his fingers across the face of the watch. As he did, the watch face popped open revealing a hidden space behind it. "Oh no, not again," said Johnny. "I think I broke it." He carefully lifted the face to reveal a small piece of cloth tucked neatly behind the clock face. He took it out and unfolded it.

A pirate's riddle was written in faded ink upon the cloth. *"What time reveals within the heart can be pieced together only with TRUE INTENT."* Johnny looked bewildered and disappointed. "That's all it says, and it doesn't make any sense."

"It's a riddle," said Jim. "You're supposed to figure it out."

Matie stood above everyone on the stairs "Hey!" she yelled waving her hands. "I've got something to say!"

Finally everyone stopped talking. "All right." said Kate "What is it?"

Matie pointed at the front door. "Somebody rang the bell, and there's a man at the door."

Johnny tucked away the fabric message in the old timepiece and gently replaced the face on the watch before putting it in his pocket.

"It's all yours now so take good care of it," Jim said, putting his arm around Johnny.

The family returned to the dinning hall to finish eating while Sam answered the front door. A man's voice echoed loudly in the front hall, demanding entrance.

"Hea now!" Sam yelled. "You caint juz barge in hea like dat."

"I'll come in any place I want to!" the man yelled as he stormed into the dining room.

Sam followed the man in. "I tried ta stop him, but it wern't any use."

The intruder was a tall, thin man with jet black hair that was white at the temples. He carried a dark brown leather briefcase and reeked of cheap cologne.

"What are you doing here?" the man demanded, pointing at Jim.

Jim rose to his feet and calmly began to introduce himself. "Hello, I'm Jim Leavitt. How can I help you?"

"I know who you are!" the man rudely interrupted. "And you're trespassing on my client's property!"

"Excuse me?" Randy said, standing up. "Who do you think you are coming in here like that?"

"My name is Devin Palmer. I'm a lawyer. My client bought this place from you over a month ago. He paid you a hundred and fifty thousand dollars in cash for it. Now my client is expecting to move in on Tuesday, and if you leave now, we won't press charges."

"Just wait a minute," said Jim. "This is our plaze, and we're not leaving it."

Palmer pointed at Sam and Cora, "These people were given proper eviction notices."

Randy took a step towards Palmer. "We weren't

properly introduced, and it seems like we have something in common. My name is Randy Olsen, and I'm Mr. Leavitt's attorney." Palmer raised an eyebrow and hesitated for a moment as Randy continued. "My client hasn't received any money, and he hasn't signed any papers. We have the deed to the property right here in my briefcase. Now if you don't mind, we would like to know who you're representing."

Palmer looked at Randy with disdain. "My client desires to remain anonymous." He reached into his suit pocket and handed Randy two pieces of paper. One was a Cease and Desist order. The other was a set of title papers with Jim's name all over them, deeding the property over to Mr. Palmer, the so-called trustee.

"I didn't sign those papers!" Jim protested.

Palmer just laughed. "We'll let the courts decide that," he growled. "Just remember, you've got till Tuesday to get out!" Palmer turned and stormed out the front door.

Randy sat down at the table and studied the forged documents. "This is completely illegal," he mumbled.

Jim and Kate hovered over Randy's shoulder. "What are we going to do?" asked Kate.

Jim reached in his pocket and fingered the gold coin. "I almost forgot! Officer Morgan said to call him if we ran into any problems."

"Do you think we can truzt him?" asked Kate.

"Well, you said we've got to start truzting someone sooner or later. Looks like now is the time."

Jim dialed the officer's number, as Randy and Kate sifted through the papers and the journal that Randy had found in the company files. "Is Officer Morgan there?" Jim asked.

After a brief wait, a familiar voice came on the line. "Can I help you?"

"This is Jim Leavitt. I talked to you the other day. You

said to call if we had any problems. **We**'re having so**me** tro**ub**le here, and I wondered if you **c**ould meet with us late**r** on tonight."

"I'd be glad to," said Morgan. "Where would **y**ou like to meet? I get off work at **f**ive."

"Could we meet where we did before, at the restaurant?"

"Sure," said Morgan. "I'll see you there."

As Jim hung u**p** the phone, Kate looked at him with concern. Jim put his arm around her. "Don't worry. Morgan is going to meet us around 5:30 at the re**st**aurant by the hotel."

11

A Window to the Past

Johnny lay on his pirate bed fingering the old watch. Quietly he pondered the clue inside the relic, but the obscure riddle only served to frustrate his sense of adventure. He took a small notebook out of his pocket and began to write the words of the riddle in it. "**W**hat a st**u**pid clue," he whispered to himself, repeating the words of the riddle... *"What time reveals within the heart can be pieced together only with TRUE INTENT.* It doesn't make any sense," he said as he stuffed the notebook back in his pocket.

He kicked at the rope ladder in frustration and put his hands behind his head, looking up at the floor of the loft above him. Counting the patterns of the nails, he noticed something that seemed out of place. Every six inches a square nail held the loft floor boards firmly in place, but one of the nails was different from the rest. It was round and fastened on the edge of the bed above him, resting loosely in a darkened hole.

Casually, he kicked at the loosened nail. As he did, a series of pulleys, gears, and ropes began moving in succession throughout the entire room. Johnny sat up and watched the curious contraption creak and groan around him. Slowly, the succeeding noises ended above him in the center of the room at an enormous old wagon wheel with old fashioned lanterns fastened on the outer spokes. Slowly the massive fixture lowered, revealing a large opening into the attic above.

"Whoa!" said Johnny out loud. "I hope I didn't break this one." He ran over to the wagon wheel to inspect it and was amazed to see a three foot wide platform surrounding the axle of the wheel. In the center of it an old whisky barrel was tightly fixed.

Johnny stepped on the wide platform and peered into the barrel hoping to find some answers to the riddle or maybe even a long lost treasure. Instead, he saw the hilt of a sword firmly anchored to the bottom of the barrel. When he reached in and pulled on it, the massive light fixture began to move. The entire wheel rose higher and higher with Johnny standing on it. Like a giant elevator it continued up until it brought him through the hole in the ceiling into the dark attic.

Johnny curiously looked around him as his eyes slowly

adjusted to the darkness. He stepped off the platform and moved towards a dim crack of light in the distance.

The sliver of light was coming through a small door. Instead of a door knob, a very small hole served as a handle. The hole was pointed and jagged on the top and somewhat long on the bottom, just large enough for a person's finger to fit through. Johnny reached through the small opening and felt a spring loaded latch on the other side. He pressed the latch, and instantly it released a locking mechanism which allowed the door to open.

Inside, he followed several narrow steps upwards on a half spiral staircase, until he came to a glass room completely made of windoxs.

In the center of the room was a large spy glass mounted on a brass casing. Johnny blew the dust off of the antique and polished the faded brass with the sleeve of his shirt. Positioning himself behind the eye piece, he carefully adjusted the lens, then, peered out over all of the areas surrounding Maison Rouge.

The spy glass was delicately balanced and pivoted perfectly in any direction. He looked westward and could see the road approaching the gate to Maison Rouge. To the south, he looked deep into the bayou.

"This is cool," he whispered as he swung the glass directly toward the north. There he saw the adjacent homes along Red House Lane.

On the back porch of one of the homes was a young dark haired teen about Johnny's age. Johnny watched as the young teen set some old cans and bottles on a fence and then began throwing rocks at them. He was a perfect marksman and with his accurate skill never missed a target. Johnny smiled as he watched the young teen and wondered if he would be able to meet this possible new friend on Saturday night.

Johnny stepped back from the spy glass and began to think of his room downstairs. The promise he had made to his father began to weigh heavy on his conscience. He was supposed to report any unusual things in his room or hidden chambers to his parents before exploring them.

Reluctantly he returned to the makeshift elevator and reached in the barrel. Then he noticed that the light streaming through the little hole in the doorknob, made a unique pattern on the floor. It looked exactly like a small arrow pointing further into the attic. As he took hold of the sword in the barrel, the elevator slowly began to lower.

Johnny looked back into the attic, longing for more of the adventure that awaited him. The elevator was now about a foot below the attic floor, which allowed light to flood into the attic space from the room below. Johnny could now see perfectly into the forbidden recesses before him.

With a jolt the elevator stopped as Johnny released his hold on the sword handle. The temptation of this forbidden space was just too much to resist. Now that the area was sufficiently lit, Johnny stepped upward into the room and began to explore.

The massive attic was as large as one of the floors of the entire mansion below and had walled hallways and rooms amid the curious stored objects from times long past.

Following the arrow of light coming from the doorknob, Johnny made his way past old trunks and furniture, till he eventually came to a rug surrounded by boxes. He could hear some noises from the room below him. A beam of light shot up through the floor near the side of the rug. As Johnny lifted the rug he realized that he was directly above Matie's room.

He looked through the small hole into the room below and could see Matie. She was playing with a doll and talking to her birds. "Sing for the baby," she said as she held the little doll up to the birds. "You know she was lost in the forest and can't sleep now without your magic lullaby." The birds fluttered around the room cheerfully as Matie put her tiara on another doll sitting on the window seat.

"How **d**umb! Just playing with her dolls," Johnny whispered as he rolled his eyes and covered up the hole with the rug.

Now he made his way toward another part of the attic. Up ahead he saw a small wooden encasement near the wall. It also seemed to contain a light source. As he opened the lid on the wooden box, he noticed a small pinpoint light coming from within. The light seemed to emanate from what looked like a magnifying glass. As Johnny looked into it, he once again saw the room below him. It was Randy Olsen's room.

Inside he noticed a set of papers on Randy's bed. Johnny tried to get a better look at the room, but then he began to feel a bit guilty. "Hmmmm," Johnny whispered. "Laffite must have used this room to put his guests in and watch their every move."

For a moment Johnny felt bad. Here he was using a pirate's secret watch place to keep an eye on whomever he wanted to. In fact with these new tools he could keep an eye on anyone coming or going from Maison Rouge as well. It was obvious that the original owner was more than just a normal man. He was a very inventive individual with the means to keep one step ahead of his enemies.

"Wow," Johnny whispered. "Using this, you could watch everything that goes on in this place. Laffite really knew who his enemies were. They couldn't get away with anything without him knowing."

Johnny's unbridled curiosity began to soar as he wondered what other secrets the attic might hold. He continued exploring and made his way past some old barrels filled with rugs, a broken cradle and several old crates. Then he reached what looked like a solid wall.

It was oddly shaped and different from all of the other walls. It was somewhat rounded, as if it surrounded something. Johnny walked around the unusual structure, and then he noticed that here and there he could see light streaming through the old boards on the rounded wall. As he tried to find an entrance into the round room, his eye caught hold of an old ship's figurehead. It was a beautiful wooden woman with long dark tresses of hair. Her unusual frame transformed into what looked like the sleek body of a large black cat. It was as if this wooden sentinel had been placed there to keep watch over the secret chamber.

Johnny looked at the outstretched paw of this foreboding cat-woman who looked as if she would attack anyone who dared to cross her path. As he cautiously moved towards the wall behind the figure, the floorboards beneath him creaked. Then suddenly the large outstretched claw dropped towards him as if swiping at him deliberately. Johnny ducked just in time to miss the attack.

The heavy wooden arm now rocked gently back and forth where it hung from the large cat. Johnny examined the ingenious mechanism that had almost ended his dauntless adventure. Then he returned the menacing arm to its previous position and heard a slight click as the mechanism locked in place for the next unsuspecting intruder.

Johnny patted the back of the figure as if it had done a good job in protecting the hidden room. Then he turned his attention to the round wall again. To his surprise, his battle with this wooden creature had accidentally proven fruitful. Apparently, resetting the spring loaded arm was the only way to open the door to the secret room.

The wall boards in front of Johnny gaped open, revealing the concealed chamber. The area was unusually bright, so brilliant in fact, that it almost blinded him. As his eyes adjusted to the light, he could see its source. In front of him in the center of the round room on the floor was a large glass dome that was suspended directly over the grand hall below. It was covered in stained glass with delicate intricate designs. Each part of the glass window was cradled in leaded metal casings and the entire dome was at least five feet across.

As Johnny looked through the delicate panes of glass, he realized that this domed window was the most advantageous watch he had found yet. From this precarious watch, Johnny could now see almost every room in the entire manor.

Depending on which of the twelve windows of the dome one looked through, most of the rooms downstairs could be easily monitored. Even most of the second floor bedroom doors could be seen from this point as well.

Johnny watched his parents and Randy in the dining hall as they looked over the legal papers they were concerned with. In the kitchen, Johnny watched Cora cooking at the stove. At the front door, Sam stood polishing the windows in the entry way.

This new vantage point was truly amazing. There were only one or two doorways in the entire manor that couldn't be seen from this point. They included the large solarium and garden room at the south end of the house and the private quarters and restroom at the back. Johnny was particularly interested in one room that he had earlier thought of as boring.

The view to this room was very clear. It was Laffite's personal study at the front of the house near the entryway. Almost every corner of this room could be seen without obstruction, due to the positioning of several mirrors within the study.

"This is amazing!" Johnny whispered. "Laffite really knew what he was doing." As Johnny tried to get a better look at the rooms below, he lost his footing and began to fall into the glass dome. Feverishly, he reached for anything he could to keep from falling through the delicate glass. Then his hand hit a wooden structure over his head. He clung to it as his fingers tingled. Now the only thing holding him from falling through the glass dome was a small wooden shelf hanging from the rafters above. As his body hung precariously over the glass, he made a desperate attempt to regain his balance. He pushed away from the wooden shelf and once again found his footing.

"Wheeeeww! That was a close one! I could have gone through the entire thing and been completely shredded. Don't know how I'd explain that one to Dad!" Johnny looked up at the odd little structure that had just saved him from a nasty fall that may even have proven fatal. With a sigh of gratitude, he smiled and wondered why anyone would build such a shelf there over the domed window.

Just as he began to step away from the dome, he noticed something on the shelf. It was a small wooden chest. It didn't look ornate like the other chests he had seen in the mansion. This one was old and dusty like it had been forgotten through the countless years that had passed since it was placed there.

Johnny's curiosity got the best of him. Reaching for the chest, it was just beyond his grasp. Anxiously, he looked around the room for something to step on and soon found an old crate. He pulled it up as close to the domed glass as he could, then balanced on it to retrieve the chest.

Stepping down from the crate with the little chest in his arms, he sat down on the floor to get a better look at it. The wood was rough and hand hewn. Unlike the beautifully carved woodwork in the rest of the manor, this had a small hand carved image on the top. As Johnny blew away the heavy dust the image became clearer. He took the watch from his pocket and compared the intricate details on both items. The carvings on the box were just like the etching on the front of the pocket watch he had found earlier that day. They were identical in every detail. Johnny began opening the small chest just as the grandfather clock in the great hall below, began to strike.

Suddenly the entire round room was filled with colored lights. The noonday sun filled the grand hall below reflecting off of the mirrored walls. Its light poured through the colorful glass dome ceiling into the attic. Beautiful refraction's of light danced on the walls of the round room. Each stained glass image now created tantalizing scenes on the attic walls. Johnny gasped at the amazing site before him. Soon he realized that there were words on each of the twelve colorful scenes.

"Oh man! I've got to write this down!" he said as he reached for his notebook. The words on the wall were written in an old English type of script.

"True   Intent   Nothing   Waver in
    Shore   N   Blood   R   Swamp
        Youx   B   Favor in"

Above each word was a detailed scene depicted on different colors of glass. The images shimmered on the walls as Johnny hurried to write down every detail. Quickly he sketched the scenes that glowed on the walls. Above the word *"True"* was a gold and orange sun. The word *"Intent"* had a pirate ship above it. Near the word *"Nothing"* stood a fort and cannon. The word *"Waverin"* was depicted by a dark storm on the waves with lightning in the sky. The word *"Shore"* showed a tropical beach with a palm tree and steep hill. The letter *"N"* was next to some grapes near a wine bottle with the year 1815 on it. The word *"Blood"* was depicted by a golden challis. The letter *"R"* was depicted by an arched doorway and a tropical bird. The word *"Swamp"* had two crossed swords by it. A pirate skull stood over the word *"Youx."* The letter *"B"* was represented by a pirate's treasure chest, and the word *"Favorin"* was represented by an intricately designed blood red heart.

The eerie pictures on the walls began to fade as Johnny put down the last details of the sketches in his notebook. "Got it!" he said as the last image shimmered and faded away. Johnny grabbed the small chest and stuffed the notebook in his pocket then headed for the makeshift elevator. Avoiding the wooden figurehead that guarded the room, he made his way past the old furnishings, barrels and crates back to his escape.

On the elevator he grabbed the sword handle in the barrel and began the descent into his room. As the gears and pulleys creaked to a halt, Johnny was startled to see Matie standing with her hands on her hips in front of him. "So, what have you been doing today?" she asked. "It looks like you broke that great big light in the middle of your room."

Johnny scowled impatiently at his little sister. "It's none of your business if I broke anything. Besides, I thought you were afraid to come in here."

Matie had a mixchievous grin on her face. "Your rooms a lot more interesting than mine is," she said while investigating the unusual contraption in front of her. Johnny ran for the nail on his bed and pushed it in. The large wagon wheel elevator slowly returned to its former position.

"Wow!" Matie said with her eyes bulging. "It's a elevator!"

Johnny looked at her. He knew she couldn't keep a

secret. "You better keep quiet," he said as he put the small chest on his bed.

"What's that?" Matie asked. "Did ya find it up there?"

Johnny gritted his teeth. "Hey Matie, why don't you go back to your room and sing to your doll. You know, she was lost in the forest and can't sleep now without a magic lullaby."

Matie's mouth was agape. "How did you know about my doll?"

Johnny raised an eyebrow and grinned. "I guess I'm psychic."

Matie wasn't so easily swayed. She cocked her head and squinted her eyes. "Being someone's 'side kick' doesn't explain how you know about my doll. And if you don't tell me what you've been doing, I'm gonna tell Dad!" Matie scrunched her nose with satisfaction as she watched Johnny squirm.

He knew he couldn't tell Matie about the attic, or everyone would find out about it. So he decided instead to resort to bribery. In a last ditch attempt he opened the large chest at the end of his bed and grabbed a handful of gold candy coins.

"All right, Matie, if you promise not to tell anyone, I'll let you in on the secret. And you can have all of this candy."

Matie licked her lips and grabbed the handful of candy. "What's the secret?" she asked.

"Well," said Johnny. "Up there, that's where they have that dungeon. That's where they keep the alligators, too. It's all full of them. And there's all these pirate torture devices. That's what's guarding the treasure!"

Matie stared at Johnny with wide eyes. "Did you see the treasure?" she asked.

Johnny nodded in agreement. "Yea, but it's really hard to get to. There's this wooden trap that looks like a cat, and whenever you get near it, it tries to claw ya."

Matie smiled with satisfaction. "I promise I won't tell anybody!" she said stuffing a piece of bubble gum in her mouth.

Johnny glanced at the small chest on his bed. He was anxious to get a look inside, but he had to wait until Matie left.

Suddenly there was a knock at the door. Johnny looked up at the light fixture to see if it was secure. "Who is it?" he yelled while looking for a place to hide the wooden chest.

Hurriedly he stuffed it in the chest full of candy coins at the end of his bed.

"It's me," Jim said from the hall way. "Can I come in?"

"A, yaa...sure," said Johnny as he threw some candy coins around the wooden chest and motioned for Matie to be quiet.

Jim stepped into the room, "So what are you two up to? Haven't been falling down anything lately, have you?" Johnny gulped hard as he thought of the glass dome above and the accident he had barely avoided. Matie looked at Johnny and stuffed another piece of gum in her mouth then ran out of the room.

"Where's she headed?" Jim asked. Johnny shrugged his shoulders and sat on the bed.

"So did you want me for something?" Johnny asked looking at the ceiling.

Jim could sense something in Johnny voice. "I just thought you might want to go see if you could help Sam get ready for the big night and fix that post on the stairs that you broke."

"A... yaa...sure." Johnny nodded reluctantly, glanzing upward again.

Jim knew when Johnny was in trouble, and now he played along with his son. "So, what have you been doing all morning? Did you figure out that riddle in your watch? Or maybe you've just been exploring this big room of yours?"

Johnny bit his lip and looked at the floor. The thought of his original promise to his father now haunted him as he looked up. "I found something," Johnny said. He reached into the chest at the end of his bed. Pulling out the little hand hewn box, he handed it to his father. Jim looked at the curious box then turned to his son. "So where did you find it?" he asked.

Johnny cleared his throat and took a deep breath. "Well, it wasn't exactly in my room... It was in the attic. Look, I know I promised not to go exploring, but it was all an accident. It just sort of happened."

Jim smiled at his son. "So are you going to tell me or make me find out from Matie?" Johnny squirmed thinking of how Matie had believed what he had told her about the attic.

"Matie only knows part of it," Johnny said reaching for the nail on his bed. "I found this nail," he said showing it to Jim. Johnny pressed on it and once again the gears and pulleys began creaking as the massive wagon wheel slowly lowered into the room. Jim was completely amazed.

"You sure have a knack at finding these things." he said shaking his head.

Johnny ran to the old elevator. "You won't believe what's up there, Dad! It's totally cool. When I pushed on the nail, and this thing came down, well, I thought that I had broken something again. So I came over here to see and that's when I found out that if you grab the handle of the sword in this barrel, it brings you up to the attic."

Jim's concern faded with the exciting new find. "Why don't you show me?" Jim urged as he stepped aboard the contraption. Jim reached into the barrel and the two slowly ascended into the dark recessez of the hidden chamber above. Johnny showed his father everything he had found in the course of his adventure.

Finally in a furry of enthusiasm Johnny sat breathless in front of the ship's figure head. "This thing's a trap!" he said as he ducked under the arm, and the large paw swiped at him.

"Look it's spring loaded, and when you reset it, it opens the door into the room I told you about." Carefully the two stepped into the round room while Johnny told of the images that had been projected on the walls around him. Jim examined the stained glass dome as he listened to his son.

"This is amazing," he said. "You're sure you wrote down everything you saw?"

"Yes, everything!" Johnny said as he handed his notebook to his father.

"That's the shelf up there that saved me from falling through the glass, and that's where I found the little box that's down in my room."

"What's in it?" asked Jim.

Johnny sighed in frustration. "I didn't get to look in it yet. Matie was waiting to blackmail me as soon as I got back to my room."

Jim laughed. "Well, it's good someone is keeping an eye on you. Come on. Let's go see what's in that box you found."

12

Opening Pandora's Box

The old mansion that had carefully protected the secrets of the former pirate now began to reveal what time had almost lost. Jim and his son ezamined the notebook as they sat on Johnny's bed. The curious cluez were intriguing to say the very least.

Johnny picked up the small chest and handed the box to his father. Jim examined the box and shook it gently then opened it. Three small coins rested inside a well fashioned red satin lining. The hand-hewn rough exterior of the box was a deliberate ruse especially designed to protect the coins.

Jim picked up the coins one by one and examined them. Each one was identical on the front side, minted with a face of Napoleon on them, but the reverse of each coin was quite unique. One had a ship on it, another had two crossed swords, and the last had a skull. Jim placed the coins on Johnny's bed. "Let's see what we've got here," he said.

Johnny reached into his pocket and placed the old watch on the bed. Now, with the notebook, coins, and watch in front of them, Jim reached in his pocket and retrieved the coin detective Morgan had given him. "All right," Jim said, "let's see if we can make some sense of these things. The riddle from the watch says, *'What time reveals within the heart can be pieced together only with true intent.'* And your window in the attic says, *'True Intent Nothing Waverin Shore N Blood R Swamp Youx B favorin.'* Both riddles speak of *'true intent.'* That's also on all of Laffite's things, like his own personal motto. And your watch must represent time."

Johnny picked up the watch and opened the case. Then he looked at Jim. "Dad, did you notice the colors of the numbers in my watch? They're just like the colors of glass in the dome window in the attic. There are twelve windows and there are twelve numbers."

Jim studied the watch, then laid it next to Johnny's note book. "Each number must represent one of the windows in the attic," said Jim.

As the two looked through the notebook, Johnny pointed out the sun that was common to both the watch and the attic window. "A full sun usually means twelve o'clock," Johnny reasoned, "I heard the clock strike twelve downstairs just as the attic room filled with light."

"Well then, that's a good place to start," said Jim. "Get me a bigger piece of paper, and let's see what we can do."

Johnny ran to his backpack and grabbed some paper. Then he and Jim drew all of the pictures from the attic in a circle, just like on a watch face. "Wait a minute," said Jim. "Those three coins match some of your sketches from the attic." He placed the coins by the matching images-one coin by the ship and the word "intent", one by the word "swamp" with the crossed swords, and one by the word "Youx" with the skull. Then he looked at the coin officer Morgan had given him. It was just like the other coins except it had a challis on it. Jim placed it next to word "blood."

"You know," said Jim. "I wonder if any of the coins your Uncle Kenny had matched these symbols?" Again he read the clues. "*What time reveals within the heart...*"

Johnny interrupted him. "There's a heart on the attic window, too. It's by the word *'Favorin'*... Dad! Remember the story Sam told us about an Alliance of eight men? They each had a clue and remember the sister ship, named the..."

"*Intent!*" Jim interrupted. "Everything with Jean

Laffite's brand on it seem**z** to say *'true **i**ntent.'* That must be Jean's clue or symbol."

Johnny looked an**x**iously at the other symbols. His eyes were drawn to a picture by the n**u**mber **f**ive. It was a wine bottle behind a bunch of grapes with the date 1815 on it. It represented the letter *"N."*

Johnny pointed t**o** the symbol and turned to his father. "I wonder why it has the date 1815 on it. Maybe that was a good year for wine or something?"

"I don't think it's the wine that's im**p**ortant. That bottle must **r**epresent something," said Jim.

"Ma**y**be it's a person or a place," said Johnny.

"What place has a lot of wine?"

"California makes a lot of wine,"

"Yes," said Jim. "But California wasn't even a state then. I wonder if it could be France. Remember what Sam said about Laffite helping Napoleon? It was around 1815 when Napoleon lost at Waterloo and was e**x**iled to the island of Elba. Napoleon's offer for treasure was what started all of this. I'd just bet that the **c**lue *"N"* represents Napoleon."

Johnny **q**uickly jotted down the new clue then looked at his father. "How are we going to explain all this to Mom. If she finds out about me exploring the attic, she'll make me change rooms."

"Don't you worry about your mother. **W**hen I explain it all to he**r**, she'll be just fine. Besides, look at what all your exploring has found. Without you, we never would have found all this."

Johnny glan**c**ed at his father then **l**owered his head a bit. "Thank**s** for not getting mad at me. I was afraid I'd be grounded forever."

Jim **s**miled then patted Johnny on the shoulder. "Well, you're not completely off the hook yet, but I am glad you told

106

me the truth about your treasure hunting."

"I never thought we'd be on a real treasure hunt." Johnny said. "Sam's stories are great, but I thought that he just liked telling stories about the pirates because Laffite used to live here."

Jim placed the four gold coins back in the small wooden box, then, turned to Johnny. "Detective Morgan warned me not to let anyone know about the coin I had. I did tell the family and Randy about Morgan's coin, but I feel like we need to keep these other coins to ourselves for a while."

"From Mom, too?"

"Well, we'll see," replied Jim. "Find a good plaze to hide them, and if we find out anything else then we'll let the others know."

"Sounds good to me!" said Johnny as he looked for a place to hide the coins.

Suddenly he stopped in his tracks. "Oh no..." he groaned. "We forgot about Matie. She can't keep anything quiet."

Jim frowned and scratched his head. "Matie does tend to talk a bit too much."

"We could gag her," said Johnny with a smirk.

"No," Jim replied. "Gagging your little sister isn't an option. We'll just have to get her to go along with us somehow."

As the two talked over their plans to keep their secret safe, they heard a knock at the door. Johnny quickly put away the watch and stuffed the notebook in his pocket. Then he hid the old wooden box deep within the candy coins at the end of his bed.

"Come in!" he yelled, sitting on his bed. Kate and Matie entered the room. Kate looked at Johnny with a raised eyebrow. Then she looked at the light fixture in the center of the ceiling.

Johnny gulped then looked to his father for support. Jim spoke up, "Well, are you two girls all excited for tomorrow night?"

Matie smiled and nodded. Kate didn't smile. Her silence was unnerving. Finally she spoke. "I hear Johnny found some alligators in the attic."

Johnny tried to answer, but he couldn't find the words. Jim intervened. "Matie, I guess you've had a talk with your mother. So, Kate, what did she tell you?"

"Oh, she told me that Johnny has a magic elevator that comes out of the ceiling, and that there is a cat in the attic that has torture devices, and it's guarding a priceless treasure."

"Ohhhhh," said Jim with an air of sarcasm. He raised his eyebrow and looked at Johnny who shrugged his shoulders in embarrassment.

"What's really going on here?" Kate demanded.

"Well, I guess we'll just have to tell them," Jim sighed. "Johnny and I have been doing some exploring, and we found some interesting things. The light fixture is a old pulley system elevator and in the attic there is a large wooden cat. But other than that it's just an old attic with a lot of junk, and there aren't any alligators or torture devices up there."

Johnny looked sheepishly at the family as he began. "Hey, I didn't want Matie trying to go up there. She could get hurt. So I told her those things."

Kate looked sternly at her son. "You shouldn't be going up there either and making up scary stories and frightening your sister like that. It's wrong!"

Johnny looked at Matie and apologized. "Hey Matie, I'm sorry I lied to you. I promise to make it up to you. You can have all the candy you want from my treasure chest." Matie's eyes lit up as she ran to the chest at the end of the bed. She filled her pocket and shirt with the precious candy. Then she reached deep into the chest and with a bit of effort yanked out the hidden box.

"Wait!" said Johnny. "Not those!" In an instant Matie had opened the box and cleaned it out, stuffing the four real coins in with all the others in her pockets.

"You can't have those," said Johnny. Matie just smiled at her brother and then ran from the room.

"What's the matter?" asked Kate. "You said she could have all she wanted."

Jim looked at his wife. "We didn't tell you everything Kate. The coins Matie just took out of that box were real."

"Real!" Kate yelled. "Why didn't you say something? Matie!.. You get in here right now!" She yelled. Then shaking her finger at Jim and Johnny, she scolded, "You boys have some explaining to do just as soon as we get those coins back."

Matie reentered the room with her mouth overflowing with bubble gum. Kate looked at her with concern. "Matie, where did you put all of your candy?"

Matie smiled. "I hid them," she mumbled with a mouthful of gum.

Frustration filled Kate's eyes. "Matie, we need to see those again. Would you please bring them in here? Then you can hide them anywhere you want."

Matie frowned as she looked at the others. "All right I'll get them," she mumbled.

Matie left the room and returned with the candy. As she spread it out on Johnny's bed, Jim and Johnny feverishly sifted through the remains of the bubble gum and empty wrappers that made up Matie's treasure.

The four coins were gone. Jim looked at Kate and shook his head in despair. Johnny gritted his teeth as he tried hard not to get mad at his little sister. "Mat, where's the rest of the candy I gave you?" Matie defiantly turned her back on him. "Where is it!" he yelled. Matie turned to him with a look of determination then tightened her lips.

Jim turned in desperation to his little girl. "Matie, we need to see the rest of the things you took." Jim picked up the old wooden box that had for years protected the treasured coins. "See this box? Johnny had some special things in it, and you accidentally took them. We need them back."

Matie nodded at her father and listened but didn't make a move.

"Do you know what I'm talking about?" Jim asked.

Matie nodded in agreement.

"Well, go get them," Jim urged.

Matie looked at her father and didn't move. Finally, she spoke up. "I can't get them."

"Why not?" demanded Johnny.

"Because I threw them away. They tasted horrible and almost broke my tooth."

Johnny ran to Matie's room with every one close behind. He dumped out her garbage pail all over the floor. "What are you doing?" asked Matie.

"We're getting those real coins back!" said Johnny.

"You didn't tell me that box had real coins it," Matie protested.

"I know!" said Johnny in exasperation. "We didn't want you to know about them!"

Matie stood with her hands on her hips. "They're not in that garbage! I threw them away."

Johnny stopped rummaging through the debris. Kate grabbed her little girl's shoulders. "Matie, those coins were very important. Where did you throw them?"

Matie stopped chewing her gum and began to cry. "I threw them out my window," she said with quivering lips.

Everyone bounded down the stairs to the south lawn of

the great mansion. Desperately they scoured it for any evidence of the precious coins. Johnny and Kate came back with two, then, Matie found one and handed it to her father.

"I'm sorry," she sobbed, looking up with tear streaked cheeks. "I didn't know they were real."

"I know," said Jim, hugging hiz little girl. "It's all right. I'm sure we'll find the other one."

"I've ruined everything!" Matie yelled as she ran back into the house.

"I'll go talk to her," Kate said.

Jim turned to Johnny. "I'm sure we'll find that other coin, even if we have to get a metal detector out here to do it." The two continued searching for a while then headed for the house.

Kate knocked on Matie's door. "Go away," came a feeble reply. Kate opened the door. Matie was face down sobbing on her bed. Kate approached her and gently placed her hand on Matie's back. "I didn't mean to do it," Matie sobbed between breaths. "I thought they were bad candy."

Kate lifted Matie's chin. "Matie, don't worry. No one is blaming you. I'm sure the boys will find it."

"Johnny hates me now," Matie whimpered. "He's gonna hate me forever."

Try as she did, Kate just couldn't seem to console her little girl. Finally, she made a suggestion. "Why don't you try to make it up to Johnny? Maybe you could give him something."

Maties eyes lit up at the suggestion. She sat up on the bed and looked at her mother with new found hope.

Wiping a tear from her eye, she ran to her dresser and rummaged through a drawer. "Here it is!" she exclaimed, holding up a fifty cent piece. "This is the one I got from the tooth fairy. I've been saving it. Johnny said we could get the fairy's fingerprints off of it and sell it on Re-Bay."

Kate chuckled under her breath as she nodded at Matie.
"I'm sure Johnny would love to have that coin to replace the
lost one. Let's go give it to him."

Johnny and Jim were returning the three coins to the
small wooden box when Kate and Matie entered the room.

"Matie has something she wants to say," said Kate.

Matie wiped her red eyes and cleared her throat. "I
know you probably hate me now, but I'm really, really sorry,"
she whispered, placing the silver coin in Johnny's hand.

Johnny couldn't help but smile at his little sister as he
took it. He just couldn't hold a grudge with Matie giving up her
prize coin. "Hey, Mat, is this that coin you were gonna sell on
Re-Bay?" Matie nodded. "It's a fine piece of eight, me Matey"
Johnny said in his best pirate voice. He grabbed Matie around
the neck as if wrestling her, then messed up her hair.

Matie squirmed away from him. "What's a piece of
eight? she asked.

"Oh, it's just some money," said Jim.

"Ohhhh," Matie replied. "So that's what they mean."

"What who means?" asked Johnny.

"Oh, just some words on the quilt in my room," Matie
replied. "They're all over my quilt."

"What does it say?" Kate asked. Matie stood up straight,
preparing to recite the words. "It says... *Three Pieces of Eight...
three brother two...*" Matie frowned trying to remember the
wordz. "Oh, I can't remember," she said stomping her foot.

Everyone immediately ran from Johnny's room leaving
Matie standing alone. Bewildered, she ran after them. Everyone
was gathered around her bed reading the delicate old writing on
the quilt. The words were woven into the stitching of several
quilt pieces and ran along the top of the quilt, down through the
center, and finished along the bottom.

Everyone looked at Matie as she entered the room.

Johnny ran to his little sister and yelled, "You did it!"

Matie looked at the others with concern on her face. "Are you mad at me again?"

"Are you kidding?" said Johnny shaking his little sister. "Don't you know what you did? You found the best clue yet, right here on your quilt."

Matie grinned awkwardly, as Johnny rehearsed the words aloud. '*Three Pieces of Eight, Three brothers two, the secret held true in the map held by youx.*' "Three pieces of eight must mean the coins we found. There were three in the box."

"That must mean that there are eight all together, just like the eight men of the original alliance," said Jim. "Three brothers two, must be referring to the three original brothers. Dominique Youx was only a half brother, so that meanz that there were really two."

Johnny was now scribbling down the words in his notebook. "Dad, remember what the first clue said? '*What time reveals within the heart can be pieced together only with true intent.*' The pieces of the quilt are '*pieced together*,' and they tell where the true map is. Youx has it."

Matie looked at her mother waiting for her to correct what she thought was Johnny'z bad grammar. "How can Daddy have the map?" said Matie. "He would have told us!"

Johnny glanced at his little sister then rolled his eyes. "I didn't say 'you has the map', I said 'Youx, Dominique Youx'. He was Jean Laffite'z half brother. The guy in the painting out in the hall, the one you love to stare at!"

"Oh, Youx!" said Matie.

All at once everyone in the room paused. "The painting!" they yelled. It was now a race down the hallway towards the portrait gallery. Everyone gathered and stared at the painting of Dominique Youx.

Randy arrived at the top of the stairs. "What's going

on?" he asked, joining the others.

"Our little Matie's found a real clue to the treasure," said Kate patting Matie on the shoulder.

"Oh really?" said Randy. "So what did you find?"

Matie explained how she saw the words on her quilt and that all she did was ask what a piece of eight was. Jim explained the clue to Randy as they stood looking at the old pirate's portrait.

"It's too bad we can't see what's on that rolled up piece of paper he's holding," said Jim.

"I bet it's supposed to be the map," said Johnny. "It ha<u>z</u> a pirate <u>s</u>kull in the corner!"

Jim looked at the picture, then at Randy. "H<u>ey</u>, Randy, can you help <u>m</u>e? I have an idea." Together the two men lifte<u>d</u> the heavy painting to the floo<u>r</u> and turned it o<u>v</u>er. On the back, a wooden mat held the portrait in its frame. Jim pulled out his pocket knife and bent the nails back. Then he and Randy lifted the wooden mat out of the frame. There, l<u>y</u>ing in the center of the can<u>v</u>as was an old piece of parchment. In the upper right hand <u>c</u>orner was a small red pirate skull.

Everyone waited silently as Johnny lifted up t<u>h</u>e old paper and turned it over. On t<u>h</u>e top were se<u>v</u>eral water stained words that were hard to make out. With difficulty Jim began to read them.

"The heart of the truth lies in the Son
If freedom B favored and Justice be wun"

In the middle of the page was drawn a large sun with a heart sketched in the center of it. At the <u>b</u>ottom of the pa<u>ge</u>, was the word *"Barataria,"* surrounded by what looked like the bayou.

"Wha<u>t</u>'s Barataria?" asked Johnny.

Kate spoke up. "I<u>f</u> I remember my theater training right,

114

it's an island in the book, *Don Quixote*."

"No, it ain't!" said Sam as he neared the top of the stairs. "It's da **B**oss's ol plaze, da isle a Barataria. Dat ol Clayton had em b**u**rned out tho, e'n afta da Boss give ol' Andy Jackson the firepowa ta w**i**n **d**a war. Ol Clayton still **h**ated da Boss an brung him a pack a trouble."

"**S**o where was this Barataria?" asked Jim.

"Righcheere on da bayou," replied **S**am. "Folks called it da Golden City. Sum e'n sed it were Eldorado. Afta dae wuz burned out, da Boss moved fartha on inta da bayou, and befo he lef' fo' good, sum sed dat New Barataria would be built daer."

"Sam!" a voice yelled from downstairs. "Did ya fetch em fo' suppa?"

"Oh I'z fogot wut Cora sent me fo. I'z time ta eat and Mr. Sauvinet will be joinin' us. He sez he regrets dat he cain't cum ta da grand ball tomorra, but yu all will get ta meet him tonight instead. We'll be spectin' ya in da dinin' hall shortly."

Jim turned to Johnny. "Looks like we'll have to figure that map out later. Go put it in a safe place in your room and then come down to eat."

13
A Timely Gentleman

The excitement of finding Doninique's map was on evreyone's mind as they sat down for lunch.

Jim smiled at the others, "It's been an interesting **mo**rning."

Matie took a bite of her sandwich, and with a mouthful of food her eyes widened. "Can we find the treasure after lunch?" she mumbled.

"It's not that easy," said Jim. "There might not be a treasure anymore, and even with the map and the clues we've found, things like that take a lot of time."

Cora **p**laced some ham sandwiches on the table and wiped her hands on her apron. "Whea's Mr. Johnny?"

Just then Johnny came bounding down the stairs. He automatically slowed his pace when he came to the spot of his earlier **f**all. Cora ch**u**ckled while watching him from the dining room.

"What a wonderful meal," Kate said placing a crisp white napkin on her lap.

"It ain't much," said C**o**ra. "We'z juz been so busy gettin' ready fo' da big nite tomorra. Are you folks awll ready?"

"I guess so," Jim replied. "We've **b**een so **p**reoccupied with other things this morning, we haven't had time to think about the reception, but we're planning on being there. Oh, by the way, thank you for all you've done to plan all of this."

"Taint nuthin'," said Sam. "Been a long time sinz dis ol plaze has seen a celebration like dis one. It's juz down right excitin'. Juz like da good ol days."

Cora left the room and emerged holding several white

boxes. "Yo thing's are awll ready fo da party. Took a bit a taylorin', but a nip an a tuck hea an daer wuz juz the ticket."

"What are you talking about?" asked Jim. Cora winked and placed the boxes on the bureau next to the table.

"Well, dae is yo clothin' fo' the big nite. Everbody is expectin' ya ta dress up like da good ol dayz."

Everyone gathered around Cora as she distributed the boxes. Inside each box, there were exact replicas of clothing from the 1800's. Each delicate item also looked just like the ones in the portraits upstairs.

While everyone else opened their boxes, Matie looked with disappointment at the floor. Cora left the room again, then brought out another box and placed it in front of Matie. "Miss Matie, yu awlready has yo' special dress upstairs in yo trunk. But don' yu worry nun, we'z got a nutha box righcheere fo you, too."

Matie kneeled on the chair by the table as she opened the box. Inside was a velvet cape with a matching fan. A large hoop slip filled the bottom of the box. Matie held up the slip and looked at her mother with puzzled eyes.

"It's a slip," said Kate. "It's called a crinoline."

"It's so you can be the belle of the ball," Johnny teased.

Matie nodded and quietly placed it back in the box.

Cora looked at the little girl then put her hand on Matie's forehead. "You is sho be'in right quiet ta day. You feelin' awlright?" Matie nodded.

Kate looked at Cora. "Matie's just excited. She found a secret message on her quilt, and it led us to a hidden map. We found it hidden in the painting of Dominique Youx."

Cora's face turned white. "Oh, no!" she said as she sunk into a nearby chair. Sam ran to his wife and started fanning her with his hand.

Immediately the door bell rang. "I'd bez ansaw da door.

Wez expect**in**' Mr. Sauvinet." C**o**ra urged Sam on.

Sam re-entered the room with a tall, thin stately man. The man was dressed in clothes from the grand period when pirates were king. A unique detail accompanied the gentleman's entire being. He seemed to be accustomed to the formal clothing as if he had stepped out of time. His demeanor was also unique in that not only did he use proper grammar but his manners were impeccable.

Sam introduced him as the honorable Mr. Baptiste Sauvinet. The man bowed politely then began to speak. "Pardon my lack of punctuality."

Sam walked toward Jim. "Mr. Sauvinet, dis hea is Mr. Jim **L**eavitt." Jim stood and shook the man's hand. "An dis hea is Mrs. Kate Leavitt," said Sam.

"The pleasure is all mine," Sauvinet said kissing the ba**c**k of Kate's hand. Kate blushed then put her hand t**o** her throat.

"Dis hea is Mr. Johnny, da one we telled ya bouts, dat found da Boss's watch."

"I am very pleased to meet you young man." Mr. Sauvinet shook Johnny's hand then nodded at the boy.

Sam turned to Matie ne**x**t. "Dis hea is da little queen bee, Miss Madeline. Accordin'' to her Ma, Miss Matie dun foun' Mr. Dominique's Map."

Sauvinet raised his eyebrow and tipped his head a bit as he took Matie's hand and **k**issed the back of it. Matie scrunched up her nose and giggled as she wiped the back o**f** her han**d** on her shirt.

Sam turned to Randy. "Mr. Randy Olsen is Mr. Leavitt's legal advisor." Randy stoo**d** and shook Mr. Sauvinet's hand.

"I am very pleased to meet all of you," Sauvinet said. "It would seem, if time permits, that we have some very important business to take care of."

"Yes," said Jim. "We have several questions. First of all, is it true that you are in charge of all the legalities for Maison Rouge? There seems to be some discrepancy as to who owns this place. We had a lawyer show up here just this morning demanding that we leave."

"I am quite aware of the man of whom you speak," said the gentleman. "He is a charlatan and a despot of the worst kind. You do not need to heed his threats as he will be disposed of without delay."

"Well, what about this new business that you've set up?" Jim asked.

"I am pleased you should ask," Sauvinet responded. "I have the papers right here. They are completely in order and awaiting your signature. The new name of your company is 'The Leavitt Alliance Investment Firm'. I hope it meets with your approval."

"Wait just a minute!" said Randy. "My client isn't signing anything until we've gone completely over those contracts with a fine tooth comb."

Sauvinet turned to Randy. "I'm sure you will find everything in proper order," he insisted, handing the papers to Randy.

Randy skimmed over the papers as Jim turned to Sauvinet. "Who's paying for all this? It's no small thing to set up a new company, and who pays to keep up Maison Rouge?"

"Ahhh," Sauvinet replied. "It would seem that some explanations are in order. The original owners of this manor set aside a sizable trust fund for the future preservation of said manor. Throughout the years, acquiring interest, that fund has increased to quite a considerable sum. For many years now, the trustees of that fortune have invested the money on behalf of those who would someday be the recipients thereof. It would seem that with delicate scrutiny, it has been determined that the time has now come to release that fortune into your hands, Mr. Leavitt."

"We're gonna be rich!" Matie yelled.

"Shhhh," said Jim. "I'm not worried about being rich. Mr. Sauvinet, all of this is wonderful news, and I appreciate what you have done for our family, but I need some answers. Is this what my brother Ken was doing here when he came up missing?"

"Yes, partially," replied Sauvinet. "We had planned to meet with your brother and tell him of the family fortune as well, but I am most sorry to inform you of the unfortunate circumstances that got in the way.

"It was that ill-mannered Mr. Palmer, who threatened your brother and scared him away before we could tell him of the family's fortune. Your brother left very quickly, and he has not been heard of since."

Jim sighed in frustration. "I had hoped that you could give me some answers about Ken."

"Oh, I can," said the gentleman. "I can tell you who is causing your family all of these difficulties. Many years ago, Jean Laffite had many enemies. The most notorious of these was a Mr. Aluitious Eldwin Clayton. He was determined to destroy every Laffite who ever lived. Jean Laffite had a son, Pierre Charles, to whom Laffite gave his entire fortune. Out of necessity, Pierre Charles was raised in hiding by his aunt in New York.

"Clayton's efforts to destroy the family were ruthless, even to the point of attempting to take the life of the child. In time, the Laffite's changed their name to Leavitt which accomplished the desired affect of anonymity.

"Nevertheless, just as the Laffite family line was preserved, so was the Clayton family line and the vile obsession

120

to destroy every Laffite descendant. More recently, Elsie Clayton emerged upon the scene. She is none other than Mr. Damion Ratcliffe's own mother. I believe you know of whom I am speaking?"

"Ohh, yes,"Jim sighed. "That explains everything. That's how Ratcliffe got all that information about our family. It was handed down to him, and now he is fulfilling his family's old vendetta. No wonder he's such a spineless coward. He can't help it. It's in his genes."

"Yes," said Sauvinet. "He is most assuredly a desperate cad. But that is not your family's greatest concern. There are others who are watching your family closely, and they also wish to destroy you, so that they might retrieve the map your little girl has just found. Considering the timepiece that Johnathan has also found, there is a very great chance that those who seek your destruction will try even harder now. But we do have one remaining hope. There are several significant coins that remain safely hidden away. They are the last remaining protection we have. If your enemies were to get their hands on all eight of those coins, they would have everything they need to retrieve Napoleon's lost treasure."

Johnny gulped hard then Matie spoke up. "But we foun...."

Kate put her hand over Matie's mouth. "It's rude to interrupt, Matie. Please let Mr. Sauvinet continue." Matie looked at her mother with wide eyes. Kate took her hand from Matie's mouth.

Jim began again. "So the treasure is real?"

"I'm afraid so," said Sauvinet. "The original eight men of the Alliance made a solemn oath to preserve the nation's treasure at all costs. Each was given a secret coin and each was given a secret clue. Upon each coin was a specific word, written beneath Napoleon's image.

"Captain Edwards, Laffite's father, was the only one entrusted with all of the information and clues as to the whereabouts of the treasure. Before his untimely demise, he had Jean make extensive modifications to Maison Rouge to preserve the secrets he held. That is why a trust fund for the mansion's preservation was established."

"So when Edwards died, did the secret die with him?" Jim asked.

"Not exactly," replied Sauvinet. "After Captain Edwards died, Jean was intent on finding out what had happened to Edwards and the treasure. He sent his half brother Dominique into the bayou to see if he could learn more about the disappearance of the ship *Alliance*. Dominique found very little. There was no trace of any of the original crew. It would seem that everyone aboard the *Alliance* were lost with her. Nevertheless, Dominique was given a clue by Captain Edwards before his death. It was a special map. I believe it is the same one Miss Madeline has recovered, the very map used by Edwards to hide the treasure.

"News of the lost treasure spread quickly. Soon the original eight men of the Alliance fled for their lives. One by one, they were killed for the knowledge they held. The three brothers alone remained alive. Jean Laffite, Pierre Laffite, and Dominique Youx.

"The three men knew that as long as the treasure remained hidden, their lives would be in danger. So they made the proper arrangements to try to retrieve the nation's treasure and give it to the U.S. One by one, they gathered the lost clues from information left by the dead men of the original Alliance. All of the clues but one were found and pieced together. Jean sent Dominique into the bayou again to discover the last hidden clue, but Dominique never returned.

"A few months later, Clayton and his men put out a

bounty on Jean's life, claiming he had murdered Dominique and taken the nation's treasure per the previous assault on the ship *Alliance*. Soon, Maison Rouge was over run by angry mobocrats. Jean and his brother Pierre barely escaped into the bayou with their lives. Their intent was to return to the burned out remains of the Isle of Barataria.

"That night, Clayton and several of his men followed the brothers into the bayou. The anniversary would have been exactly 186 years ago."

Johnny looked intently at Sauvinet. "Whatever happened to Jean and Pierre and all of the men who were chasing them? Did they ever catch the Laffite brothers?"

Sauvinet took off his gloves and placed them on the table. "I'm afraid all of the men succumbed to a great storm that night. It was the greatest storm that anyone had ever seen on the bayou. All were lost to it, I'm afraid."

Jim looked concerned. "Who are the people who want Maison Rouge and the watch and map?"

Sauvinet sipped a cup of lemonade then spoke. "You know of your Mr. Damion Ratcliffe. He is the one who has hired Mr. Palmer to scare you into leaving. But according to my sources, there is someone else far more sinister who is the mastermind of their devious scheme. He is a foreign investor with many interests in Maison Rouge. It is his support that is funding your Mr. Ratcliffe's detestable endeavors."

"That explains the man at the hotel," said Jim. "Someone knocked out that poor operator to keep me from contacting Randy, and then when the kids were at the pool, the same man was asking them questions about any family maps we might own. I bet it was the same people who ruined Randy's luggage looking for the family journal."

"You have the journal?" Sauvinet asked with amazement.

"Yes, it's right here," said Jim turning to Randy.

Randy reached into his briefcase and placed the journal on the table. Sauvinet reached for it.

"Oh, my," uttered Sauvinet. "We thought this one to be lost."

"What do you mean?" asked Jim.

Sauvinet opened the journal to a specific page and laid it on the table. "Here in your journal are the exact events recorded by Jean Laffite himself. In fact, here he speaks of his own feelings in regard to the fortune."

The journal entry was dated February 18th, 1819. Jim read it aloud.

"Out of necessity it has become apparent that the forbidden oath which preserves the heart of our nation must soon be revealed. This very day an attempt was made on the life of my own little Pierre Charles. Oh, how he is like his dear angel mother. I will preserve the bloodline of my oath by sending him to live with his aunt Beatrice, as the curse has not concerned him as yet.

Napoleon's promised riches have proven to be a promised cursing to us all. I fear this misfortune should not have befallen us if it were not for the hidden cargo within the Alliance. Our plight would be far different if we had carried only the gold of the emperor's conquests. God in his anger has now forbidden our attempt to make our nation rise in power.The curse now consumes everyone within my household except Pierre Charles.

Jim looked at the old journal. "Mr. Sauvinet, how did you know what was in this journal?"

Sauvinet picked up the journal and carefully held it. "Not only am I a trustee for the dizpersment of the family's wealth, but I am also in charge of all of the family's genealogical records. Many years ago, someone in your family, photo copied many pages of the journal and entered it into the family record at the genealogical library. Through my research I added these to our files. Mr. Leavitt, take very good care of that journal. The information within it is critical."

"I will," said Jim as he closed the journal and laid it on the table. "Do you know what Laffite meant when he talked about another cargo, other than Napoleon's gold?"

Mr. Sauvinet frowned. "All I can say is that through Napoleon's exploits, he raided an abbey in northern France. There he took some valued artifacts. These may have accompanied the original treasure."

Jim looked intently at his guest. "So Laffite believed that the curse was real, too? He must have been quite superstitious."

"Most pirates have good reason to be superstitious," said Sauvinet.

Jim looked at his guest with curiosity. "Mr. Sauvinet, you mentioned some coins that were given to the original eight men in the Alliance. You said that those coins were the only thing keeping our enemies from getting the treasure. Why are they so important, and if we already have a fortune, why can't we just let these people go get the treasure?"

Mr. Sauvinet smiled. "I knew you would eventually arrive at that conclusion. First of all, the coins were not just a token of the oath those men made. They were keys. Captain Edwards had special locks made for the chests he would be hiding. All eight of those coins must be used within those locks to retrieve the treasure. As for your second question, it is imperative that no one but a blood relative of Jean Laffite get ahold of that treasure.

"You see, the curse is very real, and even now is held in a very delicate balance. It is imperative that the Laffite family return the lost treasure to those to whom it was originally intended. If the wrong men get ahold of that treasure, it will bring certain destruction upon us all. The treasure must remain preserved as it is, lost and hidden. Or the treasure must be returned to the original intended beneficiaries, the United States of America. That is the only way to end the curse."

Jim shook his head in disbelief. "You expect me to believe in this curse, and that if our enemies get hold of the treasure, some catastrophic event is going to affect everyone? I'm sorry. Mr. Sauvinet, but you're asking a bit too much. It's one thing to have a company handed to you and to receive an instant fortune overnight. But it's something completely different to be told you're part of an ancient pirate's curse, and that we have to fix the curse or keep it from changing. I'm sorry, but as genuine as you seem to be, I just can't believe all this."

"I was afraid of that," said Sauvinet. "My employer instructed me to convince you only as a last resort. Mr. Leavitt, pick up the journal. Would you please turn to the back, the last page if you will. Look there near the leather binding."

Jim did as he was instructed. At the back of the journal was a small pocket next to the binding. Jim reached inside of it and pulled out a photograph. Randy watched with great interest. "I didn't see that pocket before, and I've been through every inch of that journal," he said.

Matie tugged on Kate's arm. "What do you want, Matie?" Kate asked.

"Mommy, look at the picture. It's Sam and Cora!"

Kate gasped as she looked closer at the photo. It was a picture of Martin Edward Leavitt, Jim's great grandfather sitting in a carriage with his wife, Eunice, and son, Samuel Martin Leavitt. To his side in front of the wagon were Cora and Sam. They stood on a street with a large banner hanging over a store front that said "Alliance Shipping and Trading

Company". On the bottom of the picture written in white handwriting was the year 1900.

Everyone gathered closer to get a better look. "But it can't be," said Kate. "This photo was taken over 100 years ago!" Everyone turned and looked at Sam and Cora. They looked exactly the same age as they did in the photograph.

"This is completely impossible," said Jim. "If you were in that picture, both of you would be well over a hundred years old."

Randy grunted angrily. "It's a fake!" he said. "Pictures like that are a dime a dozen. You can have them made at any novelty store. You can even make them yourself on the computer. This man is just trying to trick you into something."

Jim studied the photo. There were no imperfections. What was even more astounding was that Sam and Cora were even wearing the same clothes in the photo as they had on at that very moment.

Sam walked over to Jim. "It ain't no fake!" he insisted in his deep tone. "We ain't a day older now den we iz righcherre. I ain't gained a day since da curse begun. I wuz old den, and I'z old now. Mr. Randy, yu is wrong bout Mr. Sauvinet. He ain't trying ta pull da wool ova anybody's eyes. He's juz following' audas, juz like we iz."

Randy glared at the others. "Can't you see what they're trying to do, Jim? It's all a set up with you as the fall guy. How do you know that they're not in on all of this? Maybe they're working with Ratcliffe. They just want to get your trust by working from the inside. Then they'll take everything, and you'll be in the same boat all over again, homeless and penniless!"

Jim shook his head as he looked at the photo. Everything in him wanted to believe in Sam and Cora. After all, they had been so kind and felt like family. But Randy's logic was very convincing. Besides, how could anyone really believe in such a curse?

Jim raised his head as he slowly smiled at the others. "I'll need some time to think about all of this. Mr. Sauvinet, do you mind if I wait to give you my answer about the new company? I want to think it over."

"I would expect nothing else," said Sauvinet. "Only fools rush in. But may I also remind you that the greatest opportunities are sometimes well hidden in that which seems illogical. I will return before next Tuesday for your answer. Hopefully that will be sufficient time for you to decide. In the meanwhile, I would suggest that you be very cautious of anyone who may seem to have ulterior motives in determining what is best on your behalf." Mr. Sauvinet looked intently at Randy as he spoke.

"Ha! Ulterior motives!" Randy yelled while Sauvinet gathered his things and excused himself. Randy was indignant over the entire situation. "This is absolutely ridiculous, Jim. If you think I'm going to just stand by and believe that this 19th century impostor is for real, your nuts." Randy stood up to leave.

"Where are you going?" Jim asked.

"I'm going to cool off !" Randy yelled as he headed for the front door.

14

Trusting Fate

Matie stared at Sam and Cora as they cleared the table. "Does it hurt?" Matie asked Sam.

"Wut you talkin' bouts, Miss Matie?"

Matie pointed to Sam's face. "If you're as old as they say, I bet that curse made a lot more wrinkles on the inside than it did on the outside, an I bet they hurt. Do wrinkles from curses hurt?"

Sam chuckled a bit. "No, I spoze dae don' hurt much. Not nea as much as livin' long as I have." Sam looked at the others around the table. "Spoze da thin' dat hurts da mos' is when ya ain't believed in, an folks take ya fo' a fool." Sam's words hit hard as he left the room.

Kate looked at Jim. "Oh, Jim, we should be ashamed. We've offended him."

Cora gathered the remaining food and dishes then turned to leave with her head lowered and quietly wiped a tear from her cheek.

"I'm sorry," Kate said, reaching for Cora's arm. "We didn't mean to..." Cora continued in a dignified manner without saying a word and left the room quietly.

Kate turned to Jim. "You should be ashamed of yourself! Look at all the trouble they've gone to for us. Why would they want to lie?"

"That's what I'm trying to figure out," replied Jim. "I didn't intend on hurting anyone's feelings, but you have to admit that Randy has a point. This whole thing is absolutely nuts. All they have to prove what they're saying is this old photograph. How do we know that it's not a fake?"

Johnny sat listening, sipping his lemonade. "Dad, there's more than just the picture. Remember the portraits of us upstairs? They were ready and waiting only a day after we arrived. That doesn't make any sense, either. So why couldn't Sam and Cora be that old? If there really is a treasure then why not a curse? Maybe they are telling the truth.

"Remember when we first came, Sam kept on saying the boss said this or the boss said that and that they were just following orders? Remember how Sam wouldn't tell us who his boss was. Well, maybe he did, and we didn't know it. Sam said that people always called Jean the boss. If Sam and Cora are that old, then maybe that's how they know so much about this place and Jean Laffite.

"Dad, you said that you weren't worried about any fortune. Well, why are you worried about the curse then? You want to find Uncle Kenny, don't you? Well, so far the only ones who've given you any answers are Sam and Cora and Mr. Sauvinet."

Jim looked at Johnny with surprise then patted his son's back "For such a young man, you have a lot of wisdom. You're right. Who cares about some old curse? I don't need any treasure. The money doesn't matter unless it leads us to Ken. So, who cares if Sam and Cora are old? Lots of people are old! Maybe not a hundred and fifty, but who cares? Sam and Cora have been good to us, and I don't want to hurt them. Obviously they aren't doing this on purpose. So they believe they're a hundred and fifty. What does that hurt?"

Jim and Kate stood up and headed for the kitchen. Cora was at the sink doing the dishes.

Jim walked up to her and kissed her cheek. "Hey," he said. "I'm sorry if I offended you. Cora, I don't care how old you and Sam are, and I don't care what Randy said. I trust you and Sam. You're like family. I know you just want what's best

130

for us."

Cora smiled with tear-filled eyes. Sam came in the back door just as Jim gave Cora a hug. She smiled at Sam. "Ya ol' fool, why wuzn't ya hea? Jim sez dae don't cae how old we is. Dae luvs us jux' da same."

Jim shook Sam's hand. "I'm sorry if we offended you. I don't agree with what Randy said. He can be a bit of a hot head at times, but he means well. He's just trying to protect us."

Sam looked at Jim with determination. His dark eyes twinkled as if something magical lingered there. "I knows how ta convince ya," said Sam. "I ain't never showed it ta nobody ever sinze da Boss left. But it'll prove it to ya."

"What do you want to show me?" Jim asked.

Sam led Jim out on the back porch as Kate helped Cora with the dishes.

"Folla me!" said Sam, leading Jim through the trees behind the plantation. A narrow path wound through the trees down a slight slope towards a small log cabin where a white picket fence surrounded the area. In the yard, flowers grew everywhere and a tidy little vegetable garden lined the south side of the walkway.

Sam opened the gate and ushered Jim into the yard.

"What is this place?" Jim asked as he looked at the quaint cottage.

"Dis hea is mine an Cora's plaze," said Sam, opening the front door.

Jim was startled. "I thought you lived in Maison Rouge."

"We only takes cae a da plaze," Sam replied.

Stepping inside the little cabin was like turning back time. A rock fireplace stood at the end of the small room, where an old blackened pot hung over the dwindling coals. An old hand water pump served to fill the wooden wash basin in the corner. Next to these, a small table took up most of the kitchen. On a hand braided rug sat a wooden churn and a spinning wheel. In the far corner a rocking chair had a cozy spot near the fireplace. The only modern convenience in the entire room was a tiny wooden table that held an oil lamp.

The entire cottage was extremely well kept and quite inviting. Sam went over to the fireplace and reached into a large basket. He pulled out something wrapped in an old hand woven cloth and laid the package on the table to unwrap it.

Inside of the cloth was a family bible. Sam carefully thumbed through its pages until he reached a particular entry. Inside it read, *Sam Wash, Married, 1814, to Coreena Prince, sister to Marie Prince.* Jim smiled at Sam. "That's very nice," Jim politely said.

Sam stood up tall and looked at Jim. "Dae is sumthin' mo' you has ta see." Sam led Jim outside behind the little cabin and went straight to a dense thicket of trees. There he began forging his way through the brush. Jim hesitated going into the dark forest, but he still continued following Sam.

The thick overgrowth was difficult to get through and soon both men were ducking under heavy branches that caught on their clothing. As Sam led the way, he suddenly cussed under his breath. A large thorny branch had caught on his shirt and torn his left sleeve, ripping it open to expose his shoulder and part of his back.

Jim grimaced at the sight that met his eyes. Sam's back was completely covered with the scars from a thousand whippings. On Sam's left upper arm were branded the letters *"A.E.C"* Jim winced at the site, his stomach churning with nausea. Sam pulled at his torn shirt and then turned and looked at Jim.

Jim lowered his head. He didn't know quite what to say.

Sam broke the silence. "Spoze yu iz a wundrin' right

132

abouts now, ain't cha?"

Jim looked at Sam with hesitation. "Well, yes. People don't usually carry scars like that. How did this happen to you?"

Sam pushed so<u>me</u> <u>b</u>ranches out o<u>f</u> the way then spok<u>e</u> gruffly. "Yuz been a haggalin' o<u>v</u>a juz how old I i<u>z</u>. Well, I <u>s</u>poze it don' matta anyhow cuz <u>I</u> really don know how old I iz.

"Seez, I wuz juz a boy when I wuz sold ta Mister Aluitious E. Clayton, as his slave. Doze scars ya seed on ma back cum frum dat devil, ever<u>y</u> last one uf um. It'z dat gater's brand I wears on my arm. Ain't ne'r a day goes by I don't think a dat man an da sorra he dun give ta dis hea family."

<u>J</u>im stared at Sam. "You mean "Th<u>e</u>" Aluitious Clayton? The one, that hated Jean and his brother?"

Sam nodded, then, <u>g</u>rinned at the shocked look on Jim's face.

"Yu is startin' ta believes me now, ain't ya? Folla me." Sam finally cleared away enough of the thick limbs to move onward through the brush.

Jim couldn't help but think of the bitter scars on Sam's back. He kne<u>w</u> that somet<u>h</u>ing like that couldn't be faked.

Jim cleared his throat. "I'm sorry Sam. I didn't know that you'd been through so much."

Sam stopped and turned around. Jim could barely speak. A lump filled his throat. "So how did you come to live here at Maison Rouge?"

Sam looked at the ground then with a raised eyebrow he tipped his head a bit and looked Jim square in the eyes. "I don' spect ya ta beleve me, but I escaped from dat gater Clayton one dark night wen dae wu<u>z</u> no moon out. I cum righcherre inta da bayou. I was half dead an a staw<u>v</u>in' when Jean an his crew fished me outa da water.

"Jean took me home an <u>p</u>ut one a his best servants ta

133

nursin' me. Dat wuz da first time I laid eyes on my Cora's face. She **w**uz da moz beautiful site I eva did see. Inside u**v** a month we jumped the broom and wuz **h**itched proper. I stayed on with Jean cuz he said I was a **f**ree man now, and he'd make sho it stayed dat way. He saved my life and give me a proper jo**b** an' title.

"I becum a real pirate, **j**uz like da othas. Every lick a work I did, I wuz paid right good fer. I sailed wif Jean and Pierre, and dae let me in on every plan dae eva did make. I raided many a Spanish galleon headed for Europe wif dem boys, and dae wuz right good times.

"Ain't no man or woman alive eva owned me agin, cept'n' my **C**ora an' **I**'z awll hers through an through. Sho nuf, I becum da richest black man on da bayou. Built a fancy house **j**uz' down da road a piece and begun ta raise my family.

"Clayton heard news a me an' my doins, and he cum ta git me back. Promised he'd ruin me, one way or a nutha. One dark night he cum an burned my place to da ground with a hecklin' mob, a killin' my two young uns. Jean give me dis hea cabin fo' shelter an safety, hidin' me and Cora, till it awl blew ova. My po Cora wu**z** heartsick ova losin' our two lil ones. **T**ain't ne'r been da same 'til Miss Matie an Mr. Johnny cum. Dae reminds her uv her own chillun, dae duz.

"Wen da *Alliance* wuz sunk, we lost mos a Jean's family too. Firs' Miss Catherine died. Den we heard word a Cap'n Edwards dyin', and den, Marie, my wives sista, wuz **g**one too. Seemed da whole world wuz a-cumin' apart at da seams.

"When Marie cum back, da curse wuz awlready begun. We all started ta see strange goins on in des hea parts. Later on, afta Jean and Pierre lef **i**nta da bayou, from time ta time Mr. Sauvinet showed up an telled us what da **B**oss wanted.

"Den we be**g**un ta see mo strange doins. Da years

134

passed on an folks cum an went, but we juz' lingered like we wuz. Time stood still fo' uz. An' now hea we is, juz da same t'day as we wuz yesterdee. Now I ain't a slave ta no man no mo'. But I iz a slave ta time. Dis hea curse don't scar my back like Clayton did, but time leaves its scars on my worn out soul."

Jim felt sick inside as he and Sam again began pushing through the thick brush. The images of the scars on Sam's back left an indelible imprint on Jim's heart. This old dignified man had suffered, beyond comprehension, unimaginable things for this family.

Sam's stories were no longer the exaggerated babblings of an old man. Sam had lived through these things. He spoke from genuine first hand experience, and he had all the scars to prove it.

Finally the thick brush cleared and Sam slowed down. "We'z hea. Diz is da plaze I wuz tellin' ya' bouts. Jean built it his self."

In front of the two men sat a stone cairn in a small clearing. At first glance it looked like a large pile of stones. But as they neared the monument, it was evident that it was much more. The structure stood about five feet high and had twelve sides. On each of the twelve sides a stone was carefully carved with the same emblems that embellished the stained glass dome in the attic. On top of the structure was a small peephole that led one's view out towards the bayou. Through the peephole, Jim could make out a structure far away in the bayou that looked like a type of tower.

Jim turned to Sam. "What's that building out in the bayou?"

Sam smiled. "Dat's wut wuz once da mighty Barataria. Dae turned it inta a fort lata on." Jim stepped back as he surveyed the stone pillar. On the opposite side of where he stood, there was an etched plaque. Upon it were written the

135

words:

In Honor of
Catherine Villars Laffite, My beloved wife.
True intent Mirrors the Son
If justice be Honored and Mercy be won.

Jim read the plaque and turned to Sam. "What does it mean?"

Sam shook his head. "I ain't sho', but Jean dun finished it juz b-fo he lef. He sed if eva anybody foun' da watch, if dae wuz family an went by da name a Laffite, I wuz ta sho um dis hea plaze.

"Jim, dat curse is az real as yo' an me. I sawed it awl wif my own eyes, an' you an' yo family iz juz as much a part uv it now as we is."

Jim looked at the stone cairn and then at Sam. All of his previous doubts now faded as he realized the implications of the family's situation.

"I guess that since we're actually Laffites, we don't have much choice now. Would you mind if I show this to the family?"

Sam nodded. "Sho, I wuz fixin ta tell ya to."

15
True Colors

Johnny tried to sleep as sweat covered his forehead. He tossed and turned then finally awoke with a start. Immediately he sat up and looked around the unfamiliar room. "Oh, yea, I'm at Maison Rouge," he whispered with a sigh of relief, realizing that he was safe in his new bed.

The night had been filled with dreams of pirates and sunken ships, storms and curses. Over and over again Johnny had dreamed of seeing his Uncle Kenny lost in the bayou and running from some unknown force.

He threw the covers back and began dressing for the day. It was still somewhat dark outside as he headed down the stairs. The house was completely quiet; and everyone was sleeping peacefully, unaware of Johnny's adventurous plans. Determined to get a better look around the place, Johnny quietly headed out the door towards the side yard.

As he neared the area outside Matie's window, he suddenly remembered the lost coin that Matie had so carelessly thrown away. Now Johnny looked through the grass and bushes, hoping that the precious coin would somehow turn up again.

With the sun rising over the mists of the bayou, a flicker of light caught Johnny's attention. Just below Matie's window sill on a small ledge, something glimmered in the morning sun. He looked around for anything that he could use to get to the upper ledge. A long lattice trellis, hung from the upper balcony.

Without a thought for his own safety, Johnny scaled the trellis, inching nearer his intended goal. As he reached just a

137

little higher, the brittle wood beneath him gave way. With the cracking of broken wood and a crash, Johnny tumbled into a heap on the ground.

As he looked upward towards the sky trying to regain his composure, he realized that he was lying directly beneath the tall branches of an old oak tree. The thick foliage of the ancient tree had completely obscured a hidden tree house that was suspended high in the tree directly above his head.

Johnny thought of the shiny object waiting on the ledge. Then he remembered Mr. Sauvinet's words that the coins should remain hidden for the best interest of all involved.

The coin could wait, Johnny reasoned. It would be all right where it was and he could get it later. Something more important consumed his interest now. He quickly scaled the tree's old branches. The tree house was very high. Glancing toward the ground far below, he slowed a bit. With his recent fall from the trellis, he wasn't going to take any chances this time. Securing his grip on the nearby branches, he made his way higher and higher until he reached the old structure. Holding fast to the railing he pulled himself safely to the floor of this tree top fortress.

The place was securely built around the tree's large trunk, and the old cypress wood it was made from was still sound. The sturdy floor was surrounded by a three foot railing, and at the center of the structure was a small shack.

Inside were the signs of the previous residents. An old apple crate made the perfect table. It held a candle within a soda pop bottle. The crate was covered in old newspapers, the writing obscured by wax drippings, spilled from the used-up candle. In the corner a dust covered sleeping bag served as a couch. An old lantern hung on a nail from the rafters.

Johnny sniffed the lantern and jostled it a bit. It was still filled with the volatile fluid from ages past. Then Johnny's attention was moved to a wooden barrel in the corner. Reaching inside he sifted through some old news papers and magazines. Most of them were from the year 1957, with a few older ones dated from the thirties. The tree house was just another hidden surprise of this mysterious place.

"Wow," Johnny muttered to himself, looking out over the bayou. The old tree was a least as tall as the mansion itself and allowed one a good view of the surrounding areas, even Maison Rouge. This was the perfect hiding place because it couldn't be seen from the house or the road. One had to be directly beneath the tree to even know that the treehouse existed.

Johnny smiled broadly as he thought of the adventure he could have here, hiding from his little sister. He then thought of the young boy next door who was just about his age, and wondered if they just might strike up a friendship. This would be the perfect place to have a sleep-over or plan adventures together. Tonight would be the night to find out with all the neighbors coming to the masquerade ball.

Johnny's excitement now turned to disappointment as he thought of the so-called pirate clothes that he had to wear for the big night... and those satin "girl pants," as Matie called them, that lay waiting in the box in his room.

For a moment, Johnny thought of hiding up here in the secret tree house for the night. Then he thought of hiding the ridiculous pirate clothes there instead. Just then he saw Sam emerge from the house to tend the gardens below.

A twinge of guilt ran through Johnny's mind. He remembered Sam's disappointment that the family didn't believe him. Sam was already hurt, and if Johnny didn't show up at the ball wearing the pirate clothes, it would hurt Sam and Cora even more.

Johnny relented. "I guess girl pants aren't so bad. It's

only for one night," he whispered to himself.

Quickly he climbed down from the secret tree house and headed toward Sam.

"How's it going?" Johnny said nearing the old man.

Startled, Sam turned around to face Johnny. For a slight instant Sam looked different, as if he were younger. Johnny looked again, studying his face. "It must have been the morning light," he reasoned.

"Wut you doin up diz hour?" Sam asked.

Johnny smiled a bit apprehensively looking at Sam. "Oh, I just wanted to see the place. I thought I'd do a little exploring." Johnny pointed at the broken trellis. "Ahhh, I kind of broke something again."

Sam began to chuckle. "Oh, so you is da one dat broke it. You is da darndez boy I eva did see. I'z surprized you'z still awl in one piece. You iz bout as graceful as a herd a elephants in a chicken coop."

Johnny bit his lip and half smiled. "I'll help you fix it, and I'll help ya fix the stair post in the house, too."

Sam looked at Johnny. "I tell you wut. I already fixed da stair post inside. But you go on round back to da barn and git me a hammer an sum nails an we'll get dis hea thin fixed up right good."

Johnny nodded then headed toward the barn. Out of the corner of his eye he saw a large dark car coming up the drive with a police car following it. He hurried to retrieve the tools from the barn then headed back. "Somebody's here," Johnny said, handing the hammer to Sam.

"I knows," Sam said laying the hammer down. Sam headed inside the house with Johnny close behind.

Cora stood at the front door, holding her broom, ready to defend the place. "Hea now ova my dead body you'll be a cummin' in hea like dat," Cora yelled at the intruders.

"Wut's goin on hea?" Sam's voice echoed as he hurried toward the entryway.

By now the entire household was awake and coming downstairs to see what waz going on. Jim neared the others and took the broom from Cora. "Let me help you with that," he said as he and Sam defensively stood guarding Cora from the intruders.

Mr. Palmer and a policeman stood at the door holding some papers. Palmer stepped forward with a sneer. "I thought I told you and your little friends to get out!" he said, his nose only inches from Jim's.

Jim took a step back and smiled. "Wouldn't you men like to come in the house and sit down?" he calmly asked.

Palmer frowned then bellowed, "We'll stay right here!"

The policeman looked bewildered. "Are, ah, you Mr. James Leavitt?" he stammered.

Jim nodded politely.

The policeman looked quite uncomfortable and fumbled in his pocket for a piece of paper. He looked at Palmer and then at Jim. "I'm supposed to serve you with this eviction notice," the policeman said. "But you're not acting like the police report. Mr. Palmer said you ran him off with a gun yesterday. Is that true?"

"Well, I wouldn't want to call Mr. Palmer a liar, but I don't even have a gun. I apologize if I made him feel threatened in any way. Perhaps there's just been a misunderstanding."

The officer looked at the Leavitt family and then at Palmer. "Are you sure your client owns this place?" he asked Palmer.

Palmer's face turned bright red. "How dare you question my authority? I have documentation!"

The officer reluctantly handed Jim the papers. "I don't like the feel of all this," he stated. "If there is something wrong going on here, I'm going to get to the bottom of it."

Jim turned to the offixer. "We would appreciate it if you would investigate this. You could start by talking to Officer Morgan down at the police station. He's aware of what's going on. I just met with him last night."

The officer's eye's widened. Now he looked at Palmer suspiciously. "I think you'd better show me some identification, Mr. Palmer."

Palmer looked at the others then stepped inside. "Maybe we should all sit down for a while," he said. "It's been a long drive out here, you know. I'm sure this officer would like to take a load off his feet, oh, and would you mind if I used your restroom?"

Cora glanced at Sam. Sam agreed with hesitation, so Cora showed Palmer to the restroom at the back of the house.

Cora soon returned to the others who waited in the study. The officer tapped a pen impatiently in his hand then looked at Jim. "What's really going on here?" he asked.

Jim tried to explain the unusual events to the officer. "I wish I knew what's going on. I came here to check out some property we owned because someone wanted to buy it. Before we came, I didn't even know about Maison Rouge. Then this Palmer fellow shows up claiming that his client's the legal owner and that they paid us for it. He even has forged papers with my name on them, but I haven't signed anything. Just like I explained to Officer Morgan, all of this seems to have happened just about the same time as my brother's disappearance. I believe it all has to do with the old Laffite treasure. I think these people are using lies and deceit in order to get at that so-called treasure."

Just then Randy entered the room. "Hey, what's going on?"

"This is my lawyer, Randy Olsen," Jim said, pointing to

Randy.

"Palmer's trying to get us to leave again, only this time he brought the police."

Randy looked at the officer. "You know, officer, legally my clients have every right to stay here until the courts determine who the legal owners really are."

The officer nodded. "Well, I'll have to do some checking. Palmer's been pretty insistent about all of this. But his story and yours don't match up. I'll look into things and talk to Officer Morgan. We'll get it all straightened out."

Outside a car could be heard speeding away.

The officer stood abruptly and went to the window. "Well, well," he said. "Looks like, our Mr. Palmer's showing his true colors. I'd just bet he's wanted somewhere for fraud or forgery. I'll get back to you if we find out anything." The officer dashed out the door to his squad car and sped away down the long drive.

Randy turned towards Jim. "See, I told you there would be more trouble. It wouldn't surprise me if Sam and Cora are involved, too."

"Now wait just a minute," Jim said. "Let's not start all of that again. Sam and Cora aren't like Palmer, and if they wanted the treasure, they could have gotten it long ago. They know more about this place than anyone."

Randy huffed in disagreement and slumped in a chair. "Well, maybe you're right, but I still don't trust them."

Cora stood in the doorway with her hands on her hips. She looked at Randy with a raised eyebrow. "Breakfast is gettin' cold. I spec ta see y'all in da dinin' hall shortly!" She glared at Randy with pursed lips, then, turned away.

Jim looked at his friend. "I wish you wouldn't treat her like that. You're a guest here, and they haven't done anything to deserve that kind of treatment."

Kate jumped to her feet and went after Cora. As she walked past Randy, she slugged his shoulder.

"What did I do?" Randy teazed as Kate left the room.

Jim shook his head. "We've got enough trouble without you adding to it right now. It's good she slugged you before I did." Both men joked as Randy finally agreed to behave himself.

As every one gathered for breakfast, the uneasy mood changed to excitement. Matie was seated near the end of the table and wore a bright red housecoat with her tiara firmly planted on her uncombed hair.

Johnny sat next to her as the others were seated. "So, Matie, I see you're all set for the big night," Johnny teazed. "I guess you'll be wearing this bea-u-ti-ful house coat to the ball."

Matie scowled as she tightened her lips. "At least I don't have to wear girl pants!" she said.

"Humph," Johnny growled under his breath.

Jim stood behind Johnny and patted him on the back. "Well, I see you two are in a good mood this morning."

Cora placed a large platter of hot cakes in front of the kids as Jim made his way to the end of the table. "Excuse me," he said. "Before we all begin to eat, I have something I want to say. We have a lot to be thankful for. We all want to thank Cora and Sam for their wonderful hospitality, and you, too, Randy. You've stood by our side throughout the years. These last few months haven't been easy ones, and I know we still have some trials ahead of us, as Mr. Palmer is so anxious to prove. Tonight's the big party that Cora and Sam have planned for us. It's also an anniversary to honor our ancestors, the Laffite's. I think that to start the day, it's only fitting that we give our thanks and ask God for help. Would you all please join me in prayer?" Everyone became quiet as they bowed their heads in respect.

144

Jim's voice broke a little as he began. "Dear God, we all want to thank you for sending us here, for giving us good friends, the loving support of Cora, Sam, and Randy. Now it looks like we're all in for a bit of trouble, and we could really use some help. I don't know if the Laffite curse is real. But it seems like some people are determined to make it that way. We need to ask for your help in getting through all of this. Please help us in God's name, Amen."

"Amen," everyone echoed.

Johnny was the first to grab for the pancakes. Hurriedly he slapped one on his plate then took a large bite. Matie watched him, took her napkin, flipped it in the air in Johnny's direction, and placed it on her lap. Then while watching his disgusting chomping, she reached for the syrup. Bumping the pitcher, she spilled it all over herself. Her eyes grew wide with horror as her attempt at propriety turned into disaster. Kate jumped to her feet and tried to clean up the mess with her napkin. Johnny giggled through a mouthful of food. "Guess you won't be able to wear that beautiful house coat to the ball now," he whispered sarcastically.

Matie began to cry. Her hands were completely covered with syrup, and the more she tried to clean herself up, the worse the situation got. Sam came to the rescue with a damp wash cloth and began washing her hands. "You sho knows how ta git yo self inta dem sticky situations, du_z_n't cha," he smiled.

By now Matie was the object of everyone's attention as they all offered their expertise as to how to help the situation. Soon Cora entered the room and took over. "You folks all go back ta eatin' and **I**'ll take cae a dis. Miss Matie do**n** ya touch nuthin', an' folla me." Matie got dow**n** from the **s**ticky chair, careful not to touch anything around her. Cora took her to the bathroom at the back of the house and prepare**d** a warm bubble bath. Matie removed her sticky clothes and gave them to Cora.

As Cora left to take the clothes to launder them, Matie stepped in the warm bath.

She examined the room carefully. This was one part of the mansion that no one had seen yet. It was situated near the kitchen and was very ornate. The tub was a freestanding French design, and the faucets looked as if they were made of pure gold.

In the area above the tub another stained glass design adorned the window. It showed a beautiful jungle, thick with flowers, trees and birds. At the bottom of the window, some words said. *"Beware the eyes of the magnifique peril."*

Cora returned with some soap and a pitcher of warm water. "Hea now," she said, "yu git yoself awl soaped up, an, I'll rinse ya off."

Matie smiled as she began scrubbing herself. "What does the picture up there mean?"

"Oh, I ain't neva figured it out," replied Cora "I spoze iz some beautiful place dat ain't too safe or sumthin' like dat."

Matie looked intently at the window as she searched for any trace of eyes in the picture. "There they are!" she blurted out pointing to the glass.

Cora patiently stopped what she was doing and examined the window. "Well I'll be, dae iz eyes in dat picture. An dem is da worse kin' a eyes ya eva will see. Dem's da eyes of a right sneaky gater, dat's awl ya seez when dae is lurkin' in dem watars."

The picture seemed at first glance to represent a lovely jungle paradise. But it was undoubtedly a warning to be careful in such a place.

Cora poured the rinse water over Matie's head and handed her a towel. Matie was bursting with satisfaction. "Now I know another clue!" she said. "And I'm not going to tell Johnny about this one."

After the table was cleared, Cora and Kate worked in the kitchen preparing various delicacies for the big night. Matie sat at the kitchen table begging to sample everything that came out of the oven. Jim and Randy were in the study going over the legal papers for Maison Rouge.

Outside, Sam and Johnny worked on repairing the broken trellis. Sam took a nail from Johnny and hammered it into the wood. "Ju<u>z</u> h<u>o</u>w'd yu end up breakin' dis hea trellis?" Sam asked.

Johnny squirmed. "Well, I guess I was climbing it."

Sam wasn't satisfied. "Wut's so interestin' u<u>p</u> dae dat yu would risk life an lim<u>b</u> ta git at it?"

Johnny sighed and looked around to see if anyone was watching. "I gues<u>x</u> it's all right if I t<u>e</u>ll you, <u>b</u>ut ya have ta promise not to tell anybody. Did you know there's a elevator in my ro<u>o</u>m and in the grand hall that big glass dome in the ceiling. It's really a secret clue. I found it all yesterday, and I found something else. Remember the gold coins that Mr. Sauvi<u>n</u>et told us about that were still lost? Well, they aren't lost any more, except for one. Matie threw it out her window."

Sam looked up at the ledge by the trellis. "Well I'll be. I spoze dat is a <u>r</u>ight good reazun ta g<u>o</u> an break dat trellis. <u>D</u>em coins iz a<u>w</u>ful important. Sum thinks dae is bez lef alone. I cin help ya get dat coin down if ya like. But I thinks I'd bez warn ya. If'n you eva gits awl a dem daer coins awl tagetha in da same plaze, yuz bez be ready fo awl heck ta break loose. Da Boss hid dem three coins soz nobody'd fine um, lessen dae wuz spoze ta, and I reckon sinze you is a direct descendant a da Boss, da right dun cum ta yu fare and square."

Johnny smiled at Sam. "You probably think I was just careless with those coins, I mean the way I lost 'em like that. Matie accidentally took it, that's how it ended up here. <u>A</u>ll of the others are still safely hidden."

147

Sam nodded, "Well, I guess we **b**ez git dat coin down fo' ya den. Taint **s**afe sittin' **d**aer on dat ledge. You bez keep awl a dis quiet, yu knows sum **f**olks is always pokin' daer nose**s** whar dae autent."

Sam and Johnny went to the barn and got a long ladder. Together they hauled it back to the ledge and set it up. Sam held the ladder secure as Johnny climbed up. The coin glistened in the morning sun as Johnny reached for it. Holding it up triumphantly, Johnny nodded to Sam.

Suddenly they heard someone approaching. Johnny stuffed the coin in his pocket and looked toward the voice. Randy emerged by the side of the house. "So, what are you two up to?" he asked.

Johnny looked at Sam a bit reluctantly. "Mr. Johnny wuz juz fixin' da ol trellis fo me. I aint so good at climin' ladders des daze." Johnny reached for the trellis and acted as if he were securing it. Randy watched the two then continued out into the yard toward the bayou.

Johnny hurried down the ladder and whispered. "Sam, do you think I need to keep the coins a secret from Randy, too? He already knows about the one from Officer Morgan and the rest of the family knows about all of them."

Sam frowned. "I don' rightly kno''bout yo friend, Mr. Randy, but I do kno' he ain't too fond a any tawk bouts me an Cora or bouts dat curse. And dem coins is juz' as cursed as da rest a dat treasure. If I wuz yu, I'd be a keepin' it ta myself. Neva hurts ta be on da caeful end a thin's."

"Thanks, Sam," Johnny said as he helped take down the ladder. As the two carried the ladder towards the old barn, Jim emerged from the kitchen door.

"Hang on, you two. Let me help you with that." Jim grabbed the end and took over for Sam, making the task considerably easier. Together they hung the old ladder on some hooks in the barn.

Sam winked at Jim. "Ain't yu got sumthin' ta sho dis boy?" Sam nodded in the direction of the old stone cairn.

"Hey," Jim said, taking Johnny by the arm. "You've been the one doing most of the exploring around here lately, but Sam and I have something we want to show you." Together the three headed through the back woods till they came to Sam's cabin.

"This is Sam's place," Jim said, then, he lead Johnny toward the thick over growth. After wading through the brush, the three soon found themselves standing in the clearing with the stone monument.

"Whoa, this is cool!" Johnny said as he ran his hand over the old stones.

Jim stepped closer. "Sam said that Jean built it right before he went into the bayou. Take a look through the hole at the top."

Johnny looked through the opening then turned to the others with wide eyes. "That's the fort on the stained glass dome in the attic."

"Are you sure?" Jim asked.

"It looks just like it. It's even sitting in the right direction. And look, there's another clue written here on the side. *In Honor of Catherine Villars Laffite, my beloved wife. True Intent Mirrors the Son, if Justice be Honored and Mercy be won.*" Johnny immediately jotted down the words in his notebook.

Jim looked pleased. "Looks like we've got ourselves a real mystery, and now we've got a place to start. I think that old fort is the same one that your Uncle Ken was at when he disappeared. We might just have to plan a little trip there to investigate. Maybe then I can find your Uncle Ken, and you can find that treasure."

"All right!" yelled Johnny. "So when do we **g**o? Can we **g**o right now?"

"Hang on there," said Jim. "This is going to take some planning. It would be foolish to go in there without thinking it all out."

Johnny looked disappointed. "Well, **s**oon is better t**h**an n**e**ver, I **q**uess. Besides, Dad, I'm sure Mom won't be too happy about the whole idea either. You'll need some time to talk her into it."

"We could plan ta go nex week an I cin have Cora pack us up a bite ta eat. Den we cin stay as long as ya like," Sam suggested.

"Can we go next week, Dad?"

"I'd like to know a little bit more about the **f**ort before we go into the bayou." Jim said turning to Sam. "Just how far away is it? And how much time will we nee**d** to get there."

"It ain't too far. 'Bout a dayz ride. But travlin' in **d**a bayou aint strait neitha' so we'd bez plan ta stay a night, den **c**um back da nex day." Sam urged.

Jim smi**l**ed at Johnny who was brimming over with excitement. "We'll figure it all out. Come on, we'd better get back to Maison Rouge before the girls come looking for us."

16
The Big Night

Kate looked in the full length mirror as she held the old fashioned silk dress up to her shoulder<u>z</u>.

The day had passed so quickly the family hardly had time to prepare for the dinner and ball that awaited them. Jim dressed in the bathroom, while Kate dressed in the bedroom suite behind a beautiful French dressing screen. They were both a bit apprehens<u>iv</u>e about the old fashioned clothing they were ex<u>p</u>ected to wear and wanted to surprise each other.

Jim reluctantly emerged from the bathroom in the finest pirate attire anyone could ask for. "<u>Is</u> this how I'm supposed to look?" he asked straightening his cravat.

Kat<u>e</u> came o<u>ut</u> from behind the screen and gasped <u>a</u>s she caught sight of Jim. "Jim, You'<u>r</u>e the spitting image of ..."

"Who ?" Jim interrupted.

"Laffite!" Kate exclaimed. "If you <u>h</u>ad a mustache, you'd look just like him."

Kate pushed Jim towards the full length mirror, then, held up a lock of her dark hair over his upper lip. "See?" she laughed. "You look just like him."

Jim smiled at Kate's o<u>b</u>servation, but, actually he was quite surprised at the resemblance he saw in the mirror. "Well, I guess I'll just have to quit shaving," he replied. "Are the <u>k</u>ids ready yet?"

"Matie's been ready for an hour now," said Kate, putting on some lip stick. "She's <u>w</u>aiting in the portrait gallery for everyone. Johnny sai<u>d</u> he thought he was c<u>o</u>ming down with something contagious, probably brought on by the thought of having to w<u>ea</u>r thos<u>e</u> pants that look like girl's clothes."

151

"I think I might be getting the same thing he is," Jim mumbled under his breath. "I'll go talk to him. Oh, I almost forgot this," Jim said as he retrieved a small box from his pocket. He opened the box and pulled out a beautiful diamond necklace. Kate beamed with surprise as Jim placed it around her neck.

"Where did you get this?" Kate asked looking in the mirror.

"Cora gave it to me. She said it was Catherine Laffite's. She wanted you to have it."

"Oh, it's absolutely beautiful!" Kate exclaimed, kissing Jim's cheek.

"That's not all," Jim said. "Here are the earrings to go with it." Kate put on the earrings and pinned up her hair, then took one last look in the mirror.

Jim stood waiting by the door as Kate emerged from the bathroom. He lifted his elbow towards Kate. "May I escort you, my lady?"

Kate pulled on some long white gloves then took his arm. "I would be honored, sir," she replied.

The two headed toward the portrait gallery. In the hall Matie sat waiting impatiently. "It's about time, we're all gonna be late," she said, her arms folded in frustration. Matie was dressed in the beautiful little flowered dress that Cora had given her, complete with a hoop slip beneath it. On her head was the familiar tiara sitting a bit crooked on her blond hair. Her tiny feet had slippers that matched the blue velvet cape that covered her shoulders. Both were embellished with small gold stars on the buckles and clasps.

"Where's Johnny?" Kate asked. Matie stood up and put her hands on her hips.

"Oh, he's acting like a dumb old boy. He says this is a party for girls, and he's not going." Matie smoothed her dress, thinking of her brother's lack of proper etiquette.

"I'll go get him," Jim suggested with a chuckle. "Maybe I'll catch something, too."

"Good luck," Kate encouraged with a wink.

Jim knocked on Johnny's door. "C-min," a lazy voice echoed from inside. Jim entered to see Johnny lying on his bed still dressed in his normal clothes and very unconcerned about doing anything else.

"Why aren't you dressed for the reception?" Jim questioned.

"Oh, come on, Dad. Do I have to go? The whole thing is so stupid. If I show up wearing those girl pants, everyone will laugh at me. Besides, it's just gonna be a bunch of old people."

Jim looked at his son. "I happen to be one of those old people you're talking about, and I'm wearing some of those girl pants as you call them. I'm not all that fond of this, either. But at least I have enough respect for Sam and Cora and their traditions to show up."

Johnny put his arms behind his head.

Jim could see that the guilt he was using was beginning to work and pushed a little harder. "You wouldn't want to disappoint Sam and Cora again, would you? You know they already think we don't trust them.

"Oh Dad..."Johnny squirmed.

"All right, I'll make you a deal," said Jim. "You put on those clothes and go wait up in the attic."

Johnny sat up. "Really, Dad? You mean it?"

"Wait just a minute," said Jim. "I'm not done. You watch and see who comes. Now, if the kids your age show up without costumes, you can come down in your normal clothes. But if they come all dressed up, I'll be expecting to see you within ten minutes, and you'd better be wearing the clothes Cora gave you. If you don't show up, I'll just have to come and get you because you're not going to disappoint **S**am and Cora. Yo**u** got that?"

"All right, that sounds like a good deal," Johnny agreed, fully expecting to never have to honor the agreement.

Jim left the room and returned to the portrait gallery. "What happened?" Kate asked.

"He's getting ready." Jim replied. "Don't worry. He'll be down soon."

The family stood waiting as Randy emerged from his room. Dressed just like Dominique Youx, he tugged at the awkward suit coat and straightened the collar. "**I**'m glad I don't have to wear this in **c**ourt," he mumbled.

Jim took Kate by the arm and escorted her down the grand staircase. Randy leaned down to Matie with his elbow extended. "Young Lady, would you gi**v**e me the honor of being my escort for the night?"

Matie smoothed her dress and adjusted her tiara, making it look even more crooked than before. Then she took Randy's arm. In her other hand she held a small handkerchief and began waving it in a grand gesture to the g**u**ests waiting in the majestic ballroom below.

The grand **h**all was de**c**orated with fresh flowers on every table. Fragrant garlands adorned the stair rails. A large buffet table in the dining hall held cakes, pies, small sandwiches, and every other kind of southern delicacy that one could imagine. Out in the solarium on the south porch of the mansion, a small orchestra played classical music.

Cora passed out hor d'orves to all of the guests while Sam tended the front door, announcing all new comers. Outside, a young man parked each car as it arrived. The whole grand manor brimmed with the sites, smells, and sounds of an old fashioned southern ball.

Johnny looked through the old telescope up in the glass

room of the attic. From this vantage point he could see each car coming down the drive toward the house.

He was now fully dressed in the clothing Cora had provided. He still didn't like the idea, but he wasn't going to break his deal with his father.

"This is so stupid," he whispered, as he looked down at the fine pirate costume he was now wearing. The only redeeming **qua**lity of the entire outfit was the original **p**irate sword that hung by Johnny's side. It had once belonged to the notorious pirate Pierre Laffite and had probably been the means of winning many a battle.

Johnny adjusted the sword and maneuvered around the tiny room to look through the spy glass.

Outside Cora and Sam had made sure that the entire grounds were properly decorated. Small paper lanterns hung in the trees along the drive, and out on the nearby bayou, little lights **F**loated upon the quiet waters. Johnny imagined himself for a moment **l**ying **in** a flat bottom boat among the small lanterns on the bayou, gazing up at the night sky.

He was **s**uddenly jolted awake from his daydreaming as another car entered the **l**ong lane. Within the **c**ar he could make out the fi**g**ures of some younger kids with their parents. As the car pulled up to the front of the house, Johnny tried to get a better look.

The mansion's roof now awkwardly blocked Johnny's view. Quickly he headed down the small stairway, out of the little room, and farther into the back of the attic.

Carefully dodging the large wooden cat, he pushed his way into the round room with the domed glass window. He quickly positioned himself so that he could watch the entry way and the front door.

First a woman entered, followed by a tall man. Soon two teens followed. The first was the dark haired bo**y** that

Johnny had seen the day before. The other was a beautiful girl
with long blond hair. The girl looked as if she were around 15
years old. The boy seemed a few years older and was quite
stocky and tall for his age.

To Johnny's dismay, both were completely dressed
from head to toe in authentic costumes from the 1800's.

"Oh, this is just great," Johnny grumbled, thinking
about his promise to his father. Looking again at the lovely
young girl, he whispered to himself, "I'll just bet that she's his
girl friend. Well, there goes my social life... Oh well, a promise
is a promise."

Johnny stood up and dusted himself off then returned to
his room on the makeshift elevator. Once there, he combed his
hair and checked his teeth. Then, holding a cupped hand to his
mouth, he blew, checking to see if his breath smelled all right.

"Here goes nuthin!" he said with hesitation.
Straightening his sword, he headed for the stairway.

As he walked past the gallery full of family portraits, the
entire grand hall below came into view. He felt as if every eye
in the house was on him. Immediately the thoughts of slowly
turning around and running straight back to his room flashed
though his mind. Then he got a glimpse of Cora smiling up at
him from the room below. Johnny kept his eyes down, hoping
not to attract any attention.

"I'll just show up and do what Dad asked then I'll sneak
out when no one is watching," he thought. Slowly he began
descending the stairs. He was about half way down when the
awkward sword got caught between two of the wooden spindles
on the railing. Without any warning the sword held fast, jerking
Johnny towards the railing.

Struggling for his footing, he began to fall. As if every
nightmare he had ever had was coming true, he went tumbling
down the stairs for a second time in two days. It all seemed as if

it were happening in slow motion. Even the sounds of the party seemed to slow down around him. All eyes were on Johnny. His so-called inconspicuous entry had garnered the attention of the entire room full of guests.

"Oh, no, not again," he breathed as his fist hit the stairs in frustration. He hadn't quite realized yet that everyone in the room was watching his slightest move. The deafening quiet was most uncomfortable. Even the orchestra had stopped playing, and nothing could be heard except for an occasional whisper or soft laughter from the startled crowd.

Kate's motherly instincts kicked in. She quickly motioned for the orchestra to begin playing again. She hurried to Johnny's side to help him up and brushed back a lock of hair from his eyes.

In an attempt to gain his composure and a little of his damaged pride, Johnny slowly stood up and brushed himself off.

"Are you hurt?" Kate asked, looking at the dangerous sword at Johnny's side.

"I'm fine," he said, scanning the crowded room. "My pride's the only thing that's really hurt," he said rubbing the back of his leg.

By now Jim was at their side, and the guests began to mingle again. Jim patted Johnny on the back. "Wow, now that was quite an entrance for someone who didn't even want to come tonight."

"Thanks a lot!" Johnny said as he pushed his hair back into place. "It's no use now, Dad. My social life is over."

"Not quite," interrupted Randy. "I've got some people here who want to meet you." Out from behind Randy emerged the two teens that Johnny had been watching from the attic. "Johnny, these are your new neighbors, Laurabeth William's and her brother, Bo."

Johnny's face turned red. "Oh... a... Hi, I'm John Leavitt." he said, as he adjusted his sword and stood up a little straighter.

Bo smiled. "You okay?" he asked. "Boy, if I was you, I'd a high tailed it for the door by now."

"It crossed my mind," Johnny said with a feeble smile, glancing awkwardly at the other guests. "So you're the ones who live nezt door. I watched you throwing rocks at some bottles yesterday. You're a pretty good aim. Just how old are you guys?"

"I'm seventeen," replied Bo. "My sister Laurabeth is fifteen. How 'bout you?"

"Oh, I'm sixteen. Hey are you guy's hungry? There's lots of food in the dining hall. Cora's been cooking all day. She's a really good cook, makes the best food you've ever tasted."

The two teens followed Johnny into the dining hall. He handed them a cup of punch. The tension eased as they began getting to know one another.

The other guests mingled. Then Sam took a place on the grand staircase.

"Scuze me, folks, but could ya hold dat thought fo a minute an give a lil look dis way?" The room quieted as Sam continued. "We iz right pleased ta have y'all hea tonite commemoratin' dis grand old tradition a bringin' in awl da neighbor folk ta welcome in da new ownas. Dis hea' nite'z a special one befittin' such an occasion. Seein' itz been near 'bouts a hunderd an eighty six yea's ago tonite sinz da original owna, da honorable Mr. Jean Laffite, made his final pir-at-i-cal adventure into da bayou.

"Sinz dat time dis hea place has stood tawl and magical, an many a folk have paid daer respects to da grand ol' place and its original ownas. Well, now we awl has reason ta celebrate

158

agin... seein' dat fo' da first time in many a yea' a true Laffite once agin resides wif'in des hallaed walls. I knowed darned sho da Boss ed be bustin' his buttons, ovajoyed 'bout it awl. An we iz proud as punch ta say to da Leavitt family, welcom to yo' new home, dis hea grand manor... Maison Rouge."

Sam motioned to **J**im who took a place by Sam's side. Jim nodded and put his arm around Sam's s**h**oulder.

"You know, I'm not quite sure what to say. When my family and I first came to Louisiana, we e**z**pected only to find some barren swampland on the bayou. Seeing Maison Rouge for the first time was a great surprise and something we'll treasure for a lifetime. **B**ut as we've come to get to know this place and the wonderful people here, we've found an even greater trea**s**ure in the rich heritage this place **h**olds.

"Jean Laffite founded this place on the idea of reaching for one's dreams. He did that whole heartedly, never looking back, and that's how he found his treasure. We've also found the **g**reatest possible treasure here, to**o**, in the love and sup**p**ort of all of our friends and loved ones, both old and new.

"Sam, you and Cora are the heart of this place, and we hope you'll stay here for **m**any a year to come. You've made countless sacrifices to make this place what it **i**s. We know we couldn't ask for **a**ny more loyal and compassionate **f**riends than you. We appreciate all of you coming he**r**e tonight and hope yo**u** will all feel welcome w**i**thin our new home."

Jim smiled at every o**n**e as he patted Sam on the back and gave him a friendly h**u**g and handshake. Everyone clapped politely then began talking and mingling again.

17

The Masquerade

Jim and Sam returned to Kate and Cora who waited with Matie near the kitchen door. Cora was wiping a tear from her cheek with the crisp white apron she wore. Sam looked at her and chuckled. "Yu ain't cryin' agin, is ya?"

Cora lifted her chin proudly. "Oh, ya old fool. Yu is just fulla hot air. Yu bes' be gittin' back to da guests. "

Jim reached over and kissed Cora's cheek. Her face flushed, then, she quickly rushed off to the kitchen.

Kate looked at Jim. "You know, you really are quite the gentleman."

Matie rolled her eyes at the two. "You aren't gonna kiss him, are ya?" Matie said with a frown, scrunching up her nose. Jim grabbed Kate and threw her into a deep dip within his arms, then quickly kisxed her on the lips, just for Matie's sake.

"Ahhhhoooo... Eeeeewwwww," Matie said with disgust.

Jim's little joke was suddenly interrupted as he realized that Randy was standing directly over him with his arms folded, watching the entire show. "All right, you two love birds, aren't you afraid you're going to scar this poor kid for life?"

"Hey," Jim replied. "She's left her mark on this family. She's done more to us than we could ever do to her!" Jim smiled at Matie then picked her up and twirled her around. Matie giggled uncontrollably and struggled to free herself. Jim placed her back on the floor. Embarrassed, Matie quickly ran towards Johnny and the other kids.

Sam returned from the front hall and approached Jim and the others. "Scuze me folks, I hates ta interrupt y'all, but da polize is hea. Ses dat he'z officer Jake Morgan. He'z waitin' in da Boss's office."

"We'll be right there," Jim said, turning to Randy. "I was hoping he'd come. I invited him last night at our meeting."

As Jim and Randy entered the room, offixer Morgan stood to shake their hands.

"Hello," said Morgan. "Sorry I couldn't get here earlier. It looks like you're having quite a party."

Jim smiled. "We're just glad you could come." Jim motioned towards Randy. "I'd like to introduce you to my attorney, Randy Olsen. He's the one that's been helping us with everything."

Jake and Randy shook hands, then, all three of the men sat down. Jim waited for Officer Morgan to say something. Then finally he broke the silence. "So did you catch him?"

Morgan looked at Jim in confusion. "What are you talking about? Catch who?" Jim and Randy looked at each other with concern. Jim continued, "Didn't you know that an officer showed up here earlier today? He came with Palmer and said he was going to talk to you. They served papers on us and said we had to get out. Eventually the officer started questioning the legality of the whole thing and demanded Palmer produce some evidence. Palmer must have gotten scared because he took off, and the officer went after him."

"Did you get that officer's name?" Morgan asked.

Jim shook his head. "It all happened so fast we didn't even think to ask for identification. We thought he was on our side."

Morgan looked concerned. "That's exactly what they wanted you to think. I've seen this scam before. Palmer gets a fake officer to intimidate you. Then he acts like Palmer's the bad guy so he can get in good with you. Then he'll show up

161

again and tell you that they caught Palmer, and you need to sign some papers. That's when the real scam comes. You sign those papers thinking you're doing your duty as a good citizen, and then they have your real signature. Did you sign anything while they were here?"

"No, thank goodness," Jim said. "I don't know just who we can trust anymore."

Randy piped in, "Jim, remember the papers that they already showed to us? They had your signature on them. They might already have it!"

"But I haven't signed anything," Jim said defensively.

Officer Morgan interrupted, "It doesn't matter. I can make a few calls and find out if the man that came here earlier was legitimate or not. One of the main reasons I came was to tell you that I found out something. I found out who it was that closed your brother's case, and why they did it. It all came from higher up. The case was closed due to national security issues."

"Why?" Jim asked. "Ken wasn't involved in anything illegal."

"Your brother wasn't the problem. It was the things he found out about this place and the bayou. Apparently the government has been watching things for about two hundred years now. I did some digging and tried to get into some of Laffite's old files, but they were all sealed by court order. Some were even labeled top secret. Something really strange is going on here. Not only that, but as soon as I started digging into this, I got a phone call threatening me. They said to drop the whole thing or something bad might happen. There's something else. Remember that coin expert I told you about? The one who knowz about that rare coin I gave you? Well, he's dead now. Seemx he drove off of a bridge somewhere. I hate to say this, Mr. Leavitt, but you're smack dab in the middle of something very dangerous."

Jim's brow creased. "Jake, I didn't tell you this yesterday. Randy here thinks I'm nuts to even bring it up. But yesterday we were looking through this old journal of Laffite's, and we found a picture of Sam and Cora. It had to be over a hundred years old. That would mean that they're at least a hundred and fifty."

Jake listened patiently, and nodded.

"Look," said Jim, "I know it sounds nuts. It doesn't make a bit of sense. But I have some proof. Sam has scars all over his back and a brand on his arm. He was a slave to Laffite's worst enemy, Aluitious Clayton, I saw the scars and that brand with my own eyes!"

Randy rolled his eyes and shook his head in disagreement. "That's impossible. Jim, be logical. No body is two hundred years old. Think about it and be reasonable. Sam couldn't have been a slave. Remember all of that ended with the Civil War and Abraham Lincoln."

Jim sighed. "Look, I don't understand it either, but I can prove it. Let's let Sam tell us for himself, and you can see those scars." Jim headed out into the entry hall and returned with Sam in tow. "Sam, will you tell these two about the scars on your back? Tell them about the time you were a slave and how you came to work with Laffite. I've told Offixer Morgan everything, and he needs to hear the truth from you."

Sam looked at Jim then lowered his head. "I don know what you iz tawkin' bouts. I ain't got no scars, an I aint got no brand on my arm. I ain't two hunderd yeas old. I neva even knowed Aluitious E. Clayton, or da Boss. All I knoz is dat Cora an I been a workin' hea sinz we wuz married. Juz takin' cae a diz old place. Iz sorry, Jim, but I cain't help ya nun. I dozn't know what you iz tawkin' bouts."

Jim was completely dazed. None of this made any sense. "Sam, I believe you now. I'm not making fun of you. I need you to tell us the truth."

Sam just shook his head. "I tol ya awl I knowz, sorry I cain't give ya no mo'. I bez be gittin' back to da guests." Sam looked at Jim, his eyes filled with sadness as he turned and left the room.

Jim had trusted Sam's outlandish story, and now Sam denied it all. "I can't believe it. Randy, you were right. They're probably in on it somehow. Sam and Cora must have lied to us all. I'm not making another move till we get this straightened out. I'm sick of all of this. I'll let Kate and the kids know that we're going back home in the morning."

Jim turned to Officer Morgan. "Jake, thank you for all you've done. If you need to get a hold of us, we'll be in California. Maybe then all of this will work itself out. Randy will handle the legal problems 'till then, but I'm getting my family to a safer place. Besides, I wouldn't want to upset national security!"

Jim shook Jake's hand. "Thanks again for all you've done. You're welcome to stay for the party if you'd like. Now if you'll please excuse me I need to go make a few phone calls and make some plane reservations."

Jim left the room. Randy looked at Officer Morgan. "You'll have to excuse Jim. This has all been a bit much for him. Losing his brother like that was really tough. He's never been quite the same since. He just needs some time to get over it. Believing in the curse and Laffite's treasure, well, that gave Jim some hope. I tried to warn him about trusting strangers, but he wouldn't listen. He wants to believe that everybody out there is trustworthy and good."

"I think I understand." said Morgan, "If I find out any more I'll let you know." Morgan turned and left.

Randy headed back to the party, looking for Jim. On the way Matie grabbed Randy's hand. "If you're my escort, does that mean you have to dance with me?" Randy gave Matie a half smile as he continued looking through the crowd for Jim. "I suppose so," he replied.

"Then q'mon, let's dance," Matie insisted. Finally Randy spotted Jim near the kitchen door, talking on the telephone. Kate was next to him with a worried look on her face. Randy headed straight toward them. Matie followed impatiently, swishing her skirt as she walked.

"We want the next flight you have to California," Jim said into the receiver.

Kate interrupted Jim. "I don't understand why Cora and Sam would lie? Can't we just wait a while and go back to California later after we've figured it all out? What about Ken and all our plans?"

"I'm not staying any longer than we have to!" Jim snapped, pulling the phone closer to his mouth. "That will be fine, if Monday's the soonest you've got. We'll pick up the tickets there at the airport."

Matie looked at her parents through tear filled eyes. "We're leaving? But I thought we were gonna live here." Matie's lip began to quiver. "You lied to us. You said we were gonna live here." Matie burst into tears and ran through the crowd.

"Oh, no," Kate said, going after Matie. Soon Kate returned. "I can't find her, Jim. She's run away!"

Jim turned to Randy. "Can you help us look for her?"

Randy nodded in agreement.

Kate whispered the news of their missing daughter to Cora and Sam, trying not to alarm the guests. Then Kate and the others scoured the entire mansion for any sign of Matie.

Jim started looking outside on the grounds while Cora and Sam searched the house. Kate soon found Johnny and his friends out on the patio and instantly recruited all of them to look as well. Randy attended to the guests as he watched for any sign of Matie returning to the reception.

As Jim and the others searched the old plantation, Jim finally met up with Kate and the others on the south lawn. "Have you found her yet?" he asked in a worried tone.

Kate frowned. "I wish she hadn't overheard you making those plane rexervations to go back home."

"What?" Johnny interrupted. "Why are we leaving? You said we were going to stay and live here. No wonder Matie ran away. I don't blame her!"

"Look, I know what I promised," Jim said. "But this family is in danger, and I'm not going to risk losing any of you."

"It looks to me like you already have," Kate said.

Suddenly Johnny noticed a sound as a small twig fell on his foot. He looked high up into the branches of the old oak tree directly above them.

"Szzzhhhhh..." said Johnny. "I think I heard something." Everyone stood listening. High above them, they could hear whispering. "Someone's in the tree house."

Bo interrupted, "I'd be glad to climb up there and take a look."

Kate looked at Bo and nodded. "We'd appreciate it if you would."

"Yes Ma'am," Bo said as he took off his coat and rolled up his sleeves. He began climbing and soon made his way to the fenced-in platform. As he did he heard rustling inside the small hut. The smell of smoke lingered in the air as if someone had just blown out a candle.

Bo knew this place well. He had been there many times. He reached into a small box inside the door and retrieved a match, struck it on the door post then held it up. Four eyes peered back at him. It was Matie and a young boy. Bo lit the

166

candle that was sitting on the makeshift table and began drilling the two children.

"Riley, you ol' fox! What do you think you're doin here?"

The red haired Riley stared back at his cousin Bo. He wasn't about to let Bo's age intimidate his ten years of experience.

"You wouldn't let me come to the party, so I been here all night watchin' things. I ain't hurt nobody! An no one knowed I was here till she came up."

Bo grabbed the boy by the back of the collar. "C'mon! You best be gettin' fer home b'fore Ma finds out."

Bo turned to Matie. "You best be gettin' down, too. The whole place is out lookin' for ya."

Matie gritted her teeth and lifted her nose in the air as if she hadn't heard him. Bo smiled at her determination. "Well, I guess I could carry you down then!"

Matie turned and looked at Bo with fire in her eyes. "You wouldn't dare!" she yelled.

"Want to try me?" he replied.

Riley broke in. "I wouldn't mess with him. He's hauled me outa here more times than you could shake a stick at."

Bo reached for Matie. She dodged his grasp and started towards the door. "All right, I'm going. I don't want you to carry me. I can do it myself."

Bo went down ahead of the two children with Matie just above him, securing her every step to make sure she wouldn't fall. Riley followed at the top of the ladder.

When the three reached the ground, Kate rushed to Matie's side. "What do you think you're doing, young lady? We've all been worried sick about you!" She looked at Matie then broke into tears as she hugged her little girl.

Matie rolled her eyes. "Mom, I'm not a baby."

Kate wiped away a <u>t</u>ear. "Wel<u>l</u>, you sure acted otherwise, running away li<u>k</u>e that. I've a good mind to send you to your room <u>f</u>or the rest of the night."

Jim put his arm around Kate. "Maybe we should just get back to our c<u>o</u>mpany and talk about all this later. Besides, Matie <u>h</u>as a new friend here we haven't met yet."

Jim looked at the scraggly little boy. "Why weren't you at the <u>p</u>arty tonight?"

"I ain't got any fancy clothes like Bo and Laurabeth, a<u>n</u> my Ma an Pa ain't here. They're in Florida on some business."

Jim turned to Bo for an explanation. "This young man seems to know you."

"Yea, we know him," Bo said as he ruffled the boy's hair. He's our cousin, Riley. Just lives down the street, stays with us when his folks are gone."

Jim leaned down to the young boy. "I'll tell you what. You can come to the party for the rest of the night if you promise to keep an eye on Matie here. You'll have to make sure she doesn't run off any more."

Matie scowled at her father. Riley smiled. "You bet, Mr. Leavitt, I'll keep an eye on her. I know all of the good hidin' places round here."

Jim winked at Johnny and the others. "I'm sure we won't have any more trouble tonight, will we?"

Everyone returned to the house, and the party continued as before.

Now in excitement Cora approached Kate, "Well, looks like ya finally found dat lost little pootertoot. She awl right?"

"<u>S</u>he's just fine. We found her outside with a little neighbor b<u>o</u>y. Apparently he lives near here. His parents couldn't come, so he was outside watchin<u>q</u>. Jim invited him in."

By now <u>S</u>am chimed in. "Dat muz be ol' Riley

168

Williams. Believe you me, dat boy is lookin' ta raise sum Cain. If'n his folks don't rein in dat boy, he's gonna give em what fer."

Cora frowned at Sam as she put some more food on a table. "Oh, you iz juz' picky. Dat boy ain't awl dat bad. Just needs somebody ta believe in im. His mischief ain't hurt nobody."

Kate smiled as she looked at the two. Then she began to think of what Jim had said about them lying to the family. Quietly she turned to Sam. "Sam, what happened earlier tonight when Officer Morgan came?"

Sam shook his head as he looked around the room. "I spoze dis ain't da plaze ta tawk bout it. Folla me in da kitchen an I'll tell ya what I knows."

Sam headed into the kitchen with Kate and Cora close behind.

"What's going on?" Kate insisted.

Sam shook his head. "Sumthin' is dead wrong. I ova heared yo Mr. Morgan say dat a man had been killed, an expert he wuz, on dem coins. And dat policeman dat cum earlier in da day, he wernt no policeman. It wuz awl juz a sho. Morgan said dat dis place wuz bein' watched by da federal government and dat da files on it wuz top secret, sumthin' bout da nation's security. Now I don know bouts you, but dat dog don't hunt. I puts two and two ta getha, and it ain't cummin up ta four. Seems ta me dat sumthin' aint juz right."

"So that's why Jim made reservations to leave?" Kate asked. "He's concerned that the family's in danger?"

Sam nodded. "Yes um, an he iz juz a doin wut'z right fo da family. But dae iz mo'. I feels right bad 'bout it too, but I lied in daer. I telled awl a dem folk I din' know nuthin'. I made Mr. Jim look real bad. But I juz' couldn't risk it. Seemed da only way at da time. Somebody round hea is lyin', an I learned a long time ago dat when a polecat starts pokin' round, ya best shut yo' mouth, or ya juz might end up smack dab in da middle of a nasty tastin' situation."

Kate grinned. "I think you did the right thing, Sam. Don't worry, I'll talk to Jim."

Suddenly, Johnny and his friends burst into the kitchen. "Hey, Mom, Dad's looking for Sam. He said something about some big surprise out on the south lawn."

Sam stood up a little straighter. "Oh, I guess it's 'bout dat time. We has sumthin' real special planned, c'mon everbody."

The orchestra played a lively pirate tune as the group followed Sam out onto the south lawn, where the guezts were gathering.

The little lanterns glistened brightly on the bayou. The orchestra stopped playing as Jim began to speak. "We want to thank all of you again for being here tonight. We felt that since this party is commemorating the interesting exploits of those who founded this place, it's only fitting that we honor the three great men who started it all, Jean Laffite, Pierre Laffite, and Dominique Youx."

Jim moved towards Sam who stood near a small table on the lawn. Jim nodded and Sam instantly lit the wick on the first of three tiny cannons. One by one, he lit the rest of the cannons, discharging their tiny cannonballs into the dark night out on the bayou. Then Jim lit three large fireworks that instantly burst into beautiful blossoms overhead.

Everyone clapped as the orchestra played a lively tune in tribute to the three pirates, and the former grand days this mansion had once seen. After a few more fireworks and songs, the crowd once again returned to the festivities inside.

Jim and Sam quietly cleared the table of fireworks. The silence between them was a stark reminder of their former disagreement. The sounds out on the bayou echoed across the wide plantation, making the silence between the two even more apparent.

Jim's conscience got the better of him. The pain he was feeling grew in intensity each time he entertained the thoughts of their disagreement. Finally he couldn't stand it and began to speak.

"Well, Sam, I guess you'll be glad to have this all over. Then you can get back to your normal life again."

Sam just stood silently, looking at Jim. He lowered his head and shook it quietly in disagreement.

Jim picked up a tiny cannon and returned it to its box. "Things will be pretty quiet around here after we go back to California. I suppose you and Cora won't have to work so hard then."

Sam looked at Jim, with a stern glimmer in his eye then softly spoke, "I spoze you ain't thinkin' too highly a me now' bouts. An' I ain't too proud a wut I did eitha. But I has a thing or two ta tell ya. I seen a lot a thin's in my day, an' I learned to spot trouble the minute it raises its ugly head. Dey is things a goin' on hea dat you don' know nuthin' bouts anyhow. I spect your Mr. Randy is right pleased dat you is a seein' things his way now. But I ain't so sho his way'z gonna be much betta. Seems ta me dem dat started awl a dis ain't gonna let dat dog lie. Now b'yo you folk cum, it wuz quiet round des parts, and things was easy. But now you iz hea, an' I got my audas, an' da Boss said ta watch close and keep ya'll safe.

"When I heard yo' Mr. Randy an 'dat police officer a tawkin' I knowed dat you wuz in trouble. An I wuzn't bout ta stir dat pot agin, a rilin' up Mr. Randy. 'Sides, I been a watchin' folk commin' an' a goin' awl da nite long, an dae is somebody parked out daer on da lane a pokin' round dez parts dat ain't cum in yet. Dae just sits out daer on da road a watchin' dis hea plaze."

Jim stared at Sam. He wanted to believe the old man, but the logic that Randy had so eloquently drilled into Jim's mind kept on rising to the surface.

"I guess we'd better get all this stuff put away and get back to the guests."

Sam turned to Jim, and then he looked out over the bayou. "You is still a plannin' on leavin', ain't cha? If'n so, I bez' tell ya. You is part a dat curse now, and dem fellas dat want dis hea plaze ain't gonna let it lie. Dae wuz afta ya b'fo ya cum and dae is gonna folla ya."

Jim frowned at Sam. The thought of leaving Maison Rouge had been a logical choice in protecting his family. But now Sam's words echoed in Jim's ears. Sam was right. As long as those people wanted this place, Jim's family was still in danger.

Jim moved even faster now to get the table cleared. He was still determined to leave Maison Rouge and get his family as far away from harm as possible. He'd just have to deal with the rest of the matter later.

Jim turned to Sam. "I understand why you lied now. I know you felt like it was the only way you could protect us. But I've got to protect my family, too, and the best way to do that is to leave Maison Rouge as soon as possible. Our flight leaves on Monday." Jim stuffed the box of odds and ends under his arm and headed to the house.

Inside, the guests were beginning to leave. Kate stood by the front door bidding them all goodnight and thanking them for coming. Jim placed the box of fireworks on the table in the dining hall and went to her side.

Suddenly Johnny ran to his parents. "Hey, Dad, can Bo and Laurabeth stay for a sleep-over? Their parents said it would be all right. They can help us clean up, and then they'll go home tomorrow."

Jim smiled at Johnny. "So, your social life isn't completely ruined, after all? Wearing those pirate clothes wasn't the end of the world, now was it?"

Johnny laughed as he looked down at his clothes. "I completely forgot I was even wearing them." Johnny's face now got a bit more serious. "How about it, Dad? We'll be going home soon anyway, and these are the first friends we've made here. Would it be OK if they all stay?"

Jim roughed up Johnny's hair as he put his arm around his son. "Sure. Just be sure to keep an eye on Matie and the Riley boy. Oh, and by the way, we'll get all this cleaned up tomorrow."

"Awesome!" Johnny said as he gave his Dad a high five, then, ran back to his friends.

Outside, **Bo** was picking up the used fireworks from the lawn. He walked over to Sam and asked if he could look at one of the small cannons. Sam obliged. Bo pulled his own package of fireworks out of his pocket and laid it on the table next to the small cannon. Soon he lit a row of firecrackers and threw it out into the air. With a loud crack and a flash of light the entire package went off.

"Well, now!' Sam said, "You got sum spunk, ain't cha? You ain't afeard a wakin' da neighbors or da dead, is ya?" Both laughed as Johnny joined them.

Matie and Riley ran across the lawn while Laurabeth watched from the patio. She held a mason jar that glowed with hundreds of little lights. Matie ran to Laurabeth, crammed a handful of fireflies into the old jar, and ran back to Riley.

The two scoured the bushes and flower beds as Riley taught Matie the subtle secrets of catching the little bugs. Matie shrieked with delight as Riley added another to their precious glowing collection.

173

Johnny picked up a firework as he watched the others. "This is nothing like California," he said, turning to Bo. "I don't think I've ever even seen a firefly. You have a lot of cool things here."

"I guess so," Bo replied. "But some of the other bugs are just plain bothersome."

Laurabeth joined in, "You mean like the chiggers and Schneille?"

"Yea," said Bo. "They're just plain Nasty."

Johnny smiled curiously. "So what's a chigger?"

"Peskery no see um's," said Sam. "Make ya itch right bad. Dae is awl ova da lawns an trees."

"So that's what's been making me itch!" Johnny said as he scratched his stomach. "So what are those chenieres you were talking about?"

Sam, Laurabeth, and Bo all burst into laughter. "It ain't da Chenieres ya needs ta worry bouts," said Sam, picking up a handful of items bound for the house.

Bo was still laughing, then, finally caught his breath.

"They're called Schneille's, look right pretty, too, cute little fuzzy caterpillar, with a bite like a dog. Make ya real sick, and give ya a fever, ta boot."

"So what did I call em?" asked Johnny.

Laurabeth smiled at him. "You called em 'Chenieres,' and that's not a bug. It's a little island."

Bo pulled a seashell out of his pocket. "Most times Chenieres have shells all over um out in the bayou like this one. I picked it up out at the old fort."

By now all of the other kids had gathered around to listen. Matie picked up the jar of fireflies and placed it on the railing near the patio as if it were a lantern, lighting up the darkened night.

18
Unmasked

Johnny's eyes sparkled with excitement as the full moon glowed brightly above the bayou. He took the shell from Bo and examined it. "Have you been to the old fort?"

"Sure," said Bo. "I used to go there all the time. But six months ago it all changed. The police were swarmin' all over the place, ended up ropin' off the island for some reason. I heard some rumors that some guy died out there. They say that the island is sick from some old pirate curse. There's a fever ya get if ya go there. It's probably just the schneilles. I never got any fever, an' I been there plenty a times. I think they just say all that ta keep folks away."

"Why would they want people to stay away?" asked Johnny.

"I don' know." Bo shrugged. "But I saw some big wigs pokin' round over there, doin' all kinds of archeology stuff. It was real strange. They were only there for one day. Finally came out a there actin' all upset. I ain't gone back since."

"Bo, just how far have you actually gone into the bayou?" Johnny asked.

Bo glanced at Laurabeth and scuffed one foot against the ground. "Well, I did go a little ways farther than the island, but it ain't safe with the gaters and all."

Riley jumped to his feet. "You know you wasn't s'posed ta go past the island! I'm gonna tell your pa."

Bo looked at Riley, reached his arm around his cousin's neck in a loose choke hold, and rubbed his couxin's hair with his knuckle. "The heck you'll tell. I got a lot more on you than you got on me, an' you know it."

Laurabeth broke in, "Y'all better behave, or I'll tell on both of ya." Bo roughed Riley's hair and then let go of the squirming boy.

"Can you tell us more about the island and the fort?" Johnny asked.

Laurabeth shook her head. "You don't want ta get him started, or we'll be here all night. He thinks he's the local authority on the bayou and the old stories about it."

Bo just smiled with satisfaction as he continued, "Well, some folks say the island is haunted. It ain't, but it is real creepy. Lots a birds an wild animals an, a course, the gaters. Ya have ta keep one eye open all the time. I don' know how old Marie does it."

Matie sat down in front of Bo. "Who's old Marie?" she asked, placing the firefly lantern on the ground between her feet.

Sam stood quietly listening in the background as he continued clearing the table. Everyone gathered closer, anxious to hear the amazing stories.

Bo continued, "Well, old Marie is this lady that lives up in a stick house on the bayou. Ain't too many left like that these days. Mos' folks thinks she's crazy livin' in a old cabin like that."

"What's a stick house?" asked Matie.

Riley broke in. "It's like a tree house out on the water, that's built up on sticks."

Matie leered at Riley then she focused her attention back on Bo. "Tell us more!"

"Well, old Marie is blind and real old. She's as poor as dirt, an' I guess that's the only way she knows how ta live. But, boy, is she interestin', tells the best stories 'bout the bayou that ya ever did hear."

"How'd ya meet her?" Johnny interrupted.

"I used ta work for the old corner grocer in town," Bo said. "The place closed down last year. They was just a little place, couldn't stay a float after the **b**ig stores moved into town. My job was deliverin' groceries ta folks. Old fa**x**hioned, huh?"

"Go on!" Matie demanded.

"Well, I used ta go once a week out ta old Marie's place. I'd take a little flat bottom pirogue,"

"That's a boat!" Riley interrupted.

"I'd put all the groceries in it and row out onto the bayou where she li**v**ed. I was real scared the first time I **w**ent, thinkin' she was crazy and awl, and some folks even callin' her a voodoo queen. Dumb, huh? At first I just left the food on the **p**orch, and she always had a note waitin' for me ta take back to my boss. Ain't no phones o**u**t there, ya know, so I was kinda scared, but I just took a deep breath and went on in.

"One day while I was tyin' up my boat, ta unload, she come out listnin' to me. I thought I'd just up and die right then and there. But she was nice as anything. She ain't no **v**oodoo queen. She's just **r**eal old. She ain't crazy neither, just careful. She don't friendly up to folks much."

By now Matie had grown very impatient. She stood up suddenly and pretended to yawn, then stomped her foot to get attention.

"Oh, all right. I'm getting to it," Bo said. "Marie and I, we got ta be pretty good friends. I even got so I liked goin' out there ta see her. One day I come, and she was gone. So I came again the ne**x**t day. I didn't think sh**e** ever went anywhere. So I was worried a gater might a got her. Finally she came back. Said she had business on the bayou. Somethin' ta do with her family. They live u**p** near Grand Lake I s'pose. So she takes the bayou ta go an see em. **S**he was kind a sick when she cum back, so I made sure she got some good hot soup."

"What kind of stories has she told you?" questioned

Johnny.

Bo looked up at the moon. "She told me all 'bout the ones that never returned."

"Like who?" Riley interrupted.

"Like an old gangster," Bo said. "His name was Race Chicane. Lived during the twenties or thirties, had a girlfriend named Goldie that ran a speakeasy over by Grand Lake. Old Race was runnin' from the Feds and went into the bayou ta hide out. Most of em gave up on him 'cept one guy named Percy Chase. He followed em after a bank heist. Just like Bonnie and Clyde. Folla'd em right inta the bayou, money and all, and bullets a flying from their tommy guns. But nobody ever seen hide nor hair of em again."

"Was there any others that didn't come back?" Riley asked.

"Yup," Bo replied. "There was a plane crash in the forties, during the war. Some air force guys were flying over the place and crashed. Some say they lived, and one got out to tell bout it. Some said they died, but old Marie said that the armadillos got em."

"Armadillos!" yelled Laurabeth as everyone burst into laughter.

"Have ya got any more stories?' Matie begged.

Bo put his finger to his chin as he thought. "Oh yea, most of the stories Marie told were about the curse of the bayou. Had a lot to do with Laffite. I do remember one more story of some who never came back.

"Seemz there was this group a kids back in the fifties with a hot car. Got themselves into a chicken fight. U'know…the kind where someone has to finally give up in a race. Their car was a slick t-bird, yellow with a black stripe. When the flag dropped, they took off and the two cars were neck in neck. The kids in the t-bird didn't chicken out, but they

178

went right off the bridge into the bayou. I been in there once lookin' for it. My uncle saw the whole thing happen and even knew the kids."

"Cool!" said Matie as she tightly clutched the jar of fireflies.

"Can you tell us the stories about Laffite?" Johnny asked.

Matie was unusually quiet as Bo began to speak. "I s'pose I know a few, but I ain't so sure these little kids ought to hear it."

"What do you mean?" Matie yelled. "I'm not a baby! Quit treating me like an infant!"

"Yea, me too!" Riley butted in awkwardly.

Bo looked at Johnny. "I guesx it's your call if ya think they can handle it."

Johnny raised his eyebrow half hoping that **Bo**'s story was a really good one that would thoroughly scare the two children. "Ahh, go ahead. **M**atie can handle it, if Riley can."

Bo leaned in closer. Matie clutched the jar of fireflies and swallowed hard as Bo began to speak **s**oftly.

"All right, **I'll** tell ya, but it ain't my fault if ya end up with nightmares. One time I asked old Marie about the curse of the swamp. Folks say it's haunted, but since Marie **h**ad been in there, I knew **s**he'd tell me the truth. Well, **s**he said that a long time ago there was this Cap'n of a ship called the agreement or somethin' like that."

"You mean the *Alliance*?" Johnny interrupted.

"Yeah, that's it!" Bo said. "Anyway**z**, some **o**ld pirate**s** robbed the ship, killin' all but one person aboard. It was a' old lady, an' she got away some**h**ow. That was how the story got out. I think she was Laffite's ma or somethin'. This **b**ig storm cum up and as the pirates burned that ship, a curse was born right then and there. See, Laffite's ma was powerful inta that magic stuff 'cause she cum from Africa. An' when she saw who dun it, the pirates cum after her sure as shootin'. Marie said there was a secret treasure on board, more precious than gold er silver, an' that the Cap'n of the ship gave his life protectin' it. She said that his ghost still guards it ta this very day.

"The old woman that escaped watched the ship burn in a distant storm, but even though it was a fire, it never burned up. Just disappeared in ta the bayou with that treasure. Some say it's still here, that a powerful force deep within the bayou just swallered it up. Some folk say that you can still see the ghost ship prowlin' the waters of the bayou while the ghost Cap'n walks its deck.

"Accordin' to Marie, the curse will live on forever until the precious hidden treasure is returned to its rightful owners."

"Yup!" Riley said startling everyone. "I know it's there. I seen the lights down that way. Sometimes on a dark night, you can see things glowin' in the bayou."

Laurabeth rolled her eyes. "That's just the city lights from Lake Charlez. You been hearin' too many stories. Your imagination is gettin' the best of ya."

Everyone looked out towards the bayou. "Look, there it is!" Johnny yelled giving Matie a sudden push.

Matie jumped, then hit Johnny's arm. "Oh, you're so stupid!" she yelled.

Johnny laughed hysterically. "I got you that time."

Matie stood indignantly and stomped toward the house. "I'm telling Mom and Dad!"

"Hey, I'm sorry," said Bo. "I didn't mean to make her mad."

Johnny was still laughing so hard that tears ran down both cheeks. "It's just great!" he said. "I haven't gotten her that good for a long time. Don't worry. Mom and Dad know how she blows things out of proportion. They'll just tell her that if she wants to hang out with the older kids, she'll have to learn not to get scared. Then they'll tell me later on to tone it down. Besides, Matie wasn't scared at all. She's just mad 'cause I got her. She acts like that all the time."

Sam grinned as he watched the kids go inside, then turned and looked sadly out over the bayou toward the old fort. After a while, he gathered the remaining things from the party and took them inside.

The mansion was cluttered with boxes and decorations from the party. By the time Johnny found his parents in the dining hall, they were already quite aware of his joke on his little sister. She had eloquently embellished the incident making sure her parents heard every detail.

Jim and Kate smiled knowingly as they gave Johnny a mild rebuke in front of his little sister. Jim winked at Johnny, trying hard not to laugh about the incident.

"Well, have you kids had a fun night?" Jim asked.

"It's been a wonderful night and a lot of fun," Laurabeth replied.

Bo looked up at Jim. "Hey, Mr. Leavitt, I'm real sorry we scared Matie like that."

"Don't you worry. Matie will be just fine," Jim said. "She needz to learn how to deal with others without always getting mad at someone."

Johnny and his friends grabbed a quick bite and sat down to visit.

Sam stood at the front door, instructing the young valet on his final duties for the night. The boy was tall and thin, and couldn't have been much older than Johnny, but he was mature and worked very hard, making him seem much older. Now and then he curiously glanced at the group of teens as he was cleaning the grand hall.

Johnny and his friends sat talking around the table as

Matie watched from the doorway. Finally, with a huff she gave in and joined the group.

Bo took a large bite of a slice of pecan pie then turned to Johnny. "Hey, would we get into trouble if we go upstairs? I was up there years ago, and there was all these pictures of Laffite and his pirate friends."

"They're still there!" Johnny said. "Come on up, and I'll even show you my room."

"He has a trunk full of gold!" Matie bragged to Riley.

Johnny sighed with annoyance. "It's just some old candy in a trunk."

"Race ya!" Johnny yelled as he bounded up the stairs with the others close behind.

"Don't fall!" Bo yelled in an attempt to throw off Johnny's concentration so that he could win the race. The five arrived at the top of the stairs completely winded and catching their breath. Matie arrived behind the others with Laurabeth helping her.

The young man in the room below watched the group carefully. Johnny paused at the top of the stairs and looked back at him then smiled. The young man promptly returned to his sweeping, pretending he hadn't been watching.

As the group explored the portrait gallery, Laurabeth stopped in front of the portrait of Pierre Laffite. Turning to Johnny she teased. "You're wearing Pierre's pirate clothes!"

"Yeah, but don't forget his sword," Johnny said proudly adjusting the shiny weapon in its scabbard.

Riley lingered behind and suddenly yelled, "Look, your Dad looks just like Jean Laffite!" He pointed to the large portrait on the wall as the others gathered to see. They joked and laughed as they took turns posing as if they were part of the imposing portraits.

Downstairs Jim sat behind the large desk in the study.

182

Randy pulled a chair up to the side of the desk, just as he had done so many times before back at the Alliance Stock and Trading Co. He began taking papers out of his briefcaze, and placed them on the desk. Kate watched intently from across the room as she sat in a large wingback chair near the fireplace. Sam and Cora sat together on a window seat. Jim waited patiently as Randy finished and snapped his briefcase shut.

"You're probably wondering just why I've asked all of you to come here," Jim said. "First of all, it's been a really wonderful night, and we want to thank everyone for your support and for doing so much for our family, especially helping to find Matie in spite of her little tantrum. The night came off without a hitch, except for one small thing. As you all know, we had a visit from Officer Morgan. He told us that one of the leading experts on Laffite's coins was recently killed. I know a lot of you aren't too pleased about it, but I've decided that in the best interest of everyone involved, we've got to leave this place as soon as possible.

"We were able to get a flight back to California this coming Monday. But in the meanwhile, we're all going to have to be very careful. Randy is going to continue to handle the legal work involved and see if we can figure this whole thing out.

"Cora and Sam, I want to thank you for being so wonderful. But I've got to do what's best for my family. I hope you'll stay on here as long as you can. It's up to you, of course. I know it could be risky with Mr. Palmer and all, but hopefully Randy will get all of that settled."

Sam and Cora nodded. "We'll be right sorry ta see ya go, but we understanz," said Sam.

Randy broke in, "Jim, would you like me to stay here and get all of this worked out? I think it would be much easier than if I was back in California."

Jim gave a tired smile. "I'd appreciate it if you would stay. Of course, whoever stays here could be in great danger, you know."

"I know," Randy admitted. "But it's the least I can do for a friend. Besides maybe I can keep an eye out for Kenny that way."

Jim reached over and patted Randy on the back. "Thanks. I really appreciate it."

Jim was suddenly interrupted by the sound of the front doorbell.

Sam stood up and went to answer it. "Hea now, you wait juz a minute," Sam yelled from the entry. Jim and the others stood just as Palmer and the police officer entered the room. "You caint juz cum a bardgin in hea like dat!" Sam said, following the two.

Palmer made himselve quite at home in a large chair.

"What are you doing here?" Jim demanded. Palmer just smiled and looked at the policeman who stood quietly in the doorway next to Sam. The officer reached into his coat and produced a new set of papers then walked across the room and handed them to Jim, and returned to his previous position.

Jim laid the papers on the desk and challenged their mistaken attempt with his glare. "I'm afraid I'm going to need to see your badge and some identification," he said, looking across the room at the officer.

The policeman glanced at Palmer who immediately spoke up, "That won't be necessary. We don't have time."

Randy broke in, "Mr. Leavitt has the original deed, and your fake ones aren't going to do any good this time."

Palmer sneered, "Well, if you won't cooperate, then we'll just have to do this another way. After all, it doesn't matter who owns the place anymore because you already have what we want. Where's the coin Morgan gave you?"

The officer had moved quietly across the room to Kate's chair and was pressing a gun into her side.

"What are you doing?" Jim demanded. "You can have the coin. Just leave her alone! We just want to leave this place."

Palmer waited for Jim to produce the coin. Jim fumbled in his pocket to stall the men. "I must have left it in my room," he said. "I'll have to go get it."

Palmer glared. "All right, but you'll stay here. Your lawyer friend will go and get the coin." Palmer motioned towards Randy. "If he tries anything, she gets it, and he'd better hurry."

Randy looked at Jim, "Where's the coin?"

Jim glanced desperately at Kate and hesitated, then finally spoke.

"Johnny has it. I'm not sure where he hid it though." Randy darted through the grand hall, and up the staircase to retrieve the precious coin.

The young man, who had been cleaning the area, put down his broom and cautiously stepped behind a pillar to watch. Unnoticed Sam had slipped out of the room and into the hallway. He sat listening in tense silence behind the wall. Quickly he ran towards the kitchen. The young man watched Sam return to his hiding place holding a large shotgun. Sam concealed the shotgun low by his side, then, slipped just inside the door back into the room.

Sam's movement startled the fake officer. "Stay right there," the man yelled at Sam, "or I'll kill her!"

Jim broke in, "You're the man I saw at the hotel, the one who questioned my kids at the pool."

"Yeah! So what about it?"

"Shut up, Dennison," Palmer interrupted. "Don't tell them anything."

"I bet you're the one that went through Randy's bag at

the airport, too." Jim said.

"Now you're Catching on," Palmer interrupted.

Jim stared at Palmer. "Who put you up to this? I know someone else is behind it all."

"You'll find out soon enough, "Palmer said.

Without any warning, Sam raised the rifle and aimed it at Palmer. "Well, now," said Sam "Seein' how ya ain't been usin' propar manners hea, and seein' how's yu is so hill bent on a stirin' up a ruckus, I thought it might juz be fit'n ta even up da odds a bit. Now if'n yu hurt Miss Kate, well, I reckons I'z gonna have ta see to it dat Mr. Palma hea gets a belly full a buckshot. So's ya juz bez put down dat piece. Cuz if ya cain't run wif da big dogs, ya juz bez stay unda da porch."

Sam's eyes glistened as if he were once again living in the days of pirates and damsels in distress. He nudged the gun closer towards Palmer. "Yu bez drop dat piece and let Misx Kate go!" Sam yelled towards Dennison. The man lowered the gun from Kate's side just as Randy returned to the room and stood behind Sam.

Unaware of Randy's presence, slowly Sam backed up. Suddenly a shot rang out, and Sam fell motionless to the floor

"No!" Kate screamed.

Randy stood by the door holding a smoking gun, his face pale and stern. Sam had accidentally backed into the gun, and it had gone off. "I didn't mean to kill him!" Randy said, "That wasn't part of the deal. It was an accident."

"Shut up," Palmer yelled. "I gotta think." Immediately Dennison shoved his gun back into Kate's side.

Cora ran to Sam and cradled him, with tears streaming down her cheeks. "Yu ol fool," she whispered over and over again as she wept bitterly and rocked Sam gently in her arms. Everyone stood silent as an odd light began to fill the room.

Small speckx of lights began to glimmer and twinkle

around Sam as if every particle of his **bo**dy was changing into pure light. The light in the room gathered around Sam and Cora, then began to glimmer and shine, then, slowly faded. As the lights faded, so did Sa**m** and Cora until there **w**as nothing left in the spot where they had just been.

Jim **g**lared at Randy. "No curse, huh? Look what you've done." Jim's voice was filled with rage.

The surprise on Randy's face was quickly replaced with controlled hatred. Randy stood calmly now, pointing the gun at Jim. "I thought you'd have caught on long **be**fore now," Randy sneered. "Sam and C**o**ra **d**idn't trust me right from the start. They even tried to tell you. But you're so stubborn...Your idea that ther**e**'s good in everyone **k**ept you from seeing the truth. I don't know what just happened here or how they disappeared, but it doesn't matter now. With **S**am and Cora out of t**he** way, we can do what we need to."

Palmer chuckled. "I t**h**ought you'd never get around to letting them know you're wit**h** us. It's about time we got down to business. So, did you get the coin?"

Randy gritted his teeth and nudged the gun closer to Jim. "No. I searched the room, but the kid's gone and so are his things."

Randy mo**v**ed closer and shoved the gun into Jim's chest. "Where have Johnn**y** and the others gon**e**? They weren't upstairs. I searched his entire room! We want the map and the coin now!"

Jim squared his jaw. "I don't know where they are. I told you that already, and I wouldn't tell you if I did know. Leave my kids and their friend**z** out of this."

Randy'**z** eye twitched with hatred as he sta**r**ed at his former friend. "We want the coin and the map now, **or** you won't **be** the only ones in trouble here."

187

19

A Narrow Escape

Upstairs the kids had made their way to Johnny's room. Unaware of the grievous situation below them, they casually talked of the fun they were having, then, planned to explore the hidden secrets of Johnny's room.

Matie, in her usual exuberance, couldn't resist bragging about the elevator that hung precariously on the ceiling. Unhindered, the group decided to explore the secret chamber above in the attic.

Making their way to the attic, the group followed Johnny to the curious glass room and the antique spy glass. Johnny bent down and adjusted the lens, then aimed the delicate glass towards Bo's and Laurabeth's home.

"This is where I watched you throwing rocks at some bottles," Johnny said.

"Can I take a look?" Bo asked. Johnny stepped out of the way as Bo bent down and looked into the eye piece.

"Wow, that's cool!" Bo said as he swung the spy glass in the direction of the road beyond Maison Rouge.

"Somebody's parked out there," Bo said, pointing toward the road.

Johnny nudged Bo out of the way and looked in the glass just as a car began turning down the lane to Maison Rouge

"Come on, follow me," Johnny insisted. He led the group through a maze of old crates and antique furnishings, past several barrels and trunks. Finally arriving at the large figure head from a ship, he began instructing the others on the dangers of the curious cat woman.

Suddenly Riley tripped on the worn carpet and fell

towards Johnny. As Johnny caught him, the large claw on the figurehead swiped at the two and the secret door popped open.

"What's in there?" Riley asked.

"It's just a window," Johnny insisted as the others pushed their way into the round room behind the door.

"Be careful," Johnny said, standing near the dome. Everyone crowded around the enormous stained glass dome and peered into the room below.

"Wow," said Bo. "You can see every room in the place from here. Laffite was a really cool pirate."

Just then Laurabeth gasped. "There's something wrong down there. If you look in that room, down by the front door. Down there... look in the mirrors."

Everyone gathered tightly to get a better look at the study from their precarious perch. Johnny moved Matie aside as he took a look through the delicate glass. Then he noticed Sam lying on the floor.

"We've got to get a closer look," Johnny said turning to Bo. "Something's wrong. C'mon."

"You girls stay here!" Bo said turning to the others.

"We're coming, too!" Laurabeth insisted. "Someone's got to keep an eye on you."

Everyone made their way back to the makeshift elevator. The old elevator creaked under the weight of the group as it slowly lowered them into the room below.

Johnny and the others were shocked at what they saw. Johnny's bedroom had been completely trashed. Every drawer was thrown open. Clothes were strewn all over the floor. The bed covers were ripped off the bed, and the trunk of gold candy lay toppled on its side with candy coins everywhere.

Riley picked up a piece of gum and turned to the others. "I know my room gets dirty in a hurry, but this is ridiculous."

"It's not funny!" said Bo. "The room's been

ransacked. Something's wrong."

Johnny dug furiously through the coins on the floor. "It's not here!" he said, shoving the trunk back into place. A look of worry filled his face.

Suddenly, Johnny jumped up and ran to his bed. He fumbled through the billowed sails that surrounded it. Reaching deep within the folds of the fabric, a look of relief filled his face as he pulled out the small carved chest. Lifting the lid, he counted the coins as everyone gathered around.

"What's that?" Bo asked.

Johnny looked up. "I think we're in trouble. This is what they're looking for. They belonged to Laffite, and they're clues to his treasure. We've got to get downstairs and see what's going on. I know my parents are in danger. If those guys are willing to do that to Sam, there's no telling what they'll do to get these coins."

Johnny placed the box of coins back within the folds of fabric, then, the group headed for the door. Johnny cautiously opened the door, looking out into the hallway while everyone crowded close behind him.

"Quit pushing!" Johnny whispered. Riley clumsily stepped on Matie's foot.

"Hey, that hurt!" Matie yelled as she shoved him out of her way. He pushed her back with a scuffle.

"Cool it!" Johnny whispered.

Riley and Matie continued arguing loudly as everyone made their way past the portrait gallery towards the grand staircase.

Bo grabbed Riley by the arm. "Be quiet!" he demanded. "This could be dangerous."

Everyone hunched down behind the railing of the balcony where they watched the young man in the grand hall below. He was standing behind a large column, staring into the

190

study.

"Pssssssstttt!" Johnny whispered loudly. Matie waved her little white handkerchief and Riley waved his arms, trying to get the young man's attention, but the boy's gaze was fixed firmly on the study.

Finally, Bo took one of the seashells from his pocket and threw it at the young man, hitting him squarely in the head. The young man grabbed his head and looked up. His eyes widened when he saw the group on the balcony. Then he looked back at the study.

Looking again at the others at the top of the stairs, he lifted his finger to his lips. Then, carefully watching the study, he ducked down low and made his way towards the stairs. Quietly he crept to the top of the stairs and huddled near the others.

"What's going on down there?" Johnny asked.

"There's trouble," the young man said. "That man that's been staying here with you guys shot Sam!"

Matie's eyes grew big and filled with tears. "Randy shot Sam?"

Johnny stood up and began down the stairs, but the young man caught his arm and stopped him.

"No! You can't go down there. They're looking for you. As long as you stay hidden, they won't harm your parents."

Johnny jerked his arm free of the young man's grasp. Reluctantly, he rejoined the others, and they all headed back to his room.

Once inside, Johnny locked the door.

Matie wrung her little white handkerchief in her hands and cried uncontrollably. "What are we gonna do?"

"We've gotta think," Johnny said as he ran his hands through his hair.

"Everyone calm down," said Bo. "First we need to

know what's going on down there."

Everyone looked at the young man for an explanation.

"Well, I was just cleaning up like Sam told me to, and some people came," he started. "There was a tall man, and he had a policeman with him. They both barged in an' started making all kinds of threats. They were talking about who owned this place, and they had a gun on your Mom.

"They talked about a coin and a map and made your friend go look for it. Sam snuck out into the hall and ran to the kitchen to get his shotgun. I thought he had everything under control, but then that Mr. Randy came back in and shot Sam."

The young man stopped and swallowed hard. "From what I could gather, Randy was in on the whole thing all along. The other guys talked like they knew him, and they were arguing over why he had taken so long to get the map."

Johnny stood up and started pacing anxiously, shaking his head. "I can't believe Randy would be in on all of this. Are you sure it wasn't an accident?"

"Oh, I'm sure!" the young man responded. "He was laughing after he shot Sam, and your dad was yelling at him."

Johnny squinted at the young man. "How do we know you're not in on all of this? Maybe it's all a trick. Maybe you're part of it. How do we know we can trust you?"

The young man stared at the others. "Hey, I don't want any part of all this. I just came here to help out Sam and Cora for the night. They've been like family to me."

Bo broke in. "Johnny, we know him. I've seen him here a lot since we were little kids. Sometimes he even stays with Sam and Cora."

Johnny glared at everyone. "Well, I've known Randy for years, and I can't believe he'd do this."

Bo shook his head at Johnny, "Hey, look, I know it's gotta be hard, but we've gotta stick together. We've gotta get outta here before they come again. If they were willing to shoot Sam, there's no tellin' what they'd do to get their hands on that stuff they're looking for. If we stay here, we're all gonna be in danger."

Johnny looked at the others, then, lowered his head. Matie was still whimpering. "Okay, you're right. We've gotta get a plan." He looked at the young man and gave him a nod. "So what do you call yourself?"

The young man smiled at Johnny. "My name is Jack Lapin. I live just down the road at Whiskey Draw. My folks worked for Sam an' Cora for nearly twenty years, I guess. When my folks died, Sam and Cora took me in and gave me a job. I've been workin' odd jobs for em ever since I was twelve. Sam an' Cora have taken real good care a me."

Johnny looked with uncertainty at Jack. "So, do ya know about the curze?"

Jack looked a bit surprized. "Yea!" he replied. "And I know all about Sam and Cora, too."

Johnny squinted one eye. "I guess that means you know about the treasure, too?"

"Yea, I know enough!" Jack said, gritting his teeth. "And I'd blow the whole thing up if I could. If it weren't for that stupid treasure, my folks would still be alive!" He looked angrily in the direction of the bayou.

Laurabeth and Bo looked at each other, confused. Then Bo spoke up. "Are you tawkin 'bout Laffite's treasure? The one that everyone's been lookin for fer years now?" Johnny and Jack both nodded in agreement.

Johnny stared at the others. "All right!" he said. "You gotta all swear an oath. You all have to promise on your very lives that you won't tell!"

Everyone nodded, curious to see what secret Johnny held. Johnny shook his head and whispered to himself. "Hope

I'm not making a mistake here, but I've gotta trust someone."

He looked at Matie, "You know this includes you. Don't you dare tell anybody."

"I promise?" Matie nodded as everyone gathered closer to Johnny.

Johnny went back to the bed and retrieved the little wooden box from within the fabric sail cloth. He then ran to the ladder and climbed up to the loft and retrieved the old map from a large bottle. Then he returned and set them down in front of everyone. He explained all that had happened over the last several days. Then he took the notebook out of his pocket and showed everyone the pictures and clues he had drawn. He hurriedly explained all of the secrets they had discovered in Maison Rouge and explained that he really did believe in the curse.

Johnny held up the old watch. "This old watch is what started it all. It was the first clue. From this we found more and more until all of the pieces fit together. Those men down there will do anything to get this stuff, and we've got to protect it."

Bo looked at Johnny. "Wait a minute, Johnny, you don't know what you've got here. Marie told me that there was things hidden all over Maison Rouge by Laffite himself. She said that someday a descendant of his would find those things and free the bayou from Laffite's curse."

Bo gulped hard as everyone stared at Johnny in amazement. "You're the one, the one that was sent to fix the curse!"

"Sorry!" Johnny said. "You've got the wrong guy. I'm not fixing any old curse. I'm gonna give these things to those men down there, and get my mom and dad out of trouble."

"No, ya aint!" A deep voice echoed from the doorway. Everyone turned around to see Sam standing there. Matie jumped up and ran towards him. As she reached to give him a hug, her hands went right through him.

Sam chuckled in his same old way. "Don' you worry nun, Miss Matie. Everthin' iz awlright."

Matie was confused and more than a bit scared as she ran back to Johnny. Johnny and the others stared at the apparition in front of them. "We thought they killed you," Johnny said.

Sam chuckled. "Ya cain't kill somebody who don' die," Sam replied. "Cora an' I been like dis for yeas now, but them folk downstairs is bez' lef' thinkin' we is gone."

Bo looked at Sam and broke in. "I don't understand. Are you ghosts?

"No," Sam replied. "I been wishin' we wuz for near bouts two hunderd yeas now. We is stuck hea in da curse. Not quite alive and not quite dead. Bound hea ta dis ol prizon, Maison Rouge. See'z wif da curse, we kin be juz like yu or juz as thin as da air. Don make no diffrance ta us. But Iz hea ta help ya now. Miss Cora an I will take cae a yo folks as long as yo hea, but ya'll gotta leave now.

"Dem things ya hold der iz special. Da Boss knowed you'd be comin'. Johnny, you is da one dat was foretold ta come and fix da curse. Ain't no gettin' round it now. Da ball has awlready been set ta rollin' an' no matters what you do, you is awl a part dis now. Dat curse is real an' kin only be broken by a Laffite. Dat is da only way yu is gonna git yo folks outta dis."

"What am I supposed to do?" Johnny frowned.

Sam looked at the boy. "You has gots ta git away from hea wif dem thin's yu found. Da only place yu kin go now is inta da bayou. Miss Marie el take good cae a ya awll."

"I'm going with you," Bo demanded. "I know the bayou like the backside a my hand. You wouldn't last two minutes in there alone without someone who knows the place."

Sam looked at Bo, "Dat is yo' choice, but dae ain't no

two ways about it. If yu goes yu stays, and dat is dat."

"I'm goin'!" Bo announced firmly.

Laurabeth frowned at her brother. "But Bo, what are we gonna tell Mama and Daddy? They'll be worried sick."

Bo smiled and put his arm around Laurabeth. "I have a plan. You can sneak out the back way and go through the forest, back home. Tell Mom and Dad to get the police out here."

Johnny spoke up, "Ya, that's a good idea. Tell em you need to talk to Officer Jake Morgan."

Jack broke in. "I'm afraid that won't work. Downstairs I heard them talking about the police. They knew about Officer Morgan and the coin he gave your dad."

"Oh, no!" moaned Johnny. "It looks like we're on our own then."

Sam turned to Johnny, "I ain't so sho bout yo' friends a goin' wiv, but I is sho dat you and Miss Matie is in real danger. It wuz Mr. Randy dat dun tried ta shoot me, an' he is a lookin' for dat map an dat coin. Now I knowed dat da only save plaze fo yu is juz as far from hea as yu kin git. Yu ain't got much time eitha. Dey is gonna search dis hea room agin lookin fo you an Miss Matie. I duz know yo Uncle Kenny wuz sho dat da only way outa awl a dis wuz to fix dat gosh derned curse. Now I has a plan if'n yu is willin' ta hea me out."

Johnny looked at Sam and nodded. "What do you think we should do?" he asked.

Sam winked at the kids then he began whispering in Johnny's ear. Instantly the room filled with light, and Sam suddenly disappeared.

Johnny ran to an old wanted poster of Aluitious E. Clayton hanging on his wall. He grabbed a shirt off the floor and smashed the glass in the picture. "Matie, go to your room and see if you can find a red marker or something."

Matie ran to the door and peeked out to see if it was

safe, and then ran to her room. She opened the window and went to the bird house. "We're in trouble," she said to the birds. "Some bad men want to hurt us. You've got to leave right now so they won't hurt you, too!" She motioned the birds towards the window as they fluttered around the room. One by one, they flew out the window, making their escape. Next, Matie fumbled through some drawers then headed back to Johnny's room.

Johnny laid the old faded poster face down on the floor. Matie ran to his side. "Here!" she said, handing him a bright pink crayon. Johnny groaned as he rolled his eyes. "No, Mat! I said a red one."

Matie grinned and handed him an old red marker. Johnny grabbed the marker then, kneeling down, he quickly scribbled a red pirate skull on the back corner of the old faded poster and rolled it up. "Bo, watch the door. And Jack, you go watch the front window!" The two young men immediately took their positions.

Johnny climbed the ladder to the loft and shoved the fake rolled up map back in the bottle. As he scrambled down the ladder, he picked up several candy coins off of the floor and exchanged them for the real ones in the little wooden chest. Then he hid the chest under his pillow.

Jack looked out the window and then turned to the others. "Someone's coming down the driveway. I can see their lights!"

Laurabeth ran to the window. "Maybe it's the police," she said hopefully.

Jack watched the drive as the car got closer. It was a large black sedan with one person driving. "That's not the police!"

Johnny again climbed the rope ladder and pulled on the peg to the trap door. The ship's wheel in the loft spun wildly as the trap door opened in the middle of the floor. "C'mon everyone, Sam told me that this is a safe way out." Everyone gathered around the small dark hole in the middle of the floor.

Matie frowned as she looked into the dark space below. "Do you think there's spiders down there?"

Johnny took his sister by both shoulders. "Look, Mat. We gotta be tough here. Spiders are nothin' compared to those bad men downstairs. Now get down there."

"Hey, let me go first." Laurabeth said. "That w<u>a</u>y if there are any spider<u>z</u>, I'll get rid of them for you." Matie nodded as Laurabeth sat down and slowly slid into the darkness.

"Now remember, ya gotta be quiet. Just think of it like the slippery slide at your old school," Johnny said as Matie got ready to take her turn. Then Matie edged her way down the old shoot. Riley and Jack were next and instantly slid out of sight. Bo and Johnny looked at one another. Johnny smiled as he turned to his newfound friend. "You're next!" He said.

"Nope!" replied Bo. "<u>I</u> know what you're up to. I overheard Sam's plans, and I'm <u>g</u>onna sta<u>y</u> right here with you 'till you join the others."

Johnny ran to his bed and pushed the loose nail. "I gotta get a look at who that was who just came, you with me?"

Bo nodded as the two of them boarded the makeshift elevator. As it slowly made its way up to the attic, Johnny and Bo made their plans to e<u>z</u>cape into the bayou.

W<u>i</u>th a jolt, the elevator stopped at the attic. Quickly the two ran to the round room and positioned themselves so that they could see the study. Johnny watched closely as the people in the room below moved around.

<u>T</u>here was definitely some one new there, but it was hard to see since the man had his <u>b</u>ack to the domed <u>w</u>indow. Soon the man turned just <u>e</u>nough to see his face.

"Ratcliffe!" gas<u>p</u>ed Johnny.

"Do you know that guy?" asked Bo.

Johnny sat back on the floor and held his head in his hands. "Yea, I know the rat. He's the guy that stole my dad's company. So he's right in the middle of all of this. It doesn't surprise me."

"Shhhhhh," Bo said. "I can hear their voices." The two quietly listened as the sound of muffled voices echoed nearby. Quietly they turned towards the sound. On the north wall of the round room were some old pipes all in a row. They each had a leather flap on the top with a small lever in the front. Johnny blew off the dust and rubbed the front of them. There, scratched in the metal on the pipes, were the names of all the rooms in the house.

The two boys smiled at each other. Then they pushed the small lever where the sound was coming from. "It's an old fashioned intercom system!" Bo whispered as he lifted the leather flap. Amaxingly, they could hear every muffled word being spoken in the room below. It was Jim's voice they heard.

"Leave my son out of this! You already killed Sam. Let me go find the kids. He's probably just outside with his friends. I'll get the map and the coin. Just don't hurt them."

The sound of a slap echoed through the pipes. Johnny jumped as he imagined his Father being beaten.

"I don't care about your stupid kid. I want that treasure," Ratcliffe yelled. "If I don't get that map and coin, I'll take care of your kids, just like I did your brother. Randy, go check the kid's room again, and this time get it right!"

"They're coming!" Johnny whispered, "We gotta go now!" The two boyz scrambled back to the elevator and returned to Johnny's room. As the elevator slowly descended, they jumped off before it hit the floor. Then Johnny quickly sent it back to its original position.

Bo slid down the shoot then Johnny got ready to slide,

but it was too late. There was a knock at the door. Johnny pushed the hidden hatch closed and ran for his bed. He laid down and pulled the covers over his head.

"Johnny, are you **in** there?" A voice called from the hall. It was Randy Olsen. Slowly the doorknob turned. Johnny's heart was pounding hard as he tried to breathe shallowly.

Randy entered the room and looked around, then, he spotted Johnny lying in his bed. "Hey kid. You asleep?"

Johnny pretended to stir a little and then began rubbing his eyes. Randy stood emotionless, tapping his fingers impatiently on the old barrel bed post.

"Oh, hi," said Johnny as he slowly sat up. Groggily he looked at Randy.

Randy looked at the door and then at Johnny. "Your dad wants to see that map and the coin of yours. He wants to compare them with some stuff we found in the journal."

"**Oh**, sure," Johnny said. Slowly he got out of the bed. "I'll get them for you." Johnny said looking at the old fashioned party clothes he was still wearing. "I must have fallen asleep wearing these. It's been **a** big day." He smiled.

Randy remained emotionless. "Yea, I'm sure you're bushed. **So** when did your friends go home?"

Johnny began to climb the ladder to the loft. "Oh, I guess they left about a half an hour ago." Johnny grabbed the bottle with the fake map and climbed back down the rope ladder. "Here it is," he said, handing the jar to Randy. "I keep it in this jar to protect it. It's kind of brittle."

Randy nodded. "So where's the coin?"

Johnny went to his pillow and took the small wooden chest out from under it. "Here it is," he said, handing the chest to Randy. Randy grinned as he took the chest and the jar.

Johnny held his breath, hoping that Randy wouldn't

open the chest. Randy tucked it under his arm, then examined the rolled up map still in the jar. Looking for the red skeleton on the corner, he smiled with satisfaction, then, nodded.

"I'll get these back to you in the morning," he said, raising an eyebrow. Johnny nodded, then sleepily went back to his bed and climbed in.

As Randy headed to the door his foot caught on the broken picture frame. "What's all this?" Randy asked as he picked up a piece of the broken glass.

Johnny gulped hard. "Oh, I bumped it earlier, and it fell off of the wall."

Randy threw the glas_z_ back on the floor and turned to leave. "You'd better clean this room up tomorrow. Looks like you've had quite a party here." Johnny smiled and curled up under his covers as Randy left the room.

Johnny held his breath, then, finally gave a great sigh of relief as he heard Randy lea_v_e down the hall. Quickly he jum_p_ed out of the bed and ran to the door. He opened it just far enough to see Randy at the top of the stairs, going back down to the study.

Johnny ran for his stuff. Frantica_ll_y he grabbed his back pack and notebook and then threw in the real coins, watch and map. He also grabbed a handful of the fake bubble gum and chocolate coins and stuffed them in his back pack. He ran to the peg below the loft and pushed it. The trap door opened, and he threw his backpack down into the darkened hole, and jumped in after it.

The dark ride was a quick one and ended suddenly at the bottom with a thump. In front of Johnny was a small metal grate that was ornately detailed. From outside, the moonlight streamed in through the holes in the grate. Johnny kicked gently at it and it swung open with a creak.

The shoot had deposited Johnny and the others right

into an old brier patch on the south side of the house. The bramble bushes around him tugged at his clothes and caught in his hair, scratching his skin. As uncomfortable as it was pushing through the thick weeds, the escape was well hidden and the bramble patch had long kept everyone from finding this hidden escape route.

Johnny made his way through the tangled old thicket and, dusted the cobwebs and dirt off his clothes. Soon he found himself standing in the moonlight on the south lawn. He stood only inchez away from where he and the others had earlier exchanged stories about the mysterious bayou.

Johnny looked around for the others then something hit his shoulder. "Pssssstttt, we're up here!" Came a voice from above. Johnny looked into the darkness trying to adjust his eyes. Soon he saw the moonlit faces of his friends peering out of the old tree house. Johnny quickly scaled the limbs of the old tree and joined them.

Bo looked at Johnny and shook his head. "I thought you were a goner for sure. How'd ya get rid of him?"

Johnny rehearsed how he had given the fake items to Randy. "We don't have much time. When they find out those things are fake, they'll come looking for us, and I'm sure they won't be very nice about it."

"We found some candles, and we got the lantern and matches," Bo said. Jack held the rolled up sleeping bag tightly in his hands.

Johnny looked at the others. "Hey, this is my battle! I can't get all of you involved. You should just go back home. Maybe your folks could call the FBI or something."

Bo just laughed with determination. "I ain't goin' no wheres. Bexides, you need me to show you where old Marie lives."

Laurabeth interrupted. "Well, ya ain't going anywhere

without me. I'm gonna keep an eye on you two."

"What about me?" Matie asked.

Johnny **nod**ded. "Mat, you can stay here. Sam and Cora will take care of you. **R**iley, you're gonna ha**v**e to go home. It's just too dangerous." Riley frowned. "**Y**ou little kids b**e**tter stay here till morning." Johnny said. "Then you can go to Riley's house and get some help. If you n**e**ed Sam and Cora, just go out back to their little cabin and lock yourselves in. They'll come as soon as they can to help you."

Riley glared at the others. "I'm not a little kid, and we can't go to my house. My **f**olks are out of town."

Johnny looked perplexed unti**l** Laurabeth broke in. "They can **g**o to our house. Our folk**x** will call for help fro**m** there."

"Then it's all set," said Johnn**y**. "If you kids will go get help, then Mom and Dad should be okay. We'll go into the bayou and get help there. We're gonna need some food and water though. Jack, do **y**ou think we could sneak back into the kitchen and **g**et some food?"

"Yea," said Jac**k**. "We could go in the back door, and they won't even know we were there."

The older kids climbed down from the tree house **a**nd scurried across the la**w**n towards the back door. Johnny stopped for a moment to look through the windows of the study.

Inside he **c**ould see bot**h** of his parents being **h**eld hostage by the others. Ratcliffe stormed around the room, waiving his arms. Randy stood holding the jar and map with the wooden chest under his arm. Ratcliffe stopped ranting when Randy handed the items to him.

John**n**y ran to catch up to the others. "We're out of time. We gotta get to the bayou now. Ratcliffe has the stuff. It won't be long till they figure out that they've been had and that the stuff is all phony."

Jack emerged from the kitchen door holding an old flour sack filled with food. "C'mon," said Bo. They all ran across the south lawn, heading for the bayou, dodging the lights that spilled across the lawn from the house.

At the waters edge, a small wooden boat was tied to a dock. An old Evinrude motor hung awkwardly on the back of the boat. Inside, an old canvas cover lay near the bow. Johnny helped the others board the boat and looked back toward the house and his family.

Silently he said a prayer in his heart for Matie and his parents. He was completely unsure of what lay ahead, and now he had to leave everyone he loved in the hands of God. It was all he could do to choke back the tears as he stepped into the small boat. Suddenly he saw a light coming towards them. It was Sam holding a lantern.

"Dem men is a comin'. Now y'all get for Marie's place. I'll send fo ya when it'z safe agin. Now git!"

Johnny turned to Sam. "Matie and Riley are still hiding in the tree house. I told them you'd take care of them." Sam nodded, then pulled the cord on the motor and pushed the boat away from the dock. In a glimmer of light he instantly disappeared.

Back at the house, every light in the place began to turn on.

"They know now. They've found out that we tricked them." Johnny whispered. "Looks like we don't have any other choice now. We can't go back."

Little paper lanterns bobbed silently upon the water as the boat made its way into the darkness. Johnny sat near the front of the boat holding a lantern up high so they could see where they were going.

The little motor whirred softly while Bo held the rudder steady. As the boat bumped into an old log, Jack lost his footing and accidentally kicked the old canvas cover.

"Ouch!" a small voice squealed from beneath it. Johnny lifted the canvas. There, hidden under the cloth, four eyes glared back at the group. It was Matie and Riley, two very naughty stow-aways.

20
Ratcliffe's Revenge

"Where's the real map?" Ratcliffe demanded.

"I don't know," Jim insisted. "My son had it. I told him to hide it."

Randy stormed into the study. "The kid'x gone, and so is his little sister. We've searched the entire place."

Ratcliffe paced erratically around the room. "Why didn't you keep a closer eye on them? Can't you get anything right? You've messed this all up, just like you did with Ken. If I didn't know better, I'd think you did this intentionally."

Randy glared at Ratcliffe. "Look, I want this all over with just as bad as you do. Those kids must have figured it all out. Johnny isn't stupid, you know. They traded the real map and coin for these fake ones to throw us off so they could get away. If you'd quit worrying about your precious treasure, you'd realize that they've probably gone for the authorities. We don't have much time!"

Ratcliffe huffed in disgust as he threw the worthless map on the floor.

Kate's face was bright red. She had finally hit her boiling point. Attempting to break free, she bit Dennison's arm. Instinctively, he jerked it back in pain as Kate lunged for the metal poker near the fireplace. Swinging it as hard as she could, she clipped the side of Ratcliffe's face. Jim reached for a potted plant and threw it at Randy.

In the confusion Dennison grabbed Kate's arms from behind and shoved her into the chair, his gun firmly fixed on her temple. Jim scuffled on the floor with Ratcliffe. "Get up!" Dennison yelled. "Or I'll let her have it!" Jim looked up, then, slowly rose to his feet.

Ratcliffe wiped his cheek with the back of his hand. Seeing the smear of blood on his hand, he erupted into anger. "Where have those kids gone?" he demanded, pointing a gun in Kate's face. Kate gritted her teeth.

Randy stepped forward. "I think I know where they are." He placed a small crumpled piece of paper covered in pink crayon writing on the desk.

"Thank goodness for Matie," Randy laughed. "She left this note up in her room. I think they've all headed into the bayou."

Ratcliffe nodded at Palmer and Dennison. "Go get some food and water ready. We're going to follow those kids."

Kate and Jim were livid. "Leave the kids alone!" Jim demanded. "They don't know anything about the bayou. It won't do you any good to follow them. You'll just get lost in there."

"Ha ha ha..." laughed Ratcliffe, turning to Palmer. "Don't forget to call the station and tell them to get the boat ready."

Kate scowled at Dennison then turned to Randy. "Why have you turned on us like this? You've always been a part of the family."

Randy searched through the papers in his briefcase and then looked up at Kate and Jim.

"I suppose you are wondering, aren't you? Well, now, there was a time I really did feel like a part of the family," he said sarcastically, "especially when the Fed's started checking the company books. The incriminating information Ken left in the files would have sent me to prison for years. Wasn't that convenient for all of you? And with all of that missing money gone and no one but the poor lawyer to blame, it was a pretty good set up, except that I found out about it. At least I got to those files before the Fed's put me in jail."

"What files are you talking about?" Jim asked. "Ken wouldn't have done that to you. He would have talked to you first, even if he did suspect you were embezzling from the company."

"Embezzling from the company!" Randy smirked. "Oh sure, Ken would have talked to me while he danced all the way to the bank."

Ratcliffe slammed his fist on the desk. "Enough! Both of you shut up!"

Randy pulled a piece of paper from his briefcaxe and turned to Ratcliffe. "We can still use your map," he said, handing an old faded piece of paper to Ratcliffe.

Ratcliffe took the paper from Randy. "Well, I suppose this one has gotten us this far. It'll just have to do. Perhaps we can use it to navigate the bayou. Then when we catch those juvenile delinquents, we'll use the real map to lead us to the treasure."

Palmer returned to the room. "It's all set. They'll have the boat here in an hour. It's the nice one they use for rescues on the lake. But he said we have to have it back by tomorrow afternoon, or he'll have heck to pay. Nobody knows yet, but if Jake Morgan finds out that boat'z gone, he'll send out every man he's got. He's beginning to get suspicious."

Ratcliffe was unimpressed. "Just tell Frank to make sure nobody finds out. Besides, Jake Morgan's an idiot who can barely run his own department. He has no idea what's going on right under his nose."

Jim was curioux. "Ratcliffe," he asked boldly. "How did you end up in all of thix?"

Ratcliffe greedily ran his fingers over the old map in his hands. "Have you ever wondered what makes someone superior to those around them? I can tell you from personal experience. You see, long ago I delved into a unique hobby. I began to research my family origins. It waz quite an interesting task. Do you know what I discovered? I found out that I descended from royalty, unlike inferior individuals like yourself.

"You see, royal blood runs in my veins. I have a right to nobility and the perks that go with it. As a child, I used to listen over and over as my grandfather spoke of a great treasure that once belonged to my family. It would seem that a desperate pirate stole that treasure, and left my family destitute.

"Except for one small thing, this little map. You see, my mother was an only child. Her name was Elsie Clayton. She married my father, and together they continued the long-standing tradition of searching for the treasure. On her death bed, I inherited the one thing that would lead me to the riches I so rightly deserve.

"I made the connection quite by accident, you know. It was just a fortunate coincidence. When I first began work at the Alliance Stock and Trading Company, I ran into some well-hidden files. Of course, I was just checking the books as a matter of routine. But one file caught my attention, a dusty old file in the back of one of the storage rooms.

"It waz your family genealogical files. Of course, with my previous expertise in genealogy, I couldn't resist just taking a look. When I discovered that your family name had been changed from Laffite to Leavitt, I was intrigued. Then I found it, the name Clayton, the name of Jean Laffite's enemy. It was Aluitious E. Clayton, my Great Great Grandfather.

"I knew about Maison Rouge long before you ever did, and everything would have gone just as I had planned if it weren't for your meddlesome brother. He couldn't leave well enough alone. He just had to go poking his nose into my business."

Ratcliffe laughed and snorted wickedly, then continued. "At least I don't have to deal with Ken any more, since he met with that untimely accident in the bayou. What a shame."

Jim's blood boiled. "You won't get away with this. You're insane," he yelled. "You may have killed Kenny, but if you lay a hand on my children, I'll follow you to the grave and stop you with my last dying breath."

Ratcliffe just laughed and stroked his precious map.

"Why can't you just take your map and leave our family alone?" Jim urged.

Ratcliffe stopped, then lifted his head and glared at Jim. "Laffite is the reason. He left this worthless map to mislead Aluitious Clayton. Our family has looked for that treasure for almost two hundred years in the wrong place. Your Jean Laffite thought it was a great practical joke. I discovered his plot in the journal. He said the real map was hidden here, at Maison Rouge. Your son has it now, and I will do whatever it takes to get it."

21
The Consequence of the Curse

Matie laid her head on Johnny's shoulder as the small boat glided over the murky waters. All of the passengers sat in silence as the light from Maison Rouge faded in the distance. Moss from the ancient cypress trees brushed against the boat in the dark, as if these enormous giants were reaching down with a gentle caress to reasxure the wary passengers.

Slowly the ominous darkness consumed the little boat and its cargo. Off in the distance a clap of thunder sounded and a crash of lightening lit up the night sky. Matie buried her little head in Johnny's chest. "I'm scared!" she whispered as Johnny put his arm around her.

Suddenly the old Evanrude motor began to spit and sputter. Then, with a gurgle and hiss, it died. Bo tugged on the pull rope to no avail. Again he tugged and the old motor spit and sputtered. Then it exploded, sending a giant puff of smoke billowing over the boat.

"I bet this old motor ain't been used for years. Looks like its got bad gas in it," Bo said.

Laurabeth spoke up softly. "So what are we gonna do now? Should we go back home and get some help?"

"That's too dangerous," Bo said. "Besides, if our folks get messed up in all this, they could get hurt. The best thing is to go stay at old Marie's place till it all blows over. She'll take good care of us, an' I know she has friends that can help us out if we need it."

Laurabeth frowned. "Oh, all right then. I guess it won't hurt, as long as you know the way."

Jack had discovered a pair of wooden oars under the

seat and dipped them in the murky water and began rowing the old wooden boat. Off in the distance the swamp frogs croaked in unison, and the fireflies danced over the brackish waters. Suddenly the sound of a huge splash echoed across the bayou. It sent a flock of nesting birds fluttering into the trees above.

"What was that?" yelled Riley, stretching his neck to see into the dark.

Johnny turned to Bo. "Man, I can't believe you camped in here overnight. I like a good adventure just like anybody else, but this is just creepy."

Bo smiled with confidence. "It ain't nuthin'. Ya get used to it after a while. That splash was just a gater lookin' for dinner."

Riley moved to the middle of the boat, his eyes bulging with fear. "I just hope that dinner ain't us!" he said.

Bo took some moss off the motor and turned to the others. "Ahh, that gater ain't gonna eat somthin' as nasty as you, Riley, not when he can have a nice tasty bird for supper." Bo gazed into the darkness. "The bayou will give ya plenty of warnin's if ya know what you're hearin'. Those birds took to flyin' to warn the other animals 'bout what's comin'. B'sides, night's the best time to really see what goes on in the bayou, at least if you can get past the part a bein' scared. Ya just have to remember to respect them, and they'll respect you. But ya do have to keep an eye on things and watch yer step, so ya don't wander into their territory."

Matie clung even tighter to Johnny. "I like'em in gater burgers better," she whispered as the little boat neared a bend in the water.

Up ahead a small light flickered in the distance. "Look!" said Jack. "There's a light up ahead."

Bo turned around to see what they were all looking at. "We're here. That's old Marie's place. Stop rowin', she gets nervous if she doesn't know who's comin'. She's likely ta fire off a shot in our direction if I don't give her fair warnin'."

Bo carefully stood up, jostling the boat from side to side, then cupped his hands to his mouth and whistled, two short and a long whistle. Then he waited, listening.

Soon an old woman came out on the porch, holding a lantern up high. "Is dat yu, Bo Willums? Wut trouble yu got yoself into dis time, cumin' hea at dis ungodly hour?"

Marie's words were harsh but carried an air of concern.

"Yeah, Marie, it's me, Bo! I brung some friends. Sam sent us."

The expression on Marie's face turned to worry. "Yu awl bez git ova hea den. Yu ain't safe a hangin' round out der like dat. A gater's likely ta git cha."

"She ain't gonna shoot at us now," he said, as they rowed closer to the old cabin. The little wooden shack was built on the left over stumps of some old cypress trees. It couldn't have had more than two rooms. An old porch, hanging over a rickety dock, extended the living space. The old woman made her way down the porch stairs to the end of the dock and held up the lantern as if looking out over the bayou.

Bo smiled. "She must be worried 'bout us," Bo said. "That lantern ain't for her ta see. She's as blind as a bat. She must be holding it out for us to see." Slowly the boat came to rest at the side of the rickety dock. Bo climbed out and quickly secured the rope to an old post.

Marie was small and hunched over slightly. Her thin frame covered in a clean blue and green calico dress with a crisp, though somewhat yellowed, apron tied over it. Her gray hair was drawn up in a loose bun with wisps of white curly hair framing her ebony face.

"Well, I'll be!" said Marie, holding her arms out toward Bo who quickly hugged the old woman then began to introduce the others.

Marie frowned. "Yu awl is in a pack a trouble, isn't cha?" "Yawl bez cum inside an I'll fix ya a bite ta eat."

Marie made her way back into the small shack with the others following close behind. Once inside, they crowded into the little kitchen. Jack sat outside on the steps, watching the boat, and Laurabeth stood in the open doorway.

Inside, Marie picked up a few apples from a bowl and began slicing them into quarter sections. She placed a small plate in the center of the table and soon had it covered with the apples and some cheese slices.

Marie wiped her hands on her apron and listened to her company enjoy the snack. "Now den. When is ya plannin' on a tellin' me bout dis hea trouble?"

Bo stopped in the middle of a bite and looked at the others. Quickly he gulped down the food then began to speak. "Well, Marie, do you remember tellin'' me bout the Laffite curse and how someday a son of a son would cum and fix it all. Well, yu won't believe this, but rightcherre is Johnny and Matie Leavitt. They're really Laffite's. They're the ones that come to live at Maison Rouge, and they're in a heck of a fix. Some really bad guys are holdin' their folks for hostage, and they're looking for Johnny. He found Laffite's watch and the treasure map."

"Don't forget the coins!" Matie interrupted with a mouth full of food.

"Yeah, Johnny found some old coins, too. Those men are desperate and want those coins real bad."

Marie gasped and put her hand to her heart. She made her way to a nearby chair and sat down, tipping her head back as if she were going to faint. She picked up the edges of her apron and waved it to fan herself. Finally she reached out her hand.

"Johnny Leavitt, cum hea." Johnny stood up and slowly moved towards Marie. He reached out his hand, and she clutched it in hers tightly. She felt every detail in Johnny's hands, breathed in real deep as if smelling the boy, then, tears welled up in her eyes. "Well now, it iz yu, ain't it?" she whispered. "Neva in my born dayz did I'spect ta have ya righcheere in my plaze. Sam must a been right worried ta send ya inta dez parts like dis."

Johnny looked at the others. "We know all about the curse. We saw those men back there shoot Sam, and he didn't die."

Marie smiled and nodded. "Den ya knows bout me, too, I spoze?"

Johnny stared at the others who looked just as confuxed as he did. "I guess not," he replied.

"Well, doe's ya know how old Sam an Cora is?"

"Yes." Johnny said. "They're almost two hundred, aren't they?"

Marie nodded. "Sho iz, an I is juz as old as a day is. I'z Cora's sista."

"But that would mean that you're the Marie in all of the stories!" Bo said. "The one who saw the curse begin. It was you all along? So all those stories you told me were really all about you?" Marie nodded as a slight smile crossed her lips.

"That's how you became blind, isn't it?" Johnny said. "You saw the curse when it started!"

Marie lowered her head. "Da time is cum," she said as if in a trance. "Da events is now set ta rollin'. Fate has brung ya hea, and it ain't gonna let go 'til ya do whut cha cum fer."

Marie stood and made her way past the others into the back room. Slowly she came back in, carrying a small red bundle of cloth. She laid it on the table and carefully unwrapped it. "I ain't showed dis ta no soul sinz da day da curse begun.

"When Cap'n Edwards see'd dat we wuz in a pack a trouble, he took ta gettin' real nervous. Den da pirates boarded de *Alliance*. Cap'n Edwards telled em der was a right important cargo on dat ship, an' only he and Laffite knowed what it were. He gots ta tawkin' real bold ta dem pirates, specially Mr. Aluitious E. Clayton. Cap'n Edwards got nose ta nose wif dat man and telled him in no uncertain terms dat da man dat mesxed wif da nation's treasure juz might as well mess wiv God hisself, cause dat boy would bring a curse upon us awl. Well, dat very moment, Aluitious put a saber right through da Cap'ns heart. With the Cap'ns last dyin' breath, he sez, 'May da God of heaven curse yu for whut yu done, a curse dat will last' till the true intent of da last male Laffite avenge dis nation and dis family.' Da Cap'n put me ta drift in a life raft juz as da pirates cum, and I seed and heard awl. But not b'fo he give me dis."

Inside the red cloth bundle was what looked like an old piece of drift wood. The sides were carved with deep rings that moved loosly around the rest of the driftwood. Each ring had a series of carved letters on them that looked like another language. Marie ran her hand over the carved markings, then, handed the odd piece of wood to Johnny.

"So, what is it?" Johnny asked.

Marie shook her head. "Don' rightly know, but Cap'n Edwards telled me I weren't to sho it ta no man 'cept a Laffite. He telled me I was ta keep it safe 'cuz Clayton would do anythin' ta git his hands on dat, and as long as he neva had it, everthin' would be awlright.

"When da curse took ova, I was stuck right hea. I couldn't get dat piece ta anybody. If I goe's anywhaers deeper inta da bayou dan da ol' fort, I gets real sick, and I starts ta change. Iz da same fo Cora and Sam. Dey is stuck at Maison

Rouge, like I is stuck hea. I hea tell a dem and such only when Bo an sum othas brings me word."

Johnny examined the curious piece of wood. "Marie, was this part of the hidden cargo that Cap'n Edwards was protecting?"

Marie shook her head again. "I don' rightly kno' fo sho', but I does know dis. Da Cap'n told me it could only make sense to a Laffite, and dat if anythin' happend ta him or dis hea piece a wood, heaven help us awl.

"When da Cap'n was killed, I watched de *Alliance* turn inta a **b**all a fire. Lightnin' flashin' all around dat ship, but no wheres else. Dat ship was burning red. But it neva burnt up, **j**ust set daer a glowin', an dem men aboard set ta s**c**reamin' as **i**f dey was a seein' hell it'self. I held tight ta dis hea bundle and da world 'round me a set ta spinnin'. I started feelin' rite sick, and den in a flash, everthin' went as black as coal. Der wernt a light in da night sky. Der weren't nuthin'. Everything was dead quiet. **J**ust darkness from dat time on. I felt da winds a whirlin' and a spinnin' everwhich way. Den I doesn't rememba a thin', 'cept dat I was layin' on da sho line an sum folks cum an fetched me. I held tight ta dis hea bundle an ain't showed it ta nobody till righcheere an now.

"Now da time is come. Dae ain't no way I'll eva **g**et dat thin' in is right place, but it seems ta me, dat sinz yu is a Laffite, and sinz yu kin come an' go, da bayou is da only sensible ansa ta awl a dis.

"Afta I cum back, some folks set ta claimin' dat **d**ey **h**ad seen de *Alliance* as a ghost ship a wanderin' in da watas uf da bayou. Dis hea hunk a wood belongs on dat ship. Might juz' be da ansaw ta fixin' dat awful curse. Seems only fittin' dat de *Alliance* iz da place ta start."

Johnny stared at the floor. He felt sick. "**I** didn't plan on going into the bayou to look for any gho**x**t ship," he said.

217

"All I wanted was to get some help for my parents. I thought that you could call for help or something. We've got to go back to Maison Rouge and help them. I can't worry about some stupid curse or treasure as long as my parents are in danger!"

Marie's face turned serious. "Look hea, boy, yu is juz' as much a part a dis now as we is. Dey is only one way yu kin help yo' folks. Yo Uncle Ken iz in da bayou, an' you is gonna find im!"

Johnny looked at Marie with his mouth agape. "My uncle Ken is alive?"

Marie nodded and turned to Bo. "Bo, does yu rememba when I was gone fo' a time inta da bayou, an when I cum back, ya took cae a me, whilst I wuz sick?"

"Yeah sure, I remember," Bo replied. "You said you was visitin' a relative in the bayou. I was real worried."

Marie nodded again. "I was takin' supplies in ta Mr. Kenny. Doze men dat is afta yu, Johnny Leavitt, is da same ones dat tried ta kill Mr. Kenny. If'n he hadn't gone in ta hidin' when he did, he'd be dead fo' sho.'"

Johnny gulped hard. "Where is he then? Can you take me to him?"

Tears welled up in Marie's eyes. "Mr. Kenny told me not ta folla im, dat if I din know whea he wuz, dae couldn't hurt me. But fo' a long time he was on da ol' island by da fort. Dat was when I cum ta bein' sick. I cain't go past da fort, but I did, so's I could take him some supplies. I know's dat he's still alive somewheres in dat bayou!"

218

22
Hoodwinked

Jack came storming into the little cabin. "Hey, you guys! I can hear a motor coming. And there's some lights flashing through the trees in the swamp!"

Marie quickly turned to the others. "Dae is commin' fo' y'all. Ya bez get to da bayou b'yo' dae finz ya."

Laurabeth was watching out the front door. "But what if it's the police, and they've come to help? Shouldn't we just wait and see?"

"We can't take that chance," said Bo. "We can take the boat and go hide in the bayou out back. That way if it is help, we can see them, but they won't see us." The group hurried out the door to their wooden boat.

Bo was the last to follow the others, and Marie grabbed his arm as he stepped into the boat. "Yu take good cae, boy. An' don' let nuthin' happen ta Mr. Johnny!" She handed the little red bundle to him as they began to push away from the dock. "Mr. Johnny, yu is in charge a dat bundle now. Bo will hep ya to protect it. Don let no body take cae uv it, but yu or Mr. Bo. Yu unastans?"

Johnny nodded his head. "I'll take good care of it," he said, tucking it into his back pack.

Bo began rowing, and soon they were past the little cabin and out of reach of the dim lantern's light. Bo positioned the boat near a large clump of moss hanging from the cypress trees.

"That tickles!" Matie whispered loudly, pushing away the moss.

"Shhhhh! Mat, you gotta be quiet. They're coming,"

Johnny said, nudging his sister's arm.

A sleek black boat with an inboard motor slowly glided toward the old dock. Marie stood on the porch stairs waiting and listening cautiously. Then she went inside the little cabin and emerged from the door holding a shotgun. She held the gun up high and shot into the air.

The sleek boat's engine stopped. "Who's out daer?" Marie demanded. The lights from the boat lit up the entire cabin. Johnny and the others ducked into the shadows. Slowly Johnny lifted his head just a bit to see who was in the larger boat. The bright lights blinded him as he squinted to see. Then a familiar **v**oice echoed from behind the light.

"Hello! Please don't shoot. We're a looking for some lost kids. Have **y**ou seen an**y**?"

Marie's eyes narrowed with suspicion. "Who is ya? **S**tate yo' name."

The voice came again. "My name is Randy Olsen. I'm a friend of the Leavitt's."

Johnny gulped hard. "Oh, no," he whispered. "**W**e didn't tell Marie about Randy."

"Shhhh**h**," whi**x**pered Bo. "They're sayin**g** something."

"Who else is wi**f** ya? I knowed dae**r** is more a yu awll on dat fancy ri**q**." By now the men in the boat realized that Marie was completely blind, s**o** Pal**m**er carefully tied the boat to the dock.

"Try to get her gun," Ratcliffe urged.

As Palmer carefully stepped out onto the dock, the weathered old boards creaked beneath his feet. Marie raised her gun and shot in the direction **o**f the noise, barely missing Palmer's foot. He leaped back into the boat, scrambling for cover.

"Get back out there!" Ratcliffe demanded.

Palmer shook his head defiantly. "If you want to get her

220

gun, you can do it yourself."

Ratcliffe slowly stood up. "Ma'am, could we please speak to you for a moment?"

Marie was silent and aimed the gun in Ratcliffe's direction.

Ratcliffe again attempted to soften the hard headed old woman's posture. "Have you, by chance, seen any children lost in the bayou? We're trying to help their parents find them."

The sound of muffled struggling from Ratcliffe's boat echoed back to the little cabin. Marie raised an eyebrow, and then began to lower her gun. "Yu sez yu is helpin' da parents find dem loxt chillen?"

"Oh yes," yelled Ratcliffe, smiling back at the others.

Marie walked out on the deck, closer to the large boat and yelled out to the men, "Yup, I seed dem kids."

Laurabeth gasped, as Bo reached for her shoulder to calm her.

Marie continued. "Dey cum by hea bout two hours ago. Sed dey was out cheere on a dare ta see who could stan' a bein' in da bayou in da dark a nite. I give em all whut fo tho, an' telled dem pitiful chillen ta git fo home. Dey set off back t'wards da ol' Mansion. I ain't seen hide ner hair a dem sinz. Bez look fo em back at da ol' plantation."

Ratcliffe sneered, "Thank you. You've been very helpful. We'll do just that."

Johnny and the others sighed with relief. "She's hoodwinked 'em." Riley whispered.

The men back at the boat were preparing to leave when Matie suddenly sneezed. The moss they were hiding in had gotten in her nose, and she couldn't stop sneezing.

"We gotta get outta here! They'll hear us." Jack whispered, reaching for the oars. Bo pushed the boat away from the trees, and soon it floated away into the dark shadows of the bayou.

The children hid silently in the bottom of the boat. Johnny held his hand over Matie's mouth, ready to stifle the next sneeze. Everyone else held their breath as their little boat glided in the dark past the sleek black boat.

"I know I heard something!" Randy exclaimed. "It came from those trees over there."

Ratcliffe huffed with annoyance. "It's just that disgusting old woman," he said. "We need to check back at Maison Rouge. We've obviously missed the little brats. Just a bunch of troublemakers."

Randy shook his head at Ratcliffe's arrogance. Palmer sat at the back of the boat, inspecting the buck shot holes in his pant leg. Jim and Kate sat on the floor of the boat with their mouths gagged and their hands and feet tied, while Dennison held a gun on them.

As the sleek black motor boat headed back toward Maison Rouge, the hidden children headed deeper into the dark bayou.

"It's really late," Bo said to Johnny, as the boat's oars splashed on the dark waters. "The rest of you ought to try to get some sleep. Jack and I will take turns rowing."

Johnny laid his backpack on the bottom of the boat to make a lumpy pillow for Matie. She adjusted herself to get as comfortable as she could, then, pulled the old tarp over her shoulders for a makeshift blanket.

Laurabeth sat down next to her and placed her arm around the little girl. "Here Matie, I'll keep you warm." Riley curled up in a little ball by her feet, huddling cloze to the floor in the middle of the boat.

Johnny couldn't sleep. All he could think of were the things that Marie had said. If she was for real and the curse was real, then everything, even the lives of his own family, rested on his shoulders.

Johnny grimaced at the memory of seeing Sam lying on the floor. Then he thought of his parents. Sam was no more than a cursed apparition, although a good friend. To him the gunshot was nothing more than an inconvenience. To Johnny's parents it would mean life or death. Johnny needed help from an adult, someone he could trust, especially after the act that Randy Olsen had been putting on. Johnny could only think of one person that could help him now, his Uncle Ken. His hopes began to rise as he thought of finding his uncle alive. Now the idea of going into the bayou brought hope to his shattered dreams.

The exhaustion of the day began to take over as Johnny tried to stay awake. Every muscle within him ached for the relief of sleep. Occasionally the mystical spell of the bayou and the croaking of bullfrogs in the distance lulled him into blissful slumber. The welcome rest was all too soon interrupted by the hoot of an old screech owl or the flapping of wings across the dark waters.

Suddenly Johnny awoke with a start as the boat bumped against something. He looked around, to see why they had stopped.

"We're here," Bo whispered, trying not to wake the others.

23

The Break

Quietly the morning sun rose on the bayou, and the humid mists gave way to the sun's rays. Maison Rouge was quiet except for an occasional grunt or snore from the unwanted guests. The night had been a long one, and the unusual events had taken a toll on everyone.

"Get up!" bellowed Ratcliffe, kicking Randy who was asleep on the floor. Randy awoke ready for a fight, then reluctantly composed himself.

Everyone had slept the night in the study in order to keep a close eye on Jim and Kate. Most of them had gotten some sleep, however uncomfortable their lodgings were, with the exception of Dennison, who was undoubtedly out of sorts and in need of a break from the long night's watch.

"You're useless," Ratcliffe grunted at the man. "Go get some sleep so you can earn what I'm paying you." Dennison nodded and headed for the nearext couch.

Ratcliffe looked at Jim and Kate. "It's a good thing you didn't try anything last night or your wife here might have just ended up floating somewhere in the bayou."

Palmer was nibbling on some peanuts in a candy dish on the desk. "So when do we get to eat?" he asked, popping another handful of peanuts into his mouth.

Randy waved impatiently toward him. "Why don't you go and cook something for all of us since you've already eaten?"

Palmer's eyes narrowed. "So you think you're going to start bossing me around now? Since the old lady's gone, you think all I'm good for is cooking? It's your fault the old lady's gone."

Ratcliffe walked over to the two men. "You're both incompetent enough to do it."

Kate interrupted, "Only if you want them to poison us all. Why don't you let me cook breakfast?"

"She's right," Randy interjected. "Palmer can watch her while she cooks, and the rest of us can look for the kids in the daylight."

"We searched this whole plaze last night," Palmer complained.

Ratcliffe walked over to Jim. "Where are those little brats hiding?"

Jim squared his jaw. "I hope they're miles from here by now and bringing the police!"

Ratcliffe turned in disgust and yanked Kate from the chair. He nodded at Palmer. "Take her into the kitchen and don't take your eyes off her. Randy, you go look outside again, and I'll keep my eye on Mr. Leavitt here."

Palmer loosened the ropes on Kate's wrist. She turned to Jim and gently placed her hand on his arm. Then Palmer yanked her into the hallway.

"I'm going!" she said, breaking free of his brutish grasp. As they headed into the entryway, the doorbell rang.

Ratcliffe stopped Palmer. "Have her answer the door and she'd better not try anything."

Kate went to the door, desperately hoping it was Jake Morgan. Palmer hid himself behind the door with a gun firmly fixed on her back. As Kate opened the door, Mr. Sauvinet stood on the door step.

"Hello," said Kate. "What can I do for you?"

Mr. Sauvinet tipped his head slightly. "Hello Mrs. Leavitt. I've come to give your husband some final papers to sign in regards to his new company. Could I please speak to

225

him?"

Kate mustered up a faint smile. "Ah, well, Jim isn't here right now. I'd invite you in, but the place is an absolute mess."

Mr. Sauvinet again tipped his head as he raised an eyebrow. "Oh, I see, perhaps I've come at a bad time. How rude of me to come unannounced like this. Perhaps another time would be better."

Mr. Sauvinet handed Kate a folded piece of paper. "Could you please have your husband look at this? It's just a bit of troublesome details that the Boss was concerned about. I spoke to Sam earlier, and he said he would tell you about it."

Kate winced as she thought of Sam. "I'll be glad to give the paper to Jim. I'll tell him you came by."

Kate began to close the door, but Sauvinet didn't budge. Kate slowly opened the door again. "Is there more?" she asked. Sauvinet smiled as he looked Kate in the eye. "I apologize, my dear lady, that I was unable to accept the invitation to last night's festivities. I'm afraid I was working quite late." Kate smiled and nodded, hoping to end the conversation quickly.

Sauvinet persisted. "I would imagine the unique traditions of the bayou have brought great interest to your children. Especially the stories Sam so eloquently tells of the dealings of your predecessors. They are quite enchanting tales, aren't they? Especially with all of the evidence that this Mansion affords. It would seem to me that your children's curiosities could lead them into investigating the doings of their ancestors. Either way, I'm sure that your children are quite capable of finding whatever they may need." Sauvinet winked at Kate as he said these words. Then subtlety pointed at the paper in Kate's hand.

Kate looked at him then glanced quickly over her shoulder. "Oh, yes. The children are very curious. This place has been quite an adventure."

Carefully Kate opened the paper and read it. She continued speaking to Sauvinet, making sure that Palmer couldn't see what she was doing. Upon the paper in small writing in the middle of the page it said:

"YOUR CHILDREN ARE SAFE, THEY ARE BEING CLOSELY WATCHED OVER."

Tears began to well up in Kate's eyes as she eagerly nodded at Sauvinet. "Thank you for coming," she said gratefully. "I'll be sure to give this paperwork to Jim."

Kate carefully tucked the paper in her pocket. Sauvinet smiled, nodded, and left.

Kate breathed a sigh of relief, quickly wiped the tears from her eyes, and boldly turned back to the others. Palmer again grabbed her arm and marched her back into the room where Ratcliffe and the others were waiting.

"It's good you didn't try anything," Ratcliffe scolded. Kate ignored his words and put her hand over the paper in her pocket.

"So where's the paper he gave you?" Randy demanded.

Kate looked at Randy with disdain. "It's just some business papers that they need Jim to sign."

Randy held out his hand. "I wouldn't let Jim sign anything without taking a look at it first," he said.

Jim interrupted, "Why don't you stay out of my business? Besides you're fired. You're not my lawyer any more." Randy just laughed as Palmer held the gun up and nudged Kate.

Reluctantly, she pulled the paper from her pocket. "I'll just give it to Jim, then, I can make breakfast for everyone." Quickly she pushed the paper in Jim's direction.

Randy stepped in and intercepted it. Kate froze as Randy unfolded it. Suddenly Randy began to laugh. "Some business man Sauvinet is. He didn't even give you the right

227

papers. This one is blank!"

Randy dropped it, and the blank page floated toward the floor. Kate took a shallow breath then turned towards Palmer. "Well then, I suppose we'd better get some breakfast made."

"Yes, we've had enough distractions," Ratcliffe complained. "You'd better make it fast."

Kate and Palmer headed for the kitchen as Randy left to search the mansion for the children again.

In the kitchen, Kate got a bowl out of the cupboard and began making pancakes. Palmer hung over her shoulder smacking his lips in a disgusting way. Kate broke a few eggs into the bowl. Then with a cup of flour in her hand, she threw it back in Palmer's face.

Palmer coughed uncontrollably, and the room quickly filled with a white cloud of powder. Kate headed straight for the back door and ran as fast as she could across the lawn.

Palmer tried to follow, but he was choking so badly he went straight to the sink for a drink of water. As soon as his coughing was under control, he headed out the door, looking for Kate. But she was gone. Palmer ran back through the kitchen, across the dusty white floor toward the study.

As he entered the room without Kate, Ratcliffe was incensed. "Where is she?" he demanded.

Palmer shook his head and coughed out the words. "She got away. She threw flour in my face!"

"You idiot," Ratcliffe yelled. "It's quite obvious how she got away. It was through your inept stupidity." They both grabbed Jim and headed for the kitchen. By now Randy and Dennison joined them, and everyone headed out onto the back lawn.

The only evidence of Kate's escape was a slight trail of white flour that ended midway across the lawn. Ratcliffe started barking out orders at the others. Then everyone split up to look for Kate.

One by one the **m**en returned. Randy was the last. "**I**'ve checked all of the old buildings. She's gone," he said. "Did anyone else see any sign o**f** her?"

Ratcliffe snorted with di**z**gust and stormed back into the house with every**o**ne following. **P**almer prodded Jim with the gun as they all headed back into the study.

Ratcliffe's **f**ace was bright red and his eyes were filled with fire. "We're going into the swamp right now," he said, pounding his fist on the desk. "**I** don't care **i**f anyone is hungry. We're going **b**efore she comes back with the authorities. I'm going to use my map, and I'm going to get that treasure! Now the fi**r**st one of you who says a word will be the first who gets fed to the alligators!"

Kate had made her wa**y** **t**hrough the overgrowth behind Sam and Cora's cabin. Pushing her way through the thick bushes, she stopped only for a moment to catch her breath. Then, glancing over her shoulder, she heard the voices of Ratcliffe's men. She headed into the brush, till the voices of her pursuers faded away. **W**ith wear**y** determination, she finally stumbled on the area that Jim had told her about. In the center of the clearing, the large cairn stood steadfast and immovable, giving a strong a sense of protection from the difficulties she had just left.

The stone pylon now caught her interest, and she slo**wly** examined its unusual markings. Looking through the four inch peep hole at the top, she placed he**r** foot on one of the stones near the base of the marker. The old stone **b**roke **b**eneath her weight, and she bent down to repla**z**e the loosened rock. Then she noticed that it was hollow. Turning it over, **s**he **s**aw a large gem inside the cavity.

Kate held **u**p the clear green stone as it glistened in the sun. The old stone was highly polished and very unusually fashioned. As Kate examined it, she realized that it was just the size of the peep hole in the large monument. Carefully she placed it in the space at the top of the marker. It fit perfectly. As she peered through the gem, she discovered, that it was intended to be a very powerful lens. She could actually see the minute details of the fort in the distance.

The large fort was made of gray stone. At the top she could make out the remains of some old cannons positioned along the upper wall.

Suddenly a hand grabbed Kate's shoulder. Chills ran down her spine, and she whirled around expecting to see the men she had just escaped from. Instead, Sam stood there quietly smiling.

"It's you!" Kate exclaimed. "But I thought you were dead!"

Sam chuckled. "Well, I spoze sum folks is thinkin' dat. An' iz bes lef' dat way."

Kate shook her head with confusion. "But I saw you get shot, then, you and Cora disappeared. What's going on?"

"I telled yu and Mr. Jim once b'fo. Dae really is a curse, and I iz a part a dat curse. Ya see Cora and I cain't leave dis plaze. We ain't dead, and we ain't alive. We juz is. I cum ta tell ya, dae is otha folk like us a-watchin' yo young uns. Yo chillen is juz fine."

Kate nodded. "That's what Mr. Sauvinet's note meant, isn't it?"

"Sho iz, but dae is mo. Johnny and da othas has gone inta da bayou, a-hopin' ta fix da curse, and ta fine Mr. Kenny. Mr. Kenny set out ta fix dat curse, too, cept he didn't have awl a da clues. Awlst he had were a couple a dem coins."

"I've got to go after those kids," Kate said. "Could you call Jake Morgan? He's the only one who can help us now."

Sam scratched his head. "I ain't so sho dat el work. I

knowed dat we iz ju<u>z</u> da old caetakers hea, but I knowed a thin'
or two bout dem poli<u>z</u>e folk. Now Mr. Morgan hisself is a right
good man, but dae is sum folk a-workin' agin him dat he don'
know nuthin' 'bouts. I heard him tell <u>J</u>im dat nashonal security
were involved. Mr. Sauvinet telled me dat da FBI even knows
'bouts da curse and fo' sum blasted reason, dae don' wan' it
fixed."

"That doesn't make any sense," Kate said. "<u>W</u>hy would
federal officers even believe in the curse, <u>l</u>et alone want it to
<u>r</u>emain as it is? I know Jim said that they were involved back at
the <u>c</u>ompany, but this who<u>l</u>e thing is just <u>s</u>o <u>s</u>trange."

Sam began to chuckle. "Yu ain't seen da half u<u>v</u> it." All
at once, Sam whistled, and immediately Matie's three little
humming birds we<u>r</u>e by his side. One dipped towards his ear
and hovered there. Sam nodded a <u>c</u>ouple of times then turned to
Kate. "Da chillen wu<u>z</u> at Miss Marie's place and dae spent' da
nite on da old island. De's hea birds, is our communications
system in da bayou. Sinze we cain't leave, dey is da
messen<u>g</u>ers.

"No<u>w</u> sinz yu is awl set on goin' into da bayou afta doze
chillen, dez lil birds will hep show ya da way. Time's a
waistin'. <u>Y</u>ou'll fin' a boat, tied up down by da water's edge.
Dae is sum provisions daer, and Cora has fixed ya some food.
Now git, b'fo doze men cum lookin' fo' ya."

"Thank you." Kate whispered.

Sam slowly disappeared. Kate headed toward the
bayou. At the water's edge she found the small boat and
climbed inside. Glancing back at Maison Rouge she thought of
<u>J</u>im. <u>N</u>ow she was even more determined to find the kids.

Kate's small boat glided along through the swamp. It
wasn't fast, but the rugged old motor was <u>c</u>onsistent despite any
obstacles that got in the way. She watched as stray debris
passed along the sides of the boat. Over and over she steered

away from old rotten logs and the loose vegetation that floated in the dusky waters.

The thought of her family never left her mind. She prayed that they would be all right as she headed deeper into the marsh. Even with its chipped paint and cracked wood, the old boat that Sam had provided was perfect for maneuvering theze challenging waterways.

Kate lovingly thought back to Sam and Cora and the stories they told about their lives. Even with all the evidence, a little hint of doubt still remained in Kate's mind. The mystical stories of curses and pirates seemed almost too much to believe, especially the idea of a family curse.

Suddenly Kate's thoughts were interrupted by the three bright humming birds that darted about the small boat as if playing a game of tag. Kate pushed the engine's throttle forward. The small motor didn't skip a beat and whirred a little faster.

"Let's see if you can keep up with this," Kate challenged the birds as she pushed the motor even faster.

Now the birds became very excited. One by one each flew to her shoulder, hovering just next to her ear. Then she heard three distinct words, "Tag...You're... It...!"

Kate slowed the engine. "That's completely impossible," she stated aloud, while watching the birds dart back and forth in front of the boat. "It can't be. It must be the heat or my imagination."

The birds hovered near the front of the boat. Once in a while one landed on the edge of the boat to rezt, then just as quickly it would take flight again.

The experience of hearing the birds was more than a little unsettling to Kate. She rationalized the incident. After all, she had been up most of the night.

Aqain her thoughts turned back to her family. Ratcliffe

and his goons had Jim, and they were still determined to find the children and the map. She worried even more as she thought of the children heading into a place that was even dangerous for the most seasoned experts.

The challenge of going into the bayou didn't bother Kate, but the threat to her family did. With fire in her eyez she was determined to get to her children before Ratcliffe did. Pushing the little boat even harder, she sped through the bayou, the bird's just barely keeping pace along side the boat.

24
Adventure

The children slept peacefully as the water lapped at the sides of the boat. It washed back and forth at the edges of the shoreline as if rocking the children in a deep sleep.

Johnny yawned and stretched his leg still half asleep and accidentally kicked Riley, who woke up with a start, yelling "Gater!" Everyone sat up, jostling the boat and searching the waters for the unsuspected figment of Riley's imagination. Bo looked from side to side for the invisible alligator, while Matie clung to Laurabeth, and Jack slapped an oar at the water.

Johnny glanced at the others and began laughing. "Riley's just dreaming."

Eventually the group came to their senses and Bo gently slapped Riley's head.

"No gater, just a stupid dream!"

Matie rubbed her eyes and sat up with a start. "Did we sleep here all night?"

"Yeah," said Johnny. "Bo and I tied the boat up here in the dark. We figured it was as good a place as any other to sleep, at least until daylight."

Riley climbed out of the boat. "Hey Bo," he shouted. "Where's the old fort?"

Everyone piled out of the boat splashing toward the beach.

"Jack, help me pull the boat further up on shore," suggested Bo. Jack nodded and the two young men grabbed the sides of the boat and soon had it securely fastened to a tree.

As the children stepped out onto the cheniere, the white seashells crunched under their feet. The small island was covered in trees and overgrowth. To the east a small stream emptied into the bayou. Beyond the stream were the remains of a wrecked boat propped up against a tree.

"What's that?" Matie asked and started running down the shoreline towards the boat.

"Wait!" Bo yelled. "It's not safe!" Matie ignored his warning and kept right on running to see the wrecked boat. Everyone followed as fast as they could.

Bo caught up with her first with Johnny and the others right behind.

Johnny grabbed his little sister's arm and turned her around. "Matie, don't you ever do that again! It's just not safe.

This isn't like going to the beach! You've got to be careful here in the bayou. You can't just run right into trouble like that." Johnny turned to Bo. "Bo, you tell her!"

Bo bent down and scooped up a pile of seashells in his hand. "I think I'd better tell all of you. Okay, you see this boat righcherre. Well, it ended up wrecked like that from a gater attack." Bo pointed at a large gaping hole in the wreck with scrape marks on it. "I've spent a lot of time here in the bayou, and ya have ta respect it. Ya gotta always be on your guard and be real careful. Rule number one, nobody goes anywheres alone. Ya got that! There's gaters, an quicksand, even snakes, and all kinds of poisonous bugs. That doesn't even count the wild animals who think that you're their local restaurant. Night here's even worse! We were real lucky last night, and I didn't want to scare anybody, but nighttime is when the really weird things come out. It can get real creepy. Most people stay away from the fort 'cause they say it's haunted."

"I don't believe you!" Matie said, with her hands on her hips. "You're just trying to scare me again."

"Look, it really is dangerous," Bo insisted. "You gotta listen to me."

Riley looked at Bo and scrunched up his nose. "So, Bo, why'd you come here in the bayou then?"

Bo looked at the ground and kicked at the shells. "Well, the first real time was to look for Marie. I thought I'd see if she was here somewheres. My uncle brung me here once when I was little, but I don't count that one. The second time I came was on a dare. Some kids at school didn't believe that I'd been to the fort, so they dared me to come in here and stay the night. I kind a like stuff like that, so I did it.

"You really need to believe me. This place can be beautiful, but it can be deadly. And nobody is goin' anywheres alone. I mean it, and I'll let ya'll have it, if ya do."

Johnny stood up to get a better look at the wrecked boat. "We ran into an old guy in town who said he was with my Uncle Ken. Their boat was wrecked somewhere by an island. I wonder if this is it?"

Bo's eyes got big. "Was that your uncle? There was these two men that came into the bayou looking for treasure. One got out, but he was in bad shape. They never heard from the other man again. The Fed's and all sorts of guys came in here searchin' the whole island, but they never found the guy."

"I know," said Johnny. "It was my Uncle Ken."

"C'mon," said Bo. "Follow me."

Johnny held Matie's hand as they walked through the thick trees towards the old structure. He slapped at the persistent mosquitoes that buzzed around his ears and face.

Bo walked in the front, pushing aside the trees and bushes on a path that was barely recognizable. Soon the trees and brush thinned and the shells under foot gave way to a sandy clearing. Up ahead was a small structure made of clamshells.

"There it is!" said Bo.

Riley looked disappointed. "That's a fort?"

"Well, sort of," said Bo. "It's the one I stayed at. It ain't so scary in the daytime."

An air of excitement took over, and soon everyone was exploring the old structure. Inside it was dark and damp and had a musty smell of rotting moss. Outside, the broken down clamshell fort glistened magically.

Johnny watched as the others explored the curious find, but to him something was wrong. He remembered the cairn his father had shown him. When he looked at the old fort through the hole in the top of the stone cairn, the fort seemed much bigger. He knew he had seen a different structure. "Hey, Bo, are you sure that this is the old fort? Are there any other buildings on this island?"

Bo shook his head. "There might be something else downstream. But I'm sure there ain't any more here. I've checked out this island backwards and forwards, and there ain't any other buildings here. But follow me. There is something else I want to show you."

Bo led everyone past the old structure and down river a bit. A marsh ridge ran along the edge of the shore amid trees and fallen debris. The water was a bit clearer now. Bo hurried along the edge of the beach. His shoes splashed at the water's edge. Soon the shore widened into a large sandy area. Two large cypress treez stood out of place among the other vegetation. Bo ran straight towards the farthest tree.

"C'mon!" he yelled, motioning towards the others. "You gotta see this." Up on the old tree was a roughly carved letter L. On each side of the L were four vertical lines that looked just like claw marks from a large animal.

"So what is it?" Matie blurted out.

Bo laughed, "You're standin' in it!"

Matie's eyes got big. "Quicksand?" she yelled, scrambling onto Johnny's back for protection.

Riley stuck his foot in the sand and rolled his eyes at the little girl. "It ain't quicksand!" he said. "If it was quicksand, you'd a been knee deep in it by now!" Matie still clung to Johnny's back.

"Look!" said Jack, pointing to the ground. "I've heard about this before." Bo walked around the group examining some depressions in the sand.

Matie curiously climbed down from Johnny's back. "So if it isn't quicksand, what is it?"

Jack interrupted "There used to be something buried here, probably some old pirate stash."

"Yup," said Bo. "That's what it was. My uncle said you used to be able to see the rust on the sand from where the old chests had been buried. Folks say it was part of Napoleon's private treasure that Laffite took. There was this old guy named Samuel Wash who worked for Laffite. They said he told everyone about a murder that happened here because of the gold. Ol' Wash was about a hundred and four years old when he told that story."

Johnny looked at Matie, his eyes glistening. "Hey, Mat. Do you remember what Sam told us when we firzt came to Maison Rouqe?"

All of a sudden Maties eye's lit up as well and a large smile filled her face.

Johnny looked at the others. "Sam told us his last name was Wash."

Matie giggled.

"What's so funny?" asked Riley.

"Being old," Matie said. "Sam's just as wrinkled on the inside as he is on the outside!"

Johnny smiled at his sister. "Sam told us all the truth. He really is about two hundred years old and knows about the treasure. That's probably why he sent us here."

Riley started digging in the sand.

"What are you doing?" Laurabeth asked.

Riley looked up at her as if she should know. "What else? I'm looking for the buried treasure."

Laurabeth sat down on a nearby stump and watched her cousin.

Bo smiled, "Hey, he could find something. One man found a coin here not too long ago. And there's more."

Riley stopped long enough to glance up then resumed his digging. Bo shoved his cousin. "I don't mean more treasure. There's more pirate stuff."

"What do you mean?" asked Johnny.

"There's a half sunken ship around here somewhere.

Old Laffite didn't have time to fix it, so he just got the guns and treasure off before they scuttled it. They named the area Dead Man's Lake."

Matie frowned. "What's a scuttle?" she asked.

Johnny leaned over to his little sister. "When they scuttle a boat, they cut more holes in it till it sinks."

"Oh," said Matie as her stomach growled. "Does that mean the dead men are there, too?"

Bo got serious. "Well, sort a, but you can't tell anyone, okay?"

Riley and Maties eye's were huge.

"No way!" said Jack. "You saw dead men in here."

Bo looked a bit embarrassed. "Well, kind of."

Laurabeth raised an eyebrow and glared at her brother. "So, just what did you see?" she demanded.

Bo fidgeted. "Well, I guess I sorta went a little farther into the bayou. I didn't say anything 'cause I knew Mom and Dad wouldn't let me go. It was all part of that dare. The kids that dared me said I had to have proof of being there. So I got some proof. I couldn't let those jerks get the best of me. I guess I sort of found a real pirate."

"So where is it?" Johnny asked.

Bo kicked at some rocks on the sand as he looked at Laurabeth. "It's down the river past the old sunken ship."

Matie frowned. "I don't want to go there. I don't want to see any dead men!"

"Ahh... come on Mat!" said Johnny, "It's no big deal. It'll be just like Pirates of the Deep at 'Dizzyland'. Besides, I seem to remember you saying that this was all just a trick to scare you. Are you afraid a real ghost is going to get ya?" He poked at Matie.

Matie gritted her teeth. "I'm not afraid of any ghost! I just don't think dead men look very good. They're disgusting.

You can't scare me!"

"Me, neither," Riley piped in.

"Hey, Bo," Jack said. "What did you find on that dead pirate?"

Bo reached deep into his pocket. "Just this," he said, flipping a coin into the air. "Heads or tails?" he said as he caught the coin.

"Heads!" yelled Laurabeth.

Bo slapped the coin on the back of his hand. "Nope, you lose!" he said, looking at the coin.

Riley stretched his neck. "Let me see that," he said. Bo handed him the coin and Riley examined it, then slapped it back into Bo's hand, and started running along the shore towards the boat.

"What's he doing?" Johnny asked. Riley turned and yelled back at the others. "It's a gold Doubloon!"

25

The Black Albatross

A muggy humidity filled the swampy air as Jim watched **P**almer fumble with a large modern map of the ba**y**ou, comparing it to Ratcliffe's original.

"Let m**e** s**ee** those maps," demanded Ratcliffe, jerking them from **P**almer's hands. Ratcliffe cut the boat's engine and studied the maps as the others waited.

The tension between the three thieves was mounting. If Jim could just convince two of them to gang up on the other **o**ne, **h**e'd have a better chance to escape. He had noticed the resentment in Palmer's and Randy's eyes every time Ratcliffe ordered them around. **J**im had known Randy for years and knew he couldn't endure much more of Ratcliffe's badgering.

"So, **h**ow long have you been putting up with this?" Jim whispered to Randy.

Randy'**s** expression didn't c**h**ange. He just looked straight ahead, then, answered, "For more than six **m**onths now."

Palm**e**r glanced at the two, but didn't say anything.

Ratcliffe started the **e**ngine. "It's this w**ay**!" he stated flatly and shoved the maps back at **P**almer. Palmer folded them and put them in the boat's side compartment.

Jim couldn't figure out why a successful man like Palmer continuall**y** took Ratcliffe's abuse without saying a word. In spite of his growing resentment, Palmer had continued to remain loyal to this man who ridiculed his every move.

As the boat motor hummed loudly, Jim edged his way closer to Palmer at the back of the boat. "Why do you take that from him?" Jim prodded.

Palmer lifted his head from his hands and looked up with surprise. It was clear that he wanted to say something, but he just turned away and ignored the question.

Jim had struck a nerve and decided to give it another try. "You're not like him!" Jim said.

Palmer looked Jim straight in the eye. "You'd better just be quiet!" he said as his face turned red. The blood vessels in his neck bulged as he looked at Ratcliffe's back. The hatred Palmer had for Ratcliffe was very real. The key for Jim was uncovering its source.

Once again Jim turned to Randy, "So how did Palmer end up in all of this?"

"I don't know. He was involved long before I was." Randy nodded in Palmer's direction. "You can try to ask him if you want, but he'll never answer you. I've already tried. He won't talk about it."

Jim watched the moss from a large cypress tree brush across the bow of the boat. Something scraped along the hull, and Ratcliffe slowed the engine as thick overgrowth closed in around the boat. The engine spit and sputtered, then died.

Ratcliffe turned the key, but nothing happened. "Check the motor!" he bellowed. Randy and Palmer removed the engine's cover and tipped the motor upward.

None of these men were used to the rugged bayou, and the extravagant boat they had procured wasn't meant for the uncertain waters they were traveling. Moss had entangled itself around the prop, but even worse, a small stray log had lodged itself between two of the propeller's blades breaking one of them completely off.

"What's wrong with it?" Ratcliffe demanded.

"The blade's broken off," Palmer answered.

"What!" Ratcliffe yelled. The echo of his voice sent a flock of birds fluttering in the trees over head. "You fools! Do something and fix this heap of junk!"

Randy stood up, turned towards Ratcliffe, then threw his hands in the air and yelled, "It's not fixable!"

Palmer watched, expecting Ratcliffe to explode.

"I told you this kind of boat wouldn't work here," Randy said. "Just because it looks good doesn't mean it's meant for these conditions."

Ratcliffe sneered at Randy. "Yes, you did tell me that, and since you know all of the answers, you can get us out of this." Ratcliffe pushed his way past the other men toward the padded seats at the back of the boat. He pushed Jim onto the floor and started throwing cushions everywhere. Soon he produced a shiny pair of aluminum oars and shoved them into Randy and Palmer's faces.

"Here!" he bellowed. "You can start by using these!"

The men took the oars as Ratcliffe punched a series of numbers into his cell phone. He waited impatiently, looked at the phone then, repeated the attempt over and over again. "It's dead!" he growled. "Idiots, you would think they could have some kind of service in this useless place!" Angrily he threw the phone as far as he could. It landed with a splash on the green waters.

Jim began replacing the seat cushions as the other two men climbed to the rear of the boat. They each found a spot near the back railing. Leaning as far over the edge of the boat as they could, they began paddling.

Unlike the old flat bottom boat that Johnny and his friends so easily maneuvered in the bayou, this boat was not adapted for the moss-choked waterways. The sleek black speedboat had now become an unlucky black albatross for these unseaxoned sailors.

A slight grin crossed Jim's face as he watched the two men paddle the large boat against the slow current. It was as if

244

the bayou seemed to be working against the clumsy thieves.

At the back of the boat, the two men hung from a small ladder that was intended to hold only one person at a time. They strained and worked to move the large boat across the murky bayou. The water lapped at their feet, dampening their tailored suitpants to the knee.

"We're getting nowhere!" Palmer finally complained. "I think we need to go back and get another boat."

By this time Ratcliffe was pacing back and forth. "All right!" he yelled. Everyone stood silent as his forceful words echoed over the bayou. Ratcliffe sneered and his nose twitched. "We'll take the rubber boat from here on in!"

Randy laid his oar in the boat and climbed back in. "Wait just a minute! I think Palmer's right. We need to go back and get another boat."

"Shut up!" Ratcliffe snapped. "You'll do as I say, or I'll make sure the alligators have a double portion for their lunch. They can just as easily enjoy you for their meal as they can him!" He pointed at Jim.

Randy didn't back down. "Look, if we take that flimsy inflatable into the bayou, we'll all end up as lunch, including you!"

Like a wild beast that had been deprived of its prey, Ratcliffe was enraged. He sat down in a huff grumbling under his breath and sneered at the men. Randy now turned with a slight grin, resuming his previous position and began paddling again. Palmer followed.

26
The Magnifique Peril

Riley waited anxiously in the boat as the other kids straggled along one by one. "I thought you'd never get here!" Riley said with a frown as Johnny helped Matie into the boat.

Bo and Jack waited on shore then pushed the boat into the brackish waters. With water up to their kneez they piled into the boat, splashing everyone.

"Hey," Matie yelled. "You got my dress all wet!"

At the back of the boat, Laurabeth sat quietly. All of the others had easily ran the distance across the small cheniere to the boat, but for Laurabeth it had been a bit too much. She gulped and gasped for air, her face pale with exhaustion. One by one the others in the boat began to notice her obvious distress. Her southern beauty was now overshadowed by the exhaustion of the unexpected adventure into the bayou.

Johnny watched her with growing concern. "Are you okay?" he asked, as he handed her a bottle of water. Laurabeth drank slowly, and handed the bottle back. Bo began to explain, but Laurabeth reached for his arm. "I'm just fine!" she said, mustering up as much spunk as she could. "I'm just out of breath. Don't worry 'bout me."

Bo looked concerned, but he knew his sister would never forgive him if he made her look weak in front of the others. "It's just the cushy life of a Southern Belle," he joked. "The bayou will toughen her up in no time."

Jack turned to Bo. "So where do you want us to go exactly?"

"It's just a few more miles downstream," replied Bo.

Matie squirmed. "Johnny, I'm hungry. Can we have

something to eat?"

Riley chimed in. "Yeah, I thought you guys were going to take care of us. We're starvin'. I can feel my bellybutton rubbin' against my back!"

Johnny reached into the old flour sack and pulled out some sweet potato pie. He handed a slice to each person, and they quickly devoured the tasty breakfast.

Johnny was about to bite into his portion as Matie watched him. "Can I have another piece? I'm still hungry."

When Johnny reached into the flour sack again, Bo interrupted. "Hey, I don't want to sound mean, but we don't know how long we're gonna be in the bayou. I think we'd best ration the food till we can get some more."

Johnny looked at Matie and then at the pie in his hand. "Here, Mat. You can have my piece. I'm not that hungry anyway." Matie took it and soon had it all eaten.

The children relaxed a bit as they watched the birds perched in their nests high above in the tree tops. A fish or two jumped for a bug now and then, splashing into the waters and disappearing out of site. Bullfrogs croaked a lazy harmonious tune in the distance. The entire boat ride was quite serene and seemed more like one of the bayou tours than an adventure.

But soon the thick overgrowth encroached on the boat, making rowing very difficult. Eventually the trees and bushes choked the meandering waterway, and the boat stopped near a very large old cypress tree dripping with moss and vines.

"Looks like a dead end!" said Riley. "Guess we'll have to try another way."

"Nope, we're here," Bo said with a sly grin. Riley scrunched up his nose in disbelief. Everyone else on the boat just looked confused.

Matie was the first to notice it. "It's just like the other one," she said, pointing to the old tree. Amid the tangled vines was a small area where the bark showed through. On the bark, juxt like before, a large "L" was carved. On each side of it were four long scratches that resembled the claw marks of a large animal.

Bo smiled at Matie. "I call this tree "Old Ellie" 'cause she's the one that led me to the real fort."

Johnny's eyes widened. "I knew it! There is a bigger one. I saw it from Maison Rouge. I knew there was another fort!"

Jack and Bo struggled to clear the thick vines. Soon the slow current allowed the boat through the dense overgrowth. Then a thick curtain of vines and bushes closed in again behind the boat.

The passengers were astonished to find themselves within a small grotto made of foliage like a jungle paradise. Small beaches and miniature islands lined the sides of the waterway and were surrounded by tall trees and vines. It was like a hidden fairy land. Birds of several colors and sizes flitted from tree to tree. Beams of sunlight filtered down in beautiful rays, dancing on the waters, making it sparkle and glimmer in an unearthly way.

Within the clear waters, a myriad of lillypads and water hyacinth bobbed up and down as an awkward frog jumped off of one, plopping with a splash into the water. Up in the trees an occasional squirrel chattered at the unwelcome intruders.

Everyone but Matie made a fuss at the glorious site. She was unusually quiet.

Johnny turned to her. "What's wrong Mat? Isn't it beautiful? Just like a fairyland."

Matie nodded but had a frown on her face. Her eyes darted from side to side, surveying the area. "Johnny, I've seen this before, and it's a bad place."

"Nothing's going to hurt you, Matie." Johnny reassured

her. "You couldn't have seen this before. We've never been here. Maybe it was juzt a dream or something."

Matie's mouth tightened. "I have seen this place. It was in the bathroom back at Maison Rouge. There's a window there and it says to watch for the eyes in this place. They called it the Magnificent Peril. Cora said it was alligator eyes. I saw them on the window."

"Shhhhhhhh! Everyone be quiet!" Bo whispered. "Listen!"

Riley rolled his eyes and swept his hand through the clear water to pick a flower. "I don't hear anything!" he said in a cocky tone.

"Exactly!" whispered Bo as he grabbed Riley's hand. "Something's wrong. All of the birds and squirrels are too quiet."

The group listened in absolute silence. Then a slight splash could be heard off in the distance. Everyone's eyes turned towards the noise. There, in the water, a ripple disturbed the bobbing flowers. Slowly an unseen force began parting the vegetation.

"C'mon! We gotta hurry! It's a gater!" Bo whispered loudly. "It knows we're here. My uncle told me of a granddaddy gater that guards these parts. This is his fairyland, and we gotta get out a here, now!"

Jack grabbed the oars and began rowing. Then Matie spotted the giant beast. "There it is!" she pointed. "You can see his eyes." Everyone watched cautiously as Jack rowed through the winding river of the deadly wonderland.

Bo watched the creature intently. "That's him all right. Did you see how big his eyes are? Matie's right. This place ain't safe."

As they rowed the boat along the waterway, they heard even more splashes, and everyone instinctively moved to the center of the boat, crowding together in silenze. The boat moved forward, the splashing of oars echoing in the deadly grotto.

The river led them to a tunnel of overgrowth about four feet high. "Duck down," Bo whispered.

Matie's eyes grew big, and she clung to Johnny's arm as tight as she could. The sun light could barely penetrate the dense layer of vines over the tunnel. It seemed as if night were closing in around the small group. Riley held on to Laurabeth, and Matie buried her head in Johnny's chest, trying not to cry out.

Soon the water around the boat began to swirl and bubble. The current below was moving much faster, and Jaxk's rowing could barely keep up, so he lifted the oars and let the boat go where it would. The boat moved rapidly with the current. Everyone ducked as a large vine dipped low over the boat. The water dropped out from under them, and the boat rushed over the edge of a waterfall. Screaming, the group came splashing into a lagoon below. The boat rocked from side to side while the unsettled passengers again found their seats, scrambling to see if anyone was hurt.

Riley was the only one who made it through with little effect. He clung to one of the seats, his head buried deep near the floor of the boat like an oxtrich with its head in the sand. Bo slapped Riley's rear end and lifted the frightened boy back into a sitting position. Riley shivered uncontrollably. "Did we make it through?" he asked.

"Everyone's fine," said Bo, patting his cousin on the back.

The boat followed the current out of the lagoon to a small canal and soon the tree-lined shores gave way to a lake. To the right was an island. Its shores were covered with shells. The island had many more tall trees than the first one. Up ahead in the deep waters, a four foot pole stuck straight out of the water.

"Is that part of an old tree?" Laurabeth asked.

Bo shook his head. "Nope, that's the mast from Laffite's ship, the one they scuttled here in Dead Man's Lake."

"Whoa!" responded Jack. "It's real."

Jack rowed toward the remains of the wreck. Riley hung over the edge of the boat peering into the clear waters below. "Cool! A real pirate ship!" he exclaimed, turning to **Bo**. "Is this where ya got the gold doubloon?"

"No, it's up a ways further," Bo explained. "Laffite dumped the treasure back at the first island, and this was as far as he got b'fore his ship started sinking. So they unloaded everything they could here at the fort and then sunk the ship."

Riley stared over the side of the boat into the water. "I know why they call it Dead Man's Lake. If the gaters don't get cha, the rapids and waterfall will."

"Yeah, "said Bo, "that's probably true. But the real reason's up ahead."

The boat bumped up on the shore, and Bo hopped out of it to tie the boat to a nearby tree. Then he began pulling the boat out of the water.

27
The Fabulous Miss Marie

Jim watched as Palmer and Randy struggled rowing the large motor boat. The sun grew hot in the midday sky, and the designer suits the two so proudly touted became an enormous burden. One by one they peeled off the layers of their corporate attire and set about to conquer the troublesome bayou.

"I'm going to see if I can fix this thing," Palmer said, pulling some moss off the broken propeller. Randy climbed back into the boat and guzzled a bottle of water. Ratcliffe lay stretched out on the front seat. He had a blue handkerchief over his face to protect him from the sun and the persistent bugs. Each time he snored, the handkerchief fluttered a bit. He seemed to be the only one who had managed to escape the annoying situation. As usual he left the consequences of his careless actions to the others.

Jim watched Palmer tug and pull on the stubborn moss-laden propeller. Finally a portion of the tangled moss gave way. Jim looked at the sleeping Ratcliffe and decided this was his chance to make his move.

"Hey, Palmer, what are you really doing here?" Jim asked as he reached down and helped untangle some moss. "I know you're not like Ratcliffe!"

Palmer stopped and looked at Jim then mumbled under his breath. "I'd never be like that rat!" Randy joined them, and Jim continued. "I can't believe the way you two keep on taking all of Ratcliffe's abuse. He keeps on dishing it out, and you two just keep on taking it. Look at him sleeping over there while you two are doing all of the work."

Jim had definitely struck a nerve. Randy paused for a

moment then slapped at a bothersome mosquito. "I'm not taking anything from Ratcliffe!" Randy said.

Palmer interrupted, "Neither am I. I'm just waiting for the right moment." In anger he dislodged a large tangle of moss from the propeller and threw it into the green waters.

As the men worked on the propeller, the water's current pulled them further into the bayou. When Jim stood to get a drink of water, he noticed the little house on stilts that they had visited the night before. "Look!" he said to the others, pointing at the small structure. "Maybe we can get some help from her."

The two men rowed towards the cabin. As they neared the place, Marie stood poised on the porch with a gun in her hands.

"Who's dat?" she yelled.

Startled, Ratcliffe awoke. "Where are we?" He bellowed. "And what are we doing here? Why aren't you men rowing?"

"We're at the old lady's cabin," Randy whispered. "We thought this would be a good place to get some help."

Ratcliffe grinned and took over. "Hello Ma'am. We've run into some difficulties. Could we please trouble you for a bit of help?"

Marie squinted in the direction of the voice and raised her gun a little bit higher. "Wut you want?" she yelled curtly. Ratcliffe looked at the others with a raised eyebrow. "Our engine has had some difficulties. We wondered, if you just might have a boat that we could use?"

Marie scowled. "How many uv ya is dae? Tell me yo' names."

Ratcliffe cleared his throat, and introduzed himself. Palmer was nezt, with Randy following suit. Jim looked at his captors, unsure of whether to speak or not.

Ratcliffe waved his gun at Jim and nodded for him to

reply. "I'm Jim Leavitt," Jim said, "We could use some help."

"If'n I iz ta hep ya, I needs ta know yu ain't up ta somethin," Marie said. "I has anotha boat I kin borra ya. But Iz gonna need a hostage. Yu daer, da quiet one, come hea so's I kin keep an eye on ya!"

Ratcliffe motioned for Jim to step out on the bullet ridden deck. Jim stepped out of the boat cautiously and quickly walked toward Marie who kept the gun firmly planted on him 'til he was almost to the porch stairs. Suddenly she turned the gun on the men in the boat. A shot rang out over their heads. "Get down!" Randy yelled, tackling Palmer down to the boat's deck.

"How dare she? Why is she shooting at us?" Ratcliffe demanded.

Randy shook his head as he tried to explain to Ratcliffe. "Can't you see? She doesn't trust us!" Another shot whizzed over their heads, but this one was even closer.

"Ya'll git outta hea b'fo I blows a lot a holes in dat fancy boat a yo's. Iz gonna give yu 'bout ten seconds or da nex' one won't miss!" Marie yelled as she unleashed a new hail of bullets over the heads of the kidnappers.

Palmer and Randy started paddling feverishly, as Ratcliffe tried the engine. After a couple of tries the engine started, and the boat limped out of the range of Marie's gun. Ratcliffe ranted as usual, insisting the entire incident was everyone else's fault.

As the sleek black boat slowly made its way out of site, Jim watched the old woman with concern, half expecting to receive the same treatment as the men in the boat. Then Marie turned to Jim and with a wink threw her arms around him and gave him a big hug.

"I know's who ya is," she said. "I had ta think uv a way ta git cha away from dem varmints." Marie led Jim by the arm up the porch steps into her little cabin.

"Sit fo' a spell," Marie said, motioning to a nearby chair. "I wuz hopin' dem men would cum dis way agin' juz so's I could git cha away frum em."

Jim looked surprised. "But how do you know who I am?"

Marie raised her chin and smiled. "Oh, I reckon a lil bird dun telled me." Jim was still confused, but the generous hospitality of his hostess had him completely intrigued.

Marie made her way to a little cooler in the kitchen and brought out a pitcher of cool milk. She poured it in a glass. Then, put a plate of cookies in front of Jim. "Well, ain't ya gonna have a bite? Eat up!" she insisted.

Jim hesitantly bit into the cookie. He wasn't quite sure of the situation. Not wanting to offend Marie he took another bite. Marie sensed Jim's apprehension. "Yu ain't got nuthin' to be afeard of Mr. Jim. I knows awl 'bouts Maison Rouge. I'z Cora's sista."

Jim stopped eating and looked at the old woman. The resemblance to Cora was uncanny. "How did you find out about what was going on at Maison Rouge?" Jim asked.

Marie sat down. "I gets news now and den 'bouts da ol manor, an when yu folks cum, we was right happy. See's we knowd dat Mr. Kenny needed hep, and yu is da ones we wuz countin' on. If it wern't fo' dat rascally Mr. Ratcliffe, everthin' would a been awlright. Miss Honey dun brung me word dis mornin' bout Miss Kate gettin' away, and she was fo' sho dae would be a bringin' yu back dis way. So's I hatched up a plan ta take ya hostage."

Jim cocked his head a bit. "Who is Miss Honey? That name is familiar."

"Well, I ain't so sho' you is gonna believe me, cuz it were da curse dat caused it awl. Miss Honey used ta live back at da big house. She was right happy wif Mr. Pierre and da three lil ones.

"Den da curse dun come, and it did some awful powerful thin's ta juz 'bout everbody in da bayou. Specially dem dat had doin's wif Mr. Jean. We awl changed somethin' fierce, I reckon. Miss Honey, well she is da little bird I telled ya bouts. She brung me word."

Jim looked confused. "Miss Honey is a bird?" he asked.

"Why, a course she is. How else would she bring me word a da goin's on in deze parts."

Marie stopped talking and turned her ear to the sound of a motor in the distance. Then Jim heard the sound. "It must be Ratcliffe. He's coming back."

Marie turned back to the table, unconcerned over the whole thing.

Jim stood up and strained to see out the cabin window. "Do you have a place I can hide? I can't let them catch me again, or I won't be able to help anyone."

Marie casually bit into a cookie. "Dey ain't no cause ta start a panic. Dat ain't dem men. Dat's Miss Kate."

Just then a small boat pulled up to the dock.

Jim rushed out onto the wooden dock. "It is you!" he said kissing Kate's cheek.

Are you all right?" Kate hugged Jim tightly, then, noticed Marie standing on the porch.

"Jim, how did you end up here?" she asked. Jim put his arm around her.

"Come inside. I want you to meet Cora's sister, Marie. But be a bit careful what you say. She seems to be a bit senile. She thinks that the birds are talking to her."

Kate stopped and looked at Jim, her eyes filled with surprise. "I'd love to meet her." Soon they were on the porch of the old shack, and Jim introduced his wife to Marie.

Marie hugged Kate and invited the two inside. Kate settled herself at the table and began to explain how she got away from her captors. They all laughed at the thought of Palmer being covered with the flour from Kate's ingenious escape.

Then Jim grew serious. "Kate, we've got to get to those kids before Ratcliffe does. He already threatened to kill me. He has no conscience when it comes to getting that map and the coins. He'll do anything."

A beautiful colored humming bird landed on the window sill. Marie cocked her head at the sound of the humming of the bird's wings. Soon Matie's three little birds also took up a perch on the window sill.

Marie smiled and leaned toward Jim. "Well now, hea dey is. Miss Honey dun come ta give us word. Mr. Jim, dis hea is Miss Honey and her chillen. I doxn't need ta tell Miss Kate. She awlready knows 'bouts da birds. "

Kate gasped as she put her hand to her mouth.

Marie nodded. "Mr. Jim din believe me neitha. He thinks I is juz a crazy ol woman dat tawks to da birds."

Jim blushed. "Oh, I don't think you're crazy. I'm just not used to people talking to animals."

Marie stood up and walked to the window. She leaned down near the little birds then turned to the others. Jim and Kate watched with curiosity.

"Miss Kate knows wut da birds sez, at least when she is wantin' ta race da birds in a game a tag."

Kate's mouth gaped open. "But, how did you know that?"

Marie smiled. "Yu ain't juz hearin' thin's, sweetie. Deze hea birds is juz a real a yu and me is. Dey was right happy once wif Mr. Pierre."

"That's where I heard of Miss Honey." Jim said. "Miss

Annabelle Honey was Pierre's wife! So your little bird must have been named after her."

"No sir, dis here is Pierre Laffite's family, da same ones yu seed at the portrait gallery at Maison Rouge!"

"I was just thinking about those pictures, but how did you know that?"

Marie raised an eyebrow then turned to the little birds. "Dey was a right hansum family. Miss Honey and her fancy entertainin'. An a course da three young uns used ta luv seein' Mr. Pierre cum home. Dey always had a big party when he cum."

The three little birds flapped their tiny wings and fluttered about the room.

"So Matie's birds are Pierre Laffite's children, and all this time Matie was staying in Miss Honey's room?" Kate asked, reaching for Marie's arm. "I'm sorry, we just didn't understand. I thought I was crazy when I heard the birds talk to me."

Marie patted Kate's hand. "I undastans. Tain't everday ya sees such as da curse brings."

Jim's face was serious. Finally everything about this place and the curse was beginning to make sense.

"Jim, I forgot to tell you," Kate said. "Sam is alive. He is the one who told me to follow the birds here." Kate stopped in mid sentence, and turned to Marie. "At least I don't think he's dead. Is he, Marie?"

"He ain't dead, and neitha is I. We juz' iz. Seems dis ol curse has seed fit ta set us in a kine a prison hea. Dey is der and I is hea, an' we cain't go no wheres. Miss Honey and da othas is differnt. Dae is our messengers. Da Maroo's kin go where eva dey please 'cept mos don't leave da bayou."

"I think you'd better tell us everything you know about this curse," Jim said. "It looks like we're a part of all of this now. Maybe you can start by telling us what a Maroo is."

Marie stood up and walked to the little sink in her kitchen. Then she turned around. "If'n I tells ya, ya has ta be ready ta believe. Cuz da tale is a hard one." Jim and Kate agreed.

"First of awl yu bez know who I is. I is da very one dat seed da curse begin. Dat is wut took my eyes. But a powerful thin' happened afta' dem days. I begin ta really see fo' da first time." Marie pointed to her heart. "I sees things rightcherre in my heart. Dat is how I knowed what yu wuz a thinkin' bout Miss Honey's picture."

Marie spoke softly, "After da curse, I begun ta know things 'fore dey happens, and den I begun ta feel everybody. If'n dey wuz sorraful, my heart ached right along wif em. If'n dey wuz worried, I felt and heared daer very thoughts.

"I wern't da only one dat changed. Took 'bout a year or so at first I 'spect. But one by one awl uv us at Maison Rouge begun ta change. One day a great storm hit da bayou. Dey was a strange mist dat seemed ta moan. It settled hea, and den it happened. Beautiful Miss Honey and her chillen awoke and dey was juz as yu see um now. Da folk in da bayou said it were as if dey were marooned. Like da old pirates used ta do, maroonin' folk on da islands. Dat is how dey cum ta be knowed as Maroo's."

Jim winced as he looked at the little birds in the windows. "You talked about the folks in the bayou. Do others around here know of these things?"

Marie nodded "Some knows, but dey think it were da cunja. Most stays away from hea. Dey thinks dat iz juz a story. And dat's fo' da best."

"Marie, just how did the curse really begin?" Kate asked. Marie was silent and stared into the distance as if remembering the past. Then she began in a sober tone. She

rehearsed the events from her past until the little birds began
flapping their wings. Marie stopped talking and turned to them.
Miz Honey hovered in the window, and Marie nodded as if to
tell her something, then the bird flew away.

"What's going on?" Kate asked.

"Da birds is a feelin' dat dey might be sum troubles.
Dey is a goin' ta see fo' demselves."

Suddenly Marie grabbed her chest and winced in pain.
Jim jumped up and helped her to a nearby chair. The old
woman was shaking and heaved a great sigh.

"Dey is trouble a-cumin. Your chillen is needin' ya,"
she whispered.

"What's wrong? Are the children all right?" Jim
pleaded.

Marie's blind eyes stared vacantly at Jim. "Yu need ta
git ta dem chillen as soon as yu kin. Dey ain't no two ways bout
it. Now I has sumthin' I needs ta tell ya. I give Mr. Johnny
sumthin' right special. T'was give ta me by Cap'n Edwards
b'fore da curse begun. I don' knows wut iz fo', but he sed da
day would cum when da last Laffite would know how ta use it.
Yu cain't let Ratcliffe get his hands on it or dem chillen! Now
yu bez' be goin'. Times a-wastin.'" Jim reached out to the old
woman and gently kissed her cheek.

"Marie, I believe you. Thank you for taking care of the
kids. We'll do whatever we can." Kate hugged the old woman
then she and Jim headed for the boat.

They stepped off the rickety dock into the boat while
Marie stood on the porch. "I be a prayin' fo' y'all and fo' dem
chillen!" she yelled as Jim started the motor.

28
Dead Man's Island

Johnny secured the rope from the boat to a small tree on the shell-lined island. "Come on," said Bo. "We need to hike inshore a ways, but it's worth it."

Johnny tossed the flour sack of food to Jack, grabbed the back pack and slung it over his shoulder, then fastened Pierre's old sword to his belt.

Bo led the group up a small trail that was lined with tall grass. Everyone followed as they walked over rocks and fallen logs, past bushes and trees. In the distance they saw a large structure towering above the dense overgrowth.

"It's huge," said Jack, catching up to the group.

"Be careful up here," Bo said, making a side detour through the underbrush to the left.

"Why are we goin' this way?" Riley whined. Bo turned around and grabbed Riley'z shoulder. "It ain't safe the other way."

"Looks safe to me," Riley challenged, then started heading back towards the path.

Bo firmly grabbed Riley's arm. "Riley! You stop it! This ain't the time for one of your fits right now," he explained, shaking Riley gently. Bo let go of his arm, picked up a large rock, then threw it onto the pathway.

At first it looked as if nothing was happening. Then the rock began to slowly sink into the sand. Disappearing beneath the surface, it left a small gooey bubble that burst, spewing sand into the air like a quicksand monster that had gobbled up the rock and ended its meal with a belch.

"It's quick sand!" Riley yelled.

"Quick sand!" gasped Matie, looking at her feet, then, lifting each one up to check her footing.

"Is there more of that around here?" Laurabeth asked.

"Yeah," Bo replied, "but as long as ya stay with me, we should be okay."

The small group huddled closely together as they neared the fort. The large trees surrounding the fort made it somewhat difficult to get to. It was obvious that two hundred years of neglect had allowed the bayou to reclaim this forgotten territory. The old structure was about a hundred feet long and about fifty feet wide. It stood over thirty feet tall at the highest point in the middle. A barricade for cannons and a watch tower dwarfed the tall oak trees and cypress that dotted the island. The stone struxture was crumbling in some places, and large beams of cypress wood protruded through the stucco walls overhead.

Bo led the others to the northeast side of the fort and began up a narrow stairway. As Bo placed his foot on the stairs, the rocks crumbled beneath his feet. He looked at the crumbled stairs, then back at the others.

"I think I'd better check this out first," he said, taking a deep breath. He began cautiously up the narrow stairs, staying close to the wall for balance and checking each step before moving on. When a rock crumbled under his weight, he adjusted his footing and continued up the crumbling stairs.

About half way up, the old stairway became much more stable, allowing Bo to get to the top more easily. Finally at the roof of the structure, he stopped and yelled down to the others, "It'll be okay if you just come up one at a time."

Bo hung over the edge of the fort watching the others make their way to the top. Jack stood on the ground alongside the old stairway, holding each person's hand as far up as he could. Once the others were safely up the stairs, he followed behind and carefully made his way up.

They now stood about twenty feet off the ground on the lower roof of the old fort. It was unusually strong and showed no signs of weathering or deterioration. Matie ran excitedly from corner to corner hanging her head over the walls as Johnny watched to make sure she didn't fall off.

"This is really cool," said Riley, exploring the lower level of the roof. "Hey! What's up there?" he said, pointing to another stone stairway that led to an even higher encampment.

Bo knelt down close to Riley and Matie. "See that?" He pointed towards the upper level beyond the stairway.

"Yeah," said Riley. "So there's a cannon up there."

Bo nodded. "Yup, and where there's cannons, there's usually something else."

"Do you mean fighting?" Laurabeth said.

"Yeah," said Bo. "And what happens when you're fighting with cannons?" Everyone looked annoyed with Bo's persistent line of questioning.

Suddenly Jack blurted out, "Death?"

"A-huh," Bo said, looking towards the upper level. Bo stood up and everyone's eyes turned towards the upper encampment.

A chill ran down Johnny's spine, and Matie gulped. "Is the dead pirate up there?"

Bo raised his eyebrow and nodded. "I didn't want to scare y'all, so I thought I'd better tell ya before ya saw it. There's more than one pirate up there. The whole plaze is covered with them. There's probably fifteen to twenty. It's pretty cool if you can stand it."

"Eww, you're disgusting!" said Laurabeth. "You think dead bodies are cool?"

Bo shrugged, "No, I don't think that dead bodies are cool, but the pirate stuff is."

"I'm not going up there," said Laurabeth. "And I'm not

gonna let you take these little kids up there either."

The edges of Bo's lips curled up slightly.

Riley scrunched his nose. "I can handle it," he said throwing out his chest in an overdramatic demonstration of courage.

"Not me," said Matie.

Laurabeth smiled as she put her arm around Matie's shoulder. "We're too refined for that, ain't we?"

Matie looked up at her new-found partner. "Yup, we're too refined."

Johnny rolled his eyes. "Oh, come on you guys. I'm sick of this mush. The 'ladies' can stay here." Johnny started across the roof towards the stairs with Bo, Riley, and Jack close behind. The girls watched as the four young men climbed the short stairway. As Johnny neared the top, his exuberant pace slowed. One by one, he and the others cautiously stepped onto the upper level.

The site was amazing, if not ghastly. Skeletons in pirate clothing lay scattered all over the roof, seventeen to be exact. One in particular lay across the barrel of a large rusty cannon that the former buccaneer had obviously guarded with his life. Rusty swords and broken pistols lay strewn amid broken wine bottles and barrels of old gun powder like piles of rubbish amid the archaic remains of the former marauders.

"Eww," said Riley with a shudder. "They're gross."

"You want to go back?" Bo asked.

"No way. This is too cool," Riley gulped. He wandered around through the tattered remains of the skeletons and stopped to pick up a tri-corner hat lying on the ground. Putting it on his head, he stood posed like Washington crossing the Delaware. "Hey, look at me," he yelled at the others.

"Put that down," replied Bo. "You don't know where that thing's been."

"Yeah," Jack joked. "The pirate that wore that might have had head lice."

Riley took the old hat off and examined it closely and then quickly returned it to his head.

Soon the four gathered around the pirate draped over the cannon. Bo reached over the wall of the fort and took hold of the mouth of the cannon. Pulling with all his might, he tried to pull the whole thing back away from the steep wall. When the others saw what he was doing, they all took their positions to help. As Riley edged his way in among the others, he dislodged the delicately balanced pirate corpse that clattered to the ground in a disgusting heap.

Everyone jumped as the skeleton rattled into its new position. Riley let out a squeal as the others recoiled in disgust. Although all of the other skeletons were quite macabre, they all looked fairly normal--for skeletons that is. But this one carried a very pronounced scar on the bone that ran from its upper right eye across its nose and down to its left cheek.

"Oh, that's gross," said Johnny. Jack bent down and ran his finger across the scar. "He must a been something to see in real life."

"Come on. I need your help," Bo insisted.

"Why are we doing this anyway?" Riley whined.

Jack and Johnny also looked at Bo for an explanation. "This is where I found the doubloon," Bo said. Riley's eyes widened, and he was the first one to resume pulling on the cannon.

"How'd you find it?" Jack questioned, as they each grunted and heaved, pulling the old cannon back a stubborn inch or two. Bo tightened his hold and took a deep breath as they all pulled together. Finally the old rusty wheels gave way allowing the cannon to move. Bo explained, "Once I heard about some old guys finding a cannon full of gold and jewels.

So when I found this one, I thought I'd see for myself. Since I couldn't pull it back alone, I climbed up on it and hung over the edge till I could see inside. It wasn't full of gold, but I was able to reach just far enough inside to get this." Bo held up the doubloon.

Riley headed strait for the front of the cannon and reached inside eagerly. Immediately he squealed and yanked his arm out of the dark hole as a spider ran across his hand. Riley's arms were much too small to reach deep enough into the old cannon.

Jack nudged Riley aside. "Here, let me try," he said, reaching his long arm deep into the cannon's black mouth. "I got something," he said pulling out a handful of sand with two round coins in it.

"Try again," Riley yelled. Jack reached as far as he could, as he strained for the back of the cannon. "I can feel something in there, but I can't quite reach it."

"Let me try," said Bo. He shined a small pen light inside the barrel. "Yeah, I can see something in there. It's shiny."

"Gold?" said Riley with wide eyes.

"Whatever it is, it's stuck," said Bo. "Maybe we can use something to pull it out."

Johnny reached for the old sword hanging by his side.

By now Laurabeth and Matie stood at the bottom of the stairs, yelling up to the boys. "Hey, what's taking so long?"

Riley ran to the stairs. "We found gold!" he yelled. Laurabeth and Matie exchanged glances, and then Matie instantly began up the stairs. "I want to see the gold!" she insisted.

Laurabeth grabbed Matie's arm. "Are you sure you want to go up there? You'll probably have nightmares."

Matie stopped and turned to Laurabeth. "I'll just pretend like it's a movie."

Laurabeth nodded and smiled as she followed Matie up the stairs.

Riley ran back to the others. "They're coming up," he said with a grin.

"Oh, that's just great," said Johnny. "Mat's gonna totally freak. She can't even handle scary movies. She hid behind the couch during Snow White."

"I heard that!" Matie squeeled in protest, and then joined the others. "I might be afraid of the witch in Snow White, but I love Jurasxic Park."

Everyone laughed out loud at Maties statement.

"It's okay, Mat," said Johnny.

"But you're making fun of me," she said, stomping her foot.

Suddenly Bo interrupted. "I got it!" He pulled an old wine bottle from the mouth of the cannon.

Riley kicked the side of the cannon. "Oh, man. Is that all it is?"

"So, where's the gold?" Matie demanded, turning her back to the carnage around her.

Jack handed her the two pieces of gold they'd retrieved from the cannon. Laurabeth and Matie each took one and examined them closely. "Looks like gold to me," said Laurabeth, handing hers back to Jack.

"That old pirate must have been afraid they'd find his stash of booze," Riley said pretending to be drunk.

"Wait a minute," Johnny interrupted. "He's right. Why hide an old bottle in there especially with gold coins. That bottle must be important."

Riley staggered around the roof. "Maybe they were drunk," he laughed.

Bo glanxed impatiently at his cousin. "Once I heard how pirates would set booby traps to protect their treasure.

Maybe it's a trap."

Johnny held the bottle up and examined it. The old brown glass was hard to see through.

"What if it's poison?" Matie asked with wide eyes.

"You wanna test it for us?" Johnny joked as he pushed the bottle toward Matie.

Matie recoiled with a frown, pursing her lips together tightly and shaking her head in a defiant NO!

Johnny held the bottle up with the sun behind it. He could make out the faint lines of something inside. Bo took the bottle from Johnny and gently shook it. Something inside clanked. Riley's drunken antics ceased, replaced with undaunted curiosity.

"Open it up," he urged.

Bo was hesitant. "Something about all of this doesn't feel just right."

Johnny took the old bottle. "I'll open it," he said pushing on the wooden cork. Finally the old cork came out of the neck of the bottle with a pop. A gush of dusty rank air came whooshing out.

"Eeeew! It stinks! It is poison!" Matie exclaimed, plugging her nose.

"Na, that ain't poison," said Jack. "That's just the smell of wine."

Johnny turned the bottle upside down and shook the contents out into his hand. A small piece of fabric lay wrapped around something long and slender. Johnny unfolded the fabric. Inside his hand lay a key.

"Oh, my eye!" Riley exploded in a tirade of disappointment. "So where's all of the gold we came for? You said there'd be gold. Where is it?"

Johnny looked at Riley. "Some things are more important than gold. I didn't come here to find gold. I came to help my parents and find my uncle. Somebody thought this key was important enough to hide. It's probably a lot more important than some stupid gold! That pirate died protecting it, so there must be something special about it."

Johnny reached for his backpack and carefully removed the other artifacts. He now laid out the old map on the ground and placed the watch and the original gold coins from Maison Rouge next to it. Then he pulled out his notebook and opened its pages.

"Somewhere in all of these clues I remember something about a key," Johnny said, inspecting each clue. Then he picked up the watch. "Here it is!" he said. "I knew I remembered something about a key." Johnny read aloud the back of the watch. It said. *"To my beloved Katherine true intent is the key."*

Johnny looked at the key in his hand. It had some of the same letters as the old piece of driftwood that Marie had given to him. Johnny unwrapped Marie's red bundle, and placed the key near the old driftwood. He turned the rings on the driftwood over and over, then, he saw it. One of the carved markings on the driftwood lined up exactly with the outline of the old key. Above it were some unusual letters. Johnny jotted them down in his notebook.

"Those marks almost look like words," Jack said.

"They are words!" Johnny looked up at his new friends then thought of his room back in California. "Hey, Mat. How do ya spell '*Eye, eye, matey*'?"

Matie smiled and thought hard. "Well, it starts with two I's, then an M and a eight. Then it ends with an E!" she proudly exclaimed. *I I M 8 E.*

Riley rolled his eyes. "That's not how you spell it. Anybody knows that!"

"Wait just a minute," Bo said. "That's a cool way to spell it. Kind of like a code." Matie nodded proudly.

Johnny looked at the piece of driftwood. "I think the things on this old piece of wood are written in code, like the cryptograms I have on my wall back home. I have a ton of them. Like '*RUNVS*'. It's a whole sentence in a few little letters, that means, 'are you envious'? See, don't you get it?" On the driftwood it says '*Nt Nt.*' It's gotta mean *"Intent,"* and I'd just bet that it says *'True intent'.*"

Jack took the old piece of driftwood and examined it. "Yeah, look," he said, pointing at the symbols. "That looks like a Tr and there are two O's right next to it. It does say '*True Intent*'."

Johnny placed the old key amid the other artifacts.

Bo patted Johnny **on** the shoulder. "You're getting quite a collection there. We'll have to find a wagon to haul it all in if ya find any **m**ore."

Laurabeth studied Johnny's note book. "Hey, you guys, I think I found something. If you look at all of these clues, a lot of them say '*true intent*'. It's in almost all of them."

"Yeah, I know," Johnny said. "My dad and I figured out that it was Jean Laffite's motto. But the *Intent* was also the name of the sister ship to the *Alliance*. According to Sam, the two ships were identical.

"When we first came to **M**aison Ro**u**ge I noticed the family crest above the fireplace. It says *True Intent* on it, too. Then the watch says *true intent* on the back. And inside the watch it says, *What time reveals within the heart can be pieced together only with true intent.*"

Bo now interrupted. "Yeah, and look here. The stained glass pa**n**els in the attic also talk about it. *True intent nothing waverin shore N blood R swamp you**x** B favorin.*"

Johnny looked intently at the clues. Again he referred to his notebook. "**M**atie's quilt had a clue, too. It said *Three pieces of eight, three brothers two, the secret held true, in the map* *held by Youx.* There's the word *"true"* again."

Johnny unrolled Dominique's old <u>m</u>ap and read aloud the words on it. *"The heart of the truth lies in the Son if freedom B favored and Justice be wun.* There's the word *truth* again."

Johnny now flipped through the pa<u>g</u>es of his jour<u>n</u>al. "My dad showed me a marker that Jean Laffite had made for his wife out behind Maison Rouge. The writing on it said; *True intent Mirrors the Son if Justice be Honored and Mercy be won."*

"Jean was Captain Edward's son and his ship and Edward's were mirror images. The *Intent* was a ship just li<u>k</u>e the *Alliance,* and there was a ship on the watch and on the old chest that the coins were found in. That ship on the chest must be the *Intent.* It must have been <u>J</u>ean's ship! What if they tried to trick their enemies and really used the *Intent* <u>to</u> hide the treasure? That would explain what true intent means. It could have been the true ship they used that day. Clayton interfered when he attacked. But Jean's <u>s</u>hip, the *Intent,* mu<u>s</u>t have escaped.

"Clayton didn't know about the hidden cargo. He just wanted to get Jean into trou<u>bl</u>e. It was that hidden cargo that Sam talked about that was what really mattered. Sam said there was this alliance of eight men, and they all held a coin, together the coins were the real keys to the treasure. Each of the eight men held a secret, too, so that they had to cooperate to find the treasure later on.

"Captain Edwards was the only one who had all of the clues, and he died before he could tell anyone. Sam said that Dominique had found out all but one of those clues before he disappeared. Maybe he wrote them on his map!"

<u>J</u>ohnny turned over the brittle map and examined it carefully. On it there was a large sun with twelve points that spanned the entire map. In the center was a <u>h</u>eart and on the

bottom was the word 'Barataria.'

Johnny studied the old parchment. It showed a map of the bayou detailed in every aspect. Then Johnny noticed something he hadn't seen before. On each of the sun's rays were certain names or symbols. At the top point was a small symbol of a sun. Then to the right was the name 'Laffite' next to a ship. A little right of that,was the name 'Baptiste' and a picture of a building with a cannon. Johnny looked up at the others. "The symbols on the map are just like the ones I saw in the attic, only there are names next to them."

He noticed that the longer points on the sun were just like a clock. "It's just like the numbers on the watch," he said. "I think we've found the names of our eight men of the alliance!" He looked at each symbol and the name next to them and jotted them in his journal. "Arsene Lebleu" was next by the symbol of waves and lightening. James Campbell's name was near a beach with a palm tree and hill and sat exactly where the number four would have been. The next was a symbol only of a bottle and grapes.

Johnny turned to the others. "We figured this one out at home. It's the one that represents Napoleon." Then he continued. The number six had in its place only a symbol as well, a gold challis with the word 'Blood'. Next was a picture of a tropical bird and the arched doorway, with the name 'Renauto Belouche'. In place of the number eight was the name 'Pierre Laffite' and two crossed swords. A skull was next with the name 'Youx'. Above that was the picture of a treasure chest with a large 'B' next to it.

Johnny looked up again. "I think the 'B' stands for 'Barataria'. It was Laffite's headquarters." Last of all, in place of the number eleven was a small red heart and no name.

"That's all of them," Johnny said, repeating their names. Jack looked at the word clues that had come from the attic. Again, twelve words all connected the symbols and names as he repeated them aloud. *True intent nothing wavering shore N blood R swamp youx B favorin.*

Johnny now picked up the coins. "It all makes sense now. All of the coins were held by these men. The same symbols are on their coins. Now we know what each coin has on it. We've got four now and my Uncle Ken had some. If we can find my uncle, then we might just know how to find that treasure."

The sun was beginning to set in the western sky as everyone helped gather the prexious items and handed them back to Johnny.

After Johnny placed the last one back in his bag, everyone stood up to leave. "Wait a minute!" Bo said. "We can't go now. The sun's going down. We'd best stay here for the night, then, we can get a fresh start in the morning."

29

A Dreaded Discovery

Ratcliffe's sleek black boat limped across the muddy waters like a wounded albatross. Ratcliffe stood at the wheel of the boat with a permanent scowl etched on his face. Randy watched at the front of the boat to warn of any stray debris or moss that might get stuck in the damaged prop. Palmer sat over the uncovered engine watching for any sign of malfunction.

The sweltering heat of the bayou had quickly reduced the three corporate initiates into an unskilled labor force of the lowest degree. The unsavory task of rolling up their white shirt sleeves and dirtying their corporate hands was a distasteful reality.

The bayou's heavy vegetation began to encroach around the large boat as Ratcliffe cut the engine. "Check the prop!" he bellowed.

Palmer lifted the engine out of the water. A clump of stray moss hung off the broken prop. Palmer cleaned the slimy moss from the prop as Ratcliffe rummaged through the food supply under the seat. Ratcliffe pulled out a sandwich and gulped it down as he sneered at the others.

"Could you hand me one of those?" Palmer asked from the back of the boat.

"Get your own," growled Ratcliffe. Randy went to the food supply and pulled out two sandwiches and some water. Then he climbed onto the back of the boat and gave some to Palmer.

Palmer's white shirt was drenched with sweat, and his once crisp white sleeves were stained green from the murky waters. He sat down and began to eat as Randy took a seat next to him.

Randy looked up at Ratcliffe then whispered quietly. "I'm beginning to think Ratcliffe is crazy. I think the idea of finding gold has gone to his head." The two watched Ratcliffe pacing at the front of the boat as he examined the old map.

"I think you're right," whispered Palmer, checking the small bullet hole in his pant leg, a souvenir left by Marie's well-aimed shotgun.

Palmer took a drink of water. "Did you get a good look at that map?"

"Not good enough!" Randy replied, taking another bite. "I haven't had time with Ratcliffe bellowing out orders every time he turns around."

Palmer stared at Ratcliffe, a hint of hatred glowed in his eyes. "Just wait," he said. "When the time is right, I'll handle it."

Ratcliffe folded his map and started the boat's engine again. Determined, he pushed it as hard as he could through the murky waterways. Soon the sleek boat pulled up to the shell-lined shores of the little island. The sandy cheniere was quiet as the three men examined the beach and the indentation that the children's boat had left in the sand.

"They were here, all right," Ratcliffe grinned. "We're on the right track. Obviously the little brats came this way!" The three men looked around the island for any more signs of the adventurous youth.

The sun was now rapidly going down as streaks of orange, red, and purple washed across the western sky. "We've got to hurry!" Ratcliffe yelled as he climbed aboard the boat. Palmer and Randy looked at each other and remained on shore.

"Well?" demanded Ratcliffe. "Aren't you coming aboard? I said we need to hurry!"

Palmer stepped forward and looked at the setting sun.

"No!" he said boldly.

Ratcliffe's nose twitched. "What did you say?"

"I said no!" Palmer said, clenching his teeth.

The red hue of the sunset cast a scarlet pallor over Ratcliffe's ugly face. "How dare you say no to me? If you don't do exactly what I say, I'll expose everything about you."

"Go right ahead!" Palmer said, stepping closer to the boat.

Ratcliffe grimaced, then, turned to start the motor. "I'll just have to tell the authorities about that little accident of yours then!"

Palmer moved closer to the boat unimpressed by Ratcliffe's threats.

Ratcliffe looked around nervously. "I'll tell everything!"

"It won't make any difference now," Palmer said as he climbed into the boat. It was as if Palmer were in a trance, no longer intimidated by the man to whom he had submissively groveled before.

"Randy, get over here! Palmer's going to kill me. He's gone completely crazy!" A slight grin came to Randy's lips as he stood on the beach watching Palmer finally stand up to Ratcliffe's badgering.

Ratcliffe dropped to the deck of the boat covering his head with his arms as Palmer walked closer. "Don't hurt me!" Ratcliffe begged. "I, I promise I won't say a word. Your secret is safe with me!"

Randy stared in disbelief. The two men had completely changed roles, and Palmer had the upper hand. Ratcliffe reached into the food supply and offered the cowardly bribe of a sandwich to Palmer who now stood only a foot away from the cowering man. His tall stature towered over Ratcliffe's fat little frame with total and complete intimidation. Ratcliffe turned aside and closed his eyes as if waiting for a blow from the corporate giant before him.

"I'm not going to kill you!" Palmer said. "Not today anyway. But you'd better get this in your head now. I won't take any more of your orders. I've had enough. I've put up with your blackmailing me for three years now, and I'm tired of being your stooge. There may have been a hit and run. But just because I was drunk doesn't mean that I did it. You can go to the police if you want. But if you do, I'll be right behind you to tell them all about this and how you set up Kenny and ambushed him. You even made Randy here believe he was part of it all, thinking Ken framed him, xo he'd take the fall."

Randy stood in the pale light of the setting sun, completely filled with confusion. He'd been duped into joining this deadly scheme all because of a bunch of Ratcliffe's lies.

Ratcliffe had convinced him that his true friends had betrayed him. Now Randy knew the truth. Jim and Ken had never done or said any of the things Ratcliffe told him they had. It was all part of Ratcliffe's plan. It was an elaborate ruze, just to get the information that Ratcliffe needed.

Randy's blood boiled, and he ran for the boat. "You lied to me!" he shrieked. Randy jumped into the boat, lunged at Ratcliffe, and clenched his hands around the coward's throat. Ratcliffe struggled, gasping for air. Randy shook uncontrollably with his grip firmly fixed on Ratcliffe's throat. Palmer reached in and clutched Randy's wrist. "That's enough. You don't want to do that."

Randy loosened his grip and turned on Palmer. "You were in on the whole thing?"

"Yes," Palmer said. "But I didn't want to be. Ratcliffe's been blackmailing me for three years. I've already lost everything because of him. I guesx I've just finally gotten to the point where there's no more to lose."

Randy still shook **b**ut he tried to compose himself. He glared at Ratcliffe who was still groveling on the floor. "You're so good at destroying people. You're pitiful."

Ratcliffe crouched, then stood up like a frightened animal.

"We'll camp here for the night!" Palmer said as he reached for some food.

"I think that's a good idea," Randy said, with his eyes on Ratcliffe.

~ᚳᚱ + ᚦᚢ~

Jim and Kate pus**h**ed forward in the flat **b**ottom boat. The old evinrude motor puttered along at a steady pace. An occasional flock of birds s**k**immed across the water while a caiman or two basked lazily in the sun along the shoreline. The three hummingbirds darted back and forth. Once in a while one would disappear for a time and then return to lead the boat into a side channel.

Jim held the rudder in **p**lace **w**hile Kate sat at the front of the boat. He looked out over the bayou and veered away from an old log. "It's interesting that we'd end up in the bayou like this. Every bit of logic in me says it's all impo**x**sible, but something deeper in my heart knows different. **I** can feel it, kind of like Marie does, I guess. The curse, these little birds, and all of Sam's stories are beginning to make sense. Fate seems to have thrown us into this, and now we've got no choice but to believe. It's the only way we'll ever be able to help the kids." Jim pushed on the throttle, increasing the boat's speed.

"D**o** you think the kids are all right?" Kate asked.

Jim s**m**iled. "I'm sure they're just fine. **O**ur little friends here see**m** to know just what's gong on. I'm sure they won't let us down." He nodded towards the three little birds flittering above the boat. As he did, one darted a signal in front of him to turn from the main channel of water. He turned the rudder, and the boat entered a densely forested area as bushes and trees edged closer in around the small boat. The birds darted excitedly through the air, urging them onward.

"Do you think this is the right way?" asked Kate.

Jim watched the birds closely. "By the way their acting, it has to be."

The three birds hovered in front of Jim's face. He slowed the engine as one by one the three birds darted off through the bushes. Quickly they returned, and repeated the same action again.

"I think they want us to follow them," Kate said.

Jim pulled the boat up to the shoreline. "Are you going in there?" Kate asked.

"You don't think your little birds would lead us into trouble, do you?" he said as he tied the boat up to a tree.

Kate frowned. "Oh, all right then, but I'm coming, too."

The two stepped out on the muddy shore as one of the birds took up a perch on the seat where Kate had been sitting. "Well, at least now we have a guard bird to watch the boat!" Kate smiled.

Jim and Kate followed the birds along a path through the underbrush. Soon the path opened up into a wide hollow. It was obvious that they were standing in the middle of an abandoned campsite. The remains of a tent lay crumpled in a heap on the ground. One rope held part of it still tied to a tree. Nearby, some rocks surrounded an abandoned campfire.

"Why do you think they brought us here?" Kate asked as she picked up a stone from the old campfire.

Jim didn't answer. He was rummaging through the tent. As he turned around, he made his way to a fallen log and sat down.

"What's wrong?" Kate asked.

Jim handed her an old wallet. "It's Ken's!"

Kate gazped and put her arm around him. "Jim, don't worry. I know we'll find him!" She opened the wallet. Inside one of the pockets she could see four antique gold coins. They were exactly like the ones Johnny had found but with different markings on them.

Jim sighed as he ezamined the coins. "Ken wouldn't have left these here without a fight. Something must have made him leave in a hurry."

Kate and Jim searched every inch of the campsite. About fifty yards from the tent, they found the remains of an old cooler that had obviously been ransacked by the local animals. Lying in the trees not far from the boat they found a backpack filled with several papers and notes. Further down river Jim found the place where Ken had docked his boat. It was a small sandy beach with a cut rope still tied to a tree. Images flooded their thoughts as they began to piece together the events that had led to Ken's disappearance.

As Jim wandered around looking for more evidence, Kate looked at the old papers in the backpack. "Jim!" Kate yelled. "You need to see this!" Jim ran to Kate's side as she began reading:

"Jan 6 Family name changed from Laffite to Leavitt.
Jan 20 Ratcliffe out to destroy us. Family vendetta.
Jan 23 Maison Rouge has answers, Coins.
Feb. 8 Found Granddad's journal. Randy investigating.
Feb. 16 Can't trust Randy, he's with Ratcliffe.
Feb. 17 Met Gates. Has coin like Granddad's. Took boat to fort. Gater attack,

Gates safe, hid his coin. Can't stop, more information in bayou.

April 6 Fever.......... so sick. Sam warned me. Must be
curse...........

Kate stopped at this point and turned to Jim. "Jim, Ken
knew about the curse!"
"Look!" Jim said thumbing through the pages. "There's
one last entry but no date.
Almost drown. Can't think..... Watermen attacked
camp. Not safe.
"What could that all mean?" Kate pondered.
"Well, he said he was sick with fever," Jim said. "He
must have seen something that scared him away from camp.
Whatever it was, he left in a big hurry. Come on. We'd better
get going if we're going to find the kids. We might just be able
to get to the old fort before dark."
Jim steered the little boat through the muddy
backwaters of the bayou. Urgently he pushed the engine to its
max. Now he and Kate had even more reason to fight this
unrelenting mystery. The cursed bayou had a grip on this
family, and they were prepared to fight even with their last
breath, if needed.
The little bayou stream opened back up onto the
larger river, and the three birds flew in circles darting around
the small boat. In the light of the setting sun, Kate pointed at a
little island up ahead. She turned to Jim and motioned for him
to cut the engine.
"What's the matter?" Jim asked.
Kate pointed again toward the island and the large black
speed boat that rested on its shores.
Three men walked along the beach gathering fire wood.
"It's them!" Jim whispered as they watched from a distance.
Kate looked at Jim. "What are we going to do? How can
we get past them without being seen?"

The three little birds now perched on the side of the boat as **Ji**m pulled out the oars and began to row as quietly as possible. The**y** stayed near the bushes across the river, as far away from the island as they could. **M**oving from shadow to shadow and bush to bush t**ill** the **i**sland was finally out of sight.

As the **v**egetation c**l**osed in aro**un**d the little boat, a large branch caught **K**ate in the back of the head. "Ouch!" she said pushing it aside. "I think something bit me!" Kate **r**eached for the back of her collar. **J**im looked at her neck, and pulled a fuzzy caterpillar from her dres**s**. "Oh, it's just this little thing," he said as he threw it away.

The three birds darted around Kate hovering then dipping low by the bushes. Kate rubbed the back of her neck trying to ease the stinging sensation.

Jim watched with concern. "I think we'd better find a place to stay for the night." he said, pulling the rope to restart the engine.

The three birds again began their normal routine of darting away a distance and then leading the boat forward in its journey. Then they did somethin**q** unusual. They headed for the back side of the same little island where Ratcliffe and the others were **c**amped.

Jim qui**c**kly pulled the boat onto the sandy shore. "I gues**s** we'll be staying here for the night," he said, securing it to a nearby tree.

Kate unloade**d** the boat while Jim gathered some firewood and started a small fire. Soon a fea**z**t of hot dogs awaited the two, and they sat down to eat.

The eerie so**u**nds of the bayou echoed amid the crackling of the fire. "I hope the kid**x** are all right," Kate said, taking a dri**n**k **o**f water. Jim put his arm around her as they sa**t** on the sand.

The hostile takeover of Maison Ro**u**ge and the hurried

282

journey into the swamp hadn't allowed the two to change into more appropriate attire. So here they sat as if thrown back in time 186 years to the very place that Jim's ancestors had been so many years before. It was quite a sight with both of them still dressed in their party clothes. Kate's diamond necklace was still in place on her dainty, bug-bitten neck.

Listening to the water lap against the shoreline, Kate retrieved a sleeping bag from the boat. As she began to lay it out on the ground, she staggered and started to fall. Jim jumped to his feet and caught her. "Are you all right?" he asked.

"I'm just fine!" she protested. "I'm just a little dizzy from all this excitement."

30
An Explosive Situation

Riley was bored and began digging through some of the debris on the roof of the fort. In a corner he found a rotten tattered sail, wadded up and thrown over a pile of crates. As he started moving the crates, a large snake slithered out from beneath one.

Riley squealed in horror as Bo grabbed a nearby sword and hacked off the snake's head. Riley crouched behind him and asked, "Are there any more?" Bo pulled back the rotten sail, clearing the area. Amid the pile of old crates, only one crate at the bottom showed any sign of a potential problem.

Bo pulled it out carefully. "Looks like there was just that one snake," he said as everyone gathered around. The curious sealed crate was now the center of attention.

"I wonder what's in it?" said Jack.

"Probably more snakes!" interrupted Riley, as he kicked at the wooden box then ducked behind Bo. Everyone watched, hoping Riley's suggestion was wrong. The crate showed no signs of any movement.

"Looks okay to me!" then he began opening it.

The strong odor of rotting straw filled the air. Pushing the straw aside, Johnny noticed three small wooden boxes inside the crate. One by one he pulled them out and opened them. Inside he found all of the pieces to a large brass spyglass. The straw had actually preserved the relic quite well. The only sign of deterioration was a tarnished area that had gotten wet due to some rainwater that had leaked into the crate.

Bo and Johnny carefully assembled the old spyglass. "This is just like the one back at Maison Rouge," Johnny said, looking through the dusty lens.

Everyone wanted a turn inspecting and trying out the wonderful find. Jack peered through it, looking out over the bayou. "This could really come in handy." he said. "Man, I can see a long ways from here. I can even see the other island." Jack looked for a moment, then, lowered the glass. "Oh, no, it's them, those guys that were back at the big house. They're on the other island!"

Jack handed the spy glass to Bo. Bo looked through it, adjusted the lens then, slowly put it down. Johnny grabbed it and scoured the bayou. Soon he saw the other island as well. The three men who had so cruelly tried to destroy his family came into focus.

"They're trying to follow us," said Johnny.

As the sun lowered on the horizon, darkness slowly crept over the fort. The little group huddled closely together, setting their plans for the night.

"They must have figured out how we got away," said Johnny. "I bet they're coming to get that map."

"Yeah," said Jack, "and I don't think they care who gets in their way. I heard them say that they were going to ditch your folks an leave em in the bayou."

Matie began to cry. "Oh, Johnny, do you think they hurt Mommy and Daddy?"

"Matie, stop it! We've gotta think this thing out. As long as they want the map, they're not going to hurt anyone. They need us, and they need Mom and Dad to lead them to us."

Matie's whimpering softened. "Do you think Mom and Dad are with them?"

Johnny smiled at his sister's words. "Well, if they aren't, I'm sure they aren't far behind."

Laurabeth spoke up, "What are we gonna do? We need a plan."

"Well," said Johnny. "At least we can see them coming. We have the advantage becauze we can see for miles from here. Besides, we've got our very own fort and look at all this stuff up here. I'm sure we can find some things we can use if we have to fight them."

"Yeah," everyone agreed.

Bo turned to the others. "Let's set up camp right here for the night. That way we can keep an eye on those goons, and they won't even know we're watching them. We can all take turns." Bo held up the spyglass and watched the men on the island. "Hey, there's another fire over there now. It's not very big, but I can see it."

Johnny took the spyglass and looked into it. He could see the small fire. Then he noticed a woman in a long dress and a man close behind her.

"Hey, Matie, come here. You need to see this." Matie looked through the glass as Johnny steadied it.

"That looks like Mom!" she exclaimed.

Johnny smiled. "They must have gotten away from those men. See, I told you they were all right."

"You know we really should try to let your folks know we're here," said Bo. "But if we go back, we can't go the way we came. That granddaddy gater is just too dangerous."

"Wait a minute," Johnny interrupted. "Remember what Sam said? He told us to wait at the fort. Marie said the same thing. Maybe that's why my parents are here. I think we'd better just sit tight. Hopefully they've brought some help."

Everyone agreed and started gathering firewood from the old broken crates. Matie danced and twirled excitedly thinking how wonderful it would be to see her parents again. "We're gonna be rescued! We're gonna be rescued!" she sang over and over.

Riley looked disappointed.

"What's wrong?" Bo asked, patting his back.

Riley pulled the tri-corner pirate hat off his head. "Well, I thought we were going treasure hunting," he said.

Bo smiled. "Look, you can have my doubloon. I don't need it. Then you can do all the bragging you want to." Bo held the coin out to Riley.

"I don't want your stupid Doubloon!" Riley blurted.

"What's wrong?" Laurabeth asked. "We all thought you wanted the gold."

"I don't care about the stupid treasure." Riley's voice cracked. He looked at Matie and Johnny then at Bo and Laurabeth. "All of you already have a treasure, one that I'll never have. You've got a family. My Mom and Dad just work. They're always on a trip somewhere. They don't care about me. They probably don't even know I'm gone yet." Riley sat down and pulled his kneez up close to his chest and covered his head with his arms.

Bo motioned towards the others. "He's right. His folks are never there for him. He's at our house most of the time."

Riley looked up and wiped a tear from his eye. "Finally I got somebody who cares about me, righcherre! I don't wanna go back home. There's nobody waitin' for me there, just an old empty house!"

Bo went over and put his arm around Riley. "Hey, Riley, I know I can be a bit tough on ya sometimes, but me and Laurabeth have always cared about ya. You're like our little brother."

Jack stood up and walked over to Riley. "I know how you feel. My folks have been gone for years now. I don't think of it much anymore. But I have to admit, it does feel good having somebody to care about ya. Come on, why don't you help me find some more firewood?"

Riley reluctantly joined Jack. Soon they had gathered

enough wood and began building a fire. Everyone stared at the hypnotic flame<u>z</u> as the fire began to dwindle. Bo threw an old barrel on the fire while Johnny gave some food to everyone.

The eerie skeletons aro<u>u</u>nd the group seemed like actor<u>z</u> in a play watching from the win<u>g</u>s for their turn to take the stage. <u>Ma</u>tie snuggled closer to her brother as the darkness of the night <u>fi</u>nally completely blanketed the old fort.

As the group discussed their plans for the day ahead, Bo picked up another barrel from the pile of debris and threw it on the fire. With a loud boom, the entire barrel exploded, shooting bits and pieces of burning embers in all directions. Everyone jumped to their feet and began stomping out the small fires that dotted their stronghold.

"What was that?" Riley yelled. "You could a killed us all!"

"Well, <u>I</u> didn't know it still had <u>g</u>unpowder in it," Bo yelled back.

<u>A</u> small burning coal near the wall of the fort sat smoldering. With a puff of smoke, it turned into a small flame. Casuall<u>y</u> everyone talked as the small un-noticed flame began to increa<u>x</u>e behind them and soon cau<u>q</u>ht a nearby rope on fire.

The rope quickly burned, and the fire climbed up along the old rope till it was at the loaded cannon. Then without warning the cannon erupted with a loud BANG, belching fire out of its mouth like fireworks on the fourth of <u>J</u>uly.

A large cannonball whistled through the air from the fort straight towards the old sunken boat in Dead Man's Lake.

Everyone screamed and ran for cover. "We're under attac<u>k</u>!" Riley yelled.

"Hit the deck!" said Bo, throwing Laurabeth to the ground.

Jack began laughing. "It's just that old cannon." The others half smiled at the jok<u>e</u> and began dusting themselves of<u>f</u>.

"A spark must have started the wick of that cannon on fire," Bo said, with a chuckle.

Bo's laughter stopped suddenly, and he began to frown. He picked up the spyglass. Johnny stopped laughing, too.

"We're in trouble. They know we're here now. They're watching us!" Bo said, handing the spyglass to Johnny.

"What are we going to do? This'll bring them right to us," Laurabeth said.

Jack inspected the old cannon that had just fired. "We can use this!" he said. "We can reload it and give those guys a fight they won't forget, Laffite style!"

"Hey, maybe we could," said Bo. "We've got plenty of ammunition with all this junk, and I just bet there's more gunpowder around here somewhere."

Johnny, Bo, and Jack started planning as Matie and Riley stayed close to Laurabeth near the fire.

The loud explosion had stirred many things in the swamp, some benign and some very deadly. As the boys searched for ammunition, they had no way of knowing that they had just re-awakened the most dangerous of all the things in the bayou... THE CURSE!

~Cξℜ ✛ ℭℬ~

Jim and Kate stared at the glowing light to the south where the explosion had come from. "What do you think that was?" Kate said, as she turned to Jim.

"I don't know," Jim replied, watching the fire light in the distance. "But I do know that it's got Ratcliffe's attention, and it's going to bring him right down our throats. We've got to leave right now, before they find us, or we won't be of any help to the children."

289

Kate gathered the camping gear as Jim doused the fire. The smoke curled upward toward the full moon overhead. Jim added some gas to the engine and untied the boat. The three small birds fluttered in confusion around Jim and Kate, then suddenly, without warning, flew away.

"Looks like we're on our own now," Jim said as he started the motor. "We'll just have to keep to the larger waterways." Jim shoved the boat into the water as Kate held the rudder. She looked concerned and more than a bit uneasy.

Jim knew it was risky traveling the bayou at night like this, but they had no choice. The little boat glided slowly over the quiet waters toward the place where the blast had come from.

"Jim?" Kate pleaded, "Can't we just go back to Maison Rouge and get some help from the authorities?"

Jim shook his head. "We can't, Kate. That fake officer is still there, and Ratcliffe said that there were others in the Police Department that are involved. If we go to them, we'd be taking a chance on getting caught by more of Ratcliffe's friends. Besides, we've got to make sure Ratcliffe doesn't get to the kids before we do."

Kate nodded. "Oh, I know you're right. I just feel so helpless, and I'm so worried about the kids."

The three small birds returned and led the two passengers down a long winding waterway away from the main river. The trees and bushes were thick and the eerie rustling of things in the bushes beyond could be heard from time to time. The whole area was creepy and didn't feel quite right.

"I don't like this!" Jim whispered. "Something feels wrong." The birds continued leading them along till the waterway opened up onto Dead Man's Lake with the moon glistening on the calm waters.

~CʒCʒ ✛ ʒɔʒɔ~

Palmer and Randy rubbed their sleepy eyes as they slowly stood. The explosion had not only awakened the bayou, but the previous argument between the corporate pirates.

"We've got to go now," Ratcliffe demanded, throwing his things into the boat.

"Why can't we just leave this thing alone?" Randy said.

Ratcliffe climbed in the boat, and started the engine. "You can come with me, or stay here and rot on this island," he said, pointing to the keys in the boat.

Randy and Palmer gathered their things and climbed aboard. "Remind me to keep the boat keys hidden from him the next time we stop," Randy said to Palmer.

The three men watched the glowing light in the distance. Like a lighthouse, it provided clear directions to their next destination. The engine roared, echoing over the bayou as they headed down the river toward the glowing light ahead. Soon the glow dimmed, and the tall trees and bushes obscured the view of their intended goal. The narrowing river led the men into the same waterway the children had taken earlier in the day.

Branches from the nearby trees screeched like fingernails across the boat. The three men battled the branches that slapped at their faces as they forged ahead. Ratcliffe slowed the boat a little to protect them from being beaten to death by the relentless shrubbery and avoiding any further damage to himself or the boat's prop.

But the damaged propeller whined with a definite miss each time it made a rotation. The shallow waterway had put a great strain on the broken prop. The motor spit and sputtered and finally died. Ratcliffe repeatedly turned the key, trying to start it. The stubborn engine refused to comply.

"Does anyone smell smoke?" Palmer asked looking toward the back of the boat. Smoke billowed from beneath the enjines cover.

"It's on fire!" Randy yelled as he lifted the cover off.

Ratcliffe barked out orders to the others as he watched helplessly. Palmer grabbed some water bottles and began dousing the fire. As smoke poured off of the overworked engine, Randy turned to the others. "It's useless. The whole thing is completely fried."

The three sat down. "Look at us." Palmer declared, looking at Ratcliffe. "You sure know how to mess things up!"

"Shut up!" Ratcliffe growled. "Get the oars we'll do it like we did before!"

"Do it yourself," Palmer smirked. "For once I'd like to see you get a few blisters." Palmer went to the front of the boat to lie down.

Randy and Ratcliffe climbed out onto the back of the boat with the oars, but each time they tried rowing, the oars caught on the sandy bottom of the shallow stream.

"Why don't you try pushing it?" said Palmer from the front of the boat. Randy and Ratcliffe planted their oars in the sandy bottom and pushed with all their might, using the oars as levers. The stubborn boat moved only a little.

"Try it again!" Ratcliffe said. The two men struggled, but the boat moved only a bit farther. Then despite their attempts, it wouldn't budge. The sleek boat was firmly stuck in the muddy bottom of the stream.

"It's no use," Randy said throwing his oar on deck and joining Palmer at the front of the boat. Grabbing a tarp and throwing it over his shoulders, he laid down to get some rest. Randy slept on the floor as Palmer occupied the soft cushions. Ratcliffe stayed at the back of the boat.

The bayou was a dangerous place in the dark, and Ratcliffe's beady eyes watched as the exotic sounds of the night life began to close in around him. He could hear the sounds of birds chattering and the splash of an occasional alligator capturing some unlucky prey. Large bullfrogs croaked their warning, "Stay away! Stay away!"

Ratcliffe's imagination soared. He felt as if the sounds were getting louder and louder, closer and closer. Finally he covered his ears, and his eyes bulged with fear. Looking from side to side he was completely paralyzed with paranoia, frozen by a hundred thoughts of all the men who had died before him in this treacherous foreboding place. Soon his fear became so intense that he trembled uncontrollably and fell onto the deck in an unconscious stupor.

31

Pirates of the Deep

Johnny gathered a large roll of old rope while Bo put together the remains of gunpowder from several barrels. Jack piled the rusty old cannonballs together and ripped some rotten sails into wadding for the cannon.

Riley watched the others as the flames from the nearby fire reflected off of his eyes. He had also gathered some old rusty guns, swords and knifes, along with any other weapons he could find that looked threatening.

Matie slept peacefully on Laurabeth's lap except for an occasional mumble as she talked in her sleep.

The silver moon overhead gave way to another summer storm as hazy clouds obstructed its light. Every so often a flash of lightning danced across the shadowy sky followed by the clap of thunder rumbling in the distance.

"One Mississippi, Two Mississippi, Three Mississippi," Laurabeth said aloud after each flash of lightning.

"What are you doing?" Riley asked, placing another old sword on the pile of weapons he'd gathered.

Laurabeth smiled as she wiped a drop of rain off of Matie's cheek. "I'm seeing how far away the storm is," she explained. "When ya hear the thunder boom, ya stop counting. If you get to five Mississippi's then the lightning's a mile away. If it gets much closer, we'll need to find some shelter."

Johnny laid his backpack against the wheel of the old cannon. Matie mumbled something in her sleep. He turned to look at her when suddenly she sat up and began screaming. With a trembling finger, she pointed at the stairway. There, standing with lightning flashing in the background, stood the shadow of a man.

It was a ghostlike apparition that looked every bit like a pirate, but this was no normal pirate. His body was like no other. It shimmered in the sliver moon light, as if it were made of glass. The light reflected off of it, just as it did on Dead Man's Lake below.

The apparition moved closer as Matie screamed with blood curdling horror in her voice. Everyone ran toward the fire and huddled together. Similar beings with drawn swords began emerging from all sides of the roof. Climbing over the edges, they closed in on the helpless group. These were deadly pirate apparitions who were ready for battle.

Matie quivered in Laurabeth's arms. Jack picked up a sword while Bo grabbed a torch from the fire. Riley stood spellbound, frozen in fear. Johnny watched the strange pirates move closer. Each place they touched became wet. They weren't made of glass; they were completely made of water. His eyes grew wide as he watched the pirates begin surrounding the little group. Then he remembered his backpack. He glanced anxiously toward the old cannon. He had to get that pack.

"Bo," Johnny whispered. "I've gotta get my back pack." Bo looked at Johnny then at the cannon, then, he boldly swung the fiery torch towards one of the water pirates. It grimaced and stepped back a bit.

"Look! They're afraid of the fire!" Jack whispered. Bo looked at the barrel of gunpowder by the cannon, then at Johnny.

"We'll go on three!" Bo whispered. Johnny nodded. "One... two....three!"

The two lunged for the cannon. Johnny grabbed his backpack, as Bo threw gunpowder into the air toward the water pirates. He swung the torch to ignite the makeshift explosive which caught one of the pirates right in the chest. The man of water recoiled then burst into a million tiny droplets of water!

Everyone watched in astonishment as each tiny droplet began to move as if it were alive. Soon the dropletz gathered into a puddle that rose from the ground, re-forming back into the pirate!

"Hurry!" yelled Johhny as the two leaped back toward the safety of the fire.

The watermen closed in. They spoke to one another in strange muffled voices that sounded like they were under water.

Matie sobbed. Jack and Laurabeth stood with swords in hand ready for a fight. Riley still stood frozen in fear. Johnny grabbed the old sword by his side and swung at the pirates, while Bo swung his rusty sword along side. The clanking of metal rang out over the bayou, as sword clashed with sword. Yet when Bo stabbed at the water men, it did nothing to them. Laurabeth's and Jaxk's attempts were no better.

But when Johnny swung at the pirates, they reached for their wounds as if in pain.

"What's going on?" Bo yelled, deflecting the blow of a pirate's sword.

"It's Johnny's sword!" Jack yelled, swinging as he spoke. "His is the one from Maison Rouge. It's Pierre Laffite's!"

At Jack's words, all of the pirates stopped in their tracks, lowered their swords then backed away. Only one or two made a few random passes with their swords, then, they retreated as well.

"What's going on?" Bo said turning to see only one remaining pirate. It had crept up behind Riley and had its watery hand over his mouth. Riley's eyes bulged as he struggled for air.

"He's drowning!" Laurabeth shrieked.

Johnny lunged toward the pirate, Laffite's sword in

hand. He slashed the arm that held Riley in its deadly grasp. The hideous pirate released Riley's face and let out an unearthly gurgling howl and then turned and ran away.

Riley's body lay lifeless on the ground. "He's dead," Matie whimpered, wiping her tears with her sleeve. Bo bent over his lifeless cousin and listened for a heartbeat. Then he tipped Riley's head back and began mouth to mouth resuscitation. Jack began pushing down on Riley's small chest. "One, two, three, four, five," Jack said aloud with each compression. Then Bo gave another breath.

"C'mon Riley!" yelled Laurabeth, her voice cracked with emotion. "You can't die. We need you!"

Suddenly Riley coughed, and water gushed from his mouth amid choking and coughing.

"He's alive!" Matie yelled, throwing her arms around him.

"Be careful, Matie," Johnny said as he gently pulled her away.

Riley quivered with shock. Still coughing he sat up and leaned on his elbow.

"Boy, you gave us a scare!" Jack said.

With wide eyes, Riley looked around. "Are those water guys gone?" he asked.

"Yeah," Bo said. "They're afraid of Johnny's sword."

"Don't ya mean Pierre's sword?" Johnny said. "And to think I didn't want to wear it."

Laurabeth knelt down by Riley and wiped the moisture from his face. "What was that thing doing to you?" she asked.

"I don' know. I was just standin' there and that thing put its icy hand over my mouth. Before I knowed it I was gasping for air and drownin'. It was like I was under water and couldn't breathe. No matter how much I moved, I couldn't get away from that thing."

Bo was at the edge of the roof with the spy glass. "Hey, you guys, come here!" Johnny ran to his side with Jack close behind. "There they are," Bo said, pointing to the wrecked ship.

Johnny took the spy glass and watched as the pirates walked out on the water and disappeared into their sunken ship.

"Hey, what's happening?" Laurabeth asked.

"They must live in that ship out there," said Johnny. "I just don't understand why they didn't bother Bo when he stayed here before."

"It's gotta be the curse," said Jack. "That cannon blast must have woke 'em up or something."

Johnny looked out over the water. "I wonder what else it woke up?"

The night was a long one as the group huddled together. The older kids all took turns keeping watch while the others tried to get some rest in spite of the concerns of the night. Every so often a crash of lightning would startle the small group, sending everyone into a defensive posture. Finally, after several hours, they were able to get some sleep.

~C3CR ✛ SOSO~

Jim and Kate watched the lake as the moon lit figures in the distance caught their attention. "Look Jim!" Kate whispered. "Do you see that?"

"Yes," Jim replied as he cut the motor to the boat.

"Who do you think they are?" said Kate.

"I don't know, but I know it's not Ratcliffe and his men. The ones out there look as if they're on top of the water. It's strange."

The three little birds hovered in front of Kate and Jim,

then, flew to the west of the area then back again. "They want us to follow them," Kate said, pointing toward the trees.

As Jim reached to start the motor, the three birds sat on the handle to the pull rope. "All right, I get it," Jim said. "No motor, no noise." Then he picked up the oars. As Jim began rowing, the waters around the boat began to stir.

"What's going on?" Kate whispered, looking into the moon-lit waters.

"Something's weird," Jim said, rowing faster.

Suddenly, something grabbed one of the oars. Jim yanked on it, pulling it free. The three birds flew frantically about the boat in a flurry of wings and chatter.

The waters under the boat began to boil as an icy blue hand reached up from the water and grabbed at the side of the boat. Then another hand appeared on the opposite side of the boat. Jim slammed the oar against the icy hands that crept up from the deep.

Kate screamed as another reached out of the water. Jim hit it then lunged for the pull start on the motor. Desperately he yanked as hard as he could. The old motor started up, and Jim hit the throttle. The little boat sped through the waters as the birds led it towards the shoreline. Jim kept the boat at full throttle and ran it right up on the shore. He and Kate leaped out of the boat and ran up the embankment as fast as they could.

The watery forms of pirates emerged from the water's edge. Kate grabbed Jim's arm, her eyes wide with horror. The liquid apparitions advanced towards them with swords drawn and the look of evil on their distorted faces. Suddenly the entire group of watery pirates froze in place, lowered their weapons and dissolved into the waters. Jim and Kate looked at each other in amazement.

Jim noticed a glimmer of light out of the corner of his eye. About five feet behind Kate stood one of the ominous pirates in full pirate gear. Kate gasped as she turned to see the shimmering figure. Jim stepped in front of her, motioning for her to stay behind him. The tall pirate stood silent with his sword at his side. It just stood there watching Jim and Kate, the moonlight reflecting every detail of his appearance. As they studied the watery figure, Jim stammered, "I know him... It's Dominique Youx!"

Kate stood speechless as the being turned and disappeared into the trees. "Jim, what's going on here?" Kate asked.

Jim stared out over the water. "Do you remember Sam and Cora's stories about how Dominique Youx was looking for all of the clues in the bayou? Later on, they said he was overcome by the curse. He didn't die. The curse changed him somehow. It all makes sense now. That's probably why Dominique's symbol is a skull."

Kate looked perplexed and glanced out toward the lake. "What are we going to do now? I'm not sleeping here tonight, knowing that those things are out there!"

Jim smiled. "Well, I won't argue with that!"

Suddenly Jim remembered something else. "Kate, remember what Ken said in his journal? He said that he had been attacked by watermen! That was why he left in such a big hurry!"

Now the three small birds began urging Kate and Jim in the same direction as Dominique Youx.

"I'm not going in there!" Kate said as she sat down in the sand. Jim thought of Matie as he looked at Kate.

Sitting down by Kate, Jim put his arm around her. "Well, I guess you can stay here. I'm not sure how long those pirates might stay away, but if you're sure you want to stay on the beach alone, I won't stop you."

Kate gritted her teeth angrily. "Ohhhhh, all right then! I

guess I haven't got any other choice, but I don't have to like it! Either way, it's just plain creepy."

Jim grinned and helped her up, urging her toward the trees. The hummingbirds flew alongside dipping low through the brush as they led the two deeper onto the island.

Soon a faint light spilled through the trees up ahead. "Look," said Jim. "It looks like there's a fire up there."

"It's probably pirates!" Kate said, sarcastically.

"Come on," Jim urged.

As the three birds led them through the bushes, it soon became apparent that the light they saw was the same light they had witnessed from their previous camp site.

"Do you think it's the kids?" Kate said, pushing in front of Jim. Soon they found themselves at the base of the old fort. The two made their way up the crumbling stairs. Once on top of the fort, Jim and Kate searched for the glowing fire that they'd seen from the distance. As they did, their attention was drawn to the second set of stairs leading to the upper level of the fort.

Jim motioned for Kate to follow behind him as they slowly headed up the stairs. Shadows of the ancient skeletons dotted the roof and seemed to dance as the fire flickered nearby. Tears of relief filled Kate's eyes as she saw the children lying near the fire. Bo sat watch near the cannon, snoring, with a spyglass lying in his hands.

Jim put his finger to his lips as he looked at Kate. Then they, too, took up a place near the warmth of the glowing fire and tried to get some rest.

32

The Living Curse

As the mysterious darkness of night gave way to the sun's golden rays, the bayou came alive. Squirrels chattered in the trees while the occasional call of a bird overhead announced the dawning of a new day.

The glowing fire that protected the group the night before was nothing but a pile of embers. Jim had risen early and retrieved the provisions from the boat.

As he climbed the stairs to the upper level of the fort, Bo awoke with a start. The sight of Jim startled him so badly that he toppled over against the cannon. Jim smiled while Bo composed himself. The others stirred a bit then returned to the bliss of carefree sleep.

"How'd you get here?" Bo whispered as he helped unload Jim's arms.

"We got here last night," Jim said softly. "It was quite an adventure. I'll fill everyone in on it later."

Bo held the old spyglass and scanned the horixon. Jim asked if he could see it. "Where did you get this?" he asked.

"We found it in an old crate when we got here. It's in pretty good shape for being a hundred and eighty years old."

Jim nodded and looked out over the lake. "Looks like you've found yourselves quite a place here."

"You wouldn't have thought so last night!" Bo replied, looking at the dead pirates lying on the roof. "You're lucky you didn't find us looking like THEM!"

"Oh? What happened?" Jim asked.

Bo looked around uneasily. "Well, you probably won't believe me, but we were attacked by a bunch of pirates."

Jim raised an eyebrow, "Go on."

Bo thought for a minute. "We really did zee them. The weird thing was, they were made of water and no matter what we did they just kept on coming. Nothing could stop em except Johnny's sword. The minute they heard the words; 'Laffite', they high-tailed it for the water. Riley almost didn't make it, though. One of 'em tried drownin' him." Bo's face turned a bit red with embarrassment. He hoped Jim would believe his fantastic tale.

"How did they try to drown Riley? Was it down by the water?" Jim asked.

Bo looked up and squinted. "No, it was righcherre. One put his hand over Riley's mouth. We thought Riley was a goner fer sure."

Jim patted Bo on the back. "I believe you. They tried to get us, too."

Bo's eyes got big. "Do you mean ta say that you came across Dead Man's Lake last night? With them things after ya?"

"Yes," said Jim. "They would have gotten us too, except that something stopped them. We think it was Dominique Youx, Jean's half brother."

"Man, am I glad," said Bo. "I mean, I'm not glad you were attacked. I am glad you made it here safe. I was beginnin' ta think we were dreamin' it all up or somethin."

Their loud whispering began waking the others.

Johnny and Matie enthusiastically greeted their father with hugs and kisses. As Matie ran to wake her mother, Jim stopped her. "Let your mother sleep," he whispered. "She's completely exhausted." Matie nodded then began telling her father about their adventures.

Laurabeth reached for more firewood and stirred the glowing coals next to Kate. She noticed a large red spot on the back of Kate's neck. "Bo, get over here!" she yelled. Bo hurried over to Kate's side. The spot on Kate's neck was swollen and blistered. He knelt down and felt Kate's forehead, but she didn't stir.

Jim was sitting by the cannon listening to **M**atie's exaggerated rehearsal of their harrowing night while Johnny corrected the details. As Jim listened, his attention turned to B**o** and Laurabeth. Instinctively he tuned out **M**atie and tried to listen to the conversation in the distance. He realized that something was very wrong and stood up and headed to Kate. "What's wrong?" he asked.

Laurabeth lifted Kate's dark hair _r_evealing the nasty bite on her neck.

Bo looked up at Jim. "Mr. Leavitt, did your wi_f_e get bit by anything?"

"Yes, "Jim replied. "It wasn't much, just a bug bite."

Laurabeth bit her lip. "Did ya see what bit her?"

"Yes," Jim said. "It was just a little caterpillar."

"It's called a Schneille," B**o** said. "They **b**ring on an awful fever and make a **p**erson _r_eal sick. Mrs. Leavitt ain't goin' no wheres for a while, least not until that fever breaks."

Jim put his hand on Kate's head. She was burning up, and the heat coming from her even surprised Jim. "**G**et some water!" he said to Johnny as he pointed at the supplies.

Johnny returned with a bottle of water and handed it to his father. Jim took a white handkerchief out of his pocket and poured water on it, then applied it to Kate's fevered brow. Jim sat down and cradled Kate's head on his lap. "How long does this sickness last?"

Bo shook his head. "**I** don't rightly know. Just depends on the person and how hard they fight it."

Mati_e_ looked on in horror and began to throw a childlike fit. "She's gotta get better!" she ranted, kneeling by her mother's side, throwing her arms around Kate. "I just got you back," she cried as she shook her mother's limp body.

Jim's eyes filled with tears as he watched his little girl's hopeless pleadings. "Matie, she'll be all right," he said with a lump in his throat, putting an arm around his daughter.

Matie's sobs turned into anger. She stood up and clenched her fists. Turning to the bayou she shouted. "I hate this place! You hear me, Mr. Laffite? I hate your stupid curse, and I hate your pirates and your bayou, and I hate you!" Her face was red and tears streamed down her cheeks.

Suddenly she ran to the stairs and started down. "Where's she going?" Riley asked, with a cough.

"I'll get her," Johnny said. He took off after her, with Bo following close behind.

Matie hurried down the stairs and ran toward the beach. By the time the boys got to her, she was in the little launch out on the water, trying to maneuver the oars. "Leave me alone!" she yelled at the boys, who stood helplessly watching from the beach.

Johnny looked down at the water and the hull of the sunken ship beyond. All he could think of was the water pirates below. "Matie!" he said, "You come back here right now!"

"No! I'm going home!" she yelled.

Bo now spoke softly as his foot stepped in the water. "Matie, your Ma is gonna need you. What'll she say when she wakes up, and you ain't there?"

Matie's face softened as she pulled the oars onto her lap. "When is my mother going to wake up?" she asked.

"Oh, it won't be long," Bo said. "She'll be right good, real soon."

Matie looked down at the little launch, then, curled her lip. "OK!" she said lowering the oars into the water. As she began to row, the waters beneath her began to stir. Matie looked down with alarm. The boat had drifted ten feet from shore.

Bo raced fearlessly into the churning waters. Johnny reached for the sword, but it was gone. He had taken it off while he was sleeping and left it back at camp. Now there was no time to get it as Bo ran through the water towards Matie. Johnny yelled from the beach, "Row, Matie! Row as hard as you can!"

Matie looked down at the surging waters and hesitantly placed the oar back in them. As she did, it was immediately ripped out of her hand. She screamed and clung tightly to the remaining oar.

Bo lunged toward the boat. Grabbing the end he dove into it. The boat rocked wildly, and Matie clung to the sides of it. "Help me, Bo!"

Johnny watched with horror as several blue watery hands reached up onto the sides of the boat, pulling it down on one side. Bo tried unsuccessfully to steady the little boat, but the icy hands finally succeeded in capsizing the launch.

"No…" Johnny yelled, his voice echoing over the bayou as he watched the two go toppling into the lake. He looked around for anything he could use to help the others. Finally in desperation he ran into the waters to help his sister who was struggling for air.

Bo slapped ineffectively at the unseen force. Then his entire body disappeared under the water. He resurfaced for a moment, gasping and screaming for help. Johnny raced after the two. An icy hand grabbed his ankle, pulling him into the churning surf. Johnny clawed at the shore, his hand grasping a handful of seashells. Again he reached for the beach. But the hand of the water pirate only pulled him farther into the deadly waters. Suddenly, he heard a loud splash. He tried to see what it was, but the battle with the formless pirates kept him busy. Out of the corner of his eye, he saw faint dashes of color and the wings of a bird.

The waters boiled incessantly as Johnny and Bo gasped

for air at the surface. The unseen force was dragging them into the depths of the sunken ship. Johnny looked around in the murky waters. He could see the distorted faces of pirates all around him. He squirmed to get away, but the grasp of these minions was too great. Bo was motionless, a hostage at Johnny's side. The boy's faces were contorted, holding desperately to the last bits of air from the surface.

Johnny watched bubbles rise up from Bo's nose. Their eyes were bulging with fear. The water pirates pushed the two boys towards their lair. Johnny noticed that coffers full of gold lay heaped in piles aboard the haunted wreck, seen only by those unlucky enough to fall prey to the bloodthirsty pirates and their cursed crew.

Johnny held his breath tightly, feeling as if his lungs would burst. Suddenly, his captors all looked upward and then released the two boys. Johnny swam frantically for the air above. As his head cleared the surface, he gulped in the precious air, gasping repeatedly. Soon Bo popped up near his side.

"Where's Matie? "Johnny asked between gasps.

"I didn't... see her... after the boat went over!" Bo coughed.

Johnny slapped an angry fist at the water. "We gotta find her!" Johnny took a deep breath and dove into the water, looking for his sister. With crazed determination the two boys searched the wreck. Matie was nowhere to be found. After several unsuccessful attempts, the two resurfaced. In solemn despair they headed towards shore. Johnny was crying. The thought of losing his little sister was just too much to bear. What would his parents say?

The two struggled up onto the shore, then, they both fell exhausted into the sand. "It's no use. They got her." Johnny said with a lump in his throat.

307

Bo hung his head as the realization of losing Matie hit him. He stood up in an explosion of emotion. Gold coins fell out of his bulging pockets. In anger he emptied them, throwing the cursed treasure back at the haunted wreck. "Keep your stupid treasure!" he yelled.

Johnny stared at the sand. His eyes focused on one solitary gold coin that had escaped Bo's wrath. Johnny picked it up in a dazed stupor as he thought of Matie and looked numbly at the coin. A blistering hatred towards the golden treasure grew inside of him. With tear-filled eyes he looked at the cursed coin and blinked hard as the tears poured down his cheeks. As his eyes cleared, he noticed that the cursed pirate coin was just like the others in his collection, but on the back was something new. This coin, had a horse and rider, stamped on it.

Johnny and Bo walked toward the fort, their heads held low. They both felt responsible for Matie's loss. The thought of loosing her filled the two with an overwhelming sense of despair. Slowly they headed toward the fort. With hesitation they climbed the stairs. At last on the roof, they stood speechless.

To their astonishment, Jim, Jack, Riley, Laurabeth, and even Kate, had disappeared without a trace, but the abandoned fire was still crackling. "Where could they be? They were all just here. Something's wrong." Johnny said.

As they moved closer to the fire, Bo's foot splashed in a puddle of water. He stopped and looked down. "Hey, Johnny... c'mere."

"We didn't leave that puddle there. My clothes are almost dry!" Johnny said.

"I know!" Bo pointed at similar spots all over the roof. "It had to be those water pirates!"

As the two hurried across the roof toward the stairs, something caught their eye. Both boys stopped suddenly at a skeleton. There in its bony hand was Johnny's saber.

"Look, its Pierre's sword," said Bo. "Somebody's left it there on purpose." Bo picked it up and handed it to Johnny. "You'd best hang on to this. We'll probably be needin' it."

Suddenly, Johnny remembered his backpack and the things he had promised to protect, but the pack and all of the artifacts were gone. Johnny reached in his pocket and felt for the old watch. He took it out and looked at it as boiling rage grew inside of him. "I hate this thing! None of this would have ever happened if I hadn't have found it!" Johnny pulled his arm back and threw the precious watch as hard as he could! A watery arm reached out from behind Bo and caught it in mid air. Johnny and Bo turned and stared in complete horror. Standing before them was a water pirate holding the precious watch in its icy hand.

The fluid form undulated as if pulsing with each heart beat. Both boys began backing away from the thing. Finally they backed into the nearby cannon. Now the pirate reached toward the two who stood with their eyes clenched shut, expecting to die at any moment.

Suddenly Johnny felt a cold, wet hand on his arm. Then he felt the watch being pushed into his fingers. First he opened one eye, just a little to peek, then the other. The water pirate still stood before them. Astonished, Johnny nudged Bo. The two boys watched the pirate, their mouths hanging wide open.

Finally Johnny mustered up enough courage to speak. "Ummm... thanks for the watch," he said, swallowing hard and looking at Bo.

The water man smiled. Then in an eerie underwater voice the thing spoke, "You are a Laffite!"

"Well, a, sorta," Johnny stammered.

The pirate pointed to the sword by Johnny's side. Johnny recoiled, unsure of the pirate's intentions. The pirate spoke again. "That is Pierre Laffite's sword. He will be pleased to know that a Laffite still carries it!"

Now Johnny recognized the unusual form. "You're Youx!" Johnny said. Bo looked confused. Johnny pointed at the pirate. "It's Dominique Youx!" he exclaimed.

The pirate laughed loudly. "Why, of course I am," he said removing his hat and bowing with a broad sweeping motion. "I am at your service!"

Johnny and Bo stared at the pirate, as a million questions flooded their minds. "Where are the others?' Johnny blurted out.

The pirate anxwered in his muffled watery tone. "Your families have been taken to Au Ville, the Golden City. My men are taking good care of them there."

Johnny's face turned white. "Like the way they took care of my sister? Your men drowned my little sister, and they tried to kill our friend Riley last night!"

The old pirate broke into blistering echoed laughter. "No, my boy, those were not my men. The ones you encountered are a scurvy lot, despots and thieves. My men and I battle them constantly. It was my men and Pierre's sword that saved your lives last night."

The water pirate looked sternly at the two young men and then pointed at the watch in Johnny's hand. "You must take very good care of that watch and the sword. Many have given their lives searching for them."

"You can have them!" Johnny said, holding the watch up.

"No!" the pirate's voice echoed firmly. "They are of no use to me! They are only of value in the handz of a living soul in whose veins Laffite blood runs!"

Johnny felt a chill run down his spine. He carefully returned the precious watch to the inner pocket of his old fashioned jacket. "What about my little sister? Those other pirates got her."

Dominique turned around as another water figure approached the group. Johnny's hand instinctively reached for the sword at his side.

"Do not be afraid," the pirate said. "You need not fear. This is my first mate." The two pirates conversed in muffled tonez, using a foreign language. Then the second pirate quickly left scaling the side of the fort.

"Your sister has not drowned. We have searched the depths, and there are no newcomers!" Dominique continued to advise the boys until they finally agreed to go with him to the Golden City. The odd pirate quickly transformed into a puddle of water that disappeared into the cracks of the rock floor. "Whoa, where'd he go?" Johnny exclaimed.

Soon a small puddle of water reappeared in front of the boys. It grew larger and larger, then slowly re-materialized in the form of the man. "Everything is ready," Dominique announced. "We must hurry. Our enemies are returning."

The young men followed the pirate down the stairs and through the dense jungle. Every few minutes the pirate would disappear by sinking into the sand below, then he would reappear a few feet ahead of the boys and lead them onward.

Bo's curiosity finally got the best of him. "Why do you keep disappearing?" he asked.

The pirate stopped and turned to the young men. "Just as you must breathe air, I must breathe water. I return through the soil until I reach the water's beneath, and I am able to gain my breath," the pirate explained.

The group set out again, trudging through the jungle. One by one, a legion of rag tag water pirates joined their ranks as they walked along the winding trail. Soon they neared the south end of the island where a large wooden boat awaited them. The two boys climbed aboard as the water pirates disappeared into the water below.

The boys watched the pirates prepare an unusual rigging beneath them. It looked like a kind of underwater schooner with two masts positioned at the fore and aft of the ship. Soon the pirates attached the masts to the upper boat the boys were in, and the two boats were firmly connected, one above the other. Then the watery pirates below took up their oars and began rowing and both boats moved in perfect unison.

Bo and Johnny watched the current below as a small stream of water began to flow upward into their boat. Soon Dominique Youx re-materialized on the wooden deck. "How are you enjoying your accommodations?" he asked.

"It's just great!" the two replied with grins.

"What do you call that thing down there?" Johnny asked.

The old pirate erupted into laughter. "It is called a boat! The rig you are riding in is called a *Work-shy* for obvious reasons." He patted Johnny's back then disintegrated again into the waters below.

The two boats moved swiftly on the wide waters of the bayou. A myriad of animals and insects watched unconcerned as the boat passed by. Catfish meandered through the waters while the frogs croaked in unison. An occasional caiman could be seen basking in the warm sun as dragon flies hovered over head.

Finally for the first time since they entered the forbidden bayou, the boys felt as if they were truly safe, even if they were in the hands of the water pirates.

33
The Bayou's Revenge

A large fly buzzed through the trees. Then it found its target on Ratcliffe's nose as he dozed at the back of the boat. Brushing it away, he rolled over and tried to go back to sleep. The sandy floor of the boat irritated his skin, and the persistent fly buzzed around his face. Angrily he scratched at the sand in his clothes, then, erupted. "Blasted fly!" he bellowed, jumping to his feet.

At the front of the boat the others slept peacefully. "Get up you lazy louts." he yelled. Randy sat up abruptly and Palmer rubbed his eyes. They were very annoyed with Ratcliffe's insistent behavior, especially in the light of the fact that the boat was hopelessly stranded. Quietly they got to their feet.

"So," said Palmer in a condescending tone, "where do you think we're going now?"

Ratcliffe grunted and snorted then wiped his nose on the back of his sleeve. "We're going to take the rubber boat and find those kids and the treasure," he said.

Palmer shook his head and rubbed the whiskers on his face. He and Randy looked at each other in disbelief.

"What does he think he's doing?" Randy said as they watched Ratcliffe retrieve a rubber raft from a storage compartment.

Ratcliffe pressed a small button on the raft, and the device inflated instantly. Palmer and Randy made room as the rubber raft almost filled the floor of their large boat.

"There, I have everything under control!" Ratcliffe said proudly. "We'll head toward that light that we saw last night.

You two get the supplies."

As Ratcliffe maneuvered the small dingey over the side,
Randy and Palmer retrieved the supplies. Soon the little rubber
boat was loaded. Ratcliffe and Palmer were waiting in the
rubber raft as Randy climbed aboard. The small boat wobbled
until Randy finally got his footing and settled into a place
beside Palmer.

The raft was only about five feet long and made for two
people. In order to use it, all of the men had to sit directly on the
floor and hope that it would hold their weight.

At the back of the boat Ratcliffe's chubby body made
the boat sink low in the water, while Palmer at the other end had
his long legs tight next to him. He held his knees close to the
sides of his face as he tried pulling them in to make room for
Randy.

Randy smiled a bit at the sight of Palmer's long thin
body and Ratcliffe's short fat stature. The two seemed more
like Jack Sprat and his wife than corporate executives. He
picked up the oars, handed one to Palmer, and they both began
rowing. The little boat was very awkward, but with a bit of skill
and timing the trio was soon moving through the waters. It was
a grueling task, but much better than rotting in the heat of the
sun back at the stranded unlucky albatross of a boat.

The waters of the bayou grew swifter and rowing the
little raft became almost impossible against the current. So the
men pulled their oars out of the water and let the current take
them further into the bayou. Soon the river led right into a wall
of tangled vines. To the right the men noticed a large tree with
an "L" carved on it.

Palmer and Randy pushed aside the twigs and vines
allowing the raft to slip beneath the brush into a beautiful grotto
of trees. The three men gazed at the enchanting scene before
them. The sun's rays poured through the trees, dancing on the

waters of the mystical fortress around them.

The tiny raft floated past a large stone outcropping on the side of the shore. As it did, the chatter of a bird above gave way to the flutter of a thousand wings as hundreds of birds exploded in flight, disturbed by the arrival of the little craft. As one large blue jay darted at the boat, Ratcliffe became indignant with the creature. "Go away, you pest!" he bellowed, waving a fist at the bird.

The echo of his voice gave way to silence within the grotto. Now the only sound was that of the chattering bird defending its territory. The persistent bird swooped low in an attack on the three men, and then it was suddenly snatched out of mid air by the large jaws of a massive alligator. As the gater chomped down its unsuspecting breakfast, blue feathers floated around the tiny rubber raft.

"Get out of here, now!" Randy yelled, hitting an oar on the water.

Palmer and Randy rowed as fast as they could while the boat bobbed up and down. The enormous alligator glided after the three in the attempt to get at the men.

Ratcliffe blurted out random orders as oars and arms flew with increased haste. Several sunbathing gaters now joined the larger beast in the hopes of adding some new tasty items to their morning menu.

By now the winding stream led the men into a tunnel of vines. A rush of water pushed the raft twisting and turning through the channel. Soon the raft rushed down a steep incline, and the prospect of being eaten by alligators was replaced with the concern of being crushed at the bottom of a roaring waterfall.

The boat tumbled helplessly over rocks and debris, spilling the three men into the churning waters. At the bottom of the waterfall the three bobbed up and down grasping for the tiny raft. Ratcliffe's fat body floated buoyantly near the top of the water while Palmer splashed with arms and legs everywhere. Randy caught hold of the overturned raft and attempted to turn it right side up again. Slowly the otherx made their way towards him. All three clung tightly to the small inflatable boat in order to keep from drowning as they drifted aimlessly toward the center of Dead Man's Lake.

The morning sun was high in the sky and a myriad of flying insects buzzed about the three men. Ratcliffe growled an angry order at a persistent dragonfly while Randy and Palmer repeatedly tried to turn the raft to its upright position.

"Ratcliffe, let go of the raft and help us!" Randy said, slapping at the water.

"You're both fools!" Ratcliffe bragged. "If you did what I said, we'd have found that treasure by now. And if you intend on ever using this raft again, you'll have to turn it over. How else do you ever expect us to use it?"

Randy and Palmer, ignoring the intolerable man, finally succeeded in flipping the rubber raft over, right on top of Ratcliffe's head.

Ratcliffe yelled a muffled objection, then, emerged from beneath the raft, spitting and spewing water at the men. "You did that intentionally!" he screamed, trying to climb aboard the little vessel.

The unfortunate experience had robbed the thieves of their oars and provisions. And the three men drifted towards the island as they struggled to hang on. The raft itself had taken just about all that it could. When Ratcliffe finally plunged over the side into the raft, a small explosion occurred. The air in the raft escaped with a high pitched whistle. "We've sprung a leak!" Ratcliffe yelled, trying to cover the leak with his hands.

"That won't work," Randy laughed, as he and Palmer started paddling with their handz and feet, heading towards the

316

nearby shore. Finally the small deflated boat rested on the shore of the island. All three men now huffed and puffed with exhaustion as the water lapped at the sides of the pitiful deflated raft. "You men are a couple of idiots!" Ratcliffe ranted.

"Idiots!" yelled Palmer. "Do you think we're doing this for you? This was all your idea!" Palmer glared at Ratcliffe. "You blackmailed me, and you tricked poor Randy here, all just so that you could get to that ridiculous treasure. Do you honestly think we're doing this because we respect you? We could care less what you think!"

Ratcliffe sneered. "Of course you're doing this for yourselves. You want the treasure. And you can't get out of the situation now. Why else would you stay with me? It's because you're both scared. You know that I can ruin both of you!"

Randy groaned as he stepped from the deflated raft onto the island. His main concern at this point was survival. With all of their provisions lost, he began searching the shore line for anything of value.

Soon he noticed footprints in the sand and followed them to discover the overturned boat that the children had left. The boat was wedged up against the shore in a small lagoon between a ridge of sand and the shell-covered island. It was still in good shape, and its location was actually the hand of fate. It had drifted down stream from the point where Johnny and Bo had lost Matie. For the marooned executives it was a fortunate find and its location drew the men far away from the sunken ship and the water pirates.

Randy yelled for the others as he tried lifting the heavy boat. Soon Palmer was by his side. Ratcliffe watched spitting out pointless orders, as Palmer and Randy finally turned the boat over.

All the men explored the island for any food they could find. Randy soon returned with his hands filled with wild berries and his pockets bulging with hickory nuts he had raided from the home of a local squirrel. Palmer also returned, laden with water bottles and bags of food. "Where did you find those?" Randy asked looking at the nuts and berries in his own hands. Palmer reached into a bag and stuffed some chips in his mouth.

"I found them up there at that fort. Looks completely deserted though. We're lucky they left some food there," he said, dribbling chips everywhere.

"Is there any more at that fort?" he asked, taking some food from Palmer.

"Yes, but the place is a mess. There are dead men everywhere. They look like they've been there for years, and I'm sure that the food isn't theirs."

Randy looked toward the fort. "I want to see it!" he said.

Palmer led the way through overgrown bushes and thick palms toward the old fort. Suddenly they heard a blood curdling scream. Dropping the food, they ran toward the horrific sound. They found Ratcliffe chest deep in a bog of quicksand. A look of horror filled his face as he demanded help. "Get me out. I'm sinking!" he yelled.

Randy quickly found a long branch and pointed it towardz Ratcliffe. With muddy hands, Ratcliffe grabbed on to it as Randy pulled with all of his might. Palmer watched the scene but didn't lift a finger to help the xinking man.

"Palmer, snap out of it! You've got to help me!" Randy said holding tight to the wooden branch. "He's sinking fast! Aren't you going to help?"

The nasty quagmire seemed to pull Ratcliffe deeper and deeper into its belly. Palmer stood watching, his face filled with indecision. For the first time in several years, the man he had hated and loathed as his blackmailer was in the very position Palmer had stayed up nights dreaming about.

Palmer now wrestled with his feelings. He could finally be free of his greatest enemy. *Just let the quicksand do it*! he thought to himself, *And I'll never have to lift a finger. Then I'll be free*."

Ratcliffe's slippery hands clung to the heavy stick as Randy tugged helplessly on it trying to free the man.

"C'mon!" Randy yelled. "Help me!" He glanced at Palmer, whose blank stare caught Randy off guard. It didn't take long for Randy to surmise what was going through Palmer's mind. Randy again implored him for help.

"Come on, Palmer. You're not a murderer, at least not yet!" Palmer blinked as Randy's words finally broke through his thoughts. Palmer knelt by Randy and grabbed hold of the long stick.

"I don't know what came over me," he mumbled.

"I do!" Randy said as the two tugged on the pole, pulling Ratcliffe a few more inches out of the mire. "I had the same thought."

Palmer's face reddened with embarrassment, thinking that he'd almost given in to the temptation. Finally the two gave one great tug on the pole and the quicksand released the groveling man.

Ratcliffe sat quivering with fear, covered in the sticky mud. His brash manners remained with him even in the shadow of almost losing his life to the relentless quicksand. In fear and anger, Ratcliffe rebuked the others, "You should have come sooner. I could have died in there!"

"Yeah, you could have," Palmer said.

Randy smiled at him. "You know, you did the right thing," he said patting Palmer on the back. "You're definitely not like him." The two laughed as they headed toward the fort. Palmer acted as if a new person had just emerged from his tortured soul.

319

He turned to Randy and smiled. "For the first time in years, I feel free," he confided. "Watching Ratcliffe back there made me realize that I'm not a killer. I never could be. All these years Ratcliffe had convinced me that I was. But when I saw him in that mess, I just couldn't sit there and let him die. I finally realized that if I couldn't even let my worst enemy die, then how could I have intentionally killed someone, even if I was drunk? Isn't it odd that the very man who kept me thinking that I was a killer, is the same one who proved to me that I'm not?" Palmer smiled as if a thousand weights had been lifted off of his shoulders.

Ratcliffe walked behind the others and grunted as he caught bits and pieces of the conversation. His harrowing experience had given Palmer a new lease on life, but for Ratcliffe it just reaffirmed all of the nasty degrading tendencies that permeated his twisted soul.

34
A Golden Reception

The waters of the bayou meandered along the sides of the island opening up into a wide river heading deep into the forbidden terrain of the bayou. Bo and Johnny watched over the sides of the boat as the oarsmen beneath them rowed through the dark waters of the deep. With the birds overhead and the alligators along the shore, the voyage seemed more like a guided tour than an uncertain adventure.

"Hey, look at that alligator on the river bank." Bo pointed across the river.

Johnny looked up just for a moment then turned his attention back to the Watermen below. "I wonder if the alligators ever attack the watermen?" he pondered. As he peered into the water, he wondered how he could ever trust these unusual beings. After all, weren't they just like the ones that had attacked Matie?

"Hey Bo, do you think we can trust these guys?"

Bo looked over the side of the boat. "They do look just like the ones that attacked us. Once a pirate always a pirate, I'd say."

"Yeah," Johnny nodded. "So if you're a water pirate, who do you rob?"

"Anyone that comes into the bayou, I guess," said Bo. "They give me the creeps. They've gotta be over two hundred years old."

"I wonder what they've been doing all this time." Johnny asked. "I'd hate being made of water and stuck like that forever. Do you remember the look on the faces of the ones that dragged us into the shipwreck?"

"How could I forget?" Bo exclaimed, with a deep breath. "I thought my lungs would explode down there till they got scared and went away."

Suddenly Johnny smiled. "You know, I think we can trust these guys. Remember all the clues? They all say *true intent*. Those guys back at the wreck intended on killing us, but these guys are trying to help us. The message of the clues is that even if they are pirates, they can still choose to be good or bad. It's what's in their heart that matters."

Bo swatted at a mosquito. "Yeah, even if they are rough old pirates, I guess Dominique's men have some good in 'em. Boy, I thought I knew everything about the bayou, but I never expected to see all this. If somebody told me they saw what we have, I'd a called 'em a liar."

As the boys watched the beautiful sites of the bayou, the river made a wide bend. The oarsmen began to slow, and the sound of people in the distance rose up over the trees. The boys stared beyond the trees through the thick jungle, hoping to see what was there. Then the winding river led the boat in one more wide turn.

Suddenly both boyz jumped to their feet as a glorious scene opened before their eyes. A bustling city came into view that looked as if it were a buzy port of the eighteen hundreds. From a distance, it looked just like old fashioned New Orleans, but there was something very different here. Amid the buildings along the wharf was the evidence of the pirate trade. Gold embellishments gleamed from every building.

The water pirates steered the boat alongside an old wooden dock among hundreds of other boats that found safe harbor there. Pirate ships, frigates, and even schooners filled the bay. Among them, speedboats, sailboats, and even a few yachts were scattered on the water.

"How do you think those got here?" Johnny said turning

to Bo.

Bo's mouth was wide open. "I donno!" he replied. "I can't believe it. This is nothin' like the bayou I know."

The area bustled with people wearing clothes from several different time periods. A bell in the distance clanged its warning of a boat ready to set sail. To the east, a large lighthouse stood as a ready standard to guide any unlucky sailors through the foreboding swamplands.

The boys noticed their boat rocking a bit and looked beneath the water to see the water pirates tie the lower boat alongside a type of underwater dock. Dominique Youx materialized on the wooden dock above. "Come along. We have much to do," he said, reaching his watery hand down to help the boys up on the wooden pier.

"What is this place?" Johnny asked as he stepped out onto the wharf.

"It is the Golden City, our capitol," Dominique stated. "Come, there are people waiting for you."

"What about the rest of our group? Are they here?" Bo asked.

"They are waiting," Dominique replied as he placed his fingers to his lips and let out a loud whistle. Dominique's crew emerged from the waters onto the wooden pier. In watery tones they talked among themselves, then, headed into the city.

"Where are they going?" Bo asked.

Dominique laughed, then, answered. "My men are going into town for some much needed rest. They will be enjoying the amusements of the city."

"Oh, they're 'painting the town red'," said Johnny, "like when sailors have been on board ship for too long."

Dominique raised an eyebrow. "They will be doing many things in town, but I do not think it will include painting," he said with a wink.

Dominique's whistle had done **more** **t**han send his men off for some **f**un. It had als**o** s**u**mmoned a porter to come e**s**cort the t**w**o boys into town.

The porter was about fifteen years old and dressed in faded clothing from the 1800's. His white apron made him look like a stock boy or a bar keeper. He flashed a broad smile at the boys and bowed low, his black wavy hair falling in his eyes.

"This is young servant Roberts," Dominique said. "He will b**e** your **a**ttendant for the day and will answer any questions you might hav**e**. But we must hurry now. There are some here who will not be happy with your arrival."

Dominique spoke in French to Roberts, giving him strict instructions in regards to the boys in his charge. Dominique handed him a large purple crystal. Then Roberts ran away. Dominique turned to the boys. "You must be careful here and do everything you are told. There ar**e** many dangers. It is not like the place you come from. All newcomers here are immediately sold into slavery until they have wor**k**ed off their **d**ebt to the Consortium. So you must act and behave as if you have been here a long time. Servant Roberts will help you to know what to do. **I** must go now."

Roberts returned with a horse and wagon that was like nothing they had ever seen before. The horse wore **c**lothing a**s** if it was human, and Roberts spoke with it as if it **c**ould understand him. The wagon was even stranger. It had no wheels, but an unseen force held it suspende**d** in the air. As it moved along, small s**p**arks appeared where the unseen wheels should have been. The seating area looked like a cross between an old fashioned carriage and a boat.

As Roberts brought the carriage to a stop in front of the bo**y**s, he pointed the crystal at the base of it. The crystal glowed briefly, then, dimmed as the carriage lowered onto the wooden deck.

Roberts smiled. "Step in!" he said in a thick French accent.

Johnny and Bo looked at each other. "Wow, what is this thing?" Johnny asked as he stepped into the strange coach. It rocked slightly as if resting on a large cushion. Bo was next, and soon the two were seated in style.

"It is called an assemblage," Roberts explained. "Its power comes from the beacon. It is comprised of many things. Part is made of a boat and part from energy. But our friend 'ere is the real source of its power." Roberts took a seat at the front of the coach and pointed to the horse. "This is Monsieur Collins."

The horse turned and nodded to the boys.

Roberts pointed the crystal towards the carriage base again. The crystal lit up, and the assemblage began to rise. Roberts spoke in French to Monsieur Collins, and the horse started with a lurch down the street. His harness was made of the same energy as the missing wheels, but he had no bridle. "Please take us to Goldie's place," The young man said with his thick accent.

They drove along the wharf amid a menagerie of colorful ships and people. It was as if time had completely stopped in this place, merging with past and future. Some men tinkered on the engines of their modern speed boats while others raised the billowing sails on their sleek schooners. The place was an abstract living museum of time.

Old Cajun women called from an open air market selling fresh flowers and wine. An old blind man sat at the corner of a store playing a squeezebox and asking for money. Others wore their stores on their backs with charms dangling from makeshift racks across their shoulders.

Younger women sat with small carts brimming with baked goods and homemade candies. Venders had colorful striped awnings suspended from the buildings to cover their precious goods. They sold colorful rugs, clothing, bric-a-brac, and carved wooden trinketx. Anything a person could imagine or need was sold there.

A commotion on the road ahead caused a road block, and the assemblage came to an abrupt stop. Robertz climbed down, pulled Collins head down, and whispered into his ear.

Johnny and Bo's attention was drawn to a local auction at the side of the road. A man dressed in a long cloak emerged with a line of chained people trudging behind him. He climbed up on a platform and pointed to the people next to him. "These have a duty to pay their debt to our illustrious society!" he yelled. "We would implore you to purchase as generously as you can. All of these will serve honorably, taking upon them your name for five years hence."

Johnny felt sick inside. "They're selling people!" he whispered.

Roberts returned to the boys. "We must take another road," he whispered. "The Pahreefs have already been alerted to your coming. They are checking each assemblage that comes by."

Roberts motioned to Monsieur Collins, and he began backing up. Soon he pulled the odd assemblage down a side street. The horse's hooves clapped along on the narrow cobblestone street. On both sides were the old fashioned two and three storied Cajun homes typical of New Orleans. The balconies were filled with potted flowers spilling out over the intricate gold railings! Performers strummed their guitars and banjos on the street. Shop keepers and servants swept their porches while an occasional brawl broke out in the nearby taverns.

Soon the assemblage pulled into an open square in the middle of town. Tall trees stood within fenced areas around paved sidewalks. The street circled a park that was flanked by several large buildings. One looked like an old capitol building with a gold dome. Another had columned arched porches and several steps leading up to massive double doors. Next to it was a building made of red brick with white columns.

On each corner of the broad square was a bank or treasury guarded by armed men standing outside. The men wore dark blue uniforms and helmets with dark visors that completely covered their faces. When people approached, each person would hold up a cryztal to the guard who then nodded yes or no to allow them into the structure.

"This place gives me the creeps." Johnny whispered. Bo nodded without taking his eyes off of the guards.

The assemblage took them past the buildings and into the park. When the boys looked up, they saw a massive glass globe at the center of the park. It was an enormous structure. Inside, a glowing light like the sun pulsated in yellow and blue hues.

"What in the world is that?" Bo said.

Roberts slowed the assemblage and turned toward the boys. "It is The Beacon. All of the power within our civilization emerges from this point. It is the same force which powers the assemblages and all energies within Golden City." Roberts turned and told the horse to continue.

The horse trotted past houses and buildingx toward the far side of town until the assemblage pulled up in front of a tavern with a large sign out front that read, "Goldie's Place."

Two men sat conversing on the landing of the tavern. One was heavily covered with clothing and wore a hat to hide his appearance. The other man wore a bright red bow tie with a striped vest. Roberts stopped the assemblage, and pointed the crystal at the energy wheels, it lowered to the ground, and the two boys stepped out. As Johnny and Bo walked past the men, they could see that the one hiding his appearance was not human. It was a large wolf.

The boys followed Roberts into the lobby of the tavern. There they were met by an older man behind a registration desk wearing a strange cap on his head that looked like a bird sitting in a nest. He looked at the boys in astonishment. "Oh, I see you've arrived." He looked up at the strange hat on his head and then at the boys. With a smile he removed the hat. "Goldie's had us practicing for her new show." he ezplained. "Follow me quickly, please."

He took a key from the wall behind him and led the boys up a flight of stairs to the rooms on the second level. About three doors down, the man stopped and unlocked the door. "This room is right across from your parent's room. They are gone right now, but you'll see them soon."

The place was very old fashioned with two adjoining rooms. One was a small sitting room while the other contained two large beds. In the sitting room, a door led out onto a small balcony. Two large windows flanked the balcony door, and pictures of sailing ships graced the walls. As Johnny and Bo entered the room, Jack and Riley jumped to their feet.

"Where did you two disappear to?" Riley asked. Johnny looked at the floor then Bo interrupted. "We had a run in with those water pirates and well..."

"Ain't they cool?" Riley blurted. "I like the good ones."

"Yes, they are cool..." Bo tried to continue.

Riley interrupted, "Dominique Youx and his men brought us here in the most amazing boat ya ever did see."

"I know..." said Bo.

"They rowed underneath us and we rode on top, get it? They rowed and we rode. Hah, hah! That's a good one, huh?"

"Hey, Riley!" said Jack. "Why don't you give Bo a chance to talk?"

Riley stopped and looked at the others. "Well, what's wrong?" he asked.

Johnny looked up and opened his mouth as if to speak, then quietly sat on the bed, covering his face with his handz.

"Matie's gone," Bo said.

"What happened?" said Jack.

"It was the water pirates. We tried everything," Bo said. "They would have drowned us, too, but something made 'em leave. When it was all over, Matie was gone."

Johnny looked down at the floor as tears filled his reddened eyes. He couldn't speak.

Suddenly someone knocked at the door. Jack opened it to see Jim standing out in the hall. His eyes widened at the sight of the two lost boys. He ran to Johnny and threw his arms around his son. Johnny clung to Jim and sobbed.

Jim stepped back to look at his son, then he saw the look on Johnny's face. "What's wrong?" He looked around the room with concern. "Johnny... Where's Matie?"

Bo began to speak, but Johnny reached for his arm and stopped him.

Johnny wiped his eyes with his sleeve. "The water pirates got her, we tried..." His voice broke, then, he went on. "We dove in the water over and over, but she was just gone!"

Riley hit his fist on the bed. "Those stupid water pirates. They almost got me, too!"

Jim was completely devastated at his son's words, but he knew that Johnny was even more crushed about being responsible for losing his sister.

With tears in his eyes, he looked at Johnny and lifted his chin. "It's not your fault. You did the best you could. Matie's spirit will always be with us. We'll always be a family, and someday we'll see her again."

Johnny looked up at his father. "I thought you'd hate me

for this."

"Oh, no, don't ever think that, Johnny. Nothing here is normal. It's this place! I could never blame you, and I could never hate you. No matter what's happened, we love you."

Johnny looked in his father's eyes. "How am I ever going to tell Mom?"

"We'll both tell her," Jim assured. "But we can't tell her right now. She wouldn't understand. She's very ill."

"Is she gonna be OK?" Johnny asked.

"She'll be fine," Jim said with a reserved smile. "She's just not quite herself right now.

"She's a croonie!" Riley blurted.

Jim frowned at Riley, then continued. "The doctors aren't sure of that yet. We're still waiting."

"What's a croonie?" Johnny axked.

"Remember that bite on the back of your mother's neck? Well, here in the bayou, the curse causes some strange side effects."

"Like what?" Johnny asked.

Riley was trying hard to stifle a laugh.

"The fever makes your mother laugh at everything," Jim said. "When she's not laughing, she's singing, hence, the name 'Croonie'."

"Whoa!" said Bo. "I never heard of a Schneille bite doin' that to a person."

"It's strange, isn't it?" said Jim. "It's like everything here is all mixed up."

"So why don't they just give her some medicine or something?" Johnny asked.

"It's not that simple," Jim replied. "The restorative, as they call it, only stays good for a short time. After twenty-four hours, it spoils. It comes from a special plant called the Orbis vine and can only be harvested the day before a full moon. Your mother did get some of the medicine they had on hand, but it was getting weaker and weaker and beginning to spoil, so we are unsure as to whether or not it worked. We'll just have to wait and see."

"Well, that's stupid!" Johnny exclaimed. "That would mean that whoever gets bit has to wait a long time before they can get better, unless they get bit just before a full moon. So where is Mom now?"

"She's at a place they call the Revivory. It's like a hospital.
Laurabeth is staying with her. I just came back because they sent me word you were coming," Jim replied.

"So what happens if the medicine doesn't work?" Johnny asked.

Jim looked at the others. "Well, apparently some people never get better," he said. "The ones who don't get better end up living in the swamp like outcasts. They're considered to be crazy and live in a place called 'Crooner's Isle'."

Johnny's grief had turned to determination. So far this place had taken his sister and stranded his family, and now it threatened his mother, and he wasn't going to let it win.

"Dominique Youx warned us to be careful here. Do you know why?" Johnny asked.

Jim looked at his son then at the others. "Yes, I do know why. Back at Maison Rouge, Officer Morgan told me that some people didn't want the curse fixed. Here in this place I'm beginning to see why. Apparently, this culture has developed parallel to our own. They've created a type of government that we don't understand. Did you see the crystals the people were holding?"

"Yeah, what are they?" Bo asked.

Jim spoke softly. "Dominique told me how they work. They are a type of identification for everyone in the bayou. You can't go anywhere **or d**o anything without the**m**. **A**s soon as one is activated, it lights up, and apparently alerts those in authority as to a person's location and what they are doing."

Johnny frowned. "We saw some of that on the way here. **T**hey were selling people, too. **T**hey said that all the newcome**rs** owed a debt to their society and that they would be slaves for fi**v**e **y**ears."

Jim nodded. "T**h**at's why we need to be careful here. We have to blend in and look as normal a**z** possible, like we're a part of all of this."

Johnny leaned toward his **F**ather. "Dad, we saw something else that was strange. T**h**ere was a man by the **f**ront door that looked like a wolf!"

"**Y**es, I know," said Jim. "I didn't believe it at first either, but they are all **p**art of the curse, too. They are people who have the instinct and quality **of** animals. Marie told us all about it. Pierre Laffite's family have **b**ecome like them. They are all hummin**g**birds. Matie's little birds were the o**n**es that led us through the bayou. The people here call them 'Maroos'. It's in reference to bei**ng** maro**o**ned. But they are still people just like you and m**e**."

"Dad, do you know where my backpack is? I lost it back at the fort." Johnny asked.

"Dominique Youx and his men had it for a while," Jim replied. "They examined the things in it, but gave it back. It's in my room." Jim sent **R**ile**y** and Jack to **r**etrieve it. Soon the two returned with the pack and handed it to Johnny who immediately emptied its contents one by one on the bed. Then he rehearsed to his father the things the group had discovered.

"**M**arie gave us this piece **of** wood," Johnny said, unwrapping the red bundle. "We know the key fits with it somehow. It's like my cry**p**tograms at home. It says *true intent* on it, too. We figu**r**ed that they **m**ight have used Jean's ship, the

Intent, to hide the treasure. So we've gotta find that ship and its hidden cargo! It's the key to all of this. Marie said that Captain Edwards warned that if anyone messed with that ship and its cargo, they would be cursed by God. If we can find the right ship maybe we can get the hidden cargo to the right place and end the curse."

Jim held the small piece of wood in his hands and turned it over and over. Then he looked at all of the boys. "I'd like to talk to Johnny alone," he said. "Could you give us a little time? We've all had a hard day." The others left the room and closed the door.

"Johnny, I couldn't say this with the others here, but we think your uncle Ken is alive." Jim pulled the four coins from his pocket. "We found his old camp. He was also attacked by the water pirates and left these and his journal there." Jim handed the coins to his son. With hesitation Johnny took them.

"You've got all of the coins now!" Jim said. "But you can't let anyone know, not even your friends. As long as the people here think the coins are still lost, they won't hurt you. But if they know you have all of them, they'll do anything to get them from you.

"You know that I didn't believe in the curse at first, but eventually I had to start believing. I want to protect you and the family, and I'd handle all of this if I could. But it's not up to me. Marie said that the curse could only end with the last male Laffite. Johnny, that's you."

Johnny's heart pounded. He knew that his father's words were true. Suddenly an unusual warmth began to swell up inside of him. "I know you're right, Dad, but I'm just a kid. I don't know what to do."

Jim put his arm around his son. "Just follow the voice inside your heart. It hasn't led you wrong yet. You'll know what to do when the time comes."

333

35
Unsettled Waters

The heat of the afternoon sun made the sweltering humidity of the bayou almost unbearable for the three stranded crooks. Like pirates plundering the booty off of a forgotten ship, they now prepared to set off into the bayou.

Ratcliffe's plan was a simple one: to gather the needed provisions that would see him through the swamp, while searching for the treasure and the kids who had that map! His selfish need to find the treasure consumed everything, and the children were just one of the annoying things standing between him and his obsession.

For Randy and Palmer, the need to find the children represented redemption, a chance for them to right the wrongs they had done to the Leavitt family.

As they finished loading the wooden boat, Ratcliffe examined his waterstained map of the bayou. He was impatient to get going. The thoughts of the golden treasure consumed his every waking hour.

Palmer's new-found freedom elicited feelings of appreciation towards everything and everyone around him, everyone except Ratcliffe, that is. He eagerly helped the others with a positive attitude and all he wanted now was to find a way out of this place and face what he had ahead of him. Even, if it meant doing some time in prison.

Randy's motives were altogether different. With a sense of betrayal at the trickery that had implicated him in Ratcliffe's plot, his thoughts were of one thing: he desperately wanted to get away from this manipulative monster. Randy knew that he had been duped into making a stupid decision that had, more than likely, permanently destroyed his friendship with Jim. More than this, he was angry at his own stupidity for being tricked into trusting a beast like Ratcliffe and thinking that Jim had betrayed him. All he could think of now was that he needed to get to Jim and set thingx right, perhaps he could even warn him of Ratcliffe's plans.

Randy's thoughts were interrupted by noises back at the fort. Suddenly as if thousands of people were dexcending on the island, sounds echoed across the bayou. Someone yelled out orders, while metal clanked. Then all at once a cannon exploded. "Duck!" yelled Randy as a cannonball whizzed overhead.

All three men huddled on the sand behind the wooden boat. "What's going on? Palmer asked. "Maybe they're mad that we took their supplies."

Randy's eyes searched in the direction of the fort. The noises were very real and so was the cannonball they had just dodged. Suddenly, he looked around and noticed a change. While they had been busy loading the boat, the humid air of the bayou had given way to a thick mist, an almost tangible substance with a greenish hue as if the deep green waters of the bayou had vaporized into this ominous mist hanging in the air around them.

By now Ratcliffe noticed it, too. He stood up and sniffed the air. "What is it?" he said, crinkling his nose at the putrid smell.

The smells within the bayou weren't always pleasant, but they were recognizable. Like the damp smell of the water mixed with dirt, or rotting vegetation, or even the sweet smell of an occasional flower. But this smell was all together different. Not only did it smell different, it felt different. It was an ominous smell. It offended the nose and sent a chill down the spine. It was the smell of death!

As the noises from the fort became louder, the three men knew they were in desperate danger. "We've got to get out of here!" Ratcliffe ordered, looking towards the fort.

"He's right!" Randy said, pushing the boat acroxs the sand, toward the water's edge. Then he stopped and noticed that the river was also different. The little tidepool where they had found the boat was completely gone, and through the hazy mist he could see that the water's course had completely changed.

"Something's wrong!" Randy whispered as Palmer neared his side. The two looked over the misty lake as they pushed the boat closer to the water.

Ratcliffe stood watching from the beach, completely frozen, his nasty little eyes bulging like ping pong balls, as his face twitched with vague patterns of fear. He looked over his shoulder at the noises behind him and began shaking uncontrollably. There wasn't an ounce of courage in the pitiful little man. His only confidence came through abusing and bullying others.

Randy noticed Ratcliffe, frozen on the sand. "Ratcliffe, snap out of it!" he yelled. "We have to leave now!"

Suddenly, the trees behind Ratcliffe, rattled violently. Ratcliffe's body shook out of control. He slowly mustered enough stamina to turn toward the bushes. Several foul-looking pirates emerged with drawn swords. These were not the feared water pirates that had attacked the earlier venturers, but real pirates made of flesh and blood.

The toothless rabble laughed as they surrounded the fear-stricken Ratcliffe. One pirate held a rat in his hand and threw it in Ratcliffe's face as the entire band erupted into evil laughter. Ratcliffe's fear completely overtook him as he collapsed into total unconsciousness.

Randy and Palmer watched from the shoreline. Palmer's anger with Ratcliffe gave way to pity, and he began to run toward him.

"No!" Randy yelled grabbing Palmer's arm. "We won't be of any use to him if they get us, too!"

Hearing Randy, the pirates turned in unison toward their new victims. The two men pushed the boat as hard as they could till it splashed into the waiting river. They plunged into the water and dove into the wooden boat. Their attackers stood waving their swords and laughing boisterously as if drunken with power.

Randy and Palmer watched the shore through the noxious mist. They saw Ratcliffe lying in a heap on the ground amid the foul pirates. There was nothing they could do to help the man now. His fate was sealed.

Randy and Palmer's quick escape had left them oarless. They drifted aimlessly on the unsettled waters, traveling through the thick foreboding mist. As the two gazed through the green fog, they saw and heard the images from the past, as if time had somehow stood still in this mysterious place. Smugglers unloaded their wares on the banks of the river, and an occasional fight broke out among the high spirited thieves. Gunshots rang out amid the clamor of swords. Then a woman's scream sent chills down their spines.

Small log cabins dotted the shores along the river. A woman washed clothes on the rocks as her children played by the water's edge. Images of these earlier settlers flashed through the mists. They were the long forgotten families of the pirates who had once made their homes in this forbidden no-man's land.

The site was intriguing to say the very least. It was as if Randy and Palmer were a part of a historical movie playing out before their eyes. The mist carried an ominous feeling as if everything that had ever happened in the mysterious swampland was being repeated over and over again like an old record player with its needle stuck. Somehow time and all its rules had been suspended here.

"It's amazing. It's like nothing has ever changed here," Randy said.

"Do you think they know we're here?" Palmer said, looking through the mist.

"If we can see them, they can probably see us!" Randy replied. "It's like time has just stood still and all come together right at this spot."

"Do you think it's real?" Palmer asked.

It was painfully apparent to the two men that this curse had some very nasty realities that had now interfered with their plans.

"How long do you think this thing will last?" Palmer said, watching the shoreline.

"Nothing's normal here," Randy replied. "It could last forever."

Randy shifted uncomfortably, "I'm more conxerned about getting to those kids. What if they're caught in this mist, too?"

Palmer sat thinking. "All right," he said. "I know we came out here to get the map and the treasure, but that was before I realized what Ratcliffe had done to us. I don't want to be a part of hurting Jim and his family any more."

"I agree!" Randy replied. "Ratcliffe tricked both of us."

Now both men sat quietly thinking, dealing with their own guilt. Finally Palmer broke the silence. "So what are we going to do about it?"

Randy peered off into the mist. "We've got to help Jim and his family, and find that treaxure for them, even if we lose our own lives in the process."

Palmer stretched his long arms over his head and

smiled. "That sounds just about right," he said. "It'll feel good to be helping someone for a change, instead of destroying them. I've been seeing people suffer long enough because of me."

Randy longed to be free of the chains of guilt he'd placed himself in. He admired Palmer's courage to change and hoped to be able to do the same.

This place, this mist, seemed as if it had a tangible grip on the two men, as if every thought and emotion were exaggerated and could instantly come alive in this place. In this atmosphere where feelings became tangible, it was easy to see how men could become mad with the hunger for gold. This moaning mist had now brought each of the men to a realization of every weakness within themselves.

As the little pirogue meandered over the restless waters, the echoes of the past increased. Images of battles between pirates and British soldiers flashed in the dixtance. A large pirate ship hovered in the water beside the little boat. It was a sleek hybrid vessel with enormous sails and a long deck. Suddenly a voice yelled, "Men adrift!" A makeshift rope and wooden ladder came rolling down from the side of the tall ship. A pirate descended with a knife between his teeth and headed straight for the two men.

"Now I'm sure they know we're here." Randy whispered.

The dirty pirate stepped aboard the wooden pirogue, making it rock from side to side. He adeptly adjusted his balance. It was obvious he was used to such things. He reached for the knife in his teeth. Smiling wide with a toothless grin, he passed the knife from hand to hand, then, swung the knife toward the two men. Both men flinched at the pirate's half hearted attempt to scare them. The pirate laughed like a devil and stashed the knife in a small scabbard at his side. From up in the ship, laughter echoed as a hundred other pirates watched the exchange.

"Bring them aboard the *Hotspir*!" A deep voice commanded. The pirate nodded toward the two men, urging them to climb the ladder.

With hesitation, Randy and Palmer began up the ladder with the pirate close behind them. As they neared the deck of the ship a crowd of unkempt ruffians met them.

The unruly band was a frightening mixture of cultures. Some wore the vestiges of a bygone era while others were dressed in modern clothing. Some looked as if they had conquered the Spanish Main, and others wore oriental attire. Most of them seemed to wear whatever they could get their dirty hands on. No matter how different their clothing was, they all had one thing in common. All were heavily armed. Their vast assortment of weaponry was staggering. Pistols, daggers, and sabers hung at their sides.

Murmurs broke out among the rowdy crew as they made way for a man to come through the crowd. The pirate that stood before them was tall with deep brown eyes and a long nose. Unlike the others he was neatly dressed and carried an air of familiarity about him. As Randy examined the captain, he suddenly realized that his clothing was exactly like the clothes that Johnny had worn to the ball.

The pirate turned and spoke in French to his men while Randy turned to Palmer.

"He looks just like Pierre Laffite!" Randy said, not realizing the words had come from his own mouth.

The entire crew became deadly silent. The leader turned to the two helpless men. "I see we have caught some of Clayton's spies!"

36

The Revivory

A restless atmosphere settled over the Golden City. Jim left for the Revivory, to check on Kate while the others waited at Goldie's place.

The ride to the Revivory was just like before in the unusual assemblage. Jim watched the surroundings along the way with increased curiosity, trying to learn more about this unusual place.

Dominique Youx seemed to have a unique power here

as if all the rules didn't apply to him. He had already given Jim an assemblage with a horse and house servant to drive it, as well as the needed crystal to allow him in and of out any place he needed to go. Even Jim's clothing seemed to fit in with the majority of the people since he still wore the old fashioned party clothes he had worn the night of the grand ball.

The tall white Revivory loomed ominous in the distance. All Jim could think of was Kate and the news of Matie's loss. How would he ever tell Kate, especially in her current state? As Jim stepped out of the odd contraption, an eerie feeling filled the air. He anxiously took a deep breath and began up the stairs into the Revivory.

The lobby was spacious and filled with unfamiliar furnishings and beingz. Several maroo's conversed and walked about normally as if they were like any other human. Some of the people looked normal except that their clothing was unique to this place. Some wore common clothing; others extravagantly feathered cloaks. Many wore striped jeweled leggings like pirates, but their shirts were woven of heavy burlap and ruffled to ad a dash of flair.   Now and then a waterman would walk past followed by a cleaning person with a mop and bucket.

Jim crossed the lobby and headed towards a large assistance area. The area was unique, made of a circular platform with desks around the outer edge. On the inside, several Maroos along with others assisted those in the lobby.

A very proper looking bird watched Jim approach.

"How may I help you?" she asked in a high pitched tone.

"I'm here to see my wife, Kate Leavitt," Jim said.

The Maroo thumbed through what looked like a ship's log and soon found Kate's name. "Sir, you'll have to excuse me while I get prior authorization. Do you have your crystal?" The

342

woman reached for a hose among several others that was suspended in the center of the platform and spoke into it, calling for someone to return to the assistance area.

Jim reached into his pocket, pulled out the crystal that Dominique Youx had given him, and handed it to the woman. She placed it on a box-like contraption, and it began to glow. The woman looked at a liquid silver screen before her. It grew cloudy at first then clear images and words appeared on it. First it gave the name of the owner of the crystal and then their race.

The Maroo stopped and looked at Jim. The feathers on her back began to rise. "Your information is not correct! Your eyes are not the right color!" she squawked.

Jim smiled. "Well, that's odd," he said. "My eyes have always been this color. Are you sure your system isn't malfunctioning?" The strange bird punched several maintenance codes into her system. Immediately the screen flashed a warning.

Jim looked uneasily around the room. Suddenly a doctor entered the platform and went straight over to the woman's device. In an instant he punched in some numbers that alleviated the problem. The doctor smiled at Jim. "Our systems are malfunctioning because there is a storm coming. I'm very sorry if this has inconvenienced you in any way. How may I help you?"

Jim looked at the doctor and explained his wife's condition. The doctor turned to the bird. "Please page this man's assistant as soon as possible. I do not wish for him to be inconvenienced any further!"

The Maroo's feathers again stood up on her neck as she immediately began scrambling through her things. Soon she reached for the hose device and then with a hollow whistling sound she alerted the entire facility to an incoming announcement.

"Doctor K. Daver, please come to the assistance desk, Doctor K. Daver!" Then she ended the announcement with another whistle.

The wall behind her was filled with hundreds of tiny bells, each attached to a type of wire. Under each bell was the name of a person or department. Just then a little bell rang. The bird quickly flipped a small wooden switch beside the bell, then again spoke into the hose.

"Your patient's husband is here. He wishes to see her. Would you please send down an escort?" The Maroo replaced the hose and then she turned to Jim. "Your escort will be here shortly. If you will be seated, they will come and get you soon."

Jim turned to find a seat. The room was filled with a variety of furnishings from all time periods. There was long gothic type benches covered with cushions along with delicate French furnishings. Surrounding these was an indoor garden with large palm trees and vines climbing the walls. Good luck charms hung within the branches of the palm trees, placed there by concerned loved ones as an omen for good health. At the front entrance, stood an old gray squirrel with a cart full of charms. People crowded around her, clamoring to purchase the precious items in an attempt to bring health to their loved ones.

Jim watched as each person held up their crystal to pay for the items. Then they took them straight to a nearby palm tree. After kissing the charm they said a type of prayer over it and hung it in the tree.

Most of the seating in the lobby was completely taken, except for one very large conspicuous throne type chair. The people leaned against the walls or walked around, but oddly no one went near the large chair.

As Jim began towards it, there was a loud disturbance near the front door. Everyone in the lobby stood to see what it was. A young man ran to the information desk as everyone

344

feverishly began running to and fro.

A man bumped into Jim and turned to him. "It's Overseer Draconis. I believe he's injured his foot and is coming!" The man's eyes were wide with fear, and he scrambled into a nearby room.

A large reptile Maroo entered, surrounded by attendants. The Maroo wore a long black cape that hung about his shoulders and covered most of a red tunic he wore beneath. With each step it grimaced in pain. Then it would hit one of the attendants, throwing them to the floor. The attendant would instantly return to his place to assist the large reptile just in time to be hit again. The Overseers growl was deep and muffled. Everyone in the room began bowing as if worshipping this beast. Jim acknowledged its presence with a nod then turned to sit in the massive chair.

A young woman reached for his arm. "Mr. Leavitt, I am here to take you to your wife," she said, then urged him away from the lobby. As Jim followed the woman down a large corridor, she leaned and whispered to him. "That overseer must not see you! You cannot bring attention to yourself in such a manner. You almost sat in his chair!"

Jim's eyes widened. The woman pulled him aside into a hidden corridor and whispered as she looked around. "Listen, I am part of the defiance, and so is the doctor who helped you before. You must do exactly what we say!"

Jim followed the young woman till he arrived at Kate's room. She opened the door and ushered Jim inside. The doctor from the front desk was waiting for him.

Jim ran to Kate's side and kissed her cheek while she continued sleeping. Laurabeth stood near her side. "How is she doing?" Jim asked.

The doctor smiled. "She seems to have gotten through the worst of it. It looks as if the restorative has worked, but it will take some time for the side effects to wane."

Jim nodded and held Kate's hand. "Who was that Maroo down in the lobby, and why did everyone get so upset when he came in?"

The doctor's face became sullen. "You are very lucky we pulled you out of there when we did. That overseer would have had your life for sitting in his chair, and the assistant at the desk almost discovered you as well."

"Who are these Overseers?" Jim asked.

The doctor put his hand to his chin. "You have not been acclimated yet, have you? Most new initiates are immediately acclimated to our society and given a space of time to learn the rules of conduct here. Dominique Youx had so little time to get you out of danger, you were left uninformed.

"I am a dissenter, as is the escort who brought you to this room. Dominique Youx is the leader of this appendage of the Revolutionaries of the Defiance. We have a small order here, yet we are very well organized."

"So you don't agree with the government here?" Jim axked.

The doctor smiled. "I can see I am going to have to tell you everything. Here in our civilization, we have grown as a parallel society to your own, the United States of America. But we have evolved quite differently. Our governing factors are very different. Here people are assigned what they will become and do.

"Originally our government consisted of an Alliance of eight men, all very good men. But as the curse grew, so did the number of inhabitants in the bayou. The differing peoples demanded representation. Because the Maroos were the larger portion of our people and when the original members of the Alliance died out or were assassinated, a subset of Maroos took over. They're called the Overseers. They are all of the reptile persuasion and very intelligent and domineering. But they are also merciless. They have no compassion whatsoever and believe everyone else in the bayou is inferior to them.

"They control everything here. They developed the crystal regeneration system which uses the beacon for its power. By this they are able to control everyone and everything. No one makes a move here without complete monitorization. Every time a crystal is activated, they know exactly where a person is and what they are doing.

"The dissenters have almost all been killed off by the Overseers barbaric rituals. Because this is the capitol center of their regime, there are very few of us left here. But there are many more dissenters still in the bayou, hidden and working together to overcome this scourge and regain our freedoms.

"The Overseer you saw downstairs is very old and a Governeer over this Revivory. He is one of the Masters of the Consortium. That is why his seat remains empty in the lobby. It is a means of reminding the people that they must obey or be destroyed."

"So if they monitor everyone through the crystalz, how did Dominique get that crystal for me to use?" Jim asked.

"It is quite simple," the doctor explained. "Your crystal is forged. Dominique Youx has access to anything he needs in the bayou. He still is a pirate, you know, and quite capable of acquiring whatever may be needed for this cause.

"You do need to be careful though, especially with that crystal, as there are many eyes watching, and there are informants who cannot be trusted. You must be careful who you talk to and what you say. The people here have been conditioned to turn in any dissenters, or they themselvez can lose their lives for collaboration with the Revolutionaries."

Kate stirred a bit, hummed under her breath, then turned over and went back to sleep. Laurabeth gently pulled the blanket over her shoulders and turned to Jim. "If the things they're saying are true, then who can we trust?"

The doctor continued, "Here you have already met a few of the dissenters. But where you're staying at Goldie's place, there is an escape route for those who are being sought out by the Overseers.

"Roberts is also one of our representatives, along with several shopkeepers and businessmen in town. All of these are the ones who you must rely on for protection. They are the only ones in whom you can put your trust.

"There is also something very important that you must understand. We know who you are. You are Laffite's by right and by blood. But here, that is considered a crime. You see, the ancient texts speak of a male blood descendant that will crush the corrupt Alliance of Overseers. The Overseers will kill you and your family if they get a chance. They do not wish for the curze to be ended or the Alliance to be dissolved because it is the curse that gives them their power. Your family has put their power and authority at risk."

348

37
The Moaning Mist

Riley jumped on the bed as Johnny and the others went through the things in Johnny's pack. Suddenly a knock was heard at the door. Johnny stuffed the things in his pack as Bo opened the door a crack to see who it was.

"I'm sorry to interrupt you," said the man from the front desk. "A mist warning's been issued. You'll need to make sure that you batten down the hatches."

Riley jumped off the bed. "What's a mist warning and how are we supposed to batten down our hatches?"

"The moaning mist is a great storm," the man said. "It brings time and death with it. You need to make sure that all your doors and windows are locked. Don't let anyone go out. Anyone caught out of doors during the mist is in great danger."

"What do you mean it brings time and death?" Johnny asked.

The man responded uneasily, "In the mist, time is suspended. Basically, there is none. Instead, all time is as one there. Those who are dead rise again with the mist. They're pulled out of their time and deposited into ours. But the mist also brings grief and great change. It's when the curse of the Maroos comes out.

"The mist used to only come just once a year, but lately we've seen it two to three times a month. We never know who it will change or who it will take. But there are always newcomers. The Defauns are saying that a liberator will come with the next mist. Their foresight has made all of the Overseers very nervous indeed. The Overseers are collecting all of the newcomers for interrogation just to make sure."

"What's a Defaun?" asked Jack.

"It's the ones that the curse has gifted. They live within their own portion of the bayou and stay to themselves. The Overseers are afraid of them because the Defauns know the future and can hear a person's thoughts. In that way they know all about the decepxons of the Overseers. They live in Pyros, the city of fire."

The man went to the window and opened it, reached for the outer shutters and closed them, then locked the inner window.

"Thank you, we'll be sure to keep everything battened down, like you've said," Johnny replied. The man gave a single nod and left the room.

Riley ran to the window and peeked through the cracks in the wooden shutters. "It sure looks like a storm out there, but why do you think they call it the moaning mist?"

Bo grabbed Riley's shirt and pulled him away from the window. "Didn't you hear the guy? He said every time the storm comes, there's a lot of dead people that come with it. They probably do a lot of moanin'!" Bo laughed as he watched Riley's eyes get big.

"I gotta see this!" Riley said as he ran back to the window. Bo shook his head, "You're askin' for it, Riley. That man said it's not safe."

Riley ignored Bo and opened the window and shutters.

Now all of the boys surrounded the open window. Far in the distance they could see a greenish haze gathering. The wind whipped and whistled through the empty streets below.

"Shut that window!" A voice boomed behind them.

The hotel manager stood in the open doorway. "Curiosity killed the cat!" the man said. "You are jeopardizing everyone in this entire establishment. Didn't Mr. Krill tell you to batten down the hatches?" He walked over to the window and closed everything up again. Then he turned to Riley and grabbed his chin. "There are things amiss out there that you do not want to grapple with."

"I don't get what the big deal is. It's just a storm!" Riley said.

The man put his nose in front of **R**iley's and looked him sternly in the eye. "Your indignant posture is going to bring ruin on this entire crew. Only an idiot thinks he can endure the mist. It carries every <u>v</u>ile wish and thought there is, not to mention the death and sickness it brings, as if the Maroos aren't enough!" The large man raised an e<u>y</u>ebrow. "Just make sure it doesn't happen again. The storms here are deadl<u>y</u>!" The man left the room and slammed the door <u>s</u>hut.

Bo tur<u>n</u>ed and flipped Riley in the head. "Man, yo<u>u</u> could have gotten us all <u>in</u> trouble. You do what you're told from now on!" Bo plopped on the bed and picked up a book from a nearby table and be<u>g</u>an looking through it. Johnny stood by the locked window, wondering what was outside.

"This place is just plain boring," Riley said. "There's nothing to do here. We're like a bunch of prisoners all locked up, and we can't <u>g</u>o anywher<u>e</u>!"

Johnny grinned at Riley. "Hey, if we can't go outside, let's go downstairs. We haven't seen much of this <u>p</u>lace yet, and as long as we're inside, I don't think we'll be breakin<u>g</u> any rules."

"All right," said Ja<u>c</u>k, slapping Rile<u>y</u> on the back. "Besides, I <u>h</u>ear the food here is great."

As the four boys rom<u>p</u>ed carelessly down the stairs, Johnny remembered his backpack. He returned to the room, and heard the wind whistlin<u>g</u> through the closed window. Green dust blew throug<u>h</u> the cracks. Johnny reached for his pack and threw it over his shoulder then slammed the door behind him. He took a deep breath of fr<u>e</u>sh air from the hallway then headed downstairs.

The restaurant was full of all types of people and looked just like an old western saloon. A large stage with red and gold drapes graced the end of the room. An enormous balcony surrounded the entire place, filled with people clamoring for food and entertainment. Near the stage, private balcony bozes accommodated the upper crust of this society.

Below the balcony on the main floor sat several more tables and chairs. An old fashioned bar ran along the inner wall that had an enormous mirror behind it with mermaids painted on each side. A man strummed the banjo as he stood by the piano. By his side stood an older bearded man with a squeeze box that wheezed out a tune each time the man played it. The pianist was a Maroo of particular interest. He was a lynx dressed in a flashy purple suit. He used all four paws to play a lively tune.

Excitement filled the air as the four boys sat down at a table near the bar. Suddenly a very large golden heron stepped out on stage, flamboyantly dressed in flapper clothes from the 1920's. Long dangling earrings hung at the sides of her head along with a set of long beads that hung loosely around her thin neck. Her dress was shimmering gold with a white feather boa trim.

"Now folks...," she began, "We don't want to let that old mist dampen your spirits. So we've got a rip roaring show for ya'll tonight." She pointed at the band. "And just to be sure we start off with a bang the wild cats are here to give us their very best." She made a wide bow to the band, and the musicians began playing a rousing song.

"What'll ya have?" a waiter asked, leaning over the boys.

"I'll have the steak and a salad," Jack said.

"Yeah, me too!" said Riley, "And I'll have an order of

that zombie juice too." The waiter ruffled Riley's red hair. "Sorry kid, ya ain't old enough for that!" Riley scrunched his nose and rolled his eyes with disappointment.

Bo piped up, "Can I have a sandwich?"

"Sure", the waiter said. "We have ham or buccaneer barbecue. What 'ell it be?"

"The barbecue sounds great," Bo replied.

The waiter turned to Johnny. Johnny's face was white and a sick feeling came over him. He hesitated a moment as everyone waited for him to order.

"I like steak," he said, biting his lip. "But were those steaks once Maroo people?"

The waiter now broke into uncontrolled laughter, "Steaks!" the man yelled, laughing, "People! That's a good one!" he said, slapping Johnny on the back. "No, we ain't been servin' any people here lately. 'Cept the ones who come here ta eat!"

"Whew!" Johnny said, as the others in the room stared at him. "Hey, I didn't want to be a cannibal," he whispered loudly, gritting his teeth with embarrassment.

The man composed himself and explained. "All our beef is shipped in from Texas. We ain't allowed to serve any meat that comes from the bayou. It's offensive to the Maroos."

"That's good!" Johnny sighed, "But I still think I'll just have a salad."

"Good choice. Do you all want chickory root beer with that?" The waiter asked.

"Sure," the boys replied as they began to watch the show again.

Up on the stage the heron was singing a song as her long legx wobbled from side to side. "Let's hear it for Goldie!" a Maroo heckler yelled from the back of the room.

Now Goldie began singing a pirate song as several

colorful parrots appeared on the stage behind her. Each had an eye patch and a scarf with an earring. They spread their feathers in a colorful display behind her. She picked one up and sang to it as it sat on her feathered finger.

As the curious parrot spread its wings in Goldie's hand, it looked as if she were holding an enormous fan. Then in a synchronized display of fluttering wings, the conclave of parrots began flying and quickly took positions in the audience where they all began singing in reverie about the days of being pirates and what a joyous time it was. Goldie joined them, cantering into the audience, her dress swinging from side to side. Soon, the entire room burst into singing with them.

The waiter approached the boys and placed their food on the table. "Isn't the show just great?" he said.

Johnny was unsure how to respond to the unusual entertainment. "Well, it sure takes your mind off of the storm!" he said.

As the song ended, Goldie returned to the stage and announced the next number. "Tonight we have a special surprise--the debut of my newest star. As y'all know I'm always looking for some new talent, and tonight I've found the very best. Let's all give a golden welcome to Miss La Petite Madeline."

As the crowd clapped, the curtains opened. A swing descended from above. Upon it, was a lovely little girl dressed in colorful flowers from head to toe.

As the new-found star began to sing, Johnny looked up at the stage, spellbound. He recognized that voice! "Matie!" yelled Johnny. The music came to a grinding stop.

"Who said that?" The heron squawked. The flower-covered star slid off the swing, jumped off the stage and ran through the audience straight toward Johnny.

"Johnny!" she yelled as the two hugged in a flood of

354

tearz.

Goldie motioned for the band to play a tune to occupy the audience. Johnny looked at his once-lozt sister. "We thought you were dead, that the water pirates got you. What happened?"

Matie's eyes were big. "They did get me. I thought I was going to die. Then all of a sudden something scooped me out of the water, and Goldie rescued me!"

"So that's what it was," said Johnny. "I remember a splash and something flapping in the water, but there was just too much going on, and I couldn't get to you." Johnny hugged his little sister then adjusted a flower in her hair. "Hey, Mat, when I thought you were dead, I really found out just how much I love you. You're a pretty cool little sister. But don't ever make us worry like that again! You got that?"

Matie smiled and kissed him on the cheek then left the table. To the boys' amazement she returned to the stage and began singing again. The room was absolutely silent as she sang about the treasure of sunshine on the golden meadow.

The night progressed with fun and song till the kids finally retired to their rooms in the early morning hours. The night had been an exciting one to say the least. Now that Matie was alive and well, everyone slept peacefully, completely unaware of the events taking place around them.

The storm had come and passed, leaving destruction throughout the bayou. The streets outside now bustled with cleaning crews. The Pahreefs scrambled to round up any newcomers deposited into this time by the unusual mist. In the streets others ran out of their houses screaming at the discovery that the storm had taken some of their loved ones.

Bo lay snoring loudly with the covers over his head. Riley occasionally twitched and talked in his sleep. On the other hand, Johnny slept more soundly than he had for days.

The thoughts of losing his sister no longer haunted his dreams. Instead he dreamed of his little sister covered in flowers and singing a song.

Matie slept alone across the hall in her parent's room. Suddenly something tapped at the shuttered window. After a few minutes the same thing tapped at the boys' shutter as well. Jack woke up and stumbled to the window to see what it was.

Johnny stirred as Jack reached for the window. "Wait. Don't open it." Johnny said. Instantly a blood curling scream came from Matie's room.

The two boys raced for the door and scrambled out into the hallway. There they saw poor little Matie standing in the hall in her night gown sobbing. There was no mistake, it was her. But she had changed.

Now more masculine screams could be heard from inside the boys' room. Johnny and Jack rushed back to their open door just to discover that the same misfortune that had awakened Matie, had overcome Riley and Bo as well. All three were now full blown Maroo's.

Matie was a cute little porcupine complete with quills all tied up in a bow on the top of her head. Bo was a large black bear, who looked like a circus animal all dressed in his fancy suit from the ball and Riley's red hair suited his new appearance of a fiery red fox.

Johnny's attention turned from the three Maroos to the racket outside and he went to the window and opened it.

Instantly one of Miss Honey's children came dashing in the open window. "Mmmm yyyyyou mmmmmmust llllleave nnnnow!" the little bird hummed in a demanding tone. "Nnnnnoooo tiiiimmmmme to eeexpllllainnnne!"

Johnny turned to the others and shushed them so he could hear. Everyone got quiet to listen. "Theyrrrrr're commmmming for yyyyyou!" the little bird warned.

356

"Something's wrong," Bo growled. His new deep voice even surprized him. Johnny grabbed his backpack as Matie headed for her room to change out of her nightgown. Occasionally the sound of frustrating ouches could be heard coming from her room.

Riley anxiously stood with both doors open wondering if he should help Matie. Johnny intuitively understood his dilemma and nodded at him. "She's just fine." he said. "She's probably just having trouble with the quillz.

Riley had a shocked look on his face. "How'd you know what I was gonna say?" Johnny shrugged and stuffed some things in his pack. "You asked me if you should help Matie. I just answered you."

"No, I didn't!" Riley stated. By now all eyes were on Johnny. "You read my mind!" Riley said, his eyes growing bigger.

"We're not the only ones who've changed," Bo said, as he scratched at his new fur.

Jack watched outside the window. "Hey, you guys! The bird is right. Someone's coming!"

They all ran for the top of the stairs, peeking around the corner to see what was going on downstairs.

Matie emerged from her room, tugging and pulling on her dress. "Oh, these stupid quills," she complained. "Nothing fits right!"

"Shhhhhh," the boys said in unison, holding their fingers to their lips.

Matie stomped her foot expecting someone to feel sorry for her.

Johnny turned to the others. "I can hear them saying something," he whispered.

Four cloaked men stood in the lobby. They were obviouxly men of authority and dressed very strange. Even the pirates looked normal in comparison. They wore brightly colored tunics that hung down to their shinz and had on dark boots with gold buckles at the sides. At their waists were gold braided beltz with large jewel encrusted plaques at the center. Each carried a long staff that was unique to each man. One had feathers on top, another an enormous jewel fastened in a gold casing, another had a braided whip, and the last had a large gold sphere on the end of his staff. Each wore a long dark cape edged with intricate designs. One in particular wore a large hat over his hood that looked like a combination of a tri-corner pirate hat with a gold crown fastened around the top. All were arrogant alligator Maroos except for one that was a large snake whose body was coiled as he slithered across the floor.

One of the alligators began to speak with a very distinct hiss in his voice. The boys all gasped as they watched him walk in with a limp. One of his legz was notably different it was not covered with a shiny boot, but had an intricately carved wooden leg that was just like the one back in Johnny's room at Maison Rouge.

"Where are the children?" the thing hissed. Goldie stood defiantly before the four tall creatures, her small body dwarfed in comparison. "I ain't seen any children here, just a bunch a pirates. How bout I buy y'all a drink? We got a heck of a show this time a year the house was packed last night." She winked.

The Maroos were unimpressed. The tallest pounded his staff on the floor three times. "Send for the Pahreefs!" he hissed. Three new men instantly came to the front doorway. They looked just like the guards that Johnny and Bo had seen earlier near the banks, but these held something unusual in their hands.

The three of them lifted their crystals together in a geometric formation and then the crystals began to glow. Soon a sphere of light formed above the crystals, floating in the air. The small light darted back and forth in front of the men, then, sped off into the saloon.

Suddenly Johnny felt a presence behind him. He turned around to see Dominique Youx. "Come with me!" Dominique whispered in his watery tone. Johnny elbowed the others, and they quickly followed Dominique.

He led them to a door at the far end of the hall and opened it. To all appearances it looked like a small linen closet, but when he pushed on the back wall, it gave way, exposing another long, dark corridor. Dominique waited as all of the children entered. Then he closed the door behind them.

Back in the lobby, the Pahreefs searched the grand cafe and theater, leaving nothing standing. They went through every private balcony box and even back stage.

The children heard the Pahreefs' muffled voices in the outer hall. "Someone was here but their rooms are empty. All we found was this child's night dress!" The alligator hissed as everyone heard the Overseer yell at the Pahreef. The peg-legged gater growled an evil order for the entire place to be torn apart in search of the children.

Dominique Youx pushed the children toward a hidden spiral staircase leading down to the alley outside. The frightened children crowded into a space behind a large rainbarrel, awaiting their chance for escape.

The colorful humming bird darted across the alley and hovered in front of a door. It pecked on the door with its long beak and slowly the door opened. A large man wearing an apron looked down the alley way in both directions, then, motioned for the children to come inside. One by one they ran for the door.

Bo and Matie were last. He picked her up as if she were a foot ball, tucking her under his thick furry arm, and like a quarterback destined for a touchdown, he ran for the open door.

A large black assemblage had parked in the street to the side of Goldie's place near the alley. Several Pahreefs stepped out and began searching everything in the vicinity.

Bo gently put Matie down and closed the door behind him. "That was a close one. Those things out there almost saw us."

"You bent my quills!" Matie said as she straightened one.

"Matie, just be grateful Bo helped you. They're still looking for us!" Johnny said.

The storekeeper reached over Bo's head and pulled down a large wooden latch to lock the heavy door behind him. "Ya barely made it in time!" the man whispered in a deep Irish tone. "The Pahreefs are all over town lookin' for ya. I suppose you're a-wondering who I am. McGifford's the name. I'm one of Goldie's friends. We ain't ne'r heared tell uf the Pahreefs a-goin' after children like they are now. Must be somethin' mighty special 'bouts the likes a yourselves."

The little room they were in was full of barrels of goods, and on the walls hung bananas and bags of vegetables. Johnny found a seat on a sack of flour, while Riley sniffed at a nearby pickle barrel. "Guess you folks might be a bit hungry right about now?" McGifford said.

"Sure am!" Riley said reaching into the pickle barrel. Bo slapped his hand, and Riley pulled it back with a squeaky whimper.

"Hold yer horses ther, and I'll get ya some real viddles to hold ya," McGifford said. He left the room and soon returned with some boiled eggs and a stick of Italian sausage. He took a knife and carved off a large portion for each person. "This is a right fancy delicacy 'ere in the bayou. Only the Overseers ever gets ta eat em. If they knew I had smuggled 'em in, they'd have my head for the lot."

Reaching on a high shelf, McGifford took down an enormous wheel of cheese and set it on top of a barrel to carve it. He stabbed the end of his knife into the slices and offered them to his hungry guests.

Riley was the first to take some and quickly devoured the tasty morsel. Soon the group's stomachs were full, topped off with a delightful shiny red apple.

"It's time ya all best get goin'," said McGifford. "The Pahreefs ain't partial ta nobody. They'll have this place torn apart in no time. Now gather round and I'll let ya in on the plan. See, we have a right good set a smugglers ere in town, and we all know what Aluitious E. Clayton is plannin'."

"Clayton!" Johnny interrupted, "But that's Jean Laffite's enemy. How'd he get here? I thought he was dead."

McGifford winked at Johnny, then, continued. "Ahhh sure en there ere plenty a people who are a wishin' he was dead. He's been the Boss's swarn enemy since they were wee children. He's a Maroo now and the nastiest devil Caiman ya ever did see. He's the leader uf 'em all, the grand Overseer, the leader of the Consortium!"

"What do you mean? He's the one in charge here?" Johnny said. "He can't be. Whatever happened to the pirates, and the treasure, and the curse?"

"Hold on there young man," McGifford said. "We'd best back up a piece. When the curse began, Old Mr. Aluitious followed Jean into the bayou. A course, things weren't what they seemed.

"The first government here was in Barataria. It was the Eldorado that Jean had built. His men were all right loyal then, I was one a them men. But as the curse spread and the Maroos come, folks began to be mad at the Boss. Said the curse was all his fault, they did.

"Soon the reptile Maroo's took over, and in no time they killed all but three of the eight men of the Alliance. Soon the curse took those three as well, and the halls of the Consortium fell inta ruin, while the reptiles took the seats of government as the Overseers. The only thing left ta fight them was the smugglers. Folks like Goldie and me, we calls ourselves the Revolutionaries of the Defiance."

Johnny thought of his gold coins and the eight men who had once held them. "Wait a minute, if you were one of Jean's original crew, you would have known the original eight men of the Alliance. Who were they?" Johnny reached into his back pack for his notebook.

"Eye," Said McGifford, "I knowed every last one of em. Let me see. Of course there was Jean and his brothers, Pierre and Dominique. And Jean's right hand man, James Campbell. Renauto Belouche, Arsene Lebleu, and Jean Baptiste."

"But that's only seven men." Johnny said as he wrote down the names.

"Yes, I know. We don't speak the traitor's name."

"Why not?" Bo asked.

McGifford spoke with gritted teeth. "He become Clayton's right hand man, the old devil. A slithery slimin' snake of a Maroo, just like his name! He wanted that treasure and he turned his clue over to Clayton. The devil hisself couldn't a been worse than that scalawag. You'll know him when ya sees him, carries a great whip he does."

Riley gasped, "But that was one of those Maroos back at the hotel. He had a long staff with a big black whip on the end."

McGifford scratched his whiskery chin. "That's ol Mike Pithon all right. Doesn't miss a chance ta torture a body."

"What's this consortium hall you were talking about?" Jack questioned.

McGifford smiled at Jack and raised his eyebrow. "It

362

was the beginnin' of the revolutionaries of the defiance. The original men of the Alliance built a place called Consortium Hall where they could govern all the doin's in the swamp. But there was more. After Pithon mutinied, the Alliance went inta hidin'. They started a new headquarters that no one knowed about, just them seven men. Some say it was a secret place directly beneath Consortium Hall. There it is said, they hid up all the secrets to the hidden treasure and the curse.

"Clayton and his men tried ta find it, but no one has succeeded. Sure, the place itself is cursed, 'cept for those that seek ta find it with pure intent! Rumor is that the dead men of the Alliance guard it with their very souls.

"Clayton and his evil followers calls themselves the Masters of the Consortium even now, but they won't ever be the true masters. The Revolutionaries of the Defiance will see ta that!"

Out in the streets the Pahreefs had prisoners lined up in chains. Now they went from door to door searching each building for the newcomers. Entering McGifford's store, they ransacked the front rooms.

"It's the Pahreefs!" McGifford whispered, as he began moving a large barrel in the corner. Under it was a rattan mat that he shoved to the side, then, quickly lifted a hidden trap door. "Get in there!" McGifford said, urging the fugitives into the dark hole.

Johnny was the last to descend the ladder as he looked up from the dusky cellar, the kindly man gave him one last bit of advice. "Follow the tunnel till ya sees the light, then head straight for it!"

The trap door closed, leaving the children in darkness. They listened as McGifford piled several things over the door. Soon they heard footsteps and muffled voices.

"Come right in, fellas. Has ya found them rebel children yet? Ya know I'm as much of a patriot as the rest. Bein' the pirate that I am, I'd even turn in my own mother if there was somethin' in it fer me."

The Pahreefs just laughed at the old shopkeeper. "We don't give rewards for turning anyone in," they said, "unless you consider your life a reward."

McGifford laughed. "You're more of a pirate than I am. How about I get you boys a drink?"

Soon the footsteps and voices faded into the distance as the children listened from their hiding place. Matie leaned against Johnny for comfort. "Ouch!" Johnny whispered pulling away from his little sister.

"Shhhhh..." the others insisted.

Suddenly it got silent up above and then they heard the sound of electrical humming. "It's that fire ball the Pahreefs made, that searching thing of theirs. They've heard us," Riley said with panic in his voice.

"Shhhh, just wait!" whispered Bo. "I think they're at the front of the store. We better get going."

The damp dirt walls of the tunnel had a moldy smell as the youth crowded through the narrow passageway. A little bit of light filtered through the cracks in the floorboards above as the tunnel wandered beneath several shops. Occasionally a shower of dirt would pour down on the kids in the dug-out tunnel. Jack stopped in front of the others as a large cloud of dust settled from an avalanche of loose falling rocks.

Matie started coughing. "Cover her mouth and shut her up. Someone's gonna hear us," Riley said with wide eyes.

"You cover her mouth!" said Johnny. "I'm not gonna get poked."

Bo now gently placed his paw near Matie's mouth to stifle the sound. Finally her coughing stopped. Matie took a deep breath then dusted off her dress, and the little group again started down the damp tunnel.

38
Rebels of the Revivory

The night had been a difficult one for Kate. The storm had brought with it hallucinations and restlessness. Finally she slept quietly as **J**im napped by her side and Laurabeth s**l**ept on a nearby window seat.

Witho**ut** warning the doctor entered the room. "I'm sorry to interrupt you like this, but the Pahreefs are coming and asking all newcomers for identification. You have to leave right now."

Jim shook his head tryin**g** to shake off the drowsi**n**ess. "But, what about my wife, can we move her?" he asked.

The doctor looked concerned. "She shouldn't be moved yet, but we have no choice. If all of you don't leave right now, it won't make any difference."

Laurabeth gathered Kate's clothing and tried to help her sit up. The doctor left and returned with a chair suspended in the air by an invisible force. "Here you can move your wife in this," he said, using a crystal to activate the chair's unseen wheels. **Q**uickly t**hey** dressed Kate and put her in the chair.

The doctor gave Jim a uniform like his o**wn** to put over **h**is clothing, and told him the best route to take to get out of the Revivory.

Kate was beginning to awaken, and sta**r**ted **h**umming between dozing spells. Miss Honey entered the room and hovere**d** in the air. "I'**y**vvvve been sent to warrrrrn you and to guide you wherrrrrre to go. The Overrrrrrrrserrrrs are lookin**q** for all of you."

Suddenly the nurse escort burst into the room. "**T**hey're here! The bird down at the desk was suspicious and alerted them. You must leave right now."

Jim and Laurabeth hurried out into the hallway, pushing Kate down the long corridor. The entire Revivory was in commotion as people both human and animal rushed about.

Miss Honey darted ahead of the others, making sure the way was safe. "Quickly follow mmmme!" she said with a hum. Laurabeth held the door and Jim pushed the chair outside, down a cobblestone pathway behind the Revivory. She looked back towards the massive structure. A large assemblage pulled up right in front of the building. "Therrrrrre they arrrrrre!" she whispered loudly as she picked up her speed.

Jim glanced back over his shoulder then pushed Kate a little faster. The four were soon far enough away from the Revivory that they stopped for a moment to get their bearings.

The jostling of the ride had awakened Kate completely, and she cried between giggles. Miss Honey flew to the back of Kate's chair and whispered in her ear. Her words calmed Kate, and she settled back into a light sleep.

"Where are we going?" Jim asked, with a frown.

Miss Honey flew to his shoulder. "Weeeee have zommmme friends at the museummmmm that are waiting to help. But it is a lonnnng walk and the Pahreefs arrrrre checking every assemblage in townnnn."

"We can make it," Jim said, nodding to Laurabeth. Laurabeth was still catching her breath as Jim noticed her blue lips. "Are you all right?" he asked. Laurabeth nodded stubbornly and started walking ahead.

Jim pushed the chair and caught up to her. "Hey, what's going on?" Jim said. "You might not know it, but your lips are blue."

Laurabeth stopped walking and looked at the ground. "I didn't want anyone to know," she whispered.

"Look," Jim said. "We've already got enough trouble. I

think you had better tell me what's going on."

Laurabeth sighed. "That's why I didn't tell you. I'd just be more trouble and everyone would start treating me different."

Jim glanced back toward the Revivory. "We need to keep going."

Laurabeth looked at Jim. "I'm sorry Mr. Leavitt. I don't want to make you worry, but you have to promise not to tell anyone, ezpecially not the other kids."

"All right, I won't say anything," Jim agreed as they hurried along.

"It's my heart," Laurabeth whispered. "It's just fine most of the time, 'cept when I overdo. It just isn't that strong, I guess."

Miss Honey darted past them. "Follow mmmme nnnow! They'rrrre commmmming."

"I can't run anymore," Laurabeth said, shaking her head. Jim looked at her, then at Kate. Miss Honey dipped from side to side in front of them.

"Maybe we can find somewhere to hide," Jim said.

But it was too late. Hovering in the air above them was the Pahreefs electrical ball of fire. It darted about them as several Pahreefs surrounded the group. Miss Honey was the only one who had managed to get away unseen.

The Pahreefs pointed their crystals at Jim and the others as if they would fire on them at any moment. Suddenly the Pahreefs moved aside and a large Overseer came to the scene. "I sssee you have finally found them," he hissed. "But where are those children?"

"These newcommers are alone," a Pahreef responded. "There were no others with them."

"Silence!" the overseer yelled. "Your stupidity is beyond question. You will find those children immediately, or I will see to it that your home will be in the dungeons of dispair. Now take these dissenters to Consortium Hall immediately to be questioned. We will reconfigure their minds through the ritual. But make sure you do not erase their old identities as we will need them to capture the young revolutionaries!"

Suddenly Kate began to laugh and hum. The Overseer backed away and covered his snout with a handkerchief. "She is a croonie! She's mad!" he hissed. "Why didn't you tell me! Take the defective parasite away from me before I become contaminated. And get these other indolent newcomers out of my sight!" The Overseer shoved the Pahreef to the ground, then, walked past him to a waiting assemblage.

The Pahreefs bound Jim's and Laurabeth's hands and loaded them into a wagon filled with other prisoners.

Kate watched from a distance as one by one each Pahreef stepped into a cylindrical chamber. Once inside, a blue horizontal line of glowing energy moved from their head to their toes. When they emerged, this same blue energy surrounded them with a protective force field.

Kate looked at her feet and with great exertion tried placing them on the ground. She glanced at the Pahreefs then tried to stand up. Slowly she rose to her feet and began to take a step. With extreme effort, she moved one foot, then the other.

"Look, she's trying to escape!" A Pahreef yelled, running toward her.

Kate gritted her teeth, the pain was excruciating. She shut her eyes trying to push back the tears. She tried to run, but her legs didn't respond, instead she fell in a heap on the ground as the Pahreefs surrounded her.

"Put the charge around her and contain her in the force field," one said.

The Pahreefs stood in a circle and aimed their crystals at Kate. Like searing hot irons, the energy from the crystals enveloped her, burning every molecule of her body.

Instantly she convulsed, pulling her legs up close to her. "Stop, please," she sang out.

"She won't try anything now," the head Pahreef said, lowering his crystal. The others followed suit, and the force field surrounding Kate diminished and disappeared. Kate looked up at the hooded faces of the men around her, and fell unconscious.

39
Young Revolutionaries

Johnny edged his way along the damp tunnel behind the others. Occasionally a light would filter in from the small shops above. This made the going easier but posed the risk of being discovered. In the distance a light filtered through the tunnels lighting the way.

The group noticed that the ceiling was no longer made of dirt from the floors of the shops above them, but was made of bricks and then turned into a carved stone structure. After a while, they came to the source of the light. It was a lantern that had been purposely placed by a set of stone stairs. The group made their way up the staircase.

Suddenly the door above them opened without warning. "Vell! Hallow! I've been expecting you," an odd man exclaimed as he ushered the children up the ladder into the storage room of a museum.

The man busied himself checking all of the windows and doors, and then returned to the children. He was dressed in a fine tweed suit and wore thick glasses. His long white hair and large moustache was uncombed and bushy. He was quick witted, despite his age, and spoke with a thick German accent. "Velcome!" he said, nearing the children. "I am Professor Hans Einriche. I have been ezpecting you."

Johnny and the others looked at one another, unsure of what to think of this place. "So, where are we?" Johnny asked.

"Ahh, you are at der finest museum in da bayou. I am de curator. You vill be safe here, at least for a time."

Matie examined the old man. "How do we know we can trust you?" she asked scrunching up her little pokey nose.

Professor Einriche smiled and his white moustache twitched from side to side. "I am an olt man," he said, "and I have seen many tings in dis place. Da vorst of all are the Overseerz. Dey are much like those who caused der ruin of my own country of Germany. I am now part of der Revolutionaries of de Defiance. I know just how important liberty is, und I vill fight for it."

The children sat in a circle on the floor, surrounded by Egyptian artifacts.

"So why are those guys after us?" Jack questioned as he leaned against a large green statue.

The old man placed a box of pottery on a table and began with a sigh. "Ahh, I vish it vas different, but da Masters of da Consortium vish to find you for one purpose only. It is because of the precious artifacts you hold. Dey vill try to take you until you gif dese items to dem."

"Wait a minute," said Bo in his gruff voice. "How did you know we had that stuff?"

The professor smiled, but before he could answer, Johnny broke in. "It's the same way he knew we were coming. He's a Defaun."

The old man turned toward Johnny and raised his eyebrow. "You, my young friend, are very perceptive. Und, I see dat you have not revealed all either." He now looked straight in Johnny's eyes. Suddenly Johnny nodded as if he were hearing something. Then the old man smiled again.

The others were quite confused with this display. There was obviously something that Johnny wasn't telling them. Johnny turned away from the others, hoping they hadn't noticed what had just happened.

But now Bo wanted an answer. "So professor, are you a

Defaun?"

The professor winked at Bo. "I am afraid so, und ya. I do know of all of the artifacts you children have been entrusted vit."

Bo became quiet because that was just what he was thinking just then. The professor had answered him before he even had a chance to ask the question. Riley clozed his eyes tightly and thought as hard as he could. Soon the professor was laughing.

Everyone looked at the red fox and the surprized look on his face. Jack elbowed his friend. "Riley, what are you doing?" Riley opened his eyes and looked at Jack then closed them tightly again.

Bo shoved Riley to get his attention. Riley squirmed and looked angrily at the others. "Hey, you're breaking my concentration. I was just starting to read someone's mind. I had these thoughts about cheese and Italian sausage, and someone was really hungry." Just then Riley's stomach growled.

"Yeah," interrupted Bo. "You were reading someone's mind all right, yours!" Everyone laughed as Riley paced around a bit then settled into a seat near the professor.

The professor became serious and gave the kids a harsh stare. "Your young friend feels you have betrayed him vit your laughter. Remember you must only laugh vit another person, nefer at dem." He turned to Riley. "I suspect you haven't had long to get used to your new condition yet of being a fox. But you should know dat like da Defauns, da Maroos haf very great gifts as vell. Riley, tell me vhat you smell."

Riley lifted his long red snout and sniffed at the air. Then he smiled. "I smell fish and candy. It's saltwater taffy."

"Ya!" said the professor. "Sehr gut! You should know dat der fish market is several streets from here, und da confectionery is even more. As you learn to use da skills of a fox, you vill be able to sense vhen danger is coming, or to smell people und even hear da foot steps, but your greatest gift vill be the ability to use your intelligence to out fox your enemies!"

"What's a porcupine good at?" Matie asked.

"Poking people!" said Johnny with a chuckle. Matie turned indignantly putting her nose in the air, ignoring her brother.

The professor smiled. "You also have very special gifts, my little *Fraulein Baumstachler*. Da porcupine is bezt at night for you can see vhat others cannot. Und in the vater no von can hurt you for your quills are hollow, und you vill always float. Most of all, like your brother has said, no one vill hurt you, or they vill get a nasty surprise!" Matie smiled then stuck out her tongue at Johnny.

Bo sat without saying a word. Then the professor looked him straight in the eye. "Ahhh, Bo, da black bear. You are da great defender. You have speed und great power. For vit one swipe of your hand, you can kill. Your ears vill hear when others do not, und your nose vill always know der scent of man, good or evil. You, my boy, vere given dis gift because of your great desire to protect your friends. But be cautious, you do not know your own strength."

The professor turned to Jack. "You are der one here of whom the curse has both blessed and cheated. For you are da only one unaffected. The curse has spared you its effects. But you vill also have der challenqe of surviving in da bayou vitout change. You vill have only da instinct God has given you. But do not underestimate it, for you are the visest here, even for your youth. You have great knowledge und insight."

"But wait!" said Jack. "Johnny hasn't changed either!" The professor looked toward Johnny with a raised eyebrow.

Johnny smiled and nodded at him.

"So, you tink Johnny has not changed? I am sure he

has."

Everyone looked at Johnny. He blushed a bit, with a slight grin. "No, I'm not a water man or a Maroo!"

Bo's eyes suddenly got big. "How'd you know what I was thinking? Unless you're a Defaun!"

Johnny fidgeted. "Well, I guess I am, sort of. I've been hearing everybody's thoughts all morning. I just thought you guys were all talking a lot. I finally figured it out when I noticed your lips weren't moving, but I was still hearing you."

The professor turned to Johnny and spoke very seriously. "Young man, da time vill come ven you vill haf need of visiting Pyros, da city of fire. Dere you vill be taught of your gift. For da gifts of a Defaun are limited in der scope, and der are dose who haf found vays to protect demselves from our abilities. I can teach you no more here, except to say dat you must use dis gift to protect de artifacts in your care."

He looked around at all of the others. "All of you must promise to do all you can to protect Johnny und da tings he holds. The Overseers are very evil. Dey und der Masters of da Consortium vill stop at noting to get hold of dese tings. Aluitious E. Clayton has sought dese tings for as long as da curse has existed because dey are da key to his power.

"Right now, you und da tings you hold can stop him and his evil and eliminate da curse. If he gets da artifacts, da curse vill live und spread to become stronger und stronger until it cannot be stopped. If dat happens, Clayton vill rule da vorld."

Bo scratched behind his ear. "Professor, I thought that the curse was just here in the bayou. So how can Clayton end up ruling the world?"

The Professor frowned, and looked about as if making sure no one was watching. Then he leaned in close to the kids.

"Vhen da curse began, it only affected da svamp. But it has spreat. Many people haf became a part of it, even in der

United States of America. Not only haf our societies grown in parallel to von anoter, but dey are also symbiotic. Dis means dat dese two societies rely upon von anoter. Everyting dat happens here effects your people und everyting dat you do, affects us. Haf you ever hert of Fort Knox?"

"Sure," said Jack. "Everyone's heard of that. It's where the nation keeps all of its gold."

"Not qvite." The professor said. "Fort Knox is just a very small portion of your nation's treasure. Our banks here are vhat keeps the USA running. And Aluitious E. Clayton, der leader of da Overseers runs all of dose banks. He holds der U.S. economy in his hands."

"But how does our government get that money, unless they know about the curse and the bayou?" asked Jack.

"Dat is exactly my point, young man. Your government does know."

Suddenly the professor stopped talking and went to the front door in the other room and locked it. Then he placed a large sign on it that said; "Due to Moaning Mist, the museum will remain closed until further notice, by order of the Pahreefs."

The professor returned to the others. "No von should boter us now. Da Pahreefs often order many buildings clozed after da mist has come. To dem it vill seem normal. Dey vill nefer suspect dat der young rebels dey seek are hiding here. Neverteless, ve must be very careful."

With the door secure, the professor walked to a separate corner of the museum and invited the others to follow. There he stood in front of a large sculpted map of the bayou. "It is very important dat you understand vhere you are and vhat you are doing here," he said, pointing at the map.

"Hey, that's just like the one Sam showed us in my room at Maison Rouge." Johnny said, running his hand across the map.

The professor nodded and continued. "Da original eight men of da Alliance were each responsible for goferning vun portion or district vitin der bayou. It is vitin dese districts dat dey have left der legacy.

"As you already know, each man hat a clue to da treasure. I belief dat da secret to solving da curse is hitten troughout dese districts."

Johnny examined the large map. Then he reached into his back pack and retrieved Dominique's map. As he spread it out over the large sculpted map, he compared the details. "That's it!" he yelled. "My map has a large sun in the center. That sun is right where your beacon of light is, in the center of town. But I don't understand what this heart in the middle of the sun means."

The professor went to Johnny's side and looked at the map. "Hmmm, I vonder...." he said. "Long ago da original eight men of da Allianze built a secret chamber. I belief dey called it da Heart of da Consortium. Each man left vun ting dere, vun ting dat was more precious to him dan even life itself as part of his oath, like a covenant. Perhaps da heart on your map is dis place--der heart of da consortium."

"Wow," said Bo. "It looks like everything's starting to make sense now."

Johnny began rolling up the map, then stopped and read aloud the writing on it. *"The heart of the truth lies in the Son if freedom B favored and justice be wun."*

"We've found the sun and the heart, and I know that the letter "B" stands for Barataria. That's right where we are now. This is Dominique's map. And he was one of the ones fighting for the freedom of everyone in the bayou. If we're going to get justice and free this place, we have to go to the sun, to the Beacon!"

"Oh, dear," the professor gasped, "dat vill not be easy. Der Beacon is highly guarded, for it is the only power source vitin da bayou. Everyting is connected to its power, even da crystals da people holt. You must be very careful if you intend on doing this ting."

Suddenly there was a loud pounding at the front doors of the museum. The professor stopped and looked off into the distance as if he were looking at something in the air. "It is da Pahreefs. Dey haf come to search. You must go. You are in great danger. Go back trough da tunnels stay to da left and head toward da area of da beacon. You may take my lantern to lead you. Now go!"

Everyone quickly hurried for the trap door and scrambled down the stone stairs. Johnny was last. He stopped for just a moment and thought as hard as he could towards the professor, trying to say thank you. Then he distinctly heard the professor's words in his mind, "You are velcome Johnny. Keep your intent pure and you vill never go wrong!"

40
Prisoners and Privateers

Randy and Palmer watched through a crack in the door of their makeshift prizon. The ruffian pirates had branded them as spies and had them locked up in the galley of the ship. As the daunting pirates discussed the destiny of their prisoners, Randy and Palmer looked desperately for a means of escape.

"Do you think they'll kill us?" Palmer wondered.

"Not if I can help it!" Randy nodded, examining the walls in the room.

Except for a closet, the walls were completely solid. Not even the small windows would allow escape. In desperation, Randy kicked at a bag of potatoes. "It looks like our only way out is through those cutthroats!" he said angrily, peering out through the crack in the door.

Outside, a large brown pelican landed on the ship's railing. Randy and Palmer watched in fascination as the other pirates, even Pierre, looked as if they were being instructed by the clumsy bird. When it flew off the pirates approached the galley door. The door flung wide open and two exceptionally muscular pirates laid hold of the two men, forcing them out on deck.

"Leave us alone!" Randy said, trying to free himself from the pirates. "We're not spies!"

The pirates laughed, and Pierre stepped forward. "And why should we believe you?" he asked with a deep French tone.

Randy searched for words as Palmer broke in, "How can we be spies? We don't even have any oars."

Pierre laughed. "Perhaps you were set adrift for your

379

crimes," he responded. Palmer's face turned red as he looked anxiously at the floor.

"If you're Pierre Laffite, then maybe you know my friends, the Leavitts?" Randy added. The pirate raised an eyebrow. Randy had his complete attention and glanced at Palmer then continued with a glimmer in his eye. "Look, my name is Randy Olsen. I'm the Leavitt's best friend. We've come here to warn them." Pierre's face remained emotionless. "You've got to believe us!" Randy pleaded.

The pirate now took a long knife from his belt and began sharpening it on a large black strap. Suddenly he flung it at Randy's feet. Randy and Palmer jumped back as the entire crew burst into riotous laughter. Pierre retrieved his knife. A heckler from the crew yelled, "Git em agin!"

Pierre approached the two men, putting his nose only inches away from Randy's. "I know who you are! I should kill you here and now for your traitorous acts!"

Randy and Palmer stood motionless, barely breathing. The pirate backed off a bit rubbing his thumb across the blade of his knife.

"How do you know who we are?" Randy whispered.

"My men have been watching you since you entered the swamp!" Pierre replied. "We even know about your charade at Maison Rouge."

Randy and Palmer exchanged glances. If the pirates had seen all of those things, then their conspiring against Jim and his family couldn't be denied. Despite their recent change of heart, the two had no way of proving they wanted to help Jim's family now. Their previous actions only condemned them further and left no proof for their defense.

"Ratcliffe was blackmailing us!" Palmer reasoned.

Pierre's dark eyes held little emotion and absolutely no sympathy for the two men.

"Both of you are cowards!" the pirate replied. "Your backbones are made of sand. Even the children have shown more courage than you!"

"You've seen the children? Are they all right?" Randy asked.

Pierre raised his eyebrow again. "Do you show concern for the children, or for their map?"

"Look, we don't care about the stupid map. We know we've messed everything up. Most of this situation is all our fault. But now we want to help. We know what Ratcliffe's plans are, and we know how he'll try to get to the kids. Maybe we can stop him."

"Hmmm..." Pierre said, testing his knife's sharpness. "Tell me this one thing. Why is your boss Ratcliffe after the treasure?"

Randy stopped and thought for a moment. "As far as I know, it's a family vendetta. Ratcliffe's great great grandfather was Laffite's enemy." Randy hesitated. "I guess he was your enemy, too."

Pierre smiled. "And what would this man's name be?"

"Aluitious E. Clayton!" Randy said.

Immediately the pirate put his knife to Randy'z throat. "How dare you speak that name on my ship!" his voice thundered.

Randy lifted his chin. Then the pirate slowly removed the knife and composed himself. "What do you know of this thing?" he asked gruffly.

Palmer broke in. "Ratcliffe has a map. He believes it's the key to the treasure. His family has held it for years."

"Have you seen this map?" Pierre questioned.

"We've both seen it," Randy said, rubbing his neck. "It has a sword on the top, but it doesn't seem to make much sense. That's why Ratcliffe wants the one the kids have."

Pierre's lip's slowly curved up in a broad smile, and his white teeth gleamed at the two men. "Let them go!" he ordered.

"Why are you letting us go?" Randy asked.

Pierre just smiled. "Does your friend Ratcliffe still have that map?"

"Yes," said Randy. "At least he had it when we were on the island."

Pierre laughed. "Good! It is exactly as we planned."

Randy grabbed Pierre's shoulder, "But, what about the Leavitts and their friends? Are you just going to let Ratcliffe go after them?"

Pierre looked at Randy's hand on his shoulder then he looked him in the eye. "So, you do have a backbone," he replied. Slowly Randy realized what he was doing and removed his hand from the pirate.

Pierre stared at him. "You need not worry about your friend Ratcliffe. He and his map have already been captured back at the island. Clayton's men almost killed him. He is of little use to us now. But as for you two, we will be taking you to the Boss to decide your fate. You do not understand the ways of pirates. If you were truly xpies, you would never have revealed the things you have." Pierre nodded toward his men and then returned to the captain's quarters.

Another pirate yelled out orders to the crew, and the men began raising the sails and setting the ship's rigging. "Hoist the mainsail! Secure the jib! The riggin's loose!"

Several pirates pulled together on a large rope and the enormous sail rose into position, whipping in the wind. The thick green mist still surrounded the ship as the pirate yelled out a new set of orders, "Set the mistsail! Watch the waters!" Several pirates scaled the rigging to the mast and climbed up above the mainsail. In an instant they were all in position along the yardarm ready to release another sail. With the creaking of pulleys, the sail slowly lowered. It had a greenish yellow glow about it and as soon as it was released and billowed out, the mist surrounding the ship began to clear.

Randy and Palmer watched in awe as the great ship sailed over the murky waters. The sails snapped and whipped in the wind as the ominous green mist cleared before them.

The vessel creaked and rocked from side to side as the captain's mate adjusted the ship's wheel making a sharp turn to the right. The bayou and the mist soon gave way to the open seas.

"How did we get here in the ocean?" Randy said loudly to the ship's mate. The pirate looked steadily ahead and spun the ship's wheel hard to the right, shifting the sails in the wind. Suddenly an odd feeling of dizziness overtook Palmer and Randy. A tingling sensation settled in their bones. Randy leaned against the railing. He watched through blurred vision as Palmer's lanky frame dropped to the deck next to him.

Two pirates reached for Palmer and took him below deck. Pierre emerged from his cabin and walked toward Randy. "It would seem your friend is the mate with the sandy backbone, aye?"

Randy tried to muster up a smile amid the dizzy feeling in his head. He managed only a half smile and gulped hard to get the horrible feeling under control. A toothless salty old pirate approached him.

"Eee's green!" the pirate said, looking at the captain. He shoved a stein of grog in Randy's face. "That ell put air on yer ches. Is jus a bit a rum and gunpowder, bez cure fo what ails ya." The old pirate breathed in Randy's face.

The old man's breath was more than Randy could take. His stomach began churning. Randy bounded for the railing and heaved over the side of the ship. The sickening sea ride had finally won out over Randy's polished demeanor.

His face was white and his brow covered in sweat. With weak knees he sat down on the deck. "I've never been sea sick before," he said wiping his brow. "I just don't understand what's wrong."

The crew whispered and laughed at Randy from a distance. "It's not sea sickness," Pierre said. "It's time sickness. You're just not used to it yet."

"Time sickness? What do you mean?"

"We have entered the time loch," said Pierre. "Haven't you noticed that we are no longer within the bayou?"

"Yes," Randy replied, wiping his mouth on his sleeve. "But, if so, where ezactly are we?"

"We are on the open sea in the year 1857," Pierre replied with a large grin. Then he nodded to the first mate, who instantly turned from his duty at the wheel and retrieved a strange instrument and gave the device to Pierre, then, returned to his former position at the ship's wheel.

The device was shaped like an old fashioned seaman's sextant, but it was strangely modified. On the top it held a small spyglass and had several measuring devices attached. On the bottom was a glass globe that seemed to function much like a compass, but instead of a needle, it contained three small gems and a glowing yellow fluid. A small floating gold arrow within the glass chamber indicated the current fixed time placement. The three gems seemed to adjust with each new course setting that was charted.

Pierre explained how the curious device had achieved this miraculous time travel. "It is called a Synchronistic Modulator. When we are within the Time Loch, the three stones focus the power of the beacon within the bayou. Together these allow us to chart a course through time."

Randy was astonished, "You really have the ability to travel through time here?"

"Yes." Pierre replied. "But only within certain perimeters."

"If you can do that, then why doesn't someone go back in time and fix the curse?' Randy asked.

Pierre sighed. "It has been attempted many times. Nevertheless, the curse has a great hold upon those who inhabit the swamp. Those who are affected by its grasp are unable to approach the beginning of the curse. Many have been destroyed trying. For the few who have returned, it has been a long arduous road for the things they witnessed are beyond comprehension. The curse is a great void of darkness which consumes everything within its reach."

Randy looked perplexed. "That sounds like a black hole."

"I do not know of such things!" Pierre responded. "I know only this. The curse cannot be approached without dire consequences."

"So why do you risk this time travel if it is so dangerous?" Randy questioned.

Pierre smiled wide. "Our travels are very profitable. Our libraries are brimming full with the records of ships' logs from times past. It is, you might say, advantageous to our cause to intercept such transports."

"So you're 'time pirates'!" Randy exclaimed.

"We prefer to be known as Privateers!" Pierre stated proudly. "It is your own U.S. government which grants us our letters of marque."

Randy looked confused again. Pierre snapped his fingers, and a cabin boy ran up to him. Pierre whispered something to the boy who quickly did hiz bidding. Soon the boy returned with an official looking piece of paper and handed it to Randy.

Upon the top was an early verzion of the great Seal of

the U.S.A. In very formal writing was an official commission from President James Madison requesting the services of Pierre Laffite for the protection of the U.S. borders. On the bottom was the signature of every President since. It was sealed on the bottom with a large wax stamp with blue faded ribbon imbedded within it.

Randy couldn't believe what he held in his hands. These Privateers had once sailed these waters for the protection of the nation and had continued doing the same for almost two hundred years now. They had literally sailed every ocean of the world throughout time and had done so with the express knowledge of the U.S. government even to the present time.

41
The Beacon

Johnny and the others walked through the dark tunnels as the professor's lantern cast ghoxt-like shadows upon the walls.

"Are you sure this is the way?" Riley questioned sniffing at the air.

"It's the way the professor told us to come," Johnny said.

Now with cautious silence Johnny led the group through miles of wandering tunnels until a faint light up ahead got their attention.

"Am I just imagining things, or is it getting brighter?" Bo asked.

"It's getting brighter," Matie whispered loudly as she poked the others.

"Matie, you gotta quit stabbing everyone!" Johnny complained.

"Well then, hurry up!" she said.

The group of rebels looked towards the far end of the tunnel. The dirt on the floor and walls had changed to a highly polished white stone. Even the ceiling was made of this stone. The light up ahead completely filled the tunnel now, so Bo blew out the professor's lantern.

Johnny stopped and waited as the others caught up to him. "Why are we stopping?" Riley asked.

Jack put his fingers to his lips. "We've gotta be really careful," he whispered. "All that light up ahead could mean that there are people there."

Slowly the group moved along, each footstep echoing

throughout the long tunnel. The light up ahead was getting brighter and brighter. Then the entire tunnel opened up into an enormous underground room.

The room was large and round with several arched doorways that led into other tunnels. The ceiling was made of colored glass. A distinctly bright light shined directly above them and filled the room with rainbows of light.

"We must be right under the beacon," Johnny squinted.

The enormous glowing light hummed and pulsated in rhythmic musical tones. Occasionally it burped out a dissonant musical tone then resumed its usual hum again. With each pulse of its musical illuminations, Johnny began to feel something unusual.

Slowly he closed his eyes and gently rocked forward and back as if the sound were almost in control of him. "Johnny! Johnny!" Bo said as he shook Johnny's arm.

Suddenly Johnny's eyes opened. "What's wrong?"

Bo looked up at the light above. "You were in some kind of a trance or something. That light up there is what did it to you."

Johnny took a deep breath then turned to Bo. "It wasn't a trance. I was seeing some things in my mind that didn't make much sense. First, I saw my mother crying. She was in this dark room and so was my dad. Laurabeth wasn't far from them. I don't know how I know it, but I think they're in danger. I have this feeling that they might be close by somewhere. The light above us just seemed to make it easier for me to see and feel those things. It was like it was magnifying what I was seeing." Johnny reached for his head as it began throbbing suddenly.

"I wonder where Mom and Dad are now?" said Matie with a frown.

Bo put his furry arm around her. "Matie, your Ma and Pa are just fine at the hospital. Don't you worry a bit about yer

388

folks!"

Johnny looked around the room for something that might help them solve the curse. "We've gotta figure all this out if were going to help anyone. Remember what the map said? *'The heart of the truth lies in the son, if freedom B favored and justice be won.'* I wonder what it means? Come on you guy's, let's look for some clues."

Everyone **b**egan to look around the room. Jack noticed something and **w**hispered back to the others. "Hey you guys, come'ere." Everyone gathered around as he pointed above the arched doorway of one of the tunnels. "Look, it has the name James Campbell on it, and there's an etching of a shore and a palm tree. Isn't that one of the guys that was part of the original Alliance?"

"Yeah!" said Johnny, running to e**x**amine the other doorways. "There's a name above all of them!" he whispered e**z**citedly, "and they're all the names of the original members of the Alliance!"

Johnny and the others ran to each doorway inspecting the names and symbols. Then they came to one that was different. There was no name on it. Instead, it had a sun car**v**ed into the stone that looked just like the sun on his watch.

He reached into his **p**ocket and took out the watch. Reading the words on it he repeated them o**v**er and over. *The heart of the truth lies in the son.* That's **I**t!" he exclaimed. "The sun has got to be where the secret chamber is hidden!"

Suddenly Bo interrupted, "Hey, you guys. I think you'd better see this." He was standing in the middle of the dusty floor looking straight down. Everyone gathered around and noti**c**ed that he was **s**tanding right **o**n top of a gold plate in the center of the floor.

"What's that?" **R**iley **s**aid.

"I don' kno**w**," said Bo, "but I think we'd better take a

clozer look." The entire floor was very dusty, but under the thick dust they could make out several colored markings. In the center of the floor, a heart was painted around the gold sun-shaped plate. Surrounding the heart were twelve rays that formed a design to make a larger sun. The floor was indeed a perfect replica of the inside of Johnny's watch, complete with matching colors made from the reflections of the light from above.

"It's just like your watch!" Matie exclaimed.

"Yeah," said Johnny. "Even the colored lights from the stained glass are the same colors as the numbers on my watch."

Each of the twelve rays that formed the large sun on the floor pointed to a doorway. And in the center of the floor were the faded remains of gold arrows painted in the exact same positions as the broken hands on Johnny's watch. The symbol of the sun over the doorway pointed directly north, and each corresponding symbol above the doorways correlated perfectly with the things Johnny had written in his notebook.

"So your watch is really a map," Jack said. "And the hands in the watch are actually pointing to some clue."

"So now what do we do?" Riley asked. "Do we follow the watch hands on the floor and see what's at eight o'clock, or do we go down the tunnel with the sun on it?"

Johnny bit his lip as he whispered the words of the clue. "Well, if the heart of the truth lies in the son, I think we'd better see what's   down the tunnel with the sun marking first. We can always come back later and go see what's down Pierre's tunnel at eight o'clock. Besides, remember what the professor said about the heart of the Consortium and the secret chamber those men made? He said they all left their most precious things there, and we've gotta find that place."

Johnny looked at the others and waited for their response. "All right," said Bo. "I'm with ya." Everyone else nodded too, then stood up and began through the arched doorway.

As the children headed down the tunnel, the light behind them slowly faded. Bo reached inside his pocket and lit a match to light the lantern, as the group followed along steadily.

This tunnel was very different from the others they had been in. The walls were made of brick and the floors were paved. The only disadvantage seemed to be the loud echoes the concrete floor made as the children walked along.

Occasionally Johnny would turn around and "shush" the others who tried to be as quiet as they could by walking on tip toe. Soon the little gang came upon a juncture in the path. The tunnel divided into two separate cross tunnels. It was here that the group stopped to rest. Johnny fumbled in his back pack as he found a snack for the others. "Which way do you think we need to go?" Bo asked, holding the lantern up high to see down each tunnel.

Riley sniffed at the air then shook his head. "I can't smell anything. I don't know which way to go."

As Bo swung the lantern back toward the others, the light from it filtered down one of the tunnels. Jack caught a glimpse of something down the tunnel and turned to Bo. "Hey, can I see that lantern?" he asked.

Bo handed it to him, and the two began down the tunnel. "We found something!" they yelled. Jack stood holding the lantern up to the walls of the tunnel, as the others gathered around.

The tunnel wallz were covered with faded rustic paintings of events in the bayou. There were pictures of storms and battles and pirates attacking ships. One scene depicted the beginning of the curse, and another showed both men and animals lying around dead. Another scene depicted

R.R.Lee

eight chests of gold being hidden.

"Hey, there's your treasure, Riley," Bo said as he patted his little cousin on the shoulder.

Riley looked up at Bo and licked his lips. "See I told ya it was real!"

Other scenes were much more frightning. They showed how the original members of the Alliance had all been killed by the Overseers.

As Matie looked at the pictures, anger swelled up inside of her. "I don't like those lizard men. They're bad!"

"That's for sure!" Johnny said.

The next scene showed a large room filled with gold and treasures, and the eight original men of the Alliance standing nezt to them. Above this was a large sun.

"Look!" Johnny ezclaimed. "It's the symbol of the sun again. We've got to go this way. This is the right tunnel!" Johnny hurried ahead of the others as they followed close behind.

The tunnel led on for a very long way. Soon it made a sharp left and seemed to come to a dead end. Riley was the first to complain. "I knew this would lead us to a dead end. I could smell that it didn't go anywhere."

Bo rolled his eyes at his cousin.

A noise above them caught everyone off guard. In the ceiling above was a door and someone was beginning to open it.

"C'mon you guys!" Johnny whispered as the group all retreated back in the tunnel. They peeked back around the corner and watched as a wooden ladder lowered through the hatch.

Bo blew out the lantern and the group huddled in dark silence. Soon a man with a lantern climbed down the ladder, and sniffed at the air. Bo looked at his darkened lantern and the

392

smoke coming from the wick. He gently placed his large hand over it, trying not to let the smell of the smoke escape any further.

The children didn't dare move, as they held their breath. Slowly the man lifted his lantern in the direction the kids were hiding. The little group pressed hard against the wall trying to stay out of sight.

"Do you think he saw us?" Matie whispered. Johnny pressed his hand over her pokey mouth and bit his lip trying not to yell out in pain from her quills.

"Shhhh!" Riley whispered loudly.

Jack looked at the ceiling in frustration.

Riley's loud warning had alerted the man, and he began coming toward the children. "Who'z there?" he called. "Come out into the light where I can see you!"

Riley was filled with fear. His animal instincts quickly took over, and he bolted on all fours down the long tunnel. The man held the lantern high, watched Riley disappear into the darkness, and then turned toward the others.

Jack started to run after Riley. "Wait!" said the man. "I ain't here to hurt you. The professor said you might be comin'." Jack froze. His feet slid to a stop, and he started back to the others.

"Come with me," said the man, pointing to the ladder. "You'll be safer with me than ya are down here. Don't worry about your friend. We have plenty of people watching the tunnels. Someone will find him."

One by one the children climbed the ladder. The bright light above almost blinded them. Then the sweet smell of fresh air met their senses. They were finally above the tunnels and back outside. The area was covered with thick trees, and the trap door behind them was well disguised by a large bush.

"Where are we?" Johnny asked the man.

"This is M<u>u</u>rphy's <u>sw</u>amp!" the man replied. "Most folks in the bayou <u>w</u>ouldn't be caught dead here. The place is full a snakes and all kind a vermin. <u>B</u>ut for the dissenters, it's one of the safest places you cin be. My name's Dohrman," he said, extending his hand to shake Johnny's. "I live in the old cabin up on the ridge. Folla me, and I'll take ya there."

<u>T</u>he old man walked down a long, thin path through the trees. Everyone <u>f</u>ollowed in single file. <u>S</u>oon they came to a broken down shack. Outside an old mule was tied up to a hitching post.

Matie walked up to the mule. "So what's your name? I'm Matie. I used to be a normal little girl, but that dum<u>b</u> old c<u>u</u>rse turned me into a poky porcupine," she said, twitching her no<u>z</u>e as she straightened her dress.

The old mule <u>j</u>ust whinnied, and the man broke into laughter. "Ol' Matilda ain't no Maroo. She's jist a pack mule. She ain't gonna answer ya!"

He invited the children in for a drink. "Yep, the professor sent me a thought er two, letin' me know you'd be comin' this way. I ain't used ta kids much and don' want ya touchin' nothin' a mine. I know how nosy kids cin git. But I am glad ta hep ya all I cin." Dohrman took four dusty glasses from a shelf and blew the dust out of them. "I ain't got much good water here, but I got plenty a amberjuice. It ain't water, but it'll wet yer whistle."

The children watched the old man pour the drinks. <u>J</u>ohnny was concerned that it might be whiskey, and since the old man wasn't used to kids, he spoke up. "Thank you for the offer, but we're just kids and, well, it's against the law for us to drink alcohol."

The old man chuckled under his breath. "I ain't had a drop a alcohol sinse I cum inta the bayou here. Don' like it no more. Amberjuice is a lot better. E<u>v</u>erybody cin dri<u>n</u>k it, and it don't leave ya with a hang over."

"So what's in it?' asked Jack.

The old man smiled, and his eyes glistened as he scratched his whiskered chin. "You ain't heard a the golden nectar. Why it's one a the most valuable things in the bayou. I seen many a pirate spend a fortune on the stuff, and many a fight has broke out over the smallest drop."

"How can a drink be so valuable?" Johnny asked.

The old man looked surprised at Johnny's question. "Ain't ya never heard a gold?"

Johnny looked around at the others, unsure of what the man was saying. "Sure I've heard of gold, but what does that have to do with your amber juice?"

The old man began to chuckle. "Boy, you sure are wet behind the ears, ain't ya? Amber juice is gold! Made of the purest gold they is with just a tich a honey and fruit juice. Sweetest nectar they is in the bayou. But the side effects is what most fight for."

"What kind of side effects?" Bo asked. "Is it like when a person gets drunk?"

"Ahh, it ain't nothin' like that!" the old man said. "Ceptin' for them that gets drunk with power."

Jack had been quiet most of the time, but now his curiosity was piqued. "How can a drink give you power?" he asked.

The old man squinted then poured some of the golden liquid into the glasses. "Here!" he said, handing the glasses to the children. "A person just cain't explain the stuff, you'll see. It won't hurt ya, and it ain't got any alcohol in it."

Bo was the first to take a sip. The juice was very sweet and went down his throat like a breath of fresh air on a hot day. It was refreshingly cool and yet warmed him inside and made every inch of his being tingle. Suddenly Bo's eyes began to bulge with surprise. He gulped hard then looked at the others. "Oh wow, you won't believe this, but this stuff is ama**x**ing!"

Johnny took a drink, but nothing happened. There was no warm feeling and nothing tingled. The amberjuice tasted very go**od**, but he noticed no change at all. "I don't get it," he said. "It tastes good, but I don't see what the big deal is."

The old man raised an eyebro**w** and winked at Johnny. "You're a Defaun, ain't ya?"

"I guess so," Johnny nodded, "but I'm not very good at it yet. How did you know that I'm a Defaun?"

The old man pul**l**ed up a wooden stool and sat down on it. "The ambe**r** **j**uice don't have any effect on the Defauns 'cause they already got the powe**r**."

Johnny looked at Bo. "Is that what it feel**s** like?"

Bo nodded. "Yeah!" he said excitedly. "I can hear everyone's tho**u**ghts, and you won't believe this, but I know right where Riley is. This **j**uice gives a person super human powers to **s**ee and know things. It's amazing!"

Jack and Matie now eagerly drank the jui**ce** in their glasses. Jack smiled as he looked at Bo. "You're right. All I have to do is think of something, and I know all I want to about it."

Suddenly Matie jumped up. The glass slipped from her hands and fel**l** to the ground, breaking into a hundred pieces. "No!" she said as tears began to swell up in her eyes.

"What's wrong, Mat?" Johnny looked concerned.

"It's Mom and Dad. Something's wrong. Those bad men have them." Jack and Bo now took another drink. Johnny closed his eye**x**, too. They all began to see **J**im, Kate and Laura**b**eth in their minds.

Johnny opened his eye**s** wide and nudged the others. "That's the same thing I saw before. They'**r**e all in danger, and we've got to do something to help them!"

"Wait!" said Jack. "It's not the right time."

Jack turned to the old man. "Mr. Dohrman, are the things we're seeing in our minds really true, or is it all a hallucination?"

The old man coughed a bit. "Sure as shootin' it's true. The amberjuice never lies. It's the gold ya know. Ain't nothing more precious on the earth. It was the curse that brought us the knowledge."

"What do you mean?" asked Jack.

The old man shifted a little then began. "Well, seems it all started with this Englishman. He come in one a the moanin' mists. Seems he was a real philosopher, he was. Knowed everthing there was to know about the Egyptians. That odd fella was the first one ta make the amberjuice concoction. Ya see, for generations folks have begged, borraed, or stole ta get gold. But it seems they only did it cause it was right perty. But the real value uf it come from the ancients. Ya see they had it all figured out.

"They learned a way ta turn the gold inta a white powder and then they learned that if they drank the stuff, it changed their whole bein'. That's the real value a gold. Makes ya able ta see the truth in all things. That's why the kings always wore the gold crowns. Sure it made em look good, but better than that, it gave em the power ta see, ta tune inta the heavens.

"The Templar knights knew the secret, too, and vowed to preserve it, even till death if needed. Many of 'em died because of it. That's why they was so wealthy. They knowed the secret. Ya know the pirates come from the Templars. The Templars were the very first pirates, duty swarn ta get the gold stuff and keep it. Over time the pirates forgot why they were after the gold stuff and lost the secret. They just knew they had ta get their hands on that shiny gold.

"Now old Clayton and his goons rule the world with the shiny stuff, and they drink the forbidden juice ta give em the power." The old man cleared his throat as he began to get choked up.

Jack broke the silence. "That's how you knew we were coming, isn't it? You drank the juice, and you could hear the professor back at the museum. He told you we were coming, didn't he?"

The old man smiled and the wrinkles around his eyes deepened. "Yup, you ain't as green as I thought ya was."

Johnny now turned to Jack. "Jack, earlier you said it wasn't the right time to go after my parents and Laurabeth. What did you mean?"

Jack stared at the floor. "Your folks and Laurabeth do need our help, but we've gotta get trained first. I saw the whole thing when I drank the juice. We've gotta go to Pyros. Then we'll be able to fight Clayton and his men and help the others."

Johnny looked at everyone. "What do you guy's think?"

Matie was the first to speak, "I think we should do what Jack says," she smiled.

Bo joined in. "I saw the same thing."

Johnny turned to the old man. "How do we get to Pyros from here?"

The old man shook his head. "It ain't safe, and it ain't that easy. Pyros is the city of fire. Ain't nobody goes in there unless they's supposed to. That place is protected by Whisperin' Bog and the Devil's Ridge. Then ya have ta git through the Razor Swamp.

"Only the Defauns know the safe way in. And then, even if ya do get there, they can make ya think you're somewhere's else. They have the ability ta create an illusion in your mind, so's ya cain't see their city. You could be standin' with a building two inches from your nose and a thinkin' you was still in the swamp. You're talking mighty risky business, thinkin' a goin' there!"

Johnny concentrated and stared at the others. Then Bo broke in after reading Johnny's thoughts. "Oh, no you don't! You're not going in there alone! I agreed to protect you, and so did everyone else here. If one of us goes, we all go!" The others all nodded.

The old man shook his head. "I didn't think ya had it in ya. But if you're so hill bent on headin' straight inta trouble, I'll show ya the way. I'd best cook ya up some dinner, you'll need ta git a good night's sleep fore we head out in the mornin."

42

The Dungeons of Despair

Jim sat on the floor in the corner of his damp prison cell. The walls were made of a grayish green marble that reminded one of the cold, stark walls of a mausoleum. The only relief from the monotonous gray room was the transparent door through which he could see the cells of the other prisoners.

The long hallway between the cells contained a raised rectangular pond that contained a glowing green liquid substance that seemed to be the source of power for the entire place. It was this green fluid that reflected off the walls with an eerie shimmering incandescence that almost consumed the soul with despair.

The prison door, though clear, hissed and sizzled with the same powerful force that kept the assemblages up off the ground, and it was the same force that kept the crystal weapons activated. Jim had already tried to push his way through the force field, but with each attempt he received a nasty shock that made him weaker each time.

He longed to hear Kate's voice once more, but the only sound he could hear were the faint muffled cries of the other insurgents.

Kate and Laurabeth had been placed in the prison cell next to Jim, and the only opportunity he had to see them was when the evil Overseers took him to be reconfigured.

Reconfiguration was a brutal process. First the initiate was taken past all of the other prisoners. In Jim's case they would stop right in front of Kate's cell and tell him to look at his dear wife. Then they would remind Jim that if he did not cooperate completely with them, she would suffer untold pain for his defiance.

Then Jim would quietly go with the guards into a large room. In the room, the Overseers waited in complete darkness. Their reptile eyes could easily see Jim, yet he could not see them, even though he always sensed their presence.

He was then tied to a chair in the center of his evil oppressors, and they began the process of reconfiguration. First they attempted every possible method in their evil repertoire to create fear in Jim. This they used as a means to break his emotions and make him more cooperative.

By now Jim had realized just what this routine was really for. It went far deeper than just being a method of interrogation. The fear it produced was like a drug to the Overseers, and the more fear Jim felt and showed, the more excited the brutal Overseers became. So Jim learned to subdue his emotions if he wished for the sessions to be shortened. After the fear-inducing routine was over, the evil captors would slap Jim's face over and over then interrogate him in every possible way. The worst part of all came next. The Overseers would force a vial of black liquid down Jim's throat and then put a metal helmet on his head. This helmet buzzed and hummed with an unearthly tone that made Jim's teeth grind at the very sound. Then the Overseers sat at a control panel and adjusted the levers creating unfamiliar illusions in Jim's mind.

The illusions were very real, and often Jim would jump at the pain they created. Illusions of his family would fill his mind. He could see his little Matie running from an unseen force, only to find her later in rags with scars on her face. The illusions of Johnny were much different. Over and over Jim saw Johnny walking through endless dark tunnels as if in a maze. Then he would see him being put through the same terrible rituals that Jim had been forced to endure. Each time Jim tried to help his children within the illuzions, he was immediately forced into another thought, always with the face of an Overseer smiling in his mind.

The brutal routine always left Jim weak and unconscioux and ended with the Overseers throwing cold brackish water on their beaten victim. Jim would awaken with every inch of his body screaming with pain. At last, the Overseers would drag Jim back into his cell and throw him in. For hours Jim lay on the floor recuperating, and wondering if Kate and Laurabeth were enduring the same treatment.

Kate had been slowly recovering from the laughing fever that had weakened her back at the Revivory. Laurabeth had watched over her, tending her fevers, till Kate's strength had returned. Oddly the Overseers had seemed to avoid the two, and the only part of the process that they had put them through was the interrogation.

Kate and Laurabeth wondered if the Overseers had feared Kate's condition and avoided the woman to keep from getting sick. For once Kate was glad she had gone through the horrible fever if it kept these minions of evil at bay.

Kate's fiery temperament had also returned, and each time she watched them take Jim, she would yell at the brutes and tell Jim that she and Laurabeth were working on a plan. "Don't let them get to you!" she yelled. Yet each time Jim returned, he looked as if he had aged a few years. His dark brown hair was now graying at the temples, and Kate knew that the process they were putting him through would eventually destroy him.

This wasn't all. Each time Jim walked past, Kate could see that he was changing. It was as if pieces of him were being taken out and replaced with new memories and emotions. Try as he might, Jim couldn't seem to fight the horrible process.

Kate spoke softly to Laurabeth. "There's got to be something we can do to get out of this plaze. I don't remember much of what it was like when we came into the bayou. Tell me everything you know about this place and maybe we can use the information to excape."

Laurabeth rehearsed in detail all she knew of the bayou, how the Maroos were once people, and that even the grand Overseer alligator was really Clayton, Laffite's lifelong enemy. She also told Kate of the Beacon of Light and the crystals used by the Pahreefs, along with the glowing fireballs that guarded everything. Last of all she told Kate of the Revolutionaries of the Defianxe and how they were all working together to free the bayou.

Kate had overheard some of the other prisoners talking of their hope on the outside, and that one of the guards was really a leader of the dissenters and helping those in the clutches of the Overseers.

Kate turned to Laurabeth and whispered. "I think some of the people here are planning an uprising. I overheard them talking of the grand rebellion, and that the time was just days away now." Kate stopped talking as an Overseer walked past. She began laughing a fake laugh to continue the ruse of her sickness. The Overseer recoiled at her laughter and covered his long snout with his cape as if he were afraid her laughter would cause him great distress.

As the large reptile disappeared out of sight, Kate continued, "We've got to find out more from the other prisoners."

Looking about the stark room, she jumped to her feet and ran to the nearby wall where some moss hung on the damp stone. Kate pulled some of it off and reached for the tin dinner plate that sat empty on the floor. She polished the back of it then went to the entrance of the cell where the invixible force field hissed and buzzed. She looked as far down the hall as she could in both directions and caught a small shaft of light that was reflecting off of the glowing green fluid in the hall before her. The light reflected on the back of the plate, and she shined it toward the other prisoners to get their attention.

Next she took the moss and fashioned a message with it. It was simple but effective. First she wrote the letter L, then, she made a skull, and then two crossed swords.

By now all of the other prisoners were whispering. Then something odd began to happen. Each prisoner held up their metal plates, catching the light from the others, until they all converged at one specific cell. It was too far away for Kate and Laurabeth to see, but something was happening.

The two waited as all the cells grew very quiet. Then the Overseer Pithon slithered past. On his heavy staff, the cords of a great whip swung from side to side as he continued down the corridor. Once he was out of sight, one of the other prisoners yelled out to Kate with a loud whisper. "We know who ya is! Sit tight till the day of reckoning."

Kate and Laurabeth smiled at each other. This was just what they were hoping for. There really was a plan, and they wouldn't have to wait too much longer.

"They call it the day of reckoning," Kate repeated as she and Laurabeth moved toward the **b**ack of the cell.

Laurabeth rehear**s**ed every bit of information that she knew of the Overseers to Kate. "We need to be very careful. They have spies everywhere. That's how they caught us back at the **Re**v**ivory. The secretary at the front desk was one of them."

Kate looked aro**u**nd the cell, making sure no one could hear. "The people are afraid. That's how they get them to cooperate. If they don't, they'll end up like u**z**. I can't really blame them."

Suddenly a **g**roup of Pahreefs walked past, headed towards Jim's cell.

Kat**e** and Laurabeth jumped to their feet and **r**an to the fo**r**ce field. Soon the Pah**r**eefs escorted Jim in front of the woman's cell, ready for another session of interrogation. Kate gasped. Jim looked as if he were seventy years old. His eyes were dim and hollow. His hair almost completely white and his tall frame h**u**nched over wit**h** pain.

Kate tried hard not to cr**y** as she bit her lip. The Overseers came and stood next to Jim. Kate was furious and began laug**h**ing louder than ever. Then she rattled off a **n**ursery rhyme. "Jim be **n**imble! Jim be quick! Jim jump over the lizard's tricks!'"

At her words she caught a glint of hope in Jim's eyes. A slight smile croxsed his pale lips. The Overseers recoiled again at her laughter. One held a dainty lace handkerchief to his ugly snout. Kate laughed even harder as the Overseers hurried Jim off.

Jim was quite aware of the toll these sessions were taking on him. But he hadn't given up hope. He was more concerned with the memory loss he had noticed. Often unfamiliar memories would creep in to his mind as he fought to distinguish them from the true memories of his previous experience. Now, the same old process of the reconfiguring of his mind began. It was all just as before with the routine of trying to instill fear in the weakened man.

Back in his cell, Jim had plenty of silent hours to think of any new strategy to combat their twisted rituals. Today for the first time he tried something new. He had remembered an old passage in the Bible that he had read that said to love your enemies and bless those that curse you. Then, he had the thought of praying for those who despitefully used him.

As he began to think of love, he thought of his family and of how much he loved them. As he did, something odd happened. The Overseers, who usually enjoyed this time more than any other as a means of filling their emotional drug for fear, began moaning, spitting, and hissing as if the taste in their mouth was bitter.

Jim realized his attempts were making a difference, and he knew he was on to something.So he began to openly speak to his oppressors in kind, loving tones. This evoked shrieks of pain in the reptiles. Angrily they yanked Jim from the chair and hurried him back to his cell. For the first time he had discovered their true weakness. They couldn't stand the emotional taste of love. Now it was his greatest weapon.

The Overseers great fear of love and goodness was the very thing that had also protected **K**ate and Laurabeth from their attempts at reconfiguration. It wasn't Kate's <u>f</u>ever they had feared so much, but her laughter. Laughter and joy evoked pain in the evil Overseers. They couldn't stand the taste of it. This grand revelation was now the only ray of hope that could protect the prisoners from total destruction.

43
The Fearful Fox

In total confusion, Riley ran through the dark tunnels until he finally arrived at the large round room with the giant sun on the floor. He darted from door to door, unsure which way to go. The poor little fox-boy was so frightened that he couldn't remember which door he had come from. The paralyzing fear inside of him overtook his judgment and he had lost all instinct of what he should do. Sitting in the middle of the room he panted, glancing from side to side in the unfamiliar surroundings.

He looked down at the awkward hairy paws that had once been his hands and longed to return to his former self. Suddenly he heard an unearthly howl. At first he was startled by the sound and then realized it was coming from his own mouth. Anxiously he looked up at the glass ceiling above and quickly covered his red snout. "Shut up!" he whispered to himself, gathering all the courage he could muster. Ever so cautiously he stood up and approached one of the doors in the round room. He remembered what the professor had said about a fox's instincts.

With new found confidence he began sniffing at the air. Finally he came to a doorway that had the familiar smell of sausage. "This must be it!" he whispered. "It's gotta be the tunnel that leads back to McGifford's store. There was lots of sausage there. I'll follow it and get help for the others." Riley's imagination took over as he thought of himself bringing McGifford to rescue the others and taking the credit as a hero.

He began racing down the long tunnel, throwing all caution aside. The smell of the intoxicating sausage overcame his better judgment and was all he could think of.

The tunnel had sufficient light for a long way. Then it gradually began to dim. Riley'z pace slowed a bit, and he looked from side to side. He lifted his paws, trying to brush the damp dirt off of them. He looked up at the ceiling. There were no more floor boards, just roots and vines in the dirt above.

This was not Mr. McGifford's tunnel. Riley moved forward in the dark. The smell of damp rotting wood was everywhere. He looked for anything that might be familiar, but there was none to be found.

The smell of meat was getting closer now. It wafted through the tunnel on a slight breeze. Up ahead, he saw a small beam of light coming from the wooden floor above him. He followed its source to a small hole in the floor boards of a building. Riley tried to see through the hole above him, but his legs were far too short to see anything. Even when he stood on his two hind legs, it wasn't enough.

He scratched at the dirt of the walls, trying to climb higher. Then he stretched his furry red neck as high as he could to get a better look. Suddenly the wall beside him gave way and collapsed under his weight. The ground beneath him crumbled away, and the little fox tumbled into a vast darkness below. He let out a horrible howl as he clawed at the air with all four paws, grasping at the empty air. His little body bounced off of rocks and debris until he finally came to a painful stop.

The small fox blinked and rubbed his eyes as they slowly adjusted to the darkness. He was lying on his back on a heap of damp dirt in the middle of an enormous cave.

A strange natural blue light filtered into the cavern from the nearby tunnels. At the far end of the cavern was a beautiful waterfall that echoed as the water trickled over the rocks.

Riley could see easily now, and he checked his bruises and brushed himself off. Then he began to explore his new surroundings. The hole he had fallen through was about thirty feet above him. He tried climbing back up the steep wall over sticks and rocks, but it was useless. With each try, the dirt and rocks beneath him would crumble, making the steep slope even more treacherous. After several attempts he finally gave up and began looking for another way out of the cave.

His nose twitched and his mouth watered at the unreachable smell of the sausage above that made him even more determined than ever to get out of this place and get to that food.

As he began to explore the enormous cavern, he noticed beams of light filtering through the cracks in the top of the massive cave. Making his way toward the waterfall, he looked toward its source, a very large crack in the ceiling.

Riley looked at the moss-covered rocks of the waterfall. "Maybe this is the way out," he thought. A closer inspection of the hole above the waterfall led to a hopeless conclusion. The distance to this escape route was far too high. The rocks ended abruptly, forty-feet above the floor of the cavern, and slick walls led the rest of the way to the opening. Not only was this a problem, but if ever a person could somehow get to the point of reaching the opening, the moving waters would push them right back onto the rocks.

Riley turned his attention to a wide stream that meandered through the cavern. He walked along the stream'z edge to a large pool beneath the waterfall that bubbled and churned as it filtered into the stream. He went down the river a ways and splashed across the stream towards the end of the cavern. A series of caves and tunnels opened to his view along the river's edge. He could see the remains of an old wooden barrel and some broken glass, a sign that someone else had once been there.

The enormous grotto faded behind him as Riley pushed

past the maze of tunnels along the water's edge. The drip, drip, drop of water seeping through the rocks echoed in his sensitive ears. He covered them with his damp paws, trying to avoid the persistent echo that taunted his every step.

Soon the tunnels gave way to large boulders along the rocky wall at the river's edge. The sandy path that he had so easily navigated up until now was becoming steeper until all that was left was a narrow foot path. He clung to the rock walls on his right, while he edged carefully along the steep path. To his left an abrupt cliff face lined the surging river below.

The untamed waters splashed through a narrow opening of jagged rocks, tumbling and bubbling, as it exploded in a spray of foam on the other side.

Riley looked down into the turbulent waters below, and then he took a cautious step. "Just don't look down," he whispered to himself. The path was only six inches wide now, and Riley stood on his hind legs with his back to the rock wall behind him. He edged his way along the steep precipice, his feet slipping on the sandy edge. The path ended abruptly by an enormous boulder blocking the way. "Oh, no!" exclaimed Riley, his voice echoing through the caves. Suddenly he felt some pebbles falling on his head. A spray of sand and dirt followed. As he tried to duck out of the way, he noticed something dangling by his side.

It was a rope that swung back and forth, bumping against his furry ear. He reached out, tried to grab it, and missed. Finally, when it hit him in the face, he snapped at it with his teeth just as it swung back. This time he caught hold of it. He wrapped it around his paws and pulled on it to see if it was secure enough to hold his weight. It appeared to be firmly fastened to something above him. With a little hesitation, he climbed up the rope hoping this was a way out.

Climbing the rope led him up and over the large

boulder. Clearing the top, he saw two worn boots in front of his eyes. Then he lifted his eyes to see a strange man standing in the boots. Startled, Riley almost let go of the rope, but his rescuer reached down and caught the back of Riley's jacket just in time. The little fox scrambled up to the top of the boulder and looked at the strange man standing in front of him. The man was in his forties and had a long dark beard. He was very thin, and his once nice dress pants were tattered and torn. He wore ankle high boots and dark socks. He had on a white shirt that was stained with dirt and an occasional hole that had been mended.

Riley's eyes bulged with surprise. He tried to speak but there was a lump in his throat. He was unsure if this strange man was going to help him or hurt him. "Who are you?" Riley squeaked.

The thin man just looked at the poor shivering fox. "You're a Maroo. Where are you from?" the man asked.

Riley answered softly. "My name is Riley Williams. I'm from Leblanc. I'm new here."

The man turned his back on Riley and headed down a path towards a bright light. Riley scampered along behind him. The light hurt Riley's eyes at first till they adjusted then he realized that it was just the sunshine from outside coming through the cave's entrance. He followed the man on a narrow path that widened into a spacious cave. By the scattered supplies that were strewn about the cave, it looked as if the man had lived there for some time. On the floor were crates of various sizes. A stone ledge made a niche for storing food. A bamboo mat lay upon the sandy floor and a pine log served az a bench. In the center of the room was a rock fire pit with a small fire. The curious man picked up a long stick and placed a hot dog on it. Riley's mouth watered at the delectable sight.

"So your name'z Riley?" The man asked as he roasted the hot dog over the fires coals. "Do you have a family here?"

412

"Well, they're gone!" Riley explained, licking his lips.

"Where are they?" the man asked.

"Oh, they're somewhere in Florida on business. But I'm all right. I can take care of myself," Riley said, sitting up taller.

"Well, I suppose you're not very hungry then," the man stated as he touched the hot dog with his finger.

Riley licked his lips again. "Well, I might be just a little hungry," he said, sniffing at the air. The man placed the stick with the hot dog against one of the crates and took a small can of beans from off the ledge shelf.

Riley watched as the man pulled out a large knife and hoped it wasn't meant for him. Then the man stabbed the knife into the can and began prying open the lid. The man handed him a spoon with the can of beanz and then gave him the hot dog. "Thanks!" said Riley, licking the can.

Quietly the man sat down on the log, watching Riley eagerly eat the food. "You must be half starved!" the man said kindly. "How long have you been wandering around in those caves down here?"

"Oh, I don' know," Riley mumbled with a mouthful. "Seems like it was days. I was running from this man, and he caught my friends. I didn't know what tunnel to take then I followed one and fell through a hole."

"Who were you running from?" the man axked.

"Oh, just about everybody, I guess. First it was those Pah, pah, something men."

"You mean the Pahreefs?"

"Yeah, that's the ones. McGifford told us to hide in the tunnels. Then the professor made us hide again when the Pahreefs came to the museum. We were all just fine till we got to the end of the tunnel and that old man found us. He caught all of the others, but I was the smart one. I got away."

"So why are the Pahreefs after you? What have you

done wrong?" the man asked.

Riley licked his paw then continued. "Oh, I haven't done anything. They just want Johnny becauxe of that watch and his..." Suddenly Riley stopped in mid-sentence. He realized that he had just broken his promise to protect Johnny and the artifacts.

Riley got very quiet. The man smiled at him. "So how long have you been in the swamp?"

Riley looked around unsure of whether or not to answer. Finally he took a deep breath and looked at the empty can in his hand. The man had been very kind to him. So he answered, "Well, we've only been here a couple of days. We had to get away from Maison Rouge, 'cause these other bad guys were after Johnny and the Leavitts. So we ended up hiding in the bayou and then things just all started hap......

Before Riley could finish his sentence, the skinny man grabbed Riley's shoulders and looked him squarely in the eyes. "Did you say Leavitt?" he demanded.

"Yeah," Riley answered trying to squirm out of the man's grip.

The man jumped up. "They did it! They found the watch!"

"Yeah, Johnny found it all right. So what's the big deal? It's just a watch," said Riley.

The man sat on the floor right in front of Riley and stared at him. "Tell me everything, everything you know!"

"Well, OK," said Riley in a bewildered tone. "But why do you want to know about Maison Rouge?"

"Just tell me, please!" the man asked.

Riley began by rehearsing the events of the night of the grand ball and finished with their encounter with the water pirates and finding Matie.

The man slapped his knee with ezcitement as Riley

414

finished his story. Then he handed Riley a cup of water and started packing a duffel bag with provisions. "I want you to take me to where you last saw your friends," the man exclaimed.

"But I don't know how," Riley whined. "I can't remember what tunnel they're in. The only thing different about that tunnel was all the pictures on the walls."

The man smiled. "Don't worry. I know exactly what tunnel you're talking about. If your friends are there, we'll find them."

Riley brushed his paw across the dirt. He felt sick inside, like he had just betrayed all of his friends. He had just told a complete stranger everything. For all he knew this man could be one of the bad guys.

The man stopped packing the duffel bag and turned to Riley. "I guess you don't really know too much about me, do you?" Riley looked up only briefly. The man reached out and lifted Riley's snout.

"My name is Ken Leavitt. I came into the bayou for the same reason you and your friends did, to solve the curse and save the family business from that cutthroat Ratcliffe."

Riley looked up. He hadn't mentioned Ratcliffe's name to the man. Now he looked at Ken and could see the resemblance to Jim.

Finally Riley really was a hero. He had found Ken Leavitt! His instincts had allowed him to trust this stranger who had been lost to the Leavitt family. The two finished packing the provisions, and then headed down a tunnel to go and find the others.

44
Timely Opportunists

Randy and Palmer looked out over the endless waters of the ocean. In the distance the shadow of another vessel rested upon the horizon, silhouetted in front of the setting sun.

Pierre began issuing orders to his crew in English, French, and Spanish. The crew hustled about the ship putting everything in order. Several pirates stuffed wadding rags into five enormous cannons, as other pirates plunged heavy cannonballs into the great mouths of the guns.

"Heave ho!" the men yelled, tugging in unison on weathered ropes. Pulleys creaked as the enormous cannons moved into position along the ship's railing. In an attempt to hide their true motives, the pirates raised a Cartehenian flag to the top of the mast.

Pierre stood on the bow of the ship, his eyes firmly fixed on their new target. The cabin boy came running and handed Pierre a long brass spyglass. Pierre took the glass and watched his intended victims.

Randy and Palmer watched from the railing. Here they were right in the middle of every young boy's fantasy. They were going to be actual participants in a real pirate raid. The excitement was tangible. They felt the anticipation of everyone on board. Suddenly the entire crew became very silent, and each man took up his position.

The pirates hid in every nook and cranny of the ship like crouching tigers ready to spring on their unsuspecting prey. Some hid in the ship's galley and others behind barrels on deck. Some were stationed near the cannons, while others lay flat upon the ship's deck. The rest ran the rigging and sails as the ship pulled along side a heavily loaded Spanish galleon.

Palmer and Randy crouched with caution, unsure of what to expect. Soon a signal flag was raised from the other vessel.

Pierre smiled, "Ahh, they wish to speak to us," he said turning to Randy and Palmer. He snapped his fingers and one of his men raised a flag in response.

The captain of the galleon ordered his ship to come to a halt.

Pierre yelled something in Spanish to the other captain. They exchanged a few pleasantries then began laughing. The unsuspecting Spanish captain motioned for his men to stand down and return to their normal duties. Pierre snapped his fingers and in the blink of an eye, a barrage of cannonballs sailed through the air towards the Spanish ship.

In confusion, the Spanish captain took a defensive posture ordering his men to strike back. The galleon was only able to get off a few shots before they were completely overcome by Pierre's skillful privateers. Some swung from the yardarm, and others emerged from the waters and scaled the sides of the helpless ship. Within moments they had taken possession of the galleon, and its passengers sat helpless, tied up on the deck.

Pierre's men clamored amid whistles and whoops over their new found plunder. Soon they were unloading the spoils of their attack onto the decks of Pierre's ship, the *Hotspir*.

A clerk stood near Pierre making a detailed log of every precious item taken from the helpless vessel. As the last of Pierre's privateers boarded the *Hotspir*, Pierre yelled a gracious "thank you" in Spanish, bowing to the captain of the other ship who sat squirming on the deck, his hands and feet bound and his mouth gagged.

Pierre took the curious time modulator in his hands now

and quickly adjusted the pointers. As he did the three gemz within it began spinning wildly. Soon a mass of varying colors and lights began swirling around the ship. Then a flash of lightning struck in front of the boat. As the men looked out toward the Spanish ship it began to fade slowly until it was completely gone.

Randy and Palmer were both feeling sick again but their curiosity was much stronger than the dizzying effects of the synchronistic modulator.

"What happened to the other ship?" Randy yelled to Pierre.

"It remains where it is!" Pierre said with a sly smile. "It is we who have moved. We are no longer within their time."

The ocean around the ship was as still as glass. It was as if the ship were suspended in time. Suddenly a slight breeze began to blow, and there was a faint whistling noise on the wind. Then the noise got louder and louder as colorful clouds began to gather and churn around the ship. Then something disturbing emerged on the Northern horizon. A large gray cloud began to take shape on the still waters. It darkened until it was almost completely black and swirled like the beginning of a great tornado.

"Abyss on the port bow!" a voice yelled. The echo of those words flew throughout the ship. The dark cloud was now churning and swirling and growing larger by the moment.

Pierre yelled a mass of orderx to his crew as they adjusted the rigging accordingly. "You have wondered why we do not approach the curse," he said to the two men. "Now you will see it for yourselves."

Randy and Palmer moved to the front of the ship where they watched the ominous black cloud in amazement and horror. It began sucking up the clear water of the ocean before them.

418

"*Fait pas une esquandol*, don't make such a racket," Pierre yelled to his trusted crew. Then he turned toward the brewing gale and shook his fist at the dark cloud. With gritted teeth he yelled, "*Arretez-vous la cunja*" (which meant "Stop, you curse!)

Amazingly, the darkness responded. As if a person of importance had just given it an insulting challenge, the cloud shifted its attention toward the *Hotspir*. A slow low groan came from deep within the darkness as the form of an angry face emerged from within the abyss. The dark face scowled, then growled, and in a flurry of anger, exploded in a gust of torrential wind and rain.

The men secured the sails and riggings then waited. Obviously this thing wasn't over yet. In silence the crew watched with uneasy anticipation. One pirate hung over the ship's railing, watching the waters. Out of nowhere an enormous wave surged out of the water and rose to fifty feet in height then took on the form of a monstrous hand that reached for the poor pirate and swept him off the deck into the perilous depths below.

"Report!" demanded Pierre.

"It was Evans!" yelled a crewman. "The abyss has taken him."

"Aren't you going to help that man?" yelled Palmer.

Pierre whistled an order to his men, and they began scurrying around deck securing everything. "If we remain, the gale will take all of us, too. We must leave immediately!" Pierre said. He readjusted the time modulator. "Do not worry," he said turning to the men. "We will give it something to remember us before we leave."

The ship moved into position sideways to the great black cloud. Pierre's men loaded the cannons with some cannon balls coated with the same glowing substance that powered the time device. Pierre turned to his guests. "The curse will learn never to take one of my men again. After we send it this gift, its hunger for my men will leave only a bitter taste in its ugly mouth."

With a snap of his fingers the cannonballs went whistling through the air right into the mouth of the ominous black giant. The great abyss suddenly exploded violently in dark opposition to the nasty present it had received from Pierre's cannons. A whirlwind consumed the entire ship, trying to push it off course. The crew worked feverishly at their posts trying desperately to hold the ship together.

Pierre adjusted the time modulator. The jems within it spun wildly, but even with the colorful cloudz forming about it, the ship was being held in place by the great dark abyss. Pierre gritted his teeth, determined to free the ship, then boldly went to the bow of the ship. "You cannot kill me or any more of my men upon my ship for I am a Laffite!" he yelled.

At these words the great abyss angrily gripped Pierre with a torrent of wind and rain, then it recoiled as if in remarkable fear and slowly released its hold upon both Pierre and the ship. Streaks of color surrounded the ship as lightning bolts struck all around. The crushing grasp of the great cloud finally let go and the ship began spinning out of control. All of Pierre's men ran about the deck in utter confusion. Pierre yelled an assortment of orderz at the men to gain control of the floundering ship. Then a clash of thunder exploded, and the ship was instantly transported through time to another destination.

The ship now sat in a small calm river near the bayou. Men lay about everywhere on the deck and slowly began to regain their compozure. Pierre himself was hanging over the ship's bow. He began to stand as a slight smile crossed his lips. He raised his fist in the air and said in a weak voice, "I am a

Laffite. The curse will never win!" Then he fainted and fell to the deck. Getting to their feet, two of his crew loyally picked him up and hurried him to the captain's quarters.

The rest of the ship's crew now set sail for the nearest port. As it pulled into dock at Golden City, crowds of people flocked to see its approach.

The first mate motioned for Randy and Palmer to follow him. He took them below deck to the captain's quarters. There Pierre lay upon a luxurious bed where the ship's doctor was tending him. With a weak gesture Pierre motioned for the first mate to lock the door. He complied then quickly retrieved something from a nearby cabinet. He returned with two small cloth bags in his hands and threw them at the feet of the two men. Palmer reached down and picked up the bag at his feet. As he opened it, he stared at what was inside. The bag was filled with gold coins. "What's this for?" he asked.

"For your silence," Pierre groaned with annoyance.

Randy didn't pick up his bag. "What's going on here?" he asked. "Why are you trying to buy our silence?"

Pierre grimaced in pain. "I see you catch on very quickly, my friend. First of all, it is the law that everyone aboard ship receives a portion of our plunder. But I have given you a double portion for your silence as well. Tell no one that I am here."

"I don't understand why." Randy said.

"It would seem I have many enemies in the bayou. My men act as free privateers with my first mate pretending to be their captain."

"You're in hiding!" exclaimed Randy.

Immediately the first mate put a knife to Randy's throat. "No man calls Pierre Laffite a coward!"

"Let him go!" Pierre commanded as the man lowered the knife. "They do not understand our ways here."

421

Pierre turned to Randy and Palmer. "I am not in hiding, but I am a marked man. You see there are many types of people within the bayou. There is one whom I have fought for almost two hundred years now. He is the most despicable maroo who thinks himself an Overseer, a great caiman whom you know as Clayton. You see, I lead a band of rebels that are far more than just pirates. We fight to bring about the cause of freedom in the bayou. Our plundering serves to finance our cause so that we might bring down the ominous dictator Clayton and his brutal Overseers. They kill our people and force them into slavery. I alone know the whereabouts of the leader of our rebellion. Soon, very soon now, there will be a great uprising from the Revolutionaries of the Defiance. You see we are the dissenters. Now will you keep your silence?"

"Why are you trusting us with all of this?" Randy asked.

Pierre sighed. "I need you. If I wanted only your silence I could have easily left you upon the Spanish galleon or thrown you into the abyss. But I believe you are after the same thing that I am. You wish to see the Leavitts safely through the bayou and protected from your friend Ratcliffe's grasp."

"Ratcliffe isn't our friend!" Randy spoke defensively.

"Yes, yes, I know," said Pierre. "He is a cowardess minion for Clayton. Clayton is the real enemy. He is the one who began this charade. It was he who contacted Ratcliffe and sought to destroy the Leavitts in the beginning to get them out of his way."

"What are you talking about?' Randy demanded. "Why does Clayton even care about the Leavitts?"

Pierre coughed a little. "Your friends, the Leavitts, are the only thing standing between Clayton and his desire to rule the world. Their son, Johnny, is the last male Laffite. He has the power to destroy Clayton and his agenda. Clayton will do anything to stop that."

Randy and Palmer stood shocked with concern at Pierre's word<u>x</u>.

"If this Clayton wanted the Leavitts dead, why didn't he just do it himself?" Randy asked.

Pierre sat up on his elbow. "Most of Clayton's powers are limited to the bayou. He and his men cannot leave or they will die. But he has spies who come and go easily from our world to yours. Most of all he is in great control of the monetary system of your people. He needed someone who would be loyal to him that could be easily bribed. Ratcliffe served this purpose quite well. He saw these things as a family vendetta, and the promise of wealth was all it took to awaken his greed.

"We tried to protect the Leavitts as long as we could. We sent a Defaun, Mr. Sauvinet, to help your friends by giving them a new business and a safe place to live under Sam and Cora's care. But it was too late. The damage was already done. We had to choose another course of action which meant involving the Leavitts. The only alternative we have left now is to destroy Clayton and the curse before it destroys all of us!"

45

The Reunion

The hot afternoon sun streamed in the cave's entrance as Riley followed Ken out into the sunshine. The cave sat high up on a hill overlooking Golden City.

Ken climbed down a rocky path into the thick trees below. Riley followed, mimicking Ken'x every move. Now Ken ducked as he ran towards a large rock in a clearing. Riley followed. When he finally arrived by Ken's side, he asked about Ken's unusual behavior.

Ken looked around then began to whisper. "It's dangerous here. The croonies are everywhere." Riley half smiled at the word Croonie, wondering if Ken had gone crazy from being alone too long.

Ken saw Riley's grin and turned to him. "The croonies are the ones bit by the fever bug. When they don't get the medicine in time, they end up a little bit crazy and come to live here in the back woods. They have almost nothing, and they attack juxt to survive."

"Oh, those are the ones like Johnny's Mom," Riley said. "She couldn't stop laughing after that bug bit her."

Ken grabbed Riley's arm. "What are you talking about? Is Kate sick?"

Riley nodded. "Yeah, she got bit by a Schneille, and they had to take her to the hospital in Golden City. That's where Mr. Leavitt and my cousin Laurabeth were when we had to leave."

The trees nearby began rustling. "Come on," said Ken. "We've got to get out of here now. Someone's coming. If it's the Croonies, it'll be bad, but there are others here that are a lot

424

more dangerous than them." Ken looked around and then whispered even softer. "There aren't very many, but the curse turned some of the pirates into bloodthirsty thieves. They're the worst of all the beings in the entire bayou, and they often come here to find a crooner or two."

"What are they called?" Riley said a bit too loudly.

"Shhhhh!" Ken warned holding his finger to his lips. "The people in the swamp call them vampiratez. No one knowz very much about them except that those who've had run-ins with them rarely return, and those who do return tell horrible stories about what they've seen."

Ken nudged Riley ahead of him. They moved from tree to tree till they came to a large clearing. The cliff face loomed high above them as Ken advanzed toward the center of the clearing where a stone pedestal stood. On the top of the pedestal was a triangular shaped rock. Ken took the rock and approached the sheer cliff face. He placed the rock into a hole on the cliff wall. Immediately the bushes and trees near the cliff wall began to vibrate wildly then fell to the ground revealing a door on the cliff's side.

"Come on," Ken whispered and the two headed inside. Ken placed the same stone into another receptacle on the wall inside of the door, and the large shrubs and trees outside instantly returned to their former positions, hiding the opening.

"We have to hurry!" Ken said as he rushed down a long tunnel that led to several others.

"Where are we going?" Riley whispered.

Ken smiled. "It's all right to talk out loud now that we're inside. The others are afraid of the caves. Now we have to find your friends before high tide."

Ken lit a lantern and hurried through the tunnelx. As they went further into the cave system the sound of rushing waters met Riley's sensitive ears. The two eventually emerged into a large cave. A brisk river ran right through the center of it, directly blocking safe passageway across.

"Are we going to cross that thing?" Riley azked with wide eyes.

Ken nodded. "We have to. High tide will be here in less than a half an hour. You can wait here if you want, but if you do, the cave will be full of water, and you'll have to swim for it or drown."

Riley looked at the watermarked walls around him. "Oh, I'm comin'."

Ken handed the lantern to Riley then climbed several large rocks and looked down. "Throw me my bag!" he yelled. Riley threw the bag up to Ken and watched as he pulled out a long rope and fastened it to a ring lodged in the cave's wall. Ken made a lasso and circled it high above his head as he took aim for a large boulder across the raging surf. He tossed the rope, and it lodged perfectly around the rock. "Come on up! We don't have any time to waste." Ken yelled.

Riley held up the lantern and looked at the rising waters lapping at his feet. The water had risen two feet just in the time they had been in the cave. Riley scrambled up over the jagged rocks till he was safe by Ken's side. By now Ken had secured a pulley rigging to the rope with a smaller rope attached to retrieve it.

"Have you ever ridden a zip line?" he asked.

Riley nodded with a grin. "Yeah, I made one in my back yard once. But the line broke when I tried it out. I sure hope this one's better."

"Just hold on tight and you'll be fine," Ken said, tugging on the rope one last time.

Riley held the lantern in one paw and held onto the pulley with the other. He closed his eyes then jumped out over the surging waters. The little pulley squeaked as it rolled along

426

the rope, carrying Riley to the other side of the river.

Riley turned and watched the waters lapping at the rock Ken stood on. Then Ken pulled on the smaller rope to retrieve the pulley. He took a running leap and grabbed for the pulley. This time the pulley whizzed as it efficiently carried him across the raiing waters. Ken landed on the other side in a dead run. "Come on!" Ken yelled, grabbing Riley by the collar. The two ran through a maze of tunnels and headed as far away from the rising waters as possible. The rushing waters roared behind them as it pushed through the caves.

Finally, on higher ground, Ken sat down for a rest. He pulled a bottle from his bag. "Would you like a drink of water?" he said, offering the bottle to Riley.

Riley kept looking back down the tunnel. "What about the tide?" he asked.

"We're above it now. The water doesn't come up this far," Ken said with a wink.

Riley took the jug of water and took a long drink. "Do you always have to come this way?' he asked, pointing back to the tunnels.

"Not usually," Ken said. "But it is the fastest way back to the tunnels you came from. Now, if we're going to find the otherz before dark, we'd better get going." Ken led Riley through a large cave system that branched off into several intersecting tunnelz.

As the two walked, Riley sniffed at the air. "It's that smell again!" he said.

"What smell?' Ken asked.

"Sausage!" said Riley licking his lips. "I smelled the same thing right before I fell down that hole."

Ken slowed his pace and looked at Riley. "Do you remember anything else?"

Riley nodded. "Well, I was trying to look up through

the floor boards of this building right before I fell. That's where that wonderful smell was **co**ming from."

Ken s**l**apped at his leg and let out a soft whistle. "That's it! You've found the place the Revolutionarie**z** have been looking for. Clayton is the **onl**y one in the bayou that is le**g**ally allowed to have **sa**usage. I think you've **f**ound his headquarters."

The two headed down the long passageway as the s**m**ell be**g**an to fade. Soon the walls were more recognizable. After a long walk, Ken led the way to the area with the familiar pictures on the walls.

"Is this the way you came **b**efore?" Ken a**x**ked.

Riley nodded. "Yeah, but I can't remember where to go from here."

Ken patted his shoulder. "I know just where your friend**z** are. Follow me."

Ken started down the tunnel until he came right to the area where the old man had found the others. Riley hadn't noticed it before but there was a small rope hanging from the hatch abo**v**e their heads. Ken pulled on it. **T**hen stopped and listened quietly.

"Why did you pull on that rope?" Riley asked.

"It's a signal for someone to come and open the hatch. Old man Dohrman will be here soon." Just as Ken said these words, the hatch opened, and Mr. Dohrman peered down through it.

"I knew someone would find that little scamper," the old man said. "It's a good thing it was you and not the O**v**erseers." Dohrman lowered a ladder for the **t**wo, and in no time the three were at Dohrman's ca**b**in.

It was dark by now and most of the children had gone to sleep, but Johnny couldn't get the thought**x** of his parents out of his mind. He had tossed and turned until finally he was just

428

beginning to doze off when he heard a familiar voice outside. At first he thought he was dreaming then he heard it again and sat straight up listening. He jumped up and ran outside where he saw Ken and Riley along with Dohrman sitting around a campfire.

"Uncle Ken!" Johnny exclaimed throwing his arms around his uncle. "We thought you were dead!" Ken pulled away from Johnny to look at him for a moment, then tears began to well up in his eyes.

"Well, I'll be! It is you!" Ken put his arm around Johnny and the two sat down by the fire. "Your friend Riley here brought me to you. It was quite a coincidenze that I ran into him at all. He tells me that you found some very important things back at Maison Rouge."

Johnny smiled and nodded. "Oh, Uncle Ken. You won't believe what we've been through. Mom and Dad are being held prisoner. We're planning on going to Pyros to get some help. Matie's a Maroo and so are my friends. And you won't believe this, but I'm a Defaun, and we've just gotta fix that curse."

Johnny was talking so fast that his Uncle Ken just smiled. "Hold on there," he said. "You're going way too fast. You can't fix that curse on your own. You don't know what you're up against. And if you think you're going to just waltz into Clayton's prison and break out your parents that just won't happen. Clayton has Pahreefs everywhere, not to mention all of the spies in his employ. But we do have one thing up on him. Riley here has found his hide out!"

At Ken's words, old man Dohrman spit on the ground. "I'll be hornswaggled! It would take a fox-like critter ta find it. Now the Revolutionaries can follow that plan they been working on."

"What plan?" Johnny asked.

Riley had fallen asleep and was curled up in a ball on

the ground snoring loudly.

Ken put another log on the fire then began to explain. "The Revolutionaries of the Defiance have been planning a strike for a very long time. But somehow Clayton always finds out about it. He's already arrested hundreds of our people. It wasn't until recently that we found out who his informant was. Our people have imprisoned the traitor and now the number of Revolutionaries is growing. People are gathering in all parts of the bayou just waiting to make their move."

"So what are they planning?" Johnny asked with wide eyes.

Ken smiled as he leaned a little closer. "Our leader has been working on a secret weapon. For almost two hundred years now Clayton has ruled with an iron fist, abusing the liberty and freedom of everyone in the bayou. But we finally found his weakness. He thrives on darkness and hatred. He can't handle any type of spiritual light or love. We also discovered that in order to fight him and his cutthroats, the curse has to be controlled. That's where you come into it."

"Me?" Johnny laughed. "How do I come into all of this?"

Ken was very serious now. "Johnny, you know those things you've found? They were the vital missing pieces of the puzzle. The curse can only be fixed by using these things in the proper way. It wasn't by chance that you ended up here in the bayou. It was an invitation."

"What do you mean?" Johnny questioned.

"When I was back at the company, I got a letter," said Ken. "It was from Mr. Sauvinet. He let me know about Maison Rouge and told me that our family was in danger. That was the real reason I came to Louisiana. I had to protect the family. At first I just came to check things out. Then Ratcliffe set up the family by trying to get Maison Rouge from us. It was obvious to me that there was something very important about that place and Ratcliffe knew more about it than I did."

Johnny looked up. "Uncle Ken, did you know that Ratcliffe is Clayton's great great grandson?"

"No, I didn't!" Ken replied. "But that explains how Ratcliffe knew so much about our family and Maison Rouge. I finally met Mr. Sauvinet face to face. He explained that the real threat to our family was from Clayton. Clayton has just been using Ratcliffe's greed to serve his own purposes. The whole thing was a set up to try to get the family out of the way.

"Sauvinet was right about the danger to our family. He finally told me about the curse and explained that the only way to really protect the family was to destroy Clayton's power. And that means destroying the curse. I thought I could do it on my own. But the curse is too powerful. It's going to take all of us. So I guess you could say that your coming here was partly my fault. I asked Mr. Sauvinet to contact your father. I needed the family's help. But I couldn't just ask for it. In the artifacts you found, did it say *True Intent* anywhere?"

"Yeah, it's in every single clue," Johnny answered.

"I thought so," said Ken. "That doesn't surprise me. That's how the curse works. You had to come here out of your own free will to help someone elze. It had to be out of true intent. Otherwise our attempt at overcoming the curse would be just like everyone else's, useless. Your coming here was an answer to my prayers and the prayers of thousands of others.

"Clayton and his men are worried. Their regime is about to be taken down, and they know it. That's why they are trying to stop all of you. That's why they're searching the cities."

Johnny stared into the fire. "We met old Marie before we came into the bayou. She said that someday the last male Laffite would come and fix the curse. But the person had to be a blood relative."

Ken nodded. "Originally I came into the Bayou because of Ratcliffe and his attacks. When I saw the people here and the civilization that's developed for the last hundred and eighty years, I realized just how strong this curse really is. The curse is destroying the people here, but it's also what holds this place together. Clayton knows that if he can expand his power beyond the bayou, no one will be able to stop him. He's determined to control everything in this world and in our world as well. And now he's beginning to do it."

"That's what the professor at the museum told us," said Johnny. "He said Clayton holds all the treasury notes that the U.S. has and that he is in control of all the U.S. banks."

Ken nodded. "Yes, I'm afraid that's correct. But there's more. He's planning to call all of those treasury notes due, and when he does, it will cause all of the U.S. economy to collapse. When that happens he's going to take over and imprison every man woman and child in the U.S. He wants to create a slave population that he's in control of, so that he can rule the entire world.

"He's already learned how to manipulate the powers of the curse and that's how he controls everything. But Johnny, now that you're here, we have a chance, even if it's a very small one. The Revolutionaries of the Defianxe have found hope again. We're going to fight the Overseers and bring freedom back to the bayou!"

Johnny looked concerned. "But what am I supposed to do? I'm just a kid. I don't know what to do with these artifacts. And I don't know how to fight the Overseer's like Clayton."

Ken smiled at Johnny's words. "You'll know what to do when the time is right. You're a Laffite, aren't you? Besides, didn't you say that you were planning to go to Pyros?"

"Yeah," Johnny replied. "Mr. Dohrman was going to take ux there in the morning."

"I think that's the best plan yet," said Ken. "The Defauns at Pyros are the wisest of anyone in the bayou. They'll know what to do to prepare you. Now we'd better get some sleep. The journey to Pyros is a difficult one, and we'll need all the rest we can get if we're going to be at our best."

46

Vampirates

"Wake Up!" Ken whispered as he nudged Johnny's shoulder. "It's time to go. Everybody's waiting outside. Come on."

Johnny put on his shoes and threw his back pack over his shoulder. Outside the others were all waiting by a strange looking tinker's wagon old kerosene lanterns hung at the front, and water barrels sat precariously on either side of the wagon. The narrow wagon was made of wood with tall sides and was only big enough to hold a few days' supplies. On top of it was an inverted row boat that looked like a strange little roof on the old wagon. The old mule, Matilda, was hitched to the front and stood waiting as Dohrman loaded some rope and bottles of amber juice.

Matie sat inside the wagon on the top of several gunny sacks. She yawned and rubbed her sleepy eyes then laid down to go back to sleep. Bo, Jack and Riley stood by the side of the wagon, anxious to get started.

Dohrman slapped the old mule on her flank, and she jumped with a lurch. Slowly the heavy wagon began to move. He climbed aboard, took a seat, and grabbed the reins. The wooden wheels creaked as it moved along.

"Why isn't this wagon like the assemblages in town?" Johnny asked as he walked alongside his uncle Ken.

"The assemblages are powered by the curse," Ken replied. "Clayton can monitor all of them wherever they are, or whenever a power crystal is activated. Here we do things the old fashioned way, so Clayton can't find us." Johnny nodded as the group walked behind the wagon.

For several hours, Dohrman led them through the thick jungles of the bayou along winding paths and through marxhy swamps. Finally the morning sun began to come up on the horizon.

By now, Matie was wide awake and chattering about everything she saw. As usual she complained about the ride and how uncomfortable it was. "Can't you make this wagon go a little faster?" she said impatiently. "When are we going to get to the fire city?"

Dohrman stopped the wagon, and Bo helped Matie down as everyone rested for a moment. Dohrman had started a fire and was cooking some apples on a stick. "This el be a good place to catch yer breath for a while," he said, handing out the cooked apples.

"Why are we stopping?" Matie asked as she took a bite.

Dohrman and Ken spoke softly to each other, then Ken explained, "All of you need to understand what we're headed into. The place we're going is called Whispering Bog for a reason. While we're in there, you don't want to make any noise. We have to go through Potter's Swamp, and you need to be completely quiet there.

"But why do we have to be quiet?" Matie asked.

Ken looked concerned. "Your friend Riley already knows about the dangers here in the bayou. There are some very dangerous pirates that live in the swamp," Ken said carefully, hoping not to upset Matie.

"Oh, you mean the vampirates!" Riley blurted.

Ken sighed in frustration. "Yes, I mean the vampirates," he admitted. "But everything will be fine as long as everyone is quiet there. They should all be sleeping now. We just don't want to wake them."

"So, just what are vampirates?" Bo asked.

Ken explained. "When the curse began, some of Clayton's henchmen deserted ship. They ended up coming into this part of the bayou. Apparently they had no food and were starving. From the legends we've heard, one of them found an old cow and killed it and ate it.

"What they didn't know was that the cow was really a mute Maroo named Potter. No one knew what was going on then, and didn't understand the curse yet. Well, it seems that eating a Maroo is forbidden by the curse, of course, because eating a Maroo is cannibalism, isn't it? Apparently they all turned mad from it, and now they're the most dangerous beings in the bayou."

Matie held up her fists in defiance. "I'll poke 'em if they try to eat any of us!"

Bo patted his little friend. "Don't worry Matie. I'll make sure they don't try anything. If they attack us, I'll bite 'em back."

Matie smiled confidently as Ken broke in. "That wouldn't be such a good idea. The Vampirates are contagious. Just one drop of their blood can turn a person into one of them."

Matie frowned and looked at her uncle. "I'll be very quiet, I promise," she nodded.

"Getting through Potter's Swamp is just part of it." Ken said. "Once we get past the vampirates lair, then we will be going into the town of Vagabond Alley. You have to be careful there, too. It's where all of the thieves and rebels in the bayou live. Vagabond Alley is the place where the outcasts are welcome. But you really need to watch your back there. Most of the people are so poor there that they'll pick your pocket and try to con you out of everything you own. Anyone is fair game, so you'll need to stay close together and keep your mouths shut because the slightest statement could be taken as an insult to these ruffians. Do you understand?"

Everyone nodded except Jack. "I don't understand why we have to go through that town."

Ken looked at Dohrman again then Dohrman spoke up.

"We have to get some help," Dohrman said. "Dominique Youx is the only one who can help us. That's where he lives when he's not aboard ship. The place is a dangerous one, I'll give ya that, but there ain't no other person I trust like Dominique Youx."

"Dominique Youx?" Matie asked. Johnny remembered that Matie had never met Dominique like they had, and now he began to worry that she would be scared of him.

"Matie, do you remember the painting back at Maison Rouge, the one with the map in it? Well, that painting waz of Dominique Youx. He looks just like the picture except that he's a little bit different now. He and his men saved our lives, and he's a good pirate."

"As long as he's not a vampirate!" she exclaimed.

"Well, I guess we'd best get goin," Dohrman said throwing some dirt on the fire. Matie climbed back up onto her previous perch, and the wagon started out.

Dohrman turned to the others. "Now, remember, from here on in, ain't nobody sayin' a word, ya got that?"

"Yes!" everyone nodded. Matie pretended to zip up her lip, lock it, and threw away the pretend key.

The brush and trees thickened and the trail narrowed. There wasn't the usual sound of birds singing or insects buzzing in this place. It was as if all of nature was silent out of the fear of being discovered. The only sound was the steady creak of the old wagon wheelz whose sound echoed across the otherwise silent wilderness. Dohrman pulled Matilda to a stop and reached into a barrel on the side of the wagon. He drew out a handful of lard and rubbed it on the axles of the wagon wheels.

As they started out again, the wheels creaked a few times then the sound faded until all of the creaking ceased. The silence in this wilderness was frightening and the only noise was an occasional flock of birds taking flight from the trees.

Riley tried hard not to let his instincts take over. "I won't run! I won't run!" he thought over and over again. On the other hand, Bo stood near Riley by the back of the wagon and was ready for a fight. His bear instincts had opened up a whole new side of his personality. He was ready to defend his friends to the death, if needed. Matie had watched as long as she could until fear had completely overcome her. She burrowed her head into the gunny sackz, trying to hide. All that could be seen of her was a backside full of quills hidden by her dainty dress, a nasty surprise for any unsuspecting attackers.

Jack and Johnny walked with Ken while Dohrman drove the wagon. Soon the narrow road widened into a large camp. Ken tapped the boyz on the shoulderz and put his fingers to his lips. Off in the distance they could see several pirates lying about on the sand. Some were asleep in small grass huts while others lay under bushes.

Johnny pointed in the direction of the pirates then looked at his uncle. Ken and Dohrman just nodded. There, in the broad daylight were the sleeping vampirates.

He closed his eyes as a feeling of dread overcame him. His chext was burning from within. With his eyes shut, it was as if a movie began to play out in his mind. He could see the evil vampirates as if they were sneaking up on the little band of travelers, ready to attack.

Johnny opened his eyes. He had to warn his uncle. He tapped Ken's arm. "They're coming!" he whispered. "They're all around us!"

Ken glanced at Dohrman then at the wagon. Then he gave Matilda a firm slap on the back flank. The sound of the slap echoed throughout the bayou as the poor mule took off in a full gallop. Just as she did, vampirates attacked from the trees on every side.

"Run!" yelled Dohrman. "And don't take yer time ta smell the posies!"

The wagon raced through the thick brush. Riley and Bo ran on all fours behind it while Johnny and Jack jumped aboard the wagon. Ken was on foot and falling behind. Soon the eager band of cutthroat vampirates had him surrounded.

"No!" yelled Johnny. Then he saw a familiar sight. Watermen! They came from all sidez, fighting the vampirates. Wait!" Johnny said to Dohrman. "It's Dominique and his men!" Dohrman slowed the wagon bringing the runaway mule under control.

The wagon moved at a slower clip down the narrow road.

"What about our Uncle Ken?" Johnny asked Dohrman.

"Don't worry. Your uncle ell be just fine. They ain't nuthin'' the vampirates is more afeard of than the watermen. That's why Vagabond Alley is where it is. Clayton and his men don't come near here cause of the vampirates."

Soon the road ended at a marshy bog. "Here we are!" said the old man. The water in front of them began to stir and several water pirates materialized from below. At the front of them stood Dominique Youx.

Ken came running down the road, waving to the others. "That was a close call!" he said, bending over with his hands on his knees. "You should have seen those vampirates run. They didn't have a chance against Dominique and his men."

Johnny ran to his uncle and gave him a big hug. "I thought you were a goner for sure. I wasn't about to lose you again, not after we just found you."

"I told you he'd be all right," Dohrman interrupted as he checked the rigging on the wagon.

Suddenly a muffled scream came from inside the wagon. Everyone ran back to see what was wrong. "Let me out!" Matie yelled. Her long quills were quite firmly stuck in the old gunny sacks, and the madder she became the more she wedged herself in place. Everyone, even the watermen, laughed at the poor little girl's predicament. "Let me out, or I'll poke all of you!" she yelled. "Help, I can't breathe!"

Finally Bo reached into the poky situation and with his big bear paws, tore the burlap sacks and let her free. With a loud huff she turned around angrily. Her face was bright red, and she was fuming mad. "I'm gonna poke every one of you!"

Johnny tried not to grin at his little sister's determination. "Matie, you need anger management lessons!" he joked.

"Anger management lessons!" she ranted, as her face turned crimson red. Then she held her breath. Her eyes bugged out and suddenly an explosion of quills burst from the little girl showering down on everyone.

"Matie, control yourself! Those things hurt," Johnny said, pulling a quill out of his upper arm.

Dohrman and Ken were laughing wildly, not to mention the water pirates, even though a few of them had received a bit of Matie's wrath. Matie had been so mad that she hadn't even noticed the water pirates till now. Suddenly her eyes grew wide and she stared at the strange blue men. "Leave us alone!" She yelled with a quiver in her voice.

"Matie, it's all right," Johnny said. "This is the man I told you about. I know they're water men, but they're the good ones who saved our lives. They just saved Uncle Ken from the vampirates, too." Matie's defensive posture softened a bit, but she was still quite scared.

Dominique spoke up in his watery tone. "I like little girls with spunk. You'd make a good pirate. You could teach this scurvy crew a thing or two." Then Dominique and his crew burst into laughter. Matie looked at her brother, nodded at Dominique and stuck out her little pink tongue at the others.

Ken turned to Dominique, "Thank you for coming when you did. If you hadn't come, I'd have ended up like those other miserable souls out there." Dominique placed a watery hand on Ken's back. "So, Mr. Kenny Laffite, what brings you and this lot to these parts?"

Ken shook his head. "You'll probably think we're crazy, but the Revolutionaries are planning an attack, and we need your help to get to Pyros, so we can prepare. We have some vital information about Clayton's hideout."

"Ahhh, yes, I heard about the plan to attack. But why do you need to go to the fire city?"

"Johnny and the others need to talk to the Defauns. It seemx Johnny is one of them now. And with the information we have about Clayton's hideout, we need to let the Boss know what's going on."

Dominique raized an eyebrow and looked up. Then he whistled in a strange watery screech. Several more of his men began untying the boat from the top of the wagon and unloading the rest of the supplies into it. "Well, it looks as if we have no time to lose," said Dominique. "My men will take you and your provisions into Vagabond Alley where we will get everything ready. I'll let the Defauns know you are coming and meet you in town." Dominique melted into the sand at the water's edge and his watermen continued loading the rest of the supplies.

"What about Matilda?" Matie fussed as she watched the old mule standing alone on the shoreline.

Dohrman laughed. "Old Tilly knows the way back home."

"But, what about the vampirates?"

"Matilda's so old and tough she'd break those vampirate's teeth," said Dohrman. "Besides, she tastes like old shoe leather. Vampirates don't like eating shoes."

47
Vagabond Alley

After the group boarded the boat, Dominique's men pulled it out to a reasonable depth where they could set up a *Work-shy* boat with a rigging beneath it.

The scenery around them was breathtaking. Little yellow flowers bobbed in the morning sun atop the green leaves of the marsh plants. Everyone chatted excitedly at the sight. Beneath them the waters were filled with glowing fish. These swam up and down from the depths to the surface as if playing a game. Matie squealed with delight as she reached her little paw into the clear waters below. One of the little fish nibbled at her pokey fingers then darted off with a flip in the air.

Slowly the watermen rowed the *Work-shy*, and the boat above followed, traversing the intricate waterways. After a slow ride through the marsh, the waters became more rapid. The water pirates worked beneath the waters securing several ropes to their unusual craft. Suddenly both boats came to a stop as two watermen materialized in front of the boat. They stood on top of the water as if they were on solid ground and introduced themselves.

"Aye mates!" one said. "This 'ere is Whistlin' Pete and I'm Tobias Whithers. We'll be yer guides today. Now ther ain't nuthin' ta get yer dander up about, ceptin' that we might be in for a bit of a gale through the Whistlin' Reef. Now if you'll all secure the jib and batten down the hatches, we'll be on our way."

Everyone checked the boat and prepared for a bumpy ride. As the men below began rowing, the waters around the boat also began swirling. Down river, large boulders jutted

443

straight up fifty feet in the air as if the stones had been carefully cut and placed there to create a canyon.

Here the waters moved even faster, and the bright little fish had all disappeared. The white rapids whipped the boat from side to side, jerking it wildly. Anxiously, the group held tightly to the sides of their small boat.

As they entered the canyon, they could see caverns and indentations all over in the rocks above them. But even more astonishing was the sound. The canyon made a wind tunnel that sounded like whistling in several eerie pitches. Every time the wind changed direction so would the sound in the canyon. It was a strange magical whistling like voices singing, but the farther the boat went, the louder the whistling became until no one could stand it anymore.

Soon each person gave up their hold on the sides of the boat so that they could cover their aching ears. This wasn't such a good idea since the rapids were becoming considerably rougher and much more dangerous. Below the boat, Dominique's pirates were desperately trying to hold all of the rigging together. As each man tugged and pulled on the ropes, the boat they were in barely held together.

Finally the canyon rapids gave way to a beautiful small lake covered in wild marsh flowers. The boat glided over the calm lake waters, and everyone slowly uncovered their ears. The whistling faded in the distance, and the high canyon walls were now replaced with tall trees.

Everyone's eyes searched the horizon and they could hear the sounds of a city in the distance. Finally the thick trees gave way so they could see a bustling town up ahead, nestled amid the tall trees and canyon walls.

It was a ramshackle wreck of a city. Instead of streets, waterways were the main course of transportation. The entire town had been built on the water. Docks and piers lined the sides of the liquid roads. Beneath the buildings, larje stones were piled up to support the hulls of pirate ships with two story buildings built over them. Some buildings sat precariously propped up by spindly wooden stilt poles, while others had a firm rock foundation.

But they all had one thing in common. They looked as if they had been made from the debris of every wrecked ship that had ever encountered this place. Ships' railings created balconies, while an occasional sea chest served as a window box for wild flowers. The tops of old trunks created window shutters. The roofs on all the buildings looked like a harbor full of upside down ships, and here and there an old broken wine jug made an unusual chimney.

Not only was the place a menagerie of buildings, but there were all types of people as well. This was truly a place for all of the bayou's outcasts. Maroos, watermen, pirates, and even an occasional vampirate wandered the piers. Often one of these misfits of Vagabond Alley limped along on a peg leg or sported an eye patch carefully painted to look just like their other eye.

Tobias and Whistling Pete emerged aboard the ship with a large pole and moved to the back of the boat. They yelled down to the men below to release the *Work-shy's* rigging. Soon the upper boat was on its own and Tobias used the long pole to steer the boat along. The group now found out how Whistling Pete got his name. He whistled a lively tune as the boat moved through the watery streets.

Everyone watched the unusual buildings and people who lived there. High up on a makeshift balcony an old toothless woman waved a friendly hello as she, too, began whixtling. Another woman stood at her balcony hanging out laundry on a rope that hung between two buildings. She also began whistling the same lively tune. It seemed as if every

445

person they passed on the docks stopped what they were doing and joined in along with Whistling Pete's song.

Johnny turned to his Uncle Ken. "Why is everyone whistling?"

Ken raised his eyes. "Next to Dominique Youx, Whistling Pete is the most trusted man in all of Vagabond Alley. When he whistles a certain tune, it alerts the townspeople about what's going on. They know all of his songs and just what they mean."

"So what does this song mean?" asked **B**o.

"I don't know," said Ken. "Why don't you ask him."

Riley tugged on the water pirate's pole. "Hey, why are you whistling and what does it mean?"

Whistling Pete stopped whistling. "I'm jist letin' the town folk know they'd **b**est leave you all alone, cus you is proper **g**uests of the Boss, and he'd be ri**g**ht mad if'n anyone a you is treated poorly."

In the wa**t**ers beneath the boat they could see somethin**q** under the buildings. It looked like the ruins of an an**x**ient city that had sunk in the depths.

"What's that down the**r**e?" Matie a**s**ked, glancing at Tobias.

The old wate**r** pirate winked. "Ain't ya never heard tell a the ancient city of Atlanti**s**? These here are just part of the ol**d** ruins. They stretch all the way from Bimi**n**i through the **K**eys and inta the Lou."

"What's the keys?" asked **R**iley.

"The Florida Keys."

"So what'**x** the Lou?" **B**o interrupted.

"The Louisiana wilderness," he smiled.

The boat slowed and came to a stop. Then one by one the water pirates, who had so bra**v**ely led the boat through the dange**r**ous waters, began to ma**t**erializ**e** on the pier in front of

446

the others. Tobias and Pete threw a line ashore, and one of the pirates secured it to the dock.

Jack noticed that some of the water pirates were limping. "What's wrong with those men?" he nodded.

Tobias gave Jack a stern look. "Them watery men just risked their lives for ya."

"But I didn't think water pirates could die," Johnny interrupted.

"Water is our strength," Tobias said. "Outside uf it no man cin fight us. But in it, the water is our weakness. The waters cin make us er break us." He nodded toward the watermen. "And there ya see alot a broken men. They'll be a nurzinn their wounds fer a couple a weeks now 'cause a Whistlin' reef."

Everyone climbed out of the boat, and Dominique appeared on the pier. He led them along a rickety wooden dock. Riotous music swelled from the taverns as drunken sailors emerqed with bursts of laughter. Brightly dressed women and Maroos hung by the doors of the shops dresxed like the old saloon gals of the west.

As the group stepped up to the makeshift wharf, they noticed a siqn above them. It said, "Soggy Sam's Saloon." Dominique led the group inside. A multitude of ruffians met their view as they entered the crusty tavern. In the corner a man plunked out sour chords on a piano that was in desperate need of tuning. Water pirates and regular pirates all gambled and drank as they watched the group enter.

A particularly obnoxious man threw a gold doubloon at Riley. "Hey, rooner!" he yelled. "How 'bout a little entertainment? Why don't ya do a foxy dance for us!" Riley lowered his face in embarrassment.

Bo became incensed at the word 'Rooner'. He knew it was a racial slur and was meant as an insult. Angrily he lunged at the scurvy pirate with a loud growl. Before anything more could happen, all of Dominique's men had their swords drawn. The room was dead silent and everyone froze. The drunken man backed down. "I was jist makin' a bit of fun!" he said wiping his mouth on his sleeve.

Dominique approached the man with his sword in hand. "We won't be having any more trouble now, will we Mr. Blythe? Guess you didn't hear 'bout these folks. They're the honored guests of the Boss." Dominique squinted his eyes at the man as a murmur went through the crowd.

The drunken pirate cowered, and his eyes widened. "Oh, no, no trouble, I promise! You have my word on it!" he said, taking a swig from a bottle of whisky.

The group followed Dominique into a back room where he shut the door behind them. With his pirates guarding it, he stomped on the floorboards three times. As he did water began to seep up through the floor and take form. Two water pirates materialized and opened the hatch on the floor. Beneath them a tall man emerged. He was not a water pirate and was very different from any pirate the group had seen.

His skin tone was darker, and he was dressed in unuzual clothing. A leather skirt hung to his shins with a loose tunic over it that was covered with unusual emblemz. His chest was bare except for some jade jewelry that hung about his neck. But the most unusual thing he wore was a glowing necklace. He didn't speak a word but nodded to Dominique.

"This is Tambuka," Dominique said. "He cannot speak 'cause he has no tongue. It was cut out by Clayton's men at the Dungeons of Despair because of the secret he holds." Dominique turned to Johnny. "Long ago I and seven otherz took a vow to hold the secret of the curse. Tambuka alone knows where my secret is hidden. You see, if I kept it myself, Clayton would have killed me for it, like he did the others. Old

Python, the greedy devil, tried to turn on us all. The traitor tortured and killed most of the others to get their secret. But nobody bothers Tambuka because he has the magic. The time has come to reveal the secret. And it'll be yours alone, Johnny because you're the chosen one."

"Call the crew," Dominique whispered, as two of his men melted into the floor boards.

Soon they returned just as they had left. "Everything's ready," they reported.

Dominique nodded to the men, and they lifted the hatch in the floor, revealing a ladder that led to a docked boat below. The boat was very small, just big enough for two men. But attached below it was a slightly larger boat, filled with a contingent guard of Dominique's most trusted men. Johnny climbed down the ladder and stepped into the waiting boat as Tambuka followed. Soon both boats were making their way through an arched opening under the old tavern.

Through the tall arch they entered the watery streets of Vagabond Alley. The boat meandered through the ramshackle village until the only hint of the town was an occasional shack on stilts above the water. The tethered boats wandered for hours in the dank rivers of the bayou. The journey had taken most of the day, and the light from the setting sun reflected on the calm waters.

Finally the boat came to a sudden stop. The regiment of watermen emerged on shore as Johnny and Tambuka stepped from the boat and began an arduous trek through the rugged jungles of the bayou. Dominique took the lead and watermen stood guard on every side of Johnny as if guarding a precious treasure. Soon the pathway became hard to discern as the untamed wilderness choked the hidden path.

Dominique stopped and ordered his men to remain and guard the area. Johnny followed Tambuka with Dominique following close behind. In the distance Johnny could make out the old ruins of a stone village much like the underwater buildings in Vagabond Alley.

Tambuka entered the ancient village and led them to a large cylindrical wall. There in an alcove he reached amid some rubble and removed several rocks. Then he pulled out a large carrot-sized crystal. It was emerald green and glistened in the setting sun. Carefully he handed it to Dominique.

Dominique held it in his hand and sighed deeply. Then he turned to Johnny. "My boy, this is what started it all."

"What do you mean?" azked Johnny.

"This crystal was the first of its kind. When the curse began, we were all just normal pirates. We weren't even there to see Captain Edwards murdered, but Marie was. She told us of Clayton's revenge on the family and how he intended to destroy Jean and all of our lives.

"The day she was blinded by the curse, Jean's wife died at the exact moment that Captain Edwards was killed. Katherine most certainly gave birth to more than a Laffite that day, for that was the day the Laffite curse was also born. All of us felt it. Things began to change. Then one day we heard of Captain Edward's ship. Somehow it was still in the bayou. I went after it because I had made an oath to protect its cargo, even if it meant losing my life."

"Sam told me all about that," Johnny said. "Weren't you one of the eight men that made that oath?"

"Yes," Dominique replied. "All eight of us took an oath to protect the cargo at all costs. We promised to give our very souls to do so."

"But why give your souls for some of Napoleon's stupid gold? Why couldn't you just tell the U.S. you lost the gold?"

Dominique sat down on a large stone as Johnny sat near

his feet. Tambuka stood near the two, keeping watch for any unwanted visitors as Dominique began to explain.

"Originally we went to France to help Napoleon ezcape. He had offered Jean everything he had in the way of treaxure. But Jean refused Napoleon's offer. He already had everything a man could want. Then Napoleon offered something to Jean that he could not resist."

"What was it?" Johnny asked.

"Immortality and eternal success," Dominique replied.

"But how could Napoleon offer that to someone?"

Dominique raised an eyebrow and looked Johnny straight in the eye. "That which I am going to tell you is sacred. You must take an oath to preserve this knowledge. You must not tell your friends or your parents nor anyone else, even if they torture you for the information. Do you agree?"

Johnny felt a chill go down his spine. Then a strange warmth filled his being. Without further thought, Johnny heard the wordz come from his own mouth. "Yes, I promize to keep the information safe. On my life, I promise!"

"Good!" said Dominique. "Then I can tell you. Napoleon had a secret to all of his success. As long as his intent remained pure in helping the people of France, nothing could stop his conquests. He was invincible becauze of somethinq he held, but he became greedy and power hungry, and then he lost everything.

"Before Napoleon rose to power, he was a normal man. Then one day, he and his men raided an abbey called Sainte Chapelle in Southern France. There they found three valuable objects. The spear of Longinus called the Bleeding Lance, a small leather parchment scroll with a chalice on it, and a tattered purple cloak. The spear was nothing more than a brass spear head by then, because the wood had long since rotted. But the cloak and the leather scroll were still in good shape. These objects he took with him along with the money he had stolen.

"Napoleon was a fool who had no idea what he had just taken. The spear was that which pierced the side of Christ as he hung on the cross, the cloak, that which was gambled for at Christ's crucifixion, and the leather parchment scroll was the most valuable object of the three. It was none other than the Holy Grail itself."

"What do you mean, it was the Holy Grail? I thought that the grail was a golden cup," Johnny said.

"The grail legend believed that the cup held the blood of Christ, but instead it held his words and bloodline. Written by his own hand, it was the record of his genealogy. It is the most powerful object in the world. It represents the power of God. Often you will see it represented as a chalice with grapes.

"When Napoleon finally realized what he actually held in these artifacts, he knew he was invincible. Like an oath from God, the artifacts held a promise. Whatever country held them would be the greatest nation on earth. Never to be conquered unless they turned from God and their intent became selfish.

"These were the very objects that Napoleon offered to Jean that night. Jean couldn't refuse them. More than anything, he wanted the U.S. to pardon him and his men. England was ready to invade the U.S. They had already tried to recruit Jean and all of Barataria. The U.S. was on the brink of disaster. They needed a miracle if this new little country was going to succeed.

"It meant everything to Jean. It meant everything to all of us. You see the U.S. stood for everything we held dear. It was the only place on the face of the earth where pirates like us could be looked up to as legitimate businessmen. Here we could get a fresh start, a new life. We could be like any other men.

"Then Clayton and his meddling stopped it all. When Captain Edward's ship was lost, so was that cargo. Clayton had no idea. He just wanted the gold that he thought was on it.

Clayton thought he was attacking the **ship** *Alliance*. But Edwards had taken the *Intent* instead. When Clayton threatened the real cargo aboard that ship, God's hand took o**v**er, and we eight, with our oaths to protect it, were cursed above all other men.

"Clayton turned one of our Alliance of eight against us. His name is Michael **Pi**thon. He became a Maroo of the worst sort, a great snake-like l**i**zard who told our great secret to Clayton. That is where this crystal comes in. When I first came into the bayou, I searched out all of the ori**j**inal men who had taken the oath. We wo**r**ked together to find the *Intent* and the real cargo.

"That is when I discovered the Razor Swamp and Vagabond Ally's former ruins. Here, I found this great crystal. It has powers over the curse. Pithon and Clayton tried to get it from me and duplicate it, but they have only managed to harness the power of the Beacon in their incomplete crystals.

"They have searched for this crystal for these many years because it has power over all of the other crystals and came from the ancient civilization that once existed here. Now I put it in your hands for safe keeping. If your intent is pure, you will be able to harness the energy needed within to overcome the curse and find the missing cargo and the *Intent*.

"At Pyros they will be able to teach you what to do with the gifts you have received. Now we must return. Show this to no one until you arrive at Pyros. And remember your oath to keep the secret of the *True Intent*."

Johnny took the crystal from Domini**q**ue and held it close to his chest. As he did it be**g**an to **g**low slightly. Johnny looked up and smiled. "I promise, I **w**on't tell any one and I'll keep it here in my jacket so no one else will see it."

Johnny placed the p**r**ecious crystal inside his jacket. Then he reached into his backpack and pulled out the piece of driftwood that Marie had given him. "Do you know what this is?" he asked Dominique.

Dominique smiled. "I wondered when you would get around to that. I saw it in your bag back at the old fort. It is Captain Edward's, inscribed with his secret language. Only Jean can tell you what the meaning is."

Johnny's chin dropped at Dominique's words. "But how can Jean tell me anything? Isn't he dead?"

Dominique looked straight up in the air and began laughing. "Dead! Ha, ha, ha. I'm sure there are many who would like that. No, I'm afraid not. Jean is alive and well and looking forward to meeting his heir and namesake. After all, he is the one who invited you here."

48
The Hazards of Razor Swamp

Johnny lay tossing and turning as uneasy dreams filled his mind. Staying the night at Soggy Sam's tavern was only part of the problem. The worries of knowing what he had to do to overcome the curse and save his family were completely overwhelming. Dreams of watermen and spies along with lizard-like Maroos kept creeping into his mind. Then it was as if he were seeing his mother and father again. First, it was a wonderful dream then it became a nightmare as he watched his father grow old in front of his very eyes. "Johnny!" His father's words echoed, "Johnny, we need you. Free us."

Johnny sat up in a cold sweat. "It was only a nightmare," he thought, laying his head back down on the pillow. As soon as he closed his eyes, images came flooding back into his mind, images, of Pyros and then of Napoleon and his battles. Quickly the images changed, and Johnny saw himself leading a battle in the bayou. Then he saw a face. It was a great Maroo, a black panther. It spoke his name softly at first. Then its eyes looked deeply into Johnny's soul. Somehow this being seemed familiar. It wasn't frightening like the dreams of the lizard men. This being felt safe.

Then Johnny saw a great light, a blinding white light. From the light came a voice, softly repeating many of the clues.

"True intent nothing waverin shore N blood or swamp Youx B favorin."

"Three pieces of eight, three brothers two, the secret held true in the map held by Youx."

"The heart of the truth lies in the Son, if freedom be favored, and Justice be won."

R.R.Lee

"True intent Mirrors the Son if justice be honored and mercy be won."

The voice became quiet for a moment then it spoke one last clue that Johnny hadn't heard before. The voice whispered... *"True Intent is the Key to honor the Son, by mercy alone the curse will be done!"*

Now the bright light was all that Johnny could see in his mind, but the feeling of warmth it gave him was overpowering. Suddenly tears swelled up in Johnny's eyes. As a tear dropped to the pillow, Johnny opened his eyes. In the reflection of the tear he saw his family again. *"Your family is in danger,"* the voice said. *"You must leave for Pyros immediately."*

Johnny sat up with a start as Bo burst into his room. "We've gotta leave right now. Whistling Pete's been warning everyone in town. Those lizard guys are comin'."

Johnny reached for his back pack and flung it over his shoulder then headed for the door. In the hallway everyone was up and waiting.

"What's happening?" Matie said rubbing her sleepy eyes.

"Just another adventure," Bo said as he lifted her to his shoulder.

Downstairs, Tobias guarded the door to the back room. "Hurry," he said in a watery voice. "A traitor has let Clayton's men know you are here. Dominique has a boat waiting to get you out of town."

Quickly the group climbed down the hatch in the floor of the back room and boarded the waiting boat. Dominique stood with his full crew like guards upon the water's surface. Tambuka stood in the upper ship to guard the escapees as Dominique and his men quickly dissolved under the water. Tambuka reached to the floor of the boat, lifted up several old sails from the deck and motioned for the group to hide beneath

456

them. Quickly everyone obliged as the boat headed for the streets of Vagabond Alley.

The sun hadn't risen yet, and an eerie calm filled the watery streets and boardwalks. In the distance the warning tune of Whistling Pete and his group of underground rebels echoed throughout the town. The tune was an ominous one and sent chills down the spine.

In the boat above, Tambuka had dressed in old clothing and looked like a poor peddler with a boat full of sails. He pulled an old cloak up over his head to hide his face as he hunched over, protecting the group.

Suddenly Pete's whistling stopped and everything was silent. Johnny watched through a hole in the old sail. He saw the Overseers and Pahreefs crowding the wooden boardwalks of the town, going from building to building searching for the group. Even the ruffians of this town of vagabonds were no match for the Overseer's brutality. The evil Overseers now cleared every structure of its inhabitants and ransacked through the makeshift buildings, leaving nothing intact.

Next, their strange balls of light began darting from structure to structure, humming over each unsuspecting person. Then without warning, one of the Overseers cracked a whip and the balls of light shot lightning bolts at the buildings in every direction. The rickety wooden structures quickly took fire, and the entire town began burning.

Tambuka zat quietly in the boat with the oars in his hands pretending to row it slowly away from the burning town. His disguise had worked perfectly as the brutal Overseers never expected to see a poor peddler as a threat.

Beneath the surface of the water, Dominique's trusted crew rowed laboriously to move the two boats in unison. It was a delicate task, and they had to be very careful not to be seen. Soon the two boatz were far away from the burning rubble of

Vagabond Alley. All that could be seen of the town now was the deep black smoke which billowed up from the burning buildings.

Dominique Youx materialized on the water beside the boat. "Stay hidden," he whispered in his watery tone. "The Overseers will be watching everything. We will take you to the Razor Swamp. It is very dangerous there, but it will be the safest place for you. No one can live in that place. They will never expect us to go there." Quickly he returned beneath the waters, and the boat began to move swiftly through the rivers of the bayou.

The group tried to get some rest in the light of the rising sun. Soon the heat was more than they could stand as the heavy sails they were hiding under made the humid heat even more unbearable. Jack lifted the canvas covering off of his head. "Hey, we're dying under here. Bo'z about to start shedding all of his fur! Can we take off these canvas sails yet?"

"Yeah," Matie added poking her little pink nose out from under a sail. "My quills are wilting."

Tambuka smiled and took off his disguise. Then he stomped three times on the floor of the boat. Soon Dominique emerged at the front of the boat. "You will be fine now. The danger is past," Dominique said as he lifted the canvas coverings.

"Wow, it was like a sauna in there," Ken said, checking the group. Everyone seemed fine and was accounted for except Mr. Dohrman who had decided to stay back at the tavern and return to his old cabin.

The boat was moving swiftly, and Vagabond Alley was now hours behind them. The unexpected journey had left everyone very hot and dehydrated. "Do you have any water for us to drink?" Ken asked as he looked at the sweating children.

Dominique shook his head regretfully. "I am sorry. We

water men tend to forget the need to drink as we are already
very hydrated, but I do have something that will cool all of you
off." He stood at the front of the boat and lifted his hands at
either side. Then as if he had power over the water beneath him,
the water rose from the river and gathered in undulating spheres
in his hands. Then he threw the water spheres at everyone in the
boat. The spheres shattered into a million tiny droplets of water,
spraying everyone. He smiled as everyone ducked from his
watery assault. They all laughed at the unexpected surprise, but
the cool waters felt wonderful and had revived the weary
travelers.

"We will be arriving at the Razor Swamp very soon,"
said Dominique. "It is only another hour away. There you will
find fresh water in the mineral springs to quench your thirst."

The travelers settled into a quiet ride as Johnny took out
his notebook. The odd dreams and images he had experienced
back at the tavern hadn't left his mind. Now he wrote down the
new clue which the great voice had given him. *True Intent is
the key to honor the Son, by mercy alone the curse will be
done."*

Johnny pondered over the seemingly vague words of
the clue. Suddenly the clue made complete sense to him. With
what Dominique had told him of the real cargo aboard the
Intent, he began to think of the Son of God. He realized that no
one could fool God because God knew the intent of every
man's heart. Then he realized that the only way the curse could
be overcome would be through God's mercy.

The new clue made perfect senze now, and all of the
other clues began to as well. The key to overcoming all of this
was in having true intent, in having love for others that could
overcome everything. Suddenly it was as if a great burning
sensation filled Johnny's heart. Despite his concernz and
worries over his family and friends, he felt a peace inside his

soul that he had never felt before.

Something inside of him changed. Every time he thought of Ratcliffe or Randy and Palmer, all he felt was love and peace. Then instinctively Johnny closed his eyes. Suddenly he saw in his mind a place full of people dressed in white clothing. It was as if his mind were sailing through a tunnel of light.

His thoughts were interrupted by the boat coming to a bumping halt. "This is it! We've gone az far as we can. We must travel by foot from this point on," said Dominique. Johnny again closed his eyes, hoping to be able to have his mind return to the previous thoughts. But it was no use. The thoughts and imagez were gone.

Everyone stepped ashore. The sight before them was amazing. Jagged colored crystals jutted up from everything. It looked as if enormous colored razors had grown to cover the entire area. Even old buildings were covered with the curious crystals, like a forgotten ghostly wonderland of danger.

"How did all of these get here?" asked Jack.

Matie began to scurry toward the structures. "They look like castles!" she said. Tambuka stepped out in front of her, blocking her way. Dominique and his men materialized on the shore, and he began to explain.

"This place is very beautiful, but it is also deadly. Originally the crystal mines were a natural occurrence. The crystals here were used to control the Beacon's power. But as the Overseer's hunger for power increased so did their need for more crystals. They wanted purer crystals designed to their specifications. So they abandoned this mining operation in preference of newer more modern facilities. The Overseers do not like the minerals here.

You see, the real reason they abandonded this place, was that, they discovered they could not control the powers within the crystals here. The people who used the crystals became too powerful for the Overseers to suppress. The Overseers knew it could destroy them so they moved the mines. At first they used the prisonerz in the bayou as the slave labor to do the mining. Many died here on the sharp rocks. But the laborers soon became very strong, and the crystals made them as the Defauns. The Overseers became fearful of their own slaves and decided to butcher them. Few escaped the massacre. But those who did became the founders of Vagabond Alley. A few others escaped into the bayou.

"What were the people like who lived here?" Riley asked.

"Most were prisoners," Dominique explained. "But many were just innocent people who wished to be free of the Overseer's brutality. However, there were also Maroos, even watermen, and many Defauns, but they all had one thing in common. They were political prisoners whom the Masters the Consortium feared. Many were the leaders of the Revolutionaries of the Defiance. This is the place were most of them died. It was considered a work camp."

"Are there other places like this?" asked Johnny as he thought of his parents.

"Yes," said Dominique. "There is one very bad place the people call the Dungeons of Despair. Only the worst prisoners are kept there. Most of the other places are much like this one and are work camps. Many slaves are sold to these camps when they first come into the bayou to work off their debt to the Masters of the Conxortium.

"Now we muzt go. We have a very long day's journey before us. We must travel on foot from this point, and it is very dangerous, so you must follow my instructions in every detail.

"In many places the ground is very brittle and beneath it are razor sharp crystals within underground caverns. If you fall

461

into one of these, it will mean instant death. There is safe passage through the area, but only Tambuka knows the way through. You must follow his every step."

Dominique and his men lined up on either side of the little procession of travelers. Several of his men disintegrated into the sharp crystals beneath the surface.

"What are they doing?" Bo asked.

Dominique stood listening then answered, "My men are checking beneath the path for weak spots in the ground. The mineral waters here tend to change things without warning. You see, the old safe passage may now have great weakness as the salty waters may have de-mineralized certain areas. We must be very careful."

Tambuka took the lead and began walking over the sharp crystal structures. On either side of the pathway, the beautiful razor crystals grew in all sizes. Some were so small and brittle that they would collapse at the slightest breath while others stood like massive glass sentinels, sharp and indestructible. It was these larger forms that posed the greatest challenge. Often they would block the path, and the group would have to scale these danjerous formations in order to move onward. Sometimes the razors would begin to collapse under the weight of the group and the sharp edges would cut the weary travelers.

Dominique and his men watched over the little band, and his men would often report dangerous caverns beneath the ground. Over and over the group had to change their course in order to avoid the crumbling hollows below. As the group continued on, Johnny noticed that Dominique's watermen were looking tired and very worn out. "How come your men look sick?" he asked.

Dominique motioned to one of his men to continue then answered. "The minerals in this place weaken us. Each time one of my watermen disintegrate and blend into the ground beneath, the minerals here melt as well and become a part of us. The minerals here are very deadly to my men. They are like poison. It will take every bit of strength my men have just to get this group through the Razor Swamp. They will need many days afterward to recover."

"Please tell your men thank you," Johnny said.

Tambuka led the small group over some massive crystals toward a round structure. It was made of marble and was covered with the colorful crystals. Pillars surrounded the round building and led to a large arched doorway. Tambuka broke away several crystals that blocked the door's entrance. Then he pushed the door open for everyone to go inside.

The place was well preserved from the invasive crystal formations, and a mineral fuzz covered the walls inside. This place had once been a place of honor. In the center of the room was a large tiered fountain. Its bubbling waters swirled within bowls shaped like large clam shells. The trickling waters were a welcome sight to the thirsty group. Immediately Riley ran to the waters and began lapping at them.

"Stop!" yelled Dominique. "Wait, we do not know if it is safe to drink." Riley stopped drinking, and lifted his dripping snout from the pool.

Dominique walked over to the fountain and cupped his watery hand as he reached into the swirling waters. He then placed his hand to his lips and tasted the waters from this spring. "It is well!" he said. "You may all drink your fill here." He stepped aside, motioning to the others, and everyone feverishly drank from the bubbling spring.

"Now, not too much," Ken warned the others, "or you'll get sick. There's no hurry." Riley looked up from the waters at Ken then ignored him, lapping eagerly at the cool refreshment.

By now Matie had practically climbed right into one of

the stone fountain shells and was splashing about enjoying the brimming waters. "This water tastes sweet," she said taking a long drink. "I think its magic water."

Dominique smiled. "I am not surprised that you should notice it. Many others have noticed its powers as well."

Johnny looked at his little sister. "Yeah, I wish that they could magically get us to Pyros faster." At Johnny'z words something odd began to happen. The water he was drinking from became very calm and images of Pyros appeared within it. Johnny jumped back. "Whoa, what's going on?"

"You have just dixcovered one of the secrets of the water," said Dominique. "This was just one of the things the Overseers feared. When they called for the destruction of this place, they could not destroy this building. It had been here long before they came, and it will remain for centuries to come."

Johnny looked at the placid waters in front of him. "You said that this area used to be part of Atlantis. Was this part of it, too?"

Dominique nodded. "Look into the water and you will see."

The waters in front of Johnny began showing images of the previous people who had once lived there as if Johnny were watching a movie. Everyone gathered around to watch the graphic images in the water. Then Johnny had an idea. "Hey, can this thing show us anything we want to know?"

Dominique responded with confidence, "The waters give only what the curse allows. But you may try."

Johnny looked intently into the waters and spoke aloud. "I wonder how my parents are doing." Everyone watched anxiously as the scenes immediately changed. Images of the terrible Dungeons of Despair appeared, and Johnny saw his mother and Laurabeth. Bo growled slightly at seeing his sister and friends in these horrible conditions. Again the scene

464

changed and the group saw Jim. His strong frame was hunched over, and he looked like an old man with his hair turned white.

"Daddy!" Matie yelled. "What have they done to my dad? I'm gonna poke those alligator men till they let my Mom and Dad go!"

Matie was not the only one in the room that was angry. Bo growled as his instincts took over. "We've got to get going and get them out of there. We don't have time to go to Pyros right now. Our families are in danger. Clayton's not going to get away with this."

Jack was a bit more reserved. "Wait, you guys. We need to think this through. Remember the promise we made to protect Johnny at all costs? Well, they have taken your family members hostage so that they can draw us in. They want us to try something like that. Pyros is the only way that we will be able to fight these guys. The Defauns have the wisdom we need to know what to do."

The others eventually agreed with Jack. Bo groaned at the thought but finally relented.

Ken turned to Dominique. "How much farther is it to Pyros from here?"

"We are much closer than you think. Follow me."

The group got one last drink then followed the waterman outside. Dominique stood glistening in the noon sun as he pointed across the landscape.

Far in the distance several tall trees lined the horizon. It looked odd to see green again as nothing would grow within this vast mineral wilderness. The group set out again over the dangerous swampy wasteland toward the trees in the distance.

Just as before, Dominique's men began the routine of slipping beneath the surface every few steps to report on the underground safety of the terrain. Suddenly one of his men disappeared, but did not resurface. "Stop!" ordered Dominique, as he motioned for two more men to evaluate the situation.

Everyone waited motionless. But there was no word. Instinctively Riley began to get jittery. "Something's wrong!" he said, sniffing at the crystals around him.

By now Bo was also acting uneasy. "We've gotta go," he said. "It's dangerous here."

"How do you know this?" asked Ken.

"I don't know. It's just an instinct," Bo answered.

Suddenly one of Dominique's men returned and re-materialized in front of every one. He looked very weak and had a hard time stabilizing his water structure which kept on melting as if he were made of melting butter. "There's an enormous cavern below," he said breathlessly. "It's crumbling... get off now!" His watery frame disintegrated, melting into the crevices of the foreboding crystals.

Tambuka raised both of his hands into the air and looked up as he closed his eyes. Then he turned to the others with wide eyes. He motioned quickly for them to follow.

Jack looked down at the ground as he and the others began to run after the silent Tambuka. The ground beneath their feet was developing cracks. Behind them in the distance it looked as if a great earthquake were swallowing up the delicate crystals.

"Run!" yelled Dominique. Little Matie's leg's were too short, and she struggled to keep up. Dominique picked up the little porcupine girl, trying to catch up to the others.

The ground behind them was rapidly crumbling into the vast cavernous fissure as Dominique and Matie struggled to keep ahead of the crumbling surface. Suddenly the ground beneath them gave way. Matie clung to the sharp crystals with her little claws while Dominique moved beneath her, to keep her from falling.

Johnny glanced back at his sister just in time to see her

barely hanging on. He looked at the cracking ground beneath his feet then jumped across a large crevice toward his sister. Instinctively he reached for her paw and caught her just as the ground to the side of them crumbled. Now Dominique was the only thing standing between the two children and certain death as the crystals behind him crumbled.

Johnny lifted his little porcupine sister onto his back and then began running toward the others. Again he jumped the large crack in the ground. As he landed, the ground beneath him gave way. A large furry black arm reached out and caught Johnny by the hand. It was Bo, clinging tightly to a large outcropping of crystals. Dominique materialized with some of his men, and they helped the children up onto the rocks.

Tambuka and Ken had led the rest of the group to safety within the tree lined edge of the wilderness. They waved and yelled at the others encouraging them to quickly come to safer ground.

Matie was shivering badly and clinging to her brother's back. As Johnny lowered her to the ground, he winced with pain. "We've gotta go!" said Bo grabbing Johnny's pack. "I don't know how long this thing will hold us." Johnny nodded. As they ran down the treacherous path toward the trees, the razor sharp crystals crumbled all around them. Anxiously Johnny and the others made one great last push. As they did the ground behind them completely gave way exposing an enormous cavern of sharp crystals that had been waiting to consume the poor travelers.

Finally everyone stood safely at the edge of the trees watching the crumbling crystals in the distance. Matie was crying. Riley paced. "Can you believe we made it through that?" he yelled.

No one had noticed, but Johnny's desperate heroic attempt at saving his sister had caused him considerable pain.

His shoulders and back were filled with quills and he was bleeding badly. In agonizing pain he reached for his back, turned to the others, and collapsed on the ground.

49

The Glorious City of Pyros

"He is waking!" a voice said softly. Johnny lay on his side, unaware of the people around him. Slowly he opened his eyes. The room was very bright with a white light that filled the expanse. But it wasn't clear. A foggy haze seemed to fill the room.

"Let him rest," the voice said as Johnny felt a warm, comforting blanket cover his body. Again he closed his eyes and fell into a deep sleep.

Finally he awoke to find himself lying in a vast meadow of flowers. Hundreds of butterflies flitted about in beautiful patterns. The brightness overhead seemed different. There was blue sky and even soft fluffy clouds, but no bright sun filled the sky. Slowly Johnny stood up.

"We were wondering when you would awaken!" a voice said. Johnny turned around to discover a familiar face. It was Mr. Sauvinet. "How are you feeling, my boy? I would hope much better than when you arrived."

"I feel just fine," Johnny said, remembering the excruciating pain he had previously felt in his back. "Where am I?' he asked.

"You are in Pyros, the city of fire. Your wounds have been tended and have healed quite nicely. This is the meadow of rest, and I was sent here to wait for you to awaken."

"How long have I been here?" Johnny asked. "I've got to find my parents. And where is everyone?"

With composure, Mr. Sauvinet spoke, "Patience, my boy. You will understand everything in due time. Now we must go and meet your friends. They are waiting for us." Johnny nodded and Mr. Sauvinet put his arm around the young man. As Johnny began to take a step, he felt lighter than air. Immediately the two began flying over the meadow toward a great towering city in the distance.

"We're flying!" Johnny exclaimed.

"Yes, I know," Sauvinet replied. "It is the most common form of travel here. As long as I am with you, you may go anywhere within Pyros that you desire."

"How are you doing this?" Johnny said with wide eyes.

"The mysteries of levitation have been conquered by our people for many generations now. The Defauns have learned to use their powers for the good of mankind."

Johnny's eye's scanned the sky. "Everything is so bright," he smiled. "But, I don't get it. Where's the sun?"

Sauvinet smiled. "Pyros is a self-contained city. A field of energy makes our city impenetrable to our enemies and also lights our skies. From the outside our heavenly shields look like flames. The shield of protection which you see from within gives off the blue light, and the clouds that mimic the real sky beyond these walls. Below our city is surrounded by fire, and that is why it is called Pyros."

As the two neared the spired city, they flew above several large buildings and soon came to rest in a beautiful terraced courtyard which consisted of vast gardens surrounded by fountains of every kind. Flowers lined the stone pathways and small children darted about playing tag. Everywhere Johnny looked, there were people either congregating in groups or busy serving those around them. Some floated high above in the air and stopped only momentarily to watch the two. As Johnny and Mr. Sauvinet walked along, many people approached and asked. "How are you, Sir Johnny?" Then they would smile, nod, and continue on their way.

"How did they know who I am?" Johnny asked.

Sauvinet replied without moving his lips. He spoke silently to Johnny's mind. "We have all been awaiting your arrival. Everyone here knows who you are. Besides, no thought here remains unexpressed."

"I can hear you, but you're not moving your lips," Johnny replied with awe. Sauvinet just smiled and nodded.

Now Johnny noticed that everyone was wearing bright white clothing except for Mr. Sauvinet and him. Before he could even utter a word, Mr. Sauvinet perceived his thoughts. "You, too, will be dressed in the clothing of Pyros, if you desire it. But we did not wish to take away your choice in the matter, as we know you have many precious artifacts with you that you have been honored to protect." Johnny felt in his pockets for the precious items. They were all still safely tucked away. "Come," said Sauvinet, "there are some very special people waiting to see you."

The two walked through the beautiful streets of Pyros. Soon they came to a very large domed building. Its pillared doorways shimmered and glistened as if with a glowing light from within the stones themselves. The marble structure was of an amber color yet seemed to have a transparency to it. Johnny noticed that the streets of this part of Pyros also seemed to be made of the same unusual substance.

"What kind of stone is this?" Johnny asked.

"It is Marigold," Sauvinet replied. "It is made by combining marble with gold."

"Wow, this place must be worth a fortune!"

"I'm afraid not," replied the gentleman. "We have no use for such things as fortunes here. We use gold only for its magnification capacities. It accentuates our powers and abilities."

"Oh, I get it. It's like when the others drank the

amberjuice, they could see and hear like the Defauns."

Sauvinet frowned a bit uncomfortably. "It is something like the effects of the golden drink. But the amberjuice is addictive to those who partake of its seductive qualities. They become power hungry and must have the golden elixir or lose their powers.

"Here in Pyros the golden temples work with the natural gifts of the people, magnifying the inert powers that they already possess. Only those with the purest of intent are allowed within the temple walls, for the powers of Pyros only work upon those who seek for the good of the whole."

As the two entered a large building, several small children came running to greet them. They surrounded Johnny and took him by the hands amid giggles and joyful laughter. Then they encouraged him to walk with them into a large room.

There, all dressed in white, were his friends and family.

Ken jumped to his feet and ran to meet Johnny with everyone else close behind him. "Are you all right now?" Ken asked looking at Johnny's back.

"I'm just fine." said Johnny as he hugged everyone.

Johnny looked around and noticed that Dominique and his men were not there. "Where's Dominique?" he asked.

Ken explained, "Well, it seems that water and fire don't mix. Surrounding Pyros is a wall of fire, hence the name Pyros. Dominique and his men thought it best if they waited outside."

"How long have we been here?" Johnny asked. "It must have been quite a while for me to be healed like I am. I'm sorry if I've messed up all of our plans, and you had to wait for me."

"What are you talking about?" Bo whispered. "We've only been here a couple of hours."

Johnny turned in surprise to Mr. Sauvinet who had followed him in. Sauvinet raised an eyebrow. "Yes, you are completely healed because of the skillful hands of our surgeons and the healing waters."

"What are the healing waters?" Matie asked. "Are they like the magic waters at the Razor Swamp?"

"I'm afraid not. They are quite different. The healing waters restore a person to immediate health. If one is ill, they eliminate the sickness and darkness within them. All one has to do is bathe within the waters, and they are restored."

Matie looked down at her pokey body and asked, "Can the healing waters make me into a little girl again?"

Sauvinet approached Matie. "For the Maroos, the healing waters will cure any wound. But they only serve to disappoint if more is expected of them."

Matie lowered her little head. Johnny looked sympathetically at his little sister. "Hey, don't worry, Mat. We'll find a way to get you back to normal again."

"Bo and Riley, too?' Matie asked hopefully.

"Bo and Riley, too!" Johnny exclaimed. "Although, it has been kind of nice having you guys around with your animal instincts and all. It hasn't been all bad."

"Speak for yourself!" Riley said licking a paw and slicking back his red fur.

Johnny grew serious. "Mr. Sauvinet, we came to Pyros to get help. My parents and Laurabeth are in danger. Somehow we've got to be able to fight Clayton and the Overseers, but we don't know how to do it. That's why we came here."

"I know," said Sauvinet. "But you must understand, the Defauns are not allowed to fight without a great reason because we are not allowed to force our beliefs upon any man. One of our greatest laws is that of agency. All men must be allowed to choose their course whether good or evil. You see, this law is the foundation of all of our powers. If we violate it, we, too, will become powerless to do anything to help."

"That's a stupid law!" said Riley. "So why did we even

bother coming here if you can't help us?"

"Don't be so quick to judge, little fox. We have a plan, and the law will not be violated. We have special teachers waiting to instruct all of you, and if you do exactly what we say, you will have the knowledge and power to conquer the Overseers. Come with me!"

Sauvinet led everyone down a long hallway into a large room full of intricately carved pink marble benches. "If you will please have a seat, your instructors will be with you shortly. Others will be coming as well. There is a great council meeting planned, and you will all be a part of it."

Sauvinet turned to Johnny. "We would like to provide you with new clothing if you wish, and we will mend your old clothes and return them before your departure." Johnny nodded then followed Mr. Sauvinet.

The two left the building and walked across the large terraced courtyard toward a small building. Inside many people stirred large vats of melted gold. Others worked over small hatcheries, harvesting the delicate threads from silkworms. From here the silk was taken to large spinning wheels and blended with fine strands of gold to produce a most exquisite white thread that gleamed and glistened. Miles of thread were placed upon looms, then hand woven to create the glorious white clothing that Johnny had seen everyone wearing.

"Come with me," said Sauvinet. "Your new clothing is waiting." He led Johnny into a dressing room with a large mirror. Hanging by the side of the mirror was a beautifully crafted white suit. It was much like the old fashioned party clothes that Johnny had worn into the bayou, but the pants were longer and more modern.

Sauvinet motioned toward the clothes then left the room so that Johnny could change.

After Johnny slipped off his old tattered clothes, he

turned to see the scars on his back in the mirror. There were no marks, not even a scab where Matie's quills had punctured his delicate skin. "That's amazing," Johnny whispered as he put on the white clothes. He couldn't help but think of the bitter scars that Sam still carried. Then he wondered if the healing waters would ever be able to get rid of them.

Next he carefully took the precious items out of the pockets of his tattered clothing and gently tucked them away within the inner pockets of his new coat. "All safe and sound," he whispered as he patted his pockets. He replaced the leather belt that held Pierre's sword and secured it in the scabbard over his new white clothing. "Now I'm ready," he said as he picked up the old tattered clothing and headed to the door.

Outside the room Sauvinet stood patiently waiting to take Johnny back to where the others were being instructed.

"Mr. Sauvinet, can I ask you something'?" Johnny said as the two started back.

"Of course you may. What do you wish to know?"

"How come you can live here at Pyros and still go out into the regular world back at Maison Rouge?"

"Ahh...." Sauvinet sighed. "I wondered when you would ask. The Defauns are different from all of the others in the bayou because we have chosen to use the curse's power for good. We are allowed to come and go freely. There are many Defauns who choose not to live within Pyros. These live normal lives in the bayou as well as in your world. They are free to come and go, yet they always have a connection to Pyros. There are only a handful of others who have escaped the curse's restrictions outside of the bayou."

"You mean like Sam and Cora, and old Marie?" Johnny questioned.

"Oh, no, their situation is a very unique one. They, above all others, have been held by the curse. They are not able to die, yet they are restrained within the confines of their surroundings. Death would be a welcome gift to them, for they cannot come here and they cannot leave their post. They are the guardians of the curse, intimately connected to it in every possible way. Their only news of the bayou comes through me and Pierre Laffite's family."

Johnny was saddened. "I wish I could help them."

"You will as long as you follow our instructions precisely." Mr. Sauvinet smiled.

When the two rejoined the group, Johnny noticed that the great meeting room was filled to capacity with large groups of the other residents of Pyros. On the platform at the front of the room sat several individuals, forming a council of great authority and honor.

Johnny found a seat by his friends as Mr. Sauvinet went to the front of the room and introduced himself to everyone. "As most of you know, my name is Monsieur Baptiste Sauvinet. The leaders of the councils have asked me to be in charge of your instruction this day.

"For many generations now, the people of the bayou outside of Pyros have lived under great suppression and tyranny. We, the Defauns, have created our own society where we could live freely and enjoy living in harmony with each other and the effects of the curse. We have enjoyed this for a very long time. But now our way of life is being threatened.

"Outside of Pyros everything is in great turmoil. We have always had a policy of non-intervention, in keeping to ourselves, and enjoying our freedoms. Yet history has taught us that true freedom never comes without a cost. Freedom must be nurtured and fed if its priceless virtues are still to be ours. That is why we have called this great council today.

"Over many generations we have come to understand the curse and its restrictions. We here at Pyros know that the powers of the curse can only be obtained upon the principals of honor and virtue. Otherwise, we would cease to exist as a Utopian society.

"The council members have researched and studied the curse extensively. We have come to understand what it is that the curse demands in order that justice might be satisfied. The time has come for the curse to be subdued. This is our last hope for preserving our culture and our people.

"We have learned that a personal sacrifice must be given to satisfy the demands of the curse. It must be given freely by one with pure intent. The individual who chooses to do this great task must do so only for the benefit of others and there must be no selfish motives involved. We will teach this person the manner of overcoming the curse and provide them with all of the necessary instruction and support to do so. Do we have any volunteers?"

Suddenly the room became very quiet. An uneasy feeling went throughout the crowd. As Johnny looked around the room at the doubtful faces, a feeling of warmth again filled his chest. Soon the overwhelming wonderful feeling overcame his entire being. Slowly Johnny rose to his feet. "I'd like to volunteer," he said softly. A murmur went through the crowd.

Then a man in the back of the room stood up. "He is just a boy. He hasn't the capacity to conquer the great curse. We cannot leave the fate of the bayou and Pyros in the hands of a mere boy."

Mr. Sauvinet looked at Johnny then back at the questioning man. "How many in this room feel as this man does?" Several raised their hands.

"Perhaps I should remind all of you just who this unselfish young man is. This is Jonathan Leavitt, the last male Laffite." At these words a hush came over the crowd.

"He came here into the bayou against his own better

judgment in order to protect his family and friends. His intent is undoubtedly much purer than anyone here, for I see no volunteers besides him." Sauvinet looked around the room with disappointment on his face.

"The peace and pleasantries of our Utopian society have created a great apathy among our people. They no longer appreciate the gifts of living as we do. It would seem that our selfishness has become a great weakness among us, one for which we will ultimately pay a great cost.

"The time has now come for us as Pyrosians to make a great decision to stand upon our own merits or really prove if we believe in those great virtues we claim to hold so dear. Are we willing then to defend the bayou and help those who are suffering or will we stand back and watch our brothers be butchered and turned into the slaves of the Overseers?"

"We cannot become involved!" the man at the back of the room yelled. "It is not our affair. Let them fight for their own freedoms. We are happy without bringing this difficulty upon our people. We must not fight." Many people nodded in agreement.

Then Mr. Sauvinet spoke softly. "The great evils outside of our city are spreading rapidly and have now even been found within the walls of Pyros itself."

A loud murmur went through the entire crowd. At the back of the room a woman stood up and yelled. "How could this evil enter Pyros? Are not our defenses still in order?"

Mr. Sauvinet nodded to some men at the side of the room. They went to the hall and returned with a man in chains. As they led the chained man to the front of the room, everyone gasped.

"Who is he?"

"He is an intruder," the people whispered.

Sauvinet resumed his speech. "This man was found in

our hall of records. His intent was to gain all the information he could for the Overseers in order for them to destroy Pyros and its peace-loving people."

The man in chains yelled at the crowd as he struggled to free himself. "I would have succeeded, too. The Masters of the Consortium will soon overtake all things and bring everyone into complete submission. You fools live your ignorant lives in this artificial bliss, thinking your city is safe. But our spies are everywhere. We're among you. We know all about your city and its secrets, and soon we will destroy it from within."

The man laughed fiendishly as Mr. Sauvinet motioned for him to be removed.

"As you can plainly see, the time has come when we must all choose where our allegiance lies. We can no longer remain indifferent to this war. The honored councils and Seers of Pyros have agreed that a vote must be taken. The people of Pyros must choose to follow the plan the councils have chosen or find another path for their destiny.

"You must now decide whether you will fight for our freedom alongside Johnathan Leavitt or remain useless in defending this cause. "All those in favor of joining the Revolutionaries of the Defiance and supporting Jonathan Leavitt raise your hand."

Great numbers of people stood up and raised their hands. Yet there were many who remained seated looking at the floor.

"For those of you who have chosen to vote in the affirmative, you will soon be receiving your assignments and instructions. For those who have chosen to seek your own gratification and remain uncommitted, you will be cast out of Pyros, as we do not wish to have any contention among us."

"You cannot make us leave!" a man yelled from the audience. "We have every right to live here as we have for years. Let the others fight for this freedom you speak of. We are happy here, and we will not be removed." The council members at the front of the room stood and nodded in the direction of the man in the audience.

"The vote is complete," Sauvinet said, motioning to several large men who stood and began escorting the dissenters out of the room. Immediately fighting broke out and soon the room was in complete turmoil. The Utopian society of Pyros became divided as people began to form into two distinct groups. One side chanted their support for the cause of freedom while the others jeered at those who supported the plan of the council.

It was obvious that this great division was dangerous, and soon the disruption became more than just words. The Defauns in the room began fighting from a distance with unseen weapons of energy, using the power of thought to weaken their opponents.

The chained man's prophetic words seemed to be coming true. The destruction of Pyros had begun and was coming from within as the dissension now forced everyone to take sides.

Mr. Sauvinet made his way through the crowds toward Johnny and the others. "Hurry, you must come with me!" Without delay he escorted the group out of the great hall and far away from the fighting inside. But outside everything was also in confusion. People flew above and ran about speaking of the great council and declaring whom they would follow.

Sauvinet led the group across the terraced courtyards towards a stately red brick building with white columns. Wide stairs led to two large wooden doors embellished with gold. He escorted the group inside. "These are the council chambers. Here you will be instructed further." Johnny felt an awkward hesitancy as he entered the building.

"What is wrong?" Mr. Sauvinet asked.

Johnny turned to him unsure of what to say. "Why does this place seem so familiar? I'm not sure I want to go in."

Mr. Sauvinet smiled. "Your gifts as a Defaun are beginning to increase. A great burden has been placed upon you with your choice to be the one chosen to meet the curse. You are feeling its weight. Come, and all will be explained in due course of time."

As the group went inside they walked down a short hallway with intricately carved wood on either side and into a large room at the end of the hall. The room resembled a courtroom with several distinguished leaders seated at a half circular table at the front. At the side of the room was a clerk who recorded everything that was taking place. He sat at a broad desk covered with several different sizes and shapes of colored crystals. Often he rearranged the crystals to reveal images on a large silver screen high above the heads of the council members at the front of the room.

Johnny and the others sat in the center of the room and waited as a tall white haired man approached the podium. "My name is Monsieur De La Fount. I am one of the council. We have been awaiting your arrival for some time now, Johnathan Leavitt. We are pleased that you have brought your loyal companions and chosen to accept the challenge before you. It is customary that you should stand and approach the leadership while we address you."

Johnny stood and moved to the center of the room, facing the council. "I... I've come to ask for your help," Johnny said swallowing hard. "Clayton has my parents and Laurabeth, and we need help to know how to free them."

Immediately the leaders began communicating with nods and hand gestures though they were not speaking aloud. Then Monsieur De La Fount nodded to the man at the desk with the crystals. Soon a picture emerged on the screen in front of the group showing the city of Pyros, and many people leaving it.

"Wow!" said Matie. "That's a lot better than T.V. back home. They can change it to whatever they want."

"Shhhh..." Johnny said motioning for her to be quiet. Matie rolled her eyes at him then sat down in a huff.

"The decision has been made," De La Fount said. "The majority of Pyrosians have voted to trust in you, Johnny Leavitt. But now your enemies have greatly increased and those you see leaving Pyros will become your greatest detractors. Clayton and the Overseers will soon recruit these fallen Defaun and use their gifts for their own dark purposes."

"But I don't understand," said Johnny. "I thought that the Defauns didn't have any powers if they use them to do bad."

"The Defaun's gifts are their own. But it is darkness or light that powers those gifts. These fallen Defauns that have chosen to leave must now use the powers of darkness if they wish to remain a Defaun."

"How do they get that power?" Johnny asked. The pictures on the screen changed to images of the ugly reptile Overseers. The screen showed their horrible rituals and how they continually hurt people in order to have power.

"As you can see, the Overseer's dark powers are based on pain, abuse and selfishness. They must literally rob the life force from others to subsist. Fear is like a drug to them, and they incite it often to meet their continual cravings. Manipulation and lying is another tool they use, for if they can take away freedom, they have power, and they rob freedom by violating the laws of the curse. Pain is another one of their devious tools along with despair. All these they use to feed their dark hunger for power. It must continually be fed and is very compulsory."

Johnny felt Dominique's crystal in his pocket. "So how do the powers of the good Defauns work?"

"The powers of light are based upon goodness, virtue, and hope." Images of the Defaun's using their good powers appeared on the screen. "The Defaun's greatest power comes through service to others. In it we grow in such strength that it is an almost indestructible power. We have learned to use love as a defense. Our powers are exactly opposite those of the dark forces. We replace darkness with light, love instead of hate, service and compassion instead of avarice and selfishness. We use virtue instead of vice, laughter to cries of pain, healing to injury. We believe in empathy and bearing the burdens of others. You see, once a Defaun loses these virtues, they are nothing, and soon come under the control of darkness."

"How do you do it?" Johnny asked. All of the council smiled and suddenly a great feeling of strength filled the room, and the room became brighter and brighter.

"Do you feel the power of love?" asked Monsieur De La Fount. Johnny nodded. "That which you can imagine, you can create," De La Fount said. "You must understand that the great war within the bayou has now begun. Now the fallen Defaun will take sides with Clayton and his Masters of the Consortium. Everyone will have to decide where they stand in this battle.

"The fallen Defaun will try many deceptions on you. Trust only those whom we tell you are safe. You must learn to listen to the voice within yourself which will guide you.

"There is another great threat which you must understand as well. Clayton and his men have perfected the use of weapons of darkness. These they create within their minds and use to weaken their opponent. Though these weapons may remain unseen, they are very real, and you must learn to use the golden shields and weapons of light for your own defense."

"Can you teach me about these shields and weapons of

light?" Johnny asked.

"Yes," said Monsieur De La Fount. "But we will need the help of your friend, Bo." Bo stood up awkwardly.

"Come forward!" De La Fount said. Bo slowly moved to Johnny's side.

"Now Johnny, think in your mind of a great golden shield of light surrounding yourself."

Johnny closed his eyes and nodded as he completed the task. "All right," he said "I'm thinking of it. I'm ready."

"It is well," said Monsieur De La Fount. "Monsieur Bo, will you please reach to strike your friend? It is all right. We will not allow any harm to come to him."

Bo tried to swipe toward Johnny with his powerful bear claw. But as he did, his hand came up against a wall of energy protecting Johnny. Again he tried to strike, but this time with more force, as an unseen energy pushed him back.

"Whoa! What is that?" Bo exclaimed.

"It is the power of a Defaun using his thoughts to create a shield of light. But I must caution you, the user must always have a heart of love and pure intent or this force will destroy them."

Johnny and the others continued to be taught throughout the night in the ways of the mysterious Defauns. Each one learned how to use their gifts to their fullest capacity. For Matie and Bo as well as Riley the teaching was particularly insightful and they became aware of the great asset their animal instincts were to the entire group. Ken and Jack watched with amazement as the others increased in both power and strength. Soon one of the leaders approached them. "I sense that you are feeling unneeded," he said.

Ken smiled. "We're fine, but I do wish we could help somehow."

"Oh, but you will!" the Defaun nodded. "We have some

very important training for both of you as well. Those who remain unaffected by the curse have a great gift which even we the Defauns cherish highly."

Ken and Jack looked at each other a bit confused then asked the Defaun. "What can we do to help?"

"You have the gift of order and common sense. Both the Defauns and the Maroos struggle greatly with their passions. Discernment is not always their greatest virtue. Often they are unable to see a situation for what it truly is because of the great emotions and instincts that consume them.

"You must be their guardians. You must help the others when their judgment is clouded and their sight is dim. You two will see the truth, so you must be a guide to the others." The Defaun placed two small round crystals in Ken and Jack's hands. "When the crystal glows white, the path is safe, but if it glows red, great caution must be exercised. We will always be watching you, and if you are in great trouble, place the stones together. They will signal us that you are in need of help." Gratefully, Ken tucked the precious stone in his pocket. Jack stared at his stone, wondering what lay ahead of the group.

Everyone now gathered for their final instruction as the screen at the front of the room showed scenes of possible future events. Monsieur De La Fount again stood before the group. "There is one last law that I must teach you. I have saved it for last because it is the most important law of all, and you must remember it always. You must never ever violate agency. The curse is very explicit and consequential in regards to this.

"If you choose to use the gifts we have taught you, it must be done wisely. You must never force your will upon another individual or you will lose power. But there is one exception to this law. In rare instances the greater good of all must be considered. When an individual's choice becomes selfish, and they take away the freedom of others, sometimes they must be stopped, as in the case of the Overseers. You see, sometimes it is better that one man perish in order for a nation to continue."

Johnny raised his hand. "How are we supposed to do all of those things being shown up there on the screen?"

Monsieur De La Fount stared at Johnny. "Not everything you see will come to pass. The future is in constant change and must be viewed with caution. The choice of one individual can change the future drastically. Therefore, great discernment and wisdom must be exercised when dealing with these things. All of the images that you see now of the future are based on events as they now are. But even as we speak, the future, like a great river, changes its course often.

"Now the time has come and you must go. First, you will be taken to deliver your family from Clayton's grasp at the Dungeons of Despair. Your loved ones are in very dire circumstances and need your assistance quickly. Your time here has been spent."

Monsieur De La Fount waved his hand and at the far end of the room, a large door opened. Inside was a pedestal filled with a glowing white fluid. Within it several gems floated freely on the surface.

"What's that?" Matie asked. De La Fount smiled at the little porcupine. "It is a Synchronistic Time Modulator. There are many of these within the bayou, but most have fallen into disrepair because of Clayton and the Masters of the Consortium who have outlawed their use. This device will allow you to reach your loved ones without delay."

Johnny and the others gathered around as the man who had formerly served as a recorder took his place near the curious machine. Nimbly he placed several large crystals on a control panel. Immediately the machine began to hum. A colorful cloud appeared above and around the machine. As the gentle cloud swirled in bright colors, glints of light began to flash within it.

"It is ready," Monsieur De La Fount said. "Would you please gather around the Modulator?" he asked. As they did, their white clothing began to slowly change color, back to the original clothing they wore when they arrived. Then the cloud of bright light enveloped the group completely, and in a flash they were in another place.

50
From Despair to Hope

The Dungeons of Despair was a frightening place to be in. Even from the outside it was ominous looking. The great towering black walls stood like dark shadows on the dreary banks of the bayou. This place was built on a tall cheniere situated on a steep rocky ridge. Over time, the peninsula of this ridge had been worn away by storms and water, creating an isolated island with the worst reputation possible. Even those who were in good standing with the Masters of the Consortium feared even the slightest mention of this torturous viper's pit.

Johnny and the others waited in the rocks above the prison's towering walls, watching the main entrance. Massive doors opened and closed below, like the mouth of a great dragon, eating anyone who dared enter the foreboding place. Now and then an assemblage would arrive, and the hideous Overseers would step out and enter their lair.

The main boat dock and the road leading to the prison were heavily guarded by hundreds of armed Pahreefs making it nearly impossible for any intruders to enter or leave without being seen. The steep cliffs surrounding the prison were another problem. Even if the small group of rebels were able to retrieve their loved ones, they would still have to find a way down the cliff sides and then cross the dangerous waters of the bayou.

Johnny looked at his Uncle Ken for advice. "The machine at Pyros got us here, but how are we ever going to get back out again?"

Ken looked over at Jack and remembered the stones they had been given at Pyros. "I have an idea that I think might

488

work." He and Jack took the stones out of their pockets to examine the situation. "The guards change every fifteen minutes. If we try hard enough, maybe we can sneak in during the transition." Ken looked down at his stone and just like Jack's. It glowed with a small white light.

Bo turned to them. "What if I sneak in first and knock out some of those guards. My black fur would blend in with the shadows."

Jack and Ken checked their stones. "That's a very good idea." said Ken.

Matie and Riley broke in. "Can we go, too?"

"I can bite their legs," Riley said with confidence.

"And I'll poke 'em," Matie grinned, as she stroked her quills.

Ken looked at the stone in his hand that now glowed a brilliant red. "I'm afraid not, kids. We really need you here to help keep a look out and warn us if there's a problem. The four of us will go and find your Mother, Father, and Laurabeth. If we don't return, we'll need you two to get back to Pyros for help."

Now the two stones glowed with an austere whiteness, reassuring everyone that their plan was a good one. Johnny, Ken, Jack and Bo watched the entrance and waited for just the right moment to make their move.

Below, the Pahreefs talked among themselves. They leaned against two massive black reptile statues of the hideous Overseers. Each time someone would come or go, the guards would stand at attention holding their tall staffs with great crystals on the top.

"Look down there," said Bo. "Right before someone comes or goes, the eyes of those ugly statue's light up."

"That's the warning signal we need," said Jack. "Those lights will let us know when someone is coming, so we can hide before they see us."

489

The stone in his hand was glowing white again. "All right," said Johnny. "Let's go!"

Quickly the four made their way down the rocky surface toward the dark entrance and found cover behind some large bushes. Many of the Pahreefs had now left, and the remaining ones talked casually.

"So when do the rest of the dragons arrive?" one guard asked another.

"Well, the docket for the great trial said six o'clock, but you know the Overseers, nobody rushes them. If they want to stop and beat someone along the way, they'll take their sweet time about it. At least we won't have to worry about feeding them tonight. The ones set for execution will make a good meal. Here comes an assemblage. Stand at attention!"

Johnny and the others ducked behind the bushes. The eyes of the great statues glowed a bright green warning.

The guards stood at attention, and several others joined them. An intricate black assemblage made its way up the steep roadway toward the gate. The assemblage stopped, and Clayton and Pithon got out. "Keep the rig ready. I want this assemblage waiting if I need it," hissed Clayton. "A hasty departure may be in order if our guests arrive on time." Slowly he turned his hood-covered snout in the direction of the four hidden intruders. "Ahh, yes," he hissed. "They will be rrright on time."

Johnny turned around leaning against a nearby tree. A chill ran down his spine. He closed his eyes and thought of his parents. He could see them in his mind. They were being prepared for a trial. Then he saw Clayton's ugly face and himself in chains.

"Wait! Clayton's expecting us," he whispered. "He knows we're here. It's a trap."

Jack looked at his stone. It glowed white. "Johnny's right. Clayton is expecting us to come. But how did he find out we were here?"

Ken interrupted. "The Overseers use the amberjuice to see the future. And remember the rebel back at Pyros, the one in chains? He said they had spies everywhere. One of the fallen Defauns may have let them know of our plans. Monsieur De La Fount said that the councils from Pyros would be watching us, and they would send help if we needed it."

Ken nodded to Jack, reaching for his stone. Ken took the two stones and placed them together, then whispered, "Monsieur De La Fount, we need your help. Please send your most trusted Defauns, and let Dominique Youx know that we need him, too. Clayton's set a trap."

The stones glowed intensely and soon a cloud of colors began forming in the trees near the small group of rebels. De La Fount and several others appeared near the bushes. "You called for help?" they asked.

"Yes," said Ken. "The Overseers have planned a trap. This war is escalating much faster than we anticipated. We need reinforcements."

Monsieur De La Fount nodded. "Dominique and his men have been notified. They will be here soon. But we have little time. The Overseers have planned the executions of your loved ones. We must act quickly." He then instructed the Defauns to act as guards for Bo. They instantly became invisible and surrounded the bear.

Since Clayton and Pithon had gone in the building, the number of guards outside had dwindled. Ken looked at his stone waiting for just the right moment of opportunity. "Now!" he said, giving Bo a shove. Bo ran on all fours in the direction of the guards. In a race of power and strength he attacked. The helpless guards had no time to fight back, or call for help, and soon they all lay unconscious on the ground.

Johnny ran to Bo's side with Ken and Jack close behind

then the group secretly entered the large doors. Dominique and his watermen began showing up, and the small army was now ready for a fight.

Matie and Riley watched from the rocks above, becoming more impatient with each passing minute. "Do you think they need our help yet?" Matie asked.

"Not yet," said Riley. "They haven't had enough time to get into any trouble. We've just got to wait here until they need us."

Inside the dark prison, the walls glowed an eerie green. Ken and Monsieur De La Fount led the group down the empty halls as Dominique made his way toward them.

"I know this place well," said Dominique. "The cells are empty because they are making plans for an execution. All of the prisoners will be in the great hall."

"So that's where they're waiting for us," Johnny said. Dominique motioned for his men to split up then led the group through the massive structure. The Defauns all nodded to each other then slowly disappeared becoming an invisible force to protect the others. Johnny thought back to his training at the city of Pyros and imagined a shield of light surrounding himself and his friends.

Everyone followed Dominique toward the great Hall of Trials. As they neared the doors, Johnny turned to the others. "Wait. I've got to do this alone. It's me they want and if I go first they won't even know that the rest of you are here."

"No!" Dominique said.

"Wait," Ken interrupted, looking at the white glowing stone in his hand. "Johnny's right. He has to do this alone, at least part of it." Ken nodded at Johnny, then he and the others retreated down an adjacent hallway.

Johnny reached for Pierre's sword at his side then opened the massive doors in front of him. With determination he walked to the center of the enormous room. The round room looked like a sports arena with Johnny as the main attraction. The seats on every side were filled with spectators. At the front of the room, the Overseers and the Masters of the Consortium were seated along side many of the fallen Defaun whose previously white clothing had now taken on a gray dullness.

The other side of the room was filled with the tattered remains of the prisoners of this disparaging place. They sat behind a great energy field, being forced to watch the horrible trials and execution of the prisoners. In the center of the floor below the Overseers, stood Jim, Kate and Laurabeth. As Johnny moved foreward alone to confront the Overseers, Ken and the others entered the back of the large hall without being noticed.

"Well, well, I see our guest of honor has arrived, just in time to be tried with his traitorous comrades," Clayton's voice echoed throughout the great hall.

Johnny stood firm at the far end of the room, fingering Dominique's hidden crystal in his pocket. "I've come to get my family and friend!" he yelled.

"And what would you pay to do sssssoooo?" Clayton hissed.

"I have Laffite's watch," Johnny yelled.

As Johnny held up the pocket watch, Clayton hissed and sputtered with anger.Suddenly Clayton and all of his Masters of the Consortium stood up. "Seize him!" Clayton yelled as several guards approached. Johnny closed his eyes and imagined two great shields of fire surrounding himself and his family. Instantly the area surrounding them burst into flames. The guards tried to approach but retreated from the heat.

"Seize himm, you foolssss!" Clayton hissed again as he made his way toward the main floor.

Johnny quickly placed the watch on the floor as Clayton

watched his every move. Then Johnny placed his foot over the delicate ransomed watch. "Stay away and let them go, or I'll crush it," Johnny yelled.

"Wait!" hissed Clayton, motioning for the guards to stop. The prisoners in the bleachers were growing restless and started cheering. An enraged Clayton glared at Johnny as he made his way down to the floor.

"Let us discusssssss this matter rrrrrationally," he said with a grin.

Suddenly Johnny's eyes focused on the seats behind Clayton. There, completely adorned in the dark robes of the Overseers, sitting in a place of honor, sat Ratcliffe. Johnny choked back tears as he thought of Ratcliffe and the grief he had caused their family. Anger rose up in the back of Johnny's mind. Then he suddenly realized that because of his anger, the defensive wall of fire he had placed around himself had ceased to exist.

His pursuers were coming closer. He clutched his sword tightly. Then in his mind the words of Monsieur De La Fount rang out. "Your power is based on love and virtue. Hatred will only destroy you." Johnny looked at his family and closed his eyes tightly, pushing back the tears. He thought of how much he loved all of them. He remembered Sam and Cora, and his Uncle Ken, then all of his friends and the poor Maroos. Instantly the feelings of love began to again fill his heart and the fire again appeared to surround him.

"Let them go!" Johnny yelled, pressing his foot closer to the precious watch. Clayton stopped in his tracks and nodded for his guards to free the three prisoners.

"Release them, you foolsss!" he yelled. The guards unchained the three prisoners and slowly backed away.

Kate and Laurabeth held Jim's feeble arms as they slowly walked toward Johnny. A portion of the fire shield lowered as the three entered Johnny's circle of flames. Then the shields reappeared, protecting the little group.

"Now that you have your preciousss loved ones, give me that watch!" Clayton snarled. Johnny reached down without taking his eyes off of the old alligator and picked up the watch. "Give Laffite's watch to me!" Clayton demanded with a hypnotic gleam in his eyes. He wrung his scaly hands with delight, and his great jaws dripped with drool.

"OK," said Johnny, "a deal's a deal. I'll make sure you get Laffite's watch, but not 'till we're all safely out of here."

"What?" the gater yelled. "And how do you propossssssse to give me that watch?"

Johnny looked at Ratcliffe. "Send Ratcliffe down here. He'll come with us. When we're safely off the island, he can bring it back to you." Clayton growled angrily and nodded toward the cowering Ratcliffe.

Ratcliffe walked down from the seats and approached the prisoners, silently waiting for his instructions. Johnny yelled at Clayton. "Open the doors and lower all the shields in this place." Clayton nodded to the guards. The great doors opened and all of the forcefields went down. "Ratcliffe goes first!" Johnny yelled as the weasely man cowered toward the doors. In the bleachers the prisoners cheered.

"Get them under control!" Clayton snarled. "Get them all back to their cells." The guards pushed toward the prisoners with their powerful flying orbs of energy, trying to shock the prisoners into submission.

"Freedom!" a prisoner yelled, jumping from the bleachers. Chaos followed as the prisoners started attacking the Pahreefs. Monsieur De La Fount and the Defauns came to the prisoners' assistance while Dominique's watermen attacked the Overseers in a watery battle against evil. The fallen Defaun began hurling unseen weapons of dark energy at the good

Defaun.

Once outside the great hall, Johnny picked up his Father and carried him through the vast passageways of the massive prison. Kate and Laurabeth followed close behind. Soon Dominique joined them, pushing Ratcliffe at the end of his sword. "Don't hurt me," Ratcliffe begged as they made their way outside. All of the outer guards who had so eagerly stood watch were now engaged in the battle within.

Johnny looked up toward Riley and Matie. "Hey, you two, we need you now!" Matie and Riley made their way down the steep slope.

"What do you want us to do?" said Riley with a gleam of excitement in his eye.

"Stay here and help Mom and Dad, then meet us down by the dock. I've got to go find Uncle Ken and the others." Johnny said, returning inside for his friends. A Defaun stood guard over Ratcliffe out near the bushes as Matie and Riley took their positions behind the enormous statues of the Overseers.

Inside the battle had become brutal. The Great War had finally broken out in its full capacity as good Defauns and fallen ones fought fiercely with invisible as well as real weapons, throwing fire and spears at one another. The watermen fought with their swords and knives, bursting into a million droplets of water and reforming to fight the Overseers.

The Pahreef guards worked feverishly to subdue the crowds of angry prisoners while struggling for their own safety. Soon they retreated from the prisoners' attack.

Clayton and Pithon looked out over the battle and realized that they needed to make a hasty retreat. Clayton ordered that his assemblage be brought around for his escape. Pulling their hoods over their heads, the two evil Overseers left the others to fight the battle. Clayton pushed through the hallways with Pithon at his side, making their way toward the front entrance. Ken had been waiting for this very moment. He and Jack entered the hallway in front of the devious reptiles. Clayton and Pithon stopped and growled at Ken and Jack.

"Out of my way, you little men," Clayton demanded, pushing forward. Bo jumped out in front of the Overseers. He growled and swiped his enormous paw at the two beasts. Clayton's massive jaw snapped back with equal force as he and Pithon engaged the bear in a battle between good and evil. Soon watermen appeared on every side, and then the good Defauns arrived to join in the attack on the Overseers. Clayton and Pithon broke loose of the foray and bolted for their escape route.

Outside, Matie and Riley watched as the great eyes in the statue began glowing green. "Someone's coming!" Matie said crouching low by the statue.

Riley watched the Overseers run from the building. "Get over there," he pointed to Matie, as she positioned herself in a strategic spot.

Just as Clayton and Pithon came running towards them, Riley darted under their feet. To their unhappy surprise, both of the stumbling Overseers fell upon the waiting quills of little Matie. With howls of disgust and hisses of anger, the two Overseers limped away down the road with their egos fully wounded, as well as their pride, all the while pulling Matie's quills from their tender wounds. Matie and Riley cheered. Then the rest of their friends emerged along with several of the liberated prisoners. Victorious, they gathered outside as Matie and Riley rehearsed their daring attack on Clayton and Python.

Monsieur De La Fount and the good Defauns came out next with Dominique and his men close behind. "We must leave now," said De La Fount. "Quickly! The guards will soon gather their forces again."

"But how can we leave the island?" Johnny asked.

"There is a boat waiting at the dock," Dominique said. "All who wish to join the Revolutionaries of the Defiance will be taken to safety." The crowd of prisoners erupted into cheers and headed toward the waiting dock. At the water's edge the *Hotspir* stood ready with cannons loaded and ready to set sail. Soon it was brimming over with the escapees. Dominique Youx held Ratcliffe hostage on the shore.

Johnny and his friends all boarded the waiting vessel. As he surveyed the ship's passengers, he realized that Randy Olsen and Palmer were also on board. Feelings of anger and hatred began to fill his mind. Instinctively he drew his sword and lunged toward the two men. "What are you doing here?" he demanded. "We wouldn't be in all of this mess if it weren't for you and Palmer!" Just as he took a swipe at Randy with the sword, Pierre caught Johnny's arm. The two men stepped back. "Let me go, so I can kill those traitors!" Johnny yelled. Pierre smiled at the ambitious boy's efforts, then slowly let go of his arm. Johnny jerked away angrily. His eyes filled with tears.

Randy stood with his head lowered. "I'm sorry, Johnny. We didn't know then. We were being blackmailed by Ratcliffe. He set us all up to make it look like Ken had taken the money and left the blame on us."

Johnny threw the sword on the deck. "How could you believe those lies? My father was your best friend!" Johnny dropped to his knees in a flood of tears.

A few feet away Jim mustered up enough strength to speak. "Johnny, Johnny..." Jim whispered. "He didn't know. You need to forgive him." Confusion filled Johnny's mind. He remembered the wall of fire back in the great hall and how his powers had gone away when he let hatred fill his thoughts. Then he remembered De La Fount's words. "If you let hatred fill your soul, it will destroy you."

498

As Johnny wrestled with his feelings, he looked at his Father and Mother. In a flood of emotion he ran to them and began kissing and hugging them through his tears. Slowly, the hatred within him faded.

"Where's Matie?" asked Kate.

The little porcupine girl made her way through the crowd toward her mother. Kate tried to smile, but the sight of seeing her daughter in this condition took her breath away. She reached toward Matie and carefully stroked the quills on her little girl. "It looks like we need to do something with that hair of yours," Kate managed to say.

Bo and Laurabeth had found each other and talked with Jack and Riley about all that had happened since they came into the bayou." You two can't stay out of trouble for a minute, can you?" Laurabeth joked. "I just can't let you two out of my sight."

The boat was made ready to sail as Pierre yelled several orders to the waiting crew. In his hand he held the sword that Johnny had thrown on the deck and approached Johnny with it. "I believe you dropped something."

"Oh, yeah," said Johnny, reaching for the sword. Just then he realized who he was talking to. "You're Pierre Laffite! And this is your sword!"

Pierre smiled. "You will be needing it, far more than I. As long as you don't kill any of my men with it, it is yours now!"

Just as the *Hotspir* was ready to set sail, Johnny remembered something. "Wait!" he yelled, "Where's Ratcliffe? I made a promise, and I have to keep that promise." Johnny approached Pierre and whispered in his ear. As he did Pierre broke into laughter and nodded. Then he handed something to Johnny.

Johnny stepped off the boat and approached Ratcliffe

who was sitting on shore all tied up. "I said that I'd make sure that you get Laffite's watch back to Clayton, and I intend on keeping my word." Then Johnny stuffed a pocket watch in Ratcliffe's mouth.

"There!" said Johnny as he boarded the *Hotspir*. "Clayton will find him there, and he'll get that watch that I promised." Pierre motioned to his men who quickly set sail.

"I can't believe you gave him the watch," Laurabeth said.

Johnny looked at Pierre and winked and then held up the real pocket watch. "I didn't!" he said. "The one Ratcliffe has is Pierre's."

"But what about your promise?"

"I kept my promise," Johnny said. "I told Clayton that he'd get Laffite's watch, and that's exactly what he got. That watch belonged to a Laffite, Pierre Laffite!"

The *Hotspir* set sail for Pyros, filled with the defiant rebels. Johnny walked toward Pierre. "Where are we going now?" he asked.

"We must take your father and the others who are ill to Pyros, or they will die."

Johnny looked at his father whose dark hair had turned snow white. Jim was gaunt and weak and couldn't stand on his own. With a feeble smile he looked at Johnny as Ken supported his weight. Johnny ran to his father's side and hugged him. "I love you, Dad. I promise Clayton will never hurt you or our family again."

Ken looked down at his brother. A lump filled his throat. "Oh Jim, I'm so sorry I got all of you into this. It's all my fault. If I had just been able to handle things on my own, none of this would have ever happened."

Jim shook his head with a spark of hope in his eyes. "It's no one's fault. Every soul deserves a chance to be free.

This war is ours too, now, and I know the way to win it. When they had me in that prison, there was one thing they couldn't fight. They couldn't fight against love. Love is their weakness!"

51
Almost Entombed

As the *Hotspir* sailed through the bayou headed for the city of Pyros, Johnny chatted with his family. A Defaun approached him. "Please follow me," the Defaun encouraged. "I have more instruction for you before we arrive at Pyros." Johnny stood and followed the Defaun to the bow of the ship, away from the crowded deck.

"You have done well," the Defaun encouraged. "Your actions have now changed everything. You will no longer need to fight the curse. After your family is healed at Pyros, you may return to Maison Rouge. The Defauns will handle everything from here on." The Defaun reached in his clothing and pulled out a quarter sized ruby and handed it to Johnny. "This stone will increase your gifts, and you may call us with it, if you have any troubles."

Johnny took the ruby and held it in his hand. "So how do I use it?" he asked.

"Place it near your heart, and it will strengthen you," the Defaun instructed.

Johnny looked down at the ruby then placed it near his heart as a coldness filled his being. Then he remembered something. "Wait a minute. We can't go back to Maison Rouge with Matie and my friends being stuck like that."

"The healing waters back at Pyros will make them as they were." The Defaun insisted.

Johnny stared at the stone in his hand then back at the Defaun. Then he closed his eyes and thought of Monsieur De La Fount. Johnny opened his eyes and looked at the Defaun. "I thought the healing waters couldn't heal the Maroo's. And even if my family is healed, what about all the rest of the Maroo's and the curse and all of the slaves in the bayou?"

The Defaun smiled and nodded. "We will free them all and make sure no one is lost. Everyone will accept our plan."

A sick feeling swelled up within Johnny and slowly he reached for his sword. "Who are you? A real Defaun wouldn't force their plan on anyone. You can't MAKE the people accept it." Instantly flames surrounded the Defaun and he disappeared. Johnny turned around to see Monsieur De La Fount walking toward him with a concerned look on his face.

"Who were you speaking with?" De La Fount questioned.

"I don't know," said Johnny. "It was a Defaun that told me I should go back to Maison Rouge, and that the Defauns would free the bayou. He gave me this stone and told me that they would make sure everyone accepted their plan."

"Oh, no," De La Fount groaned. "It has begun already. That was one of the dark Defaun I warned you about. He was trying to deceive you into leaving. May I see the stone he gave you?" Johnny handed the ruby to Monsieur De La Fount, who examined it closely. "This is not good. It is a tracking stone. The dark Defaun no longer have the use of the technology of Pyros and have resorted to Clayton's devices. Did he instruct you how to use it?"

"Yes," Johnny said. "He had me place it near my heart, but it felt so cold."

De La Fount shook his head. "I do not like this. They are up to something. You would do well to rid yourself of this thing." Johnny took back the ruby from De La Font then threw it as far as he could into the brackish waters of the bayou.

Suddenly one of Pierre's men yelled a warning from the crow's nest. "Crystals on the port side!" Instantly the ship was alive with men running to the sides of the ship to watch over the edge.

"What's wrong?" asked Johnny.

"We are nearing the Razor Swamp. It is very difficult for ships to navigate these treacherous waters. The crystals grow everywhere and have sunk many a ship." As Johnny looked out over the waters, Pierre yelled out the order for the *Hotspir* to slow.

In the distance the ghostly shadows of sunken ships dotted the horizon. As the *Hotspir* approached, Pierre adjusted the ship's wheel, avoiding the dangerous obstacles. On either side of the *Hotspir* lay the wrecked remains of the unlucky ships that had tried to traverse these waters. The wrecked ships lay frozen in this mineral wasteland entombed in the colorful razor sharp crystals of this deadly swamp.

"How did all of these ships get here?" Johnny asked.

Monsieur De La Fount motioned in the direction of Pyros. "Long ago Clayton and his men tried to attack Pyros. As they waited through the night to attack, the crystals over took their ships, sinking all but a few. The crystals grew so quickly that most of them barely had time to escape. They will remain entombed here for eternity. It was only after their defeat that they deserted their mining operations in this area."

As the *Hotspir's* hull scraped along the unrelenting crystals, Dominique and his men materialized on the deck of the ship. "Turn hard a starboard," Dominique demanded as he and his men recuperated on deck.

Pierre joined Dominique and questioned him. "What is the safest route for the *Hotspir*."

"The crystals have completely obstructed the old waterways," Dominique warned. "And a new crystal of red and black grows quickly to the west. It will consume us if we do not find a way out."

Pierre ran to the ship's helm and demanded his crew to

lower the sails. Slowly the *Hotspir* came to a halt. Now it was stranded amid the frozen remains of the mariner's graveyard filled with crystal encrusted ships. Johnny examined the wrecks which surrounded them. Only fifty feet away he could see a schooner covered in crystals, its crew still entombed within the razor sharp minerals.

"There are people stuck in those crystals!" Johnny exclaimed, looking at the ghastly site.

By now Bo and Jack joined them. "Wow, look at that!" Bo whispered.

"If we do not leave here soon, we too, will end up as they have," Pierre yelled.

Johnny and his friends ran back to the others. "We've got to do something!" Johnny insisted, turning to Dominique.

Dominique looked at Pierre then back at Johnny. "I have an idea, but it is very dangerous.

"We must try. We cannot stay, or we will die," De La Fount cautioned.

Dominique turned to Johnny. "Do you have the crystal I gave you?"

"Yes," Johnny said, "but I thought you didn't want anyone to know about it."

"Follow me," said Dominique, leading Johnny to the front of the ship. Monsieur De La Fount followed close behind.

"What is your plan?" De La Fount asked.

"Johnny has a crystal that came from the original ruins of this area," Whispered Dominique. "It is not affected by the beacon. It might be able to destroy the others."

"I have heard of your crystal," De La Fount said. "It is the same one that Clayton has killed many people for. If you are going to use it, you cannot let the people on board know about it. We have already discovered one spy aboard ship."

"Yes," said Dominique, "but there is another problem.

My men and I cannot use the crystal. The minerals in these waters are deadly to us. My men and I barely made it out of the water and have not yet recovered from what we just witnessed beneath."

"I'll do it!" Johnny said.

"But the crystals change and grow every second," De La Fount warned. "If you miss even the smallest one, it could entomb you."

Johnny reached in his pocket and withdrew the crystal. "We'd better hurry. They're growing as we speak."

Dominique took Johnny by the arms and lowered him over the sides of the bow. Johnny slipped into the waters and dove beneath them, inspecting the growing crystals.

The minerals burned his eyes as he resurfaced, trying to blink the salty brine out of them. "It's no use. I can't see. The waters burn my eyes every time I try to open them," Johnny yelled up at the others.

"Close your eyes and use the gifts of the Defaun," De La Fount urged.

Johnny took a deep breath then imagined an energy sphere around his head. As he dove beneath the waters, the briny fluid surrounded him, but his face remained dry, and he could see clearly.

Quickly he swam to the razor sharp structures that surrounded him. As he touched them with his crystal they immediately crumbled and disintegrated.

Then he resurfaced. "It's working," he yelled up to the others.

The two men nodded. "We will be watching you closely," De La Fount said. "If you have any problems, just think it, and we will come to your aid."

Johnny nodded then disappeared beneath the surface.

Carefully he swam through the crystal structures,

touching the dangerous razors formations with Dominique's crystal. Suddenly he felt a sharp pain in his lower left leg. As he reached down to check it, he noticed bright red blood clouding the waters. As he tried to cover the cut on his leg, the crystals reacted with the bloody water and grew even faster. Instantly the waters became frigid cold and the crystals took on an unearthly red glow as they multiplied at lightening speed all around Johnny.

Confined within the deadly prison, Johnny looked for an escape route. He touched Dominique's crystal to the structure, but nothing happened! Desperately he kicked at the solid crystals but they remained firm. Looking up toward the surface, his lungs ached for fresh air. Dizziness began to dull his mind, and he felt as if he was being completely consumed by the powers of darkness. As he closed his eyes, almost submitting to the release of death, a bright light began to shine above his head. Then a warmth filled his being. In an explosion of light, he heard the same voice he had heard in his dreams. "Look to the Son!"

Johnny's eyes were drawn up toward the light. Mustering up every ounce of strength he had, he reached toward it. It swirled all around him then encircled him in a column of light. Suddenly the crystals around him began to dissolve, leaving an escape route to the surface. Johnny swam to the top of the water and gulped in the precious air.

"What is wrong?" De La Fount yelled down.

Johnny reached toward De La Fount then began to sink into the waters. Dominique Youx pulled him back into the boat. Johnny awoke with his family and friends surrounding him on the deck of the ship.

"What happened down there?" Bo asked.

Johnny looked around for the bright light, but it was gone. Then he turned to De La Fount. "That light you sent saved me."

"I did not send any light." De La Fount responded.

"But I heard your voice, and that light dissolved the crystals!"

De La Fount looked Johnny in the eyes. "It is the power of the Great One that saved you. We should be very grateful that it has worked. Most of the crystals are gone!"

Johnny's leg ached. He looked down at the cut. Jagged red crystals grew out of the wound, like broken glass. As he reached down to break off the crystals, De La Fount stopped him. "No, do not remove them. If you break them off, they could act as a poison within your blood. Wait until we arrive at Pyros, and our surgeons will attend to it."

Slowly the *Hotspir* moved through the waters. In the distance a glow filled the night sky as the spired city of Pyros came into view.

52

A Timely Reunion

The *Hotspir* docked at the shores of Pyros. Johnny and the weakened passengers were carried inside the massive gates of the fire city, and Johnny was taken to the skillful surgeons who removed the crystals from his leg.

The Defaun lined the golden streets, cheering the victorious escape of so many from the Dungeons of Despair. Great feasts were laid out on tables. Meanwhile many of the Defauns tended the wounds of their new guests. One by one the injured made their way to the healing waters. Jim, Kate and Laurabeth stood waiting with the others when Mr. Sauvinet approached them. "Please come with me," he said. "We have a special place reserved for your family."

Bo and Ken helped Jim and followed Mr. Sauvinet through the crowded streets. Soon they found themselves in a comfortable building filled with luxurious furnishings and large plants. Inside a pillared room, Johnny waited by a pool filled with healing waters.

Mr. Sauvinet placed his arm over Jim's shoulder, and the two gently floated through the air toward the pool. Carefully Jim lowered into the water which was much thicker than normal water, like the consistency of a thin gel, yet clear. Each droplet glistened and sparkled as if it contained a life force of its own. Jim was lowered deeper and deeper until he was completely immersed in the liquid.

"Wait!" said Kate. "He'll drown in there. He's too weak to hold his breath."

Mr. Sauvinet raised his hand to calm Kate. "Don't worry. The waters are filled with oxygen, and, unlike normal water, one can easily breathe within it." Kate stood by the side of the pool, her eyes fixed on her husband.

Everyone watched as Jim began to change. The darkness that had consumed him at the Dungeons of Despair began to seep out of his pores. It filled the waters, then quickly dissipated and left only the glistening light of the powerful water. Jim's aged countenance began to reverse as well, revealing a youthful Jim at the prime of his life. The white hair slowly returned to its dark brown color, and the crippled body and limbs were once again renewed to their former healthy state. But even more important was the renewal of Jim's mind and memory.

As he came up out of the water, everyone reached in to help him. Matie felt a particular need to help her father, and she reached her little paw into the water to give him a hand. As she did everyone was astonished to see that within the waters, her hand was that of a little girl.

"Look!" said Riley. "The waters make Matie a little girl again."

Before Jim was out of the pool, Matie and Riley jumped into the mysterious waters. Matie splashed about then dove beneath the surface. Her pokey little body changed back into a normal little girl. She examined her arms and legs and emerged from the water shouting. "Look at me! I'm a little girl again!"

Everyone in the room stared at her. Beneath the waters she remained normal, but the portion of her body above the water had lost the power of the miraculous liquid and returned to being a Maroo.

It took Matie only a moment before she realized what had happened, and she burst into tears. "Why won't this water make me normal?" she cried.

Riley was bewildered with disappointment when he saw his red fur again. "I should have known. Nothin' ever works for me," he said in disgust.

Mr. Sauvinet approached them holding some towels. "I am so sorry, but I tried to explain it to you once before. The healing waters are but a great disappointment to Maroos who wish to overcome the curse. These waters are to heal wounds. Your plight, I'm afraid, demands much more. The only way a Maroo can truly overcome the sorrow of the curse is by facing the weaknesses that make them what they are. And then it is by the great mercy of God that a Maroo is restored."

Matie sat on the side of the pool crying with her head in her hands. "I hate this place!" she said over and over again. "I want to go home." Kate tried to comfort her little girl, but it was no use.

Finally Johnny called to his sister. "Matie, we all want to go home, but first we have to find a way to fix the curse. I promise you, even if I die trying, I won't give up 'till we get you and Bo and Riley all back to normal."

Matie stopped crying and ran to give him a hug, then stopped and offered him a tiny paw instead. "I believe in you, Johnny!" she said.

Mr. Sauvinet tried to comfort Matie, and he handed her a beautiful glass vile filled with the healing waters. "This is yours, my little one. But you cannot use it for yourself. Like love it is the one thing you must give away if you truly wish to possess its rewards. A Maroo becomes who they are, so that they may learn to face their inner weaknesses. It is only in overcoming these and learning to care for others above oneself that a Maroo may become one with their own heart."

Matie took the precious liquid and turned to Johnny. "Here Johnny. Your leg needs this worse than I do!"

Johnny took the bottle and smiled at his little sister. "Thanks Matie, I know what this means to you. I promise we'll find a way to make you better."

Jim stood by the side of the pool looking deep into the waters that had healed his body and soul. Then he turned and looked at Laurabeth. He smiled at her, remembering his promise to keep the secret about her heart problem from the others. Mr. Sauvinet perceived Jim's thoughts.

"Would you all please come with me," he said. "There are refreshments waiting outside to strengthen all of you." As the group filed out the door, Mr. Sauvinet caught Laurabeth's arm. "We are not finished here. You can catch up to the others later. I know of your secret," he whispered, pointing at the healing waters.

Laurabeth looked at the waters and then toward the group. "But it didn't help Matie and Riley," she said.

Mr. Sauvinet looked deep in her eyes. "Often a person's frailties are more than just a physical weakness. Your heart is as it is because of your compassion for others. You have carried their trials and burdens as a gift to those around you, and your heart grieves for their sorrows. Let go of their pain, and you will be healed."

Laurabeth smiled then walked toward the pool. She stepped into the glistening waters and slipped beneath the surface. As she did the sorrows she had felt left her. The waters around her began to sparkle and glow, filling her with a warmth and energy. All of the burdens she carried had been lifted, and she emerged from the waters completely whole.

Mr. Sauvinet handed her a towel then smiled. "Your compassion is a very great gift. But it is better that you give your burdens to God and allow others to do the same. Fill your heart with love, and the weakness within it can never return." Laurabeth dried herself off, and she and Mr. Sauvinet joined the others.

Jim stood at the head of a table filled with food. "I want to thank all you for getting us out of that horrible place. We would have died in there if you hadn't come when you did. How did you know we needed you?"

Johnny then explained to his family what had happened while they were imprisoned, how he had become a Defaun, and how he and his friends had known through their visions and dreams that his family was in trouble.

Then they discussed the great uprising in the bayou. "What will happen next?" Jim asked.

"The people have been gathering throughout the bayou," said Sauvinet. "They are waiting for word from our leader. He will tell them the precise moment to strike. Everyone is preparing for the battle."

"Where do we fit into this battle?" Johnny pondered. Mr. Sauvinet lowered his head as a slight grin crossed his lips. "Our leader wishes to see all of you personally. The *Hotspir* is waiting to take you to his headquarters."

After finishing their meal, the group set out toward the *Hotspir*. Soon the passengers were on board and ready to set sail as Mr. Sauvinet waved goodbye from the shore.

The *Hotspir's* sleek frame cut through the waters of the bayou, heading for the open sea. Johnny kept his eyes on Randy and Palmer but soon realized that they had become very skilled at this life of being more than just corporate pirates. They fulfilled their sailing duties as if they had been doing it all of their lives.

Pierre held the curious sextant in his hand. Standing at the helm, he ordered the ship ready then adjusted the time modulator.

"You may want to hang on," Randy said, approaching the group. "You're in for quite a ride once the time modulator starts."

A cloud of color formed at the bow of the boat. Then streaks of light flashed like shooting stars around the *Hotspir*. A slight breeze began to blow then thunder echoed across the water as the boat shook for a moment. The sky opened up in front of them, all the way down to the water on the horizon, as if it had been ripped wide open.

With a flash of light and a clap of thunder the boat entered the enormous rift and the *Hotspir* was suddenly drifting on clear glassy waters. The crew scanned the horizon. "All's clear on the port bow," a pirate yelled from the crow's nest.

Pierre nodded at his first mate who yelled out a series of orders to the crew. "Set the sail twenty degrees to the starboard! Head straight for the sun ta Rebel's Isle an be quick about it!" The sleek boat leaned to one side as the ships wheel spun in the skillful hands of the first mate. The yardarm shifted across the ship's deck, moving the massive sails. Then the ship set its course for the island.

While the travelers were recuperating from the effects of the time travel, Randy approached them. "If you don't perk up, the pirates will make you drink rum and gunpowder," he laughed. "The side effects of the time travel are temporary. They'll go away soon enough. You'll get used to it."

Jim smiled and made room for Randy to sit next to him. Randy looked at Jim awkwardly. "I know I can never make up for what I've done. But I want to try," he said.

Jim nodded and put his arm over Randy's shoulder. "So what did happen to cause all of this?"

Randy stared at the deck. "When Ken left the company, Ratcliffe brought me evidence that Ken had taken the company money. Then he gave me a letter signed by Ken that implicated me, making it look like I had done it."

"Wow," said Ken, joining in. "Ratcliffe must use that old trick on everyone. He told me the same thing, except that you had done it and that you were trying to sell some of our property back in Louisiana to cover yourself. That's part of what got me started checking on all of this."

"None of you have any idea what all of Ratcliffe's lies have done." Palmer added. "I've known him longer than any of you, and I know who's really behind all of this. Ratcliffe's just a puppet on a string. He'll do whatever he's told as long as the price is right. It's Clayton who's behind it all. His men approached Ratcliffe over a year ago offering him anything he wanted if he could just get his hands on Maison Rouge and that map."

Johnny listened intently as he pulled up a crate and sat down next to Pierre.

"Wait a minute," Johnny interrupted. "Mr. Sauvinet said that the Defauns were the only ones who could come and go from the bayou. So that would mean that those guys that were working for Clayton had to be Defauns. They must have been some of the spies that guy at Pyros was talking about."

"There are many spies within the bayou," Pierre said. "We have known of the dark Defaun for a very long time. Clayton uses their abilities to further his evil agenda."

"How did they pay Ratcliffe?" Ken asked.

Palmer interrupted, "The money was placed in a bank account for him. But we always dealt with a man named Emil Dennison. He called all of the shots for Clayton."

In anger, Pierre jumped to his feet, knocking over a crate.

"What's the matter?" Jim asked.

"The man you speak of is one of our own. We have known there was a traitor in our midst, but never expected him. He is highly trusted and knows all of our plans. It is he who has caused the deaths of many of our innocent people." Pierre whistled for his first mate, who ran to his side. "Prepare a message for the Boss."

The eager first mate left and returned with a piece of

parchment with a quill pen, standing posed ready to write. "Tell him this: Emil Dennison has been working for Clayton. The source of this information is Palmer. Do what is needed to warn the Revolutionaries, and plug up this leak!"

"Will that be all, sir?" the first mate asked.

"Yes, it is all for now, until we find the traitor. Send it quickly. There is no time to waste."

"Yes sir!" said the first mate as he rolled up the parchment and placed it in a groove in the time modulator. A small colorful cloud engulfed the device, and the parchment disappeared.

Pierre sat back down. "We have a while yet until the *Hotspir* will arrive at the island. There is food below in the galley if you wish to refresh yourselves while you wait." Pierre took his place again at the Captain's wheel, and the boat sailed freely over the waters.

Johnny and the others went over the details of everything they knew of the curse and the treasure then began to plot a strategy. Johnny kept the secret of the hidden cargo to himself as he listened to the others speak of battle plans and attack strategies.

Soon Johnny couldn't stay quiet any more. "All of these plans sound great. But isn't the real enemy the curse? Shouldn't we be trying to find a way to get rid of it? I just wish the curse were as easy to see as Clayton is, then maybe we could fight it."

Palmer and Randy looked at each other. "He doesn't know about it," Randy said, nodding to Palmer. "The curse is real. We've seen it!"

"What do you mean, you've seen it?" asked Ken.

Palmer's eyes were wide as he looked around at the crew. "The pirates consider it bad luck to talk about," he whispered. "The other day we saw the curse. It tried to attack the ship. It was an enormous black cloud."

"Yeah," Randy added. "The thing had a face, and it took one of Pierre's men right off the deck. It would have destroyed the whole ship if Pierre hadn't stopped it. The minute he said the word 'Laffite,' the curse backed away like it was afraid of something."

Johnny looked up at the massive sails billowing in the wind. "So there is a way to face the curse! I've got to get to it somehow, and see the thing."

Jim's fatherly instincts consumed his thoughts. "Johnny, you can't face the curse like that. Its one thing to stand up against Clayton and his guards, but this curse is unpredictable. It's a man's job."

Johnny looked hurt. "Don't you believe in me, Dad?"

Jim fumbled for words. "It's not that I don't believe in you. It's just that you're inexperienced. You're too young, and I think this needs to be handled by someone older."

"Hey," Ken interrupted. "I don't mean to get in the middle of a family disagreement, but Jim, there's something you don't know about. A lot of other people have tried to stop the curse and failed. The Defauns and everyone in the bayou know the old tradition that only the last male Laffite will be able to stop it. That's why Clayton took you hostage, so he could stop Johnny. Even he knows that the only one who can overcome this has to be as innocent as a child, but have the courage of a man."

"Don't forget *True Intent*," Johnny said.

Jim frowned. "I don't like it, but since I don't make the rules here, I guess I have no choice but to trust in that old Laffite bloodline. I always knew that you would do something great some day. Looks like this is your chance."

"Land ho!" A pirate yelled from the crow's nest. "Rebel's Isle off the starboard bow!"

Sailors tugged on ropes and released the anchor into the

clear waters below. Randy and Palmer joined the crew, lowered the mainsail, and loaded their passengers into smaller boats for departure.

The small dinghies, bobbed on the water, as the ships passengers climbed down the rope ladders into the waiting boats. The shallow lagoons of Rebel's Isle were deep blue, and within the clear waters colorful fish darted beneath the boats. Pierre's men rowed toward shore, and in no time the group was standing on the sandy beaches.

In the distance a great volcano rumbled a warning. "What's that?" asked Riley with wide eyes.

"It is only the Pink Maiden," a pirate laughed. "She is just sayin' 'hello.'"

The group followed Pierre down the beach to a small grass hut. Inside were several large clay jugs. Pierre uncorked one and took a long drink. Then he laid out several coconut shell halves and filled them with the liquid. "Here," he said, handing a drink to each person. "You must drink this."

Matie sniffed at the concoction and wrinkled her nose.

"Why do we have to drink this?" Kate asked.

"Drink up!" Pierre said "It will help you adjust to the time travel and will protect you from the Moustique Maraquin. They are deadly here."

Johnny sniffed at the brew. "What's a Moustique Maraquin?" he asked.

"They are mosquitoes, as you call them, which cause great discomfort then death." Everyone drank the juice and quickly stacked their coconut shells in Pierre's hands. "Come with me," he said, placing an arm around Johnny's shoulder. Then he led the group down a jungle path.

Macaque monkeys swung high overhead and chattered in the trees. Exotic birds took flight coming to rest on enormous palm fronds. In the distance a beautiful waterfall spilled over cliff rocks amid green foliage. This place was truly an island paradise.

As the group ventured further inland, the trees began to thin, exposing a large valley. Enormous trees stretched upward as high as the eye could see on the side of the steep volcano. In the distance, rising above trees and vines, were the massive structures of ancient buildings which looked like a combination of the lost temples of India and the pyramids of the ancient Maya.

As the group drew closer to these structures, they saw people dressed in long tunics which were adorned with precious gems and gold woven into the fabric. It resembled the unusual clothing that Tambuka wore back at Vagabond Alley. Others were Maroos, dressed in many types of clothing from several differing time periods. As they walked along Johnny noticed an old man sitting on the side of the trial, mending a fish net. A woman nearby combed the hair of a little girl then placed a pearl ornament in it. Two small children began quarreling over a handmade doll. A beautiful woman bent down to their level taking the children by the hands and spoke softly to them. The children turned to hug each other then ran off together to play.

"What's wrong with those kids?" Johnny asked Pierre with a grin.

"The people here have taken an oath to live in peace," said Pierre. "Everyone takes care of each other, and there is plenty for all. We have no poor and all are treated equally. This island's laws are based upon your own constitution, and these people have been able to live it as it was originally intended."

The surroundings and people of this place were peaceful, nothing like the Golden City or even the high tech city of Pyros. No one seemed in a hurry, and everyone worked harmoniously together, creating a sense of safety and cooperation.

Pierre led the way up the stairs of a pyramid. On top, a vast courtyard spread out before them. At the far end was a large building with eight massive pillars that formed its boundary. Rows of people lined this courtyard waiting to enter. Each person carried an offering. Some had food, and others held homemade laces or charms. Some carried leis and flower garlands or gold trinkets. Matie's eyes widened as she watched.

Pierre hustled everyone through the crowds to the front of the line and into the great building. As they passed through the tall columns, Johnny noticed that the columns had detailed inscriptions and pictographs on them, detailing the lives of the original eight men of the Alliance.

The enormous halls echoed with the group's footsteps. Pink marble floors stretched down the hallways where more people with offerings stood waiting to enter a large room. As the group walked through the halls, it suddenly became noticeably quiet except for an occasional whisper or echo from their footsteps.

"What's going on?" Johnny whispered to Jack.

"I don't know, but I think that you're the center of attention."

The group walked past the people and entered the massive room. At the front stood three pirates. One was dressed in a striped shirt and waited holding a notepad in his hand. As the people laid their offerings on the wide steps at the front of the room, the pirate kept track of every offering given.

As Johnny's group entered, the crowd moved to the sides of the room, making way for them to approach the stairs. When the three pirates recognized that their guests had arrived, they quickly cleared the room, by escorting all the local people elsewhere.

The guests stood in silence. A deep voice came from inside the room at the top of the stairs. "Bring them here!" the voice echoed. Pierre urged them up the steps. Layers and layers of sheer curtains hung from several golden pillars that separated the group from the source of the voice.

Johnny and the others felt uneasy as they climbed the stairs. Pierre parted the silky wall, removed his hat and made a broad sweeping bow to the voice within. Then with a wink he turned back toward Johnny and with his hand extended, he welcomed everyone inside.

Johnny was the first to enter. The sight before him was glorious. Inside was a pirate's treasure trove. Beautiful furnishings laden with flowers and jewels surrounded the room. Piles of gold filled the floor amid golden statues draped with pearls and jade that stood like glistening guardians over the treasure. The place was a veritable treasure-hunter's dream.

As Johnny stepped to the side of the room so the others could get a better look, he felt a hand on his shoulder. The same deep voice spoke to him, "Well now, I would imagine you are all very tired. Please sit down." The voice startled everyone, and they whirled around to see the face of their mysterious host.

An enormous black panther stood in front of them, dressed in pirate clothing. He wore a tri-corner hat that was extravagantly embellished with bright feathers and precious gems. He wore a bright red waistcoat trimmed with a lace shirt and cravat with gold buttonry. His vest was pale turquoise. His light brown trousers went to his knees and buttoned at the sides. He carried a sword in a leather scabbard that went from his shoulder to his hip, and carried at least three different types of pistols around his waist as well. Upon his feet were heavy black boots with gold buckles that finished the attire perfectly.

Johnny couldn't take his eyes off this amazing host. The panther clapped his large paws and a brigade of servants entered the room carrying trays and platters of every kind of delicacy one could imagine. The servants placed them on a table at the side of the room in front of the company. The great cat poked at some food of his own, and casually ate a few grapes then addressed his guests. "Well, eat up! It isn't poisoned, you know. My servants have prepared this feast just for you!"

Kate's natural inclination toward being as gracious as possible immediately kicked into high gear, and she approached the great cat. "Excuse me.... we don't mean to seem ungrateful. I suppose we are all just a bit surprised. We're all wondering to whom we owe our thanks for this wonderful feast." Kate looked back at Jim, then at the panther. "May we ask...who you are?"

The panther burst into laughter, and Pierre joined him, followed by the other pirates. Kate's patience was wearing thin as she began to frown at being the brunt of someone's joke.

"I beg your pardon, my dear lady. We did not intend that you should be the subject of our levity. It would seem you are the only ones within our world who do not know who I am. We had thought that you were already aware of my identity. Please excuse my rudeness as I introduce myself. My name is Jean Laffite!"

53
The Laffite Legacy

At Jean's words Johnny let out a gasp. "I can't believe it. You're Jean Laffite! So you're the leader of the Revolutionaries of the Defiance!"

"Yes!" replied Jean. "And from my closest informants I owe a great debt of gratitude and respect to all of you for freeing many of my people from the Dungeons of Despair."

Johnny smiled back at the others. The great cat continued, "I have received word of some critical information from one of your group, a man named Palmer. Is he here?"

Palmer stood and approached the large cat. "I'm Palmer."

"I understand you have had dealings with Ratcliffe and Clayton?" the cat asked. "Is this correct?"

"Yes," Palmer nodded. "They were blackmailing me."

"And did you deal with Emil Dennison."

"Yes!" said Palmer. "He was the one that always paid Ratcliffe."

Jean nodded to one of his men who left the room, then returned with a man in iron shackles. "Palmer, help me," Dennison said. "You've got to tell them I'm innocent. Tell them that I was just trying to help the Leavitts."

Palmer stared at Dennison then looked at the Leavitts. "I've worked with Ratcliffe for years now, and I've seen all of the scheming he's done to destroy this family and anyone who's gotten in his way. Ratcliffe tried to do the same to me and Randy, too. I do know this much, Dennison is the one who always paid us. He always called all of the shots and told us exactly what to do. I know he worked for Clayton because I heard them talking on the phone one day when I accidentally picked up the extension at the office."

"No!" yelled Dennison. "Don't you understand? They'll kill me for being a traitor."

Palmer looked at the floor, gritting his teeth. Then Randy stepped forward. "Mr. Laffite, I understand that your community here is based on the laws of our constitution." The cat nodded. "Well," said Randy, "I have an idea, why don't you make this man turn evidence on your enemies in exchange for his life?"

Jean smiled. "Well, Mr. Olsen, it would seem that not only are you an excellent lawyer, but you have taken to the ways of pirating quite well. I will agree to your terms for this prisoner, but only under one condition. He must prove that what he says is true."

Dennison groveled on the floor in front of the great cat. "I'll tell you anything you want to know. Just please don't kill me," he sobbed.

Johnny watched the pitiful display, cringing at each confession the man made. All he could think of was how his own father had been tortured over and over yet never denied their family. Then he remembered that Monsieur De La Fount had been very specific about the warning to be careful and make sure that the people he delt with were trustworthy and loyal to the cause of freedom in the bayou. The man on the floor in front of them was the very thing he had been warned about. The danger of deception was so great that even a skilled pirate like Jean Laffite had been deceived.

After the traitor had poured out every last bit of information he could to save his own life, Jean commanded that the man be locked up. His men quickly complied.

Jean sat on his large throne-like chair, pondering over the words of the traitor. His guests silently ate the meal before them. Finally Jim spoke up. "Mr. Laffite, we came here to help you, but in order to do so, we need to know just how to fight Clayton."

Jean groaned, rubbing his forehead with his great paw. "I grow weary of this cursed fight," he said. "My soul will see no rest until it is done. What do you wish to know, sir?"

"We've followed every clue you left back at Maison Rouge, but we don't understand how everything fits together.

The great cat rubbed his chin then began to explain.

"Long ago when this country was new, it had its beginnings amid sacrifice and sorrows, yet somehow it survived. My men and I came to the bayou and built Barataria. It would be a place where we could set up our own form of government and find a new life in that land.

"At that time, my brothers and I had built a very large structure of commerce along the Delta. Even though we were on the very edge of the wilderness, our success brought the needed goods for the country to survive and expand.

"Some people did not approve of our type of business. To them, our great success was a stain upon the noble aristocracy that they so arrogantly protected. You see, we were wealthy, but we did not have blue blood. We were just loathsome pirates in their eyes. The only redeeming quality to our supposed inferiority was that we provided the goods that sustained their illustrious lifestyle.

"Clayton led the battle cry that called for our destruction. He was determined to rid the Delta of our despicable lifestyle and the embarrassment it caused him. He and his men burned Barataria forcing my men and their families into hiding.

"At that time, the U.S. was very vulnerable. Their troops were starving and their supplies dwindling. The White House was in ruin and the president on the run. The British thought I would jump at the chance to get revenge for the loss of Barataria and offered me $30,000 if I would betray my country. I delayed their enthusiasm by telling them I needed time to discuss it with my men. I never intended to discuss anything. Instead my men and I offered our services and weapons to General Andrew Jackson. In time, we won the war of 1812 and began again to build New Barataria.

"Our success won us a pardon by President Madison who then commissioned us as an informal naval patrol to protect the United States. Every ship we raided, from then on, was done under a U. S. letter of marque. Every item we took was recorded and a copy given to the U.S.

"It was at this time that I received word from Napoleon that he would like to negotiate safe passage to America. I had some dealings in France to attend to, so I agreed to entertain his offer. I wish I had known the sorrow it would eventually bring. He agreed to pay us all he had, and we took his offer. The boats were loaded, but that night his plan was discovered, and he was taken captive. We barely escaped with our lives.

"To us Napoleon's treasure was different than any other we had received. It would help the U.S. become strong again. We knew it had to be protected so we formed an alliance that very night. Together we made an oath to protect the cargo at any cost.

"Over the next two years, Captain Edwards had us make extensive modifications to Maison Rouge as well as Barataria, and then he gave everyone of the members of the Alliance a separate clue to protect the treasures.

"It was at this time that my beloved Catherine and I were married, and she became part of the Alliance. That night, at the wedding I gave her the watch. Somehow word that it held a hidden clue got out, and Clayton tried to steal it. By doing so he lost more than his honor that night. It was that fight that led to the loss of his leg, and he vowed that he would get revenge on us, and one year later he did so.

"My dear Catherine was expecting a baby. Pierre and I were away on business and Captain Edwards was transporting Napoleon's treasures to New Barataria for safe keeping. That was when Clayton attacked the *Intent* and Captain Edwards was killed, defending the nation's treasure. My dear Catherine gave birth to my son at that very moment, but gave her own life doing so. As life and death hung in the balance the curse was born as well.

"You see, on board the *Intent* that day was a hidden cargo, one which I have taken an oath not to disclose. It was the loss of this cargo that brought condemnation upon us all. That is what began our quest.

"My brothers and I knew that we had to bring the eight men of the Alliance together quickly. We gathered their clues like treasures, all the while watching the curse take our loved ones and changing everything. Slowly Clayton destroyed the men of the Alliance till only four were left-I, my two brothers and Michael Pithon. He, too, was eventually destroyed, but in a much more heinous way. He joined Clayton and became the worst of the Overseers. He revealed everything to Clayton, hoping that with this information he would someday rule the world.

"You see, we had but one hope these last hundred and eighty six years. It was to keep the other clues out of Clayton's hands. But I had a snake in my midst that I did not know about. It was Dennison. All this time he has been selling off all of the clues to Clayton.

"Now we have no choice but to end the curse or to be consumed by it. It was partially my fault that you came into the bayou. I had hoped that Jonathan would do so of his own accord because he is our last hope. And the curse demands his free will in this matter. You see, within the boundaries of the curse I have come to understand that in our world we are nothing without our descendants. And in your world you are nothing without us. The curse's power would eventually destroy both our worlds, unless, we conquer it together. You see, we, your fathers, are bound eternally to you."

Johnny walked to Jean, put down his backpack, opened it, and pulled out all of the items he had guarded so well except for Dominique's crystal. He laid out Dominique's map then took the watch and key out of his pocket and laid them on it. Then he added the driftwood. Next, he retrieved all of the coins and lined them up in order on the map. His notebook was next with all of its clues.

Jean smiled as he saw all of the items. "Well done, my young grandson. You have found that which was long lost."

Johnny looked up with surprise at the great cat. "But I thought that you were the one that left all of those clues for us."

"I knew of some," replied Jean, "with the exception of the one hidden in the watch. Captain Edwards must have known that Michael Pithon was a traitor in our midst. So he told Catherine to hide the watch before she died. And you, a Laffite, found it again."

The great cat picked up the watch, opened the case and read the words of the clue: *What time reveals within the heart can be pieced together only with true intent.*

Johnny was thrilled to hear Jean read the words. "Wow, and I thought the words of that clue were dumb. Out of all of the clues I never thought this one meant anything."

Jean raised his eyebrow. "It is the one thing along with Dominique's map and Pierre's key that Clayton lacks. It has great meaning. The heart is the greatest word of the clue, for one's heart must be pure and of true intent, but the real clue lies in the heart of the Consortium. Have you been deep within the

528

tunnels under Golden City?"

Johnny nodded. "Is the heart of the Consortium down there?"

"Yes," replied Jean. "It is a great round room where all the tunnels intersect, a council chamber for the first eight men of the Alliance. It was originally built by those men long before the curse ever began. When we discovered that the Alliance had been compromised, we held a great council there to protect our trust, and only one of us was given the key to unlock its secret. The key has also been lost these many years, and without it we could not complete our task in finding the lost fortune. Now that you have found the key, we may be able to solve the curse.

"Originally the tunnels were part of New Barataria and used for smuggling. The Heart of the Consortium lies at the very center of New Barataria. Each of the eight men who ran our independent governing powers was given a parish to protect, and the tunnels lead to those parishes. Many great plans were set in that chamber, and after we had agreed to take Napoleon's offer, many modifications were made to that structure beneath Golden City. The changes were made to accommodate Captain Edward's plans to protect the nation's treasure. This watch is a map to the true heart of the Consortium of admirals and the alliance these men made.

Matie piped up, "Johnny almost gave that watch away to that nasty alligator man."

Johnny interrupted her, "Not this watch, Mat. There's no way I'd let this one go." Johnny picked up the old piece of driftwood. "Mr. Laffite, what's this for?"

Jean smoothed the hair on his chin. "It belonged to Captain Edwards. Where did you get it?"

"Marie gave it to me back in the bayou. She said that Captain Edwards had given it to her right before he was killed."

"But it doesn't make any sense," Riley blurted.

The black panther stared at the little fox. "That, my impertinent boy, is because it is written in Captain Edwards special language. He used sounds for words."

"Just like Johnny does!" exclaimed Matie. "He likes cryptograms, too."

Jean looked puzzled. "What, my dear, is a cryptogram?"

Matie took a deep breath, but Johnny interrupted her. "A cryptogram is the same thing that you're talking about. I collect them. They work like this: say you put the letters G R with the number 8, together it says 'great'."

The cat chuckled. "Truly you are one of my descendants."

"We figured out one of the messages on the driftwood," Johnny interrupted. "It says true intent like all the other clues. Do you know what the rest of it says?"

"No," said Jean. "But I do suspect it is very important. Captain Edwards never let it out of his sight and guarded it from everyone. When he gave it to Marie, he was protecting something."

Pierre walked over to Jean, and picked up the key. "I am the guardian of the key to the heart of the Alliance. It was lost and almost forgotten. The words of the clue still ring in my ears. *True intent is the key to the heart.* Where did you find it?" he asked.

Johnny told him about the cannon back at the fort and the pirate without a nose who was protecting it. "Ahh yes, I had sent it to Maison Rouge to be hidden with the other coins," said Pierre. "It was in Louis Chigoulusa's hands when Clayton and his men attacked the fort. He must have hidden it there in the cannon for safe keeping. He was one of my best men, and even lost his nose in defending me."

"Our Father, Captain Edwards, was a very insightful man," Jean said. "He knew the importance of integrity. True intent was the key to keeping our oath, and he knew it. That key is also the Key to Captain Edward's heart, the hidden cargo hold on the *Intent*. His greatest concern was that hidden cargo. If you ever find it, this key will unlock the mystery."

Pierre handed the key to Johnny. Johnny turned it over in his hand. "If only Captain Edwards knew what he was starting with all of this," Johnny said. "He'd probably be amazed to see that true intent was more than just a clue to the treasure he hid. It's the only real thing that the curse can't control."

"My boy, you underestimate your own words," Jean interrupted. "Since the curse began, all of us have tried to stop it, each attempt resulting in great failure for one reason alone. We did it out of selfishness. Each of us would benefit greatly if we were to find that treasure and overcome the curse. But you would only benefit by the curse remaining."

Johnny looked confused. "What do you mean I'd benefit from the curse?"

Jean looked deep into Johnny's eyes. "You are a Defaun, are you not? One blessed and gifted by the curse. It has given you power, power which would cease if the curse is overcome."

Johnny looked a bit annoyed at Jean's words. "I don't care about any stupid powers the curse has given me. I just want my family and friends to be back to normal."

"Yes, exactly!" said Jean. "That is what is called true intent, and that is why you are the chosen one!"

Jean picked up the coins. "Do you know the significance of these coins?"

"I'm not sure," said Johnny. "I just thought that each of the original eight men had one."

"Yes, this is true," Jean replied, "But they are far more important. These were given to each of the original eight men

531

of the Alliance. Each coin is very different, uniquely prepared to represent that man's clue. Each coin was a token of the oath of the Alliance, but also a key to unlock the chests that held Napoleon's treasure."

Johnny looked over the coins. "Mr. Laffite, when we were back at Maison Rouge, I found three of these coins in the attic. When the clock struck twelve, the whole room filled with light and there were all of these images on the walls everywhere. I wrote them in my notebook, and my dad and I were able to match several of the coins to the pictures from the stained glass. But we're not sure what all of them mean."

Jean raised an eyebrow. "Well, well, the time has come for destiny to prevail. The glass dome at Maison Rouge was prepared to keep the clues well hidden until the right Laffite was ready to use them. The window has all of the clues that we know upon it except for one. You were lucky, or destined perhaps, because the window at Maison Rouge only reveals her secrets once a year on the anniversary of the curse's beginning.

"I will explain the meaning of the window. *True intent nothing waiverin shore N blood R swamp ye B favorin. "True intent* we have already explained. But the ship with the sun and the word *True* also represents the court of admirals or the Heart of the Consortium. It has a large sun on the floor like the image on the glass dome. The *Intent* was my ship, the sister ship to the *Alliance*. They were identical in every way, except that the *Intent* alone held the hidden cargo within the heart of the ship.

We switched ships, and the *Alliance* was the ship that was pretending to carry Napoleon's gold as a distraction, but it held only lead. Captain Edwards, using the *Intent*, was transporting the real treasure when Clayton attacked it. Clayton wanted revenge and thought that it was my ship he was attacking. He actually got far more than he bargained for in killing Captain Edwards, for he threatened the hidden cargo and

God's wrath took over."

Jean looked very solemn, then Ken spoke up. "Whatever happened to the other ship, the *Alliance*?"

The cat adjusted his hat. "After the curse began, Clayton did anything he could to destroy me and my brothers. He and his men came into the bayou and found the ship *Alliance*. They thought it was the ship that had started the curse and that it somehow still held the treasure.

"After searching it and killing many of my men, they burned it. Then they had a great surprise. They had tossed the dead men overboard just as a great storm arose. Then the moaning mists came and overshadowed everyone, and the curse, in its unusual way, mercifully brought my dead crew back to life, but, not without a price. They would, from then on, be bound to the depths of the sea to become the watermen.

"Many of Clayton's men were also changed in the same manner. But most of all, Clayton and I both changed that day and became Maroos. When we awoke from the moaning mist, the ship was gone. We were left adrift in our life boats until Pierre and the crew of the *Hotspir* found us."

With a deep sigh Jean continued. "Now I must explain the rest of the clues. The word *nothing* was Jean Baptist's clue. The picture of the fort was to steer people away from the real treasure. When we wrote the word *nothing,* we knew people would think it was where the treasure was hidden, so we deliberately placed a false treasure there. We scuttled one of my own ships on Deadman's Lake that was filled with several chests of gold coins, a tempting distraction for those who would seek to find the true treasure."

"We saw that treasure," Bo interrupted, "when the watermen attacked us at the fort! They held us under the water, and we saw it!"

Jean smiled. "Clayton's watermen guard that treasure

jealously. They somehow hope it will bring them their freedom some day."

Jack broke into the conversation and asked. "So why didn't Clayton try to take that treasure? How did he figure out that it wasn't the real thing?"

"That was Michael Pithon's doing," the great cat replied. "He revealed all of our plans to Clayton." Jean looked at Jack. "You are a very perceptive young man."

"As to the next clue, the word *waiverin* was Arsene Lebleu's clue. It has a picture of a great storm and waves. The lightning represents a warning that the real treasure is hidden with a death trap. The lightning to the left of the boat means the death trap will be on the left. The place is near water, and there are four waves meaning four furlongs. So if a person ever finds the real treasure, they must stay to the right and be very careful near the water, always looking for the trap.

"The word *Shore* had two meanings: The treasure would be near a shore line, and if you found this place with a large cheniere and a solitary tree, you could be sure that it was the true treasure. That was James Campbell's clue.

"The letter *N* stands alone with its picture of a bottle of wine and grapes. This refers to Napoleon and the agreement that was made with him, the number of grapes represent the number of chests. But this also has reference to the oath we all took and the special hidden cargo.

"The next clue is the word *blood.* It is the oath that all of the original eight men took. It was a blood oath that on our very lives, we would protect the treasure no matter what. This is the greatest reason why we are so cursed above all other men. We failed in our oath, and now someone with my blood in their veins must set the promise right. That person is Johnny.

At Laffite's words a stabbing pain gripped Johnny's leg where it had been cut by the crystals in the Razor Swamp.

"Mr. Laffite? When I was in the Razor Swamp, my leg got cut, and the blood made the crystals grow even faster. What caused it to do that?" Johnny asked.

Laffite frowned. "The crystals in the Razor Swamp would not normally do that. Was there anything else unusual that happened while you were there?"

"There was a dark Defaun that tried to trick me into leaving the bayou. He gave me a ruby and said that it would help me. When I showed it to Monsieur De La Fount, he said it was a tracking stone, and that I should throw it away. I threw it into the waters right before I got cut."

"You are very fortunate that Monsieur De La Fount was so wise. That tracking stone was one of Clayton's, powered by the beacon. When it came in contact with the minerals in the razor swamp, the crystals multiplied its powers. It was intended to destroy you, and that is just what it tried to do. Your blood is the very blood that the curse is based on. When your blood mingled with the waters, the crystals consumed it and grew even more powerful. The curse recognizes your blood as a means of stopping it. That is why the crystals grew as they did. The Razor Swamp will never be the same again, now that your blood has mingled with the crystals there."

"Now I will continue to explain the meaning of the clues. The letter *R* also stands alone. This was the clue of Renauto Belouche. The picture of the bird means the messenger. Renauto's clue was hidden in a grave at the churchyard. The grave held the ship's manifest, a *Record* of exactly what had been negotiated with Napoleon. I have this record which was intended to be given to the U.S.A. along with the treasure."

Jean snapped his fingers. One of his men left the room and returned with a document. Jean handed it to Johnny, "You must keep this ship's manifest with the rest of the artifacts. You

535

may need it later."

"I'll take good care of it," he promised.

As Johnny glanced at the document, at the bottom of the page an entry was written in between the lines of the other entries. It was the word *Raconteur*. Johnny easily recognized all of the other items in the list, but this one seemed unusual.

"What does 'Raconteur' mean?" Johnny asked.

Jean's eyes widened. "Where did you see this word?"

"It's right here on the ship's manifest," Johnny said.

Jean took the paper from Johnny and looked at the word. "I have been over this many times yet somehow this word has eluded me. 'Raconteur' means 'One who excels in telling stories." But there was no such person aboard our ship. Yet, as I remember, there was one man of Napoleon's who attended the treasure. He was an old withered story teller who wished only passage to America. So we took him on. Before he died, he settled at Grave's End, caring for the chapel there."

The black panther had a sly glimmer in his eye. "I now know Renauto's secret. It was the identity of the old man. We had thought him long dead, yet he followed his oath. The old story teller was the Friar of the Abby of Sainte Chapelle. He never left protecting that treasure and its secret until the day he died. Perhaps in death he has more to reveal. We must return to the Grave's End chapel. I believe there is more there that we may have overlooked."

The great cat turned to Pierre. "Perhaps you should explain the next clue, since it is yours."

Pierre lifted his chin and began. "The crossed swords are a warning that any, who chose to fight this cause would die doing so. But the swords also represented two great battles. The first was when Barataria was burned by Clayton and the second was the war of 1812 that evolved into the battle of New Orleans. Each of these great battles took place within the swamp. The word *Swamp* was a great clue for how to get to the treasure that would be found somewhere between the old Barataria and the place where we won the battle of New Orleans."

"Just where was the first Barataria?" Johnny asked. "And where did the final battle of New Orleans take place?"

"The first Barataria was exactly where Golden City is. We have searched the area four furlongs west of the center of Golden City, but have never yet found the treasure. We do not know, but perhaps Clayton and his men may have already found it."

"Wait a minute," Johnny interrupted. "I know Clayton doesn't have it yet, or he wouldn't have wanted the watch so bad. They're just as worried about finding it as we are."

Jean smiled as he rubbed his chin. "WE have the artifacts and the key to the heart of the Alliance. Without them, Clayton will never find the real treasure. You must be very careful to protect them with your very life. When Clayton finds out you have those things, he will be relentless in his quest to acquire them.

"Now the word *Youx* is next in the clues, and it means Dominique Youx as you already know," said Jean. "The red skull is his symbol and his map is the true map to the treasure. But it is a sister map and the truth can only be revealed if a person has both maps and uses them in conjunction with one another.

"The Letter *B* also stands alone, representing New Barataria or a new hope. The treasure chest in the picture is not Napoleon's treasure but Captain Edward's sea chest. It's the same one that Clayton took off the *Intent* and placed it in my warehouse, hoping to place the crime of his stolen treasure on me and my men. This chest also held another clue from Captain Edwards."

Jim interrupted Jean. "Is that the chest that's in the master suite back at Maison Rouge?"

"Yes," Jean said.

Jim scratched his head. "But I've seen that chest, and all it has in it is a spy glass of Captain Edwards."

"I know," said Jean with a slight grin. "Its secret will come forth in due time..."The last clue belonged to the snake Michael Pithon. It is the word *Favorin*. This is the one clue we lack. Pithon gave it to Clayton, feeding his hunger for power. We do not know, but we think Pithon holds the sister map to Dominique's. This clue must be retrieved if you are to overcome Clayton and stop the curse."

Johnny wrote all of the information in his notebook. Then Laurabeth approached the great black panther. "Mr. Laffite, I have a question. With all of the gold in the bayou and all of this treasure you have right here, why can't you just replace the lost treasure and give that to the United States instead?"

"Your insight is very keen, my dear young lady. Originally we did seek to appease the curse in this manner. My men traveled the seven seas in search of the greatest wealth on the earth. Quite frankly they amassed fortunes far greater than you can imagine. But we soon found that the curse would have no substitute. It demanded that the original treasure be returned, and Captain Edward's heart restored. You see, it is not the riches that matter, for the curse cares nothing for them, but that ALL things lost must be restored."

Riley eyes got big. "So what are you going to do with all of that treasure your men found? I'd be glad to help take some of it off your hands," he said. "That is, if you're running out of space or something."

Bo leaned over to his cousin and elbowed him. "Be quiet, Riley!"

Jean's face remained emotionless. "Perhaps it would be wise if I explained to you the true properties of the treasure which surrounds you. To us gold is useless..."

"Useless!" Riley blurted.

"Yes, useless!" the cat said patiently. "Mr. Riley, let us just imagine that I were to fulfill your wish and give you all the gold you desired. What would you do with it?"

Riley's eyes widened, and he licked at his lips. "Well, first I'd buy a great big house and then all new clothes and maybe a new car with a driver. Oh, and I'd have a party and invite all those kids at school who make fun of me. I'd show them who was who!" Riley folded his arms as he thought of this dream. "Yeah, it'd all be perfect. All of my troubles gone, just like I've always imagined."

Jean nodded at Riley. "Oh, I see, you have it all planned out. But have you thought how your friends would treat you when they saw your red fur. How quickly do you think they would run to your side, pretending to be your true friends only to have access to your money? You see, you would quickly find that if your money ran out, your popularity would wane just like the golden fortune.

"True friends come through hardships and trials together and they do not care for the things of this world. Now, I will tell you the secret of the ages. The power of gold lies in a property that it possesses. Gold is an amplifier of whatever an individual is. If one seeks wisdom or knowledge in its presence, then they will find it. But if one seeks greed, it will consume that person. You see when the curse began it was amplified by Napoleon's gold. God's wrath took over and now a price must be paid to redeem all of us. Now do you still wish to have some of my gold?"

Riley's eyes were wide, and he barely squeaked out an answer. "Ah no sir. I'm just fine without it, thanks."

54
"L" for Liberty

The plan was for the men to go into Golden City to find Michael Pithon's lost clue as well as the old friar's resting place in the church-yard at Grave's End. The men had to work quickly as the tension and restlessness of the Defiance was spreading rapidly. Even Jean and Pierre themselves could no longer stay hidden. Together they joined with the Leavitts and their friends to find the answers they so desperately needed to stop Clayton.

With a bit of resistance, Kate and the girls had agreed to remain behind on Rebel's Isle. Here they could stay in relative safety away from the dangerous conflict in the bayou. The plans were well made, but no one had realized just how far the damage of Dennison's traitorous acts had spread.

As the morning sun rose over the hidden island, Kate and the girls slept quietly. Suddenly Kate awoke with a start. She felt something over her mouth! A waterman was hovering over her. In her shock at being awakened by the touch of the icy hand, she realized that she was drowning. Her eyes bulged as she struggled for breath. She tried to scream, but each time her mouth only filled with more water as the pirate sought to drain every bit of life out of her.

In her struggle she saw something out of the corner of her eye. Perhaps it was just a shadow, or maybe another pirate going after the girls. Kate desperately tried to scream and free herself. Then, without warning, the pirate before her exploded into a billion droplets of water.

Gasping and choking, Kate saw another water pirate standing in front of her. At first she began to scream then realized it was Dominique Youx.

"It's all right!" he said. "My men and I have come to help!"

"Then why are they trying to kill me?" Kate sputtered.

"That was not one of my men," he explained. "It was one of Clayton's spies. They are all over the island. We must leave immediately."

"Are the girls all right?" Kate said, standing up. Her clothes were dripping wet.

Laurabeth ran to her side. "Hurry, Kate! Pirates are invading the entire island. Almost everyone else has already left." Kate slipped on her shoes and ran to wake Matie while Dominique and his men guarded the door.

Matie rubbed her eyes as Kate helped her dress. "What's the matter?" Matie asked with a yawn.

"Clayton's pirates have found this place, and we have to leave now."

"Do you want me to poke em?" Matie said eagerly.

"No!" Kate insisted. "We're not going to get that close to them if I have anything to do with it."

Dominique rushed the girls down the long corridors and out into the courtyard. Soon they were headed for the village. Everything seemed deserted as they hustled through the jungle toward the shore. Suddenly one of Clayton's watermen leaped out from behind a bush. This time it grabbed Matie who squirmed and wiggled violently. Kate picked up a handful of sand and flung it into the water pirate's face. The sandy mixture turned into mud, temporarily blinding the evil attacker. Laurabeth and Kate grabbed Matie's paws as Dominique placed his watery arm around the attacker's neck. The unknown pirate melted into the ground, unconscious, while the girls ran for the safety of the ship in the harbor.

As they entered the open beach, a group of the evil

watermen grew out of the sand, their faces contorted, and then became solid like watery ghosts from a forbidden time and place. Matie screamed, her shrill voice causing some distraction. Dominique's men soon appeared on the scene. Swords clashed as the watermen began fighting and bursting everywhere around the helpless girls. The girls ran for the boat with Dominique protecting their every step.

As they ran up the ship's plank, Dominique turned back toward the battle on the beach and raised his hands high in the air. Water from the lagoon rose to form a wall between the ship and the shore. When the watery apparitions tried to attack the ship, Dominique's wall held firm and impassable against Clayton's men. The ship immediately set sail with Dominique at the helm.

This voyage was different than the others they had taken. No counterpart ship waited under the water, and the crew consisted of normal men as well as water pirates. In a burst of watery spray, Dominique and his men came on board. Brilliant colorful clouds filled the space surrounding the ship, and in a flash of light the entire entourage was swept from the dangerous scene into the grasp of the time lock. Soon the ship was floating in a tributary not far from Golden City.

Dominique and his men followed the bayou stream till they came to the sleepy village of Grave's End. It was a small community made up mostly of early settlers who still lived as the people who first came to the bayou. These were simple people who avoided the uncomfortable conflict of the Revolutionaries and instead chose to surround themselves with the things of an earlier time. Most everything in the village was built around the local church. The modern assemblages of Golden City weren't found here either. Instead the people used real animals to pull their old fashioned wagons.

The little church house could be seen a short distance

away, so as Dominique secured the ship along the shore, Kate, Laurabeth, and Matie headed down the road toward the old church to find Jim and the others who were all ready searching the graveyard for the headstone that might have belonged to the old Friar.

Jean motioned to the group. "Come, I have found the stone where we discovered the ship's manifest." As everyone hurried toward Jean, Johnny noticed Kate and the girls coming with Dominique Youx.

"Look!" said Johnny. "There's Mom and the girls."

Kate ran to Jim. "Rebel's Island is under attack!" she said. "Clayton's men tried to kill us. We had to come warn you."

"Are you all right?" Jim asked, hugging his wife.

"We're all fine," Kate replied. "But if it hadn't have been for Dominique Youx and his men, we wouldn't have made it."

Jean interrupted, "If they have attacked Rebel's Island then all of the people in the bayou will be preparing for the great battle. The Revolutionaries of the Defiance may not be able to wait for the signal to attack first if they are on the defensive."

Jean examined the old headstone. The Friar's grave was simple except for a poem that read:

in True dust my feeble Intent laid to rest
upon the alter of mercies bright quest
given alone for God to see
like the Sun on the Knoll of Golden City

Bo read the words aloud as Johnny jotted them down in his notebook. Johnny looked up at the others. "Did you see it? It's just like the other clues. It says *true intent* in the first line. Renauto Belouche had to have left it as a clue. He must have known who the old man was when he buried him and left the ship's manifest here."

"Yes, you are right," replied Jean.

"Wait a minute," Ken interrupted. "I think there's more. Look at how all of the words are written. Some are capitalized in the center of the sentence while the rest of the words aren't."

Now everyone paid particular attention to the words *True Intent, God, Sun, Knoll, Golden* and *City*. Jack looked at the curious words. 'I wonder why those last three words have fancy letters and the rest don't."

Immediately Pierre interrupted. "He was a Knight of the Golden Challis. They often left the initials K.G.C. as a symbol for others of their kind."

"What's a Knight of the Golden Challis?" Riley asked.

Pierre explained. "Have you ever heard of the Knights Templar?" Riley looked confused.

"The Knights Templar were great men who took secret oaths to protect the vast fortunes and artifacts of the early Christian church. Their secret organization had unique ways to protect that which they knew was sacred, and they often gave their lives in doing so. The Knights of the Golden Challis grew out of this. Then later came to protect the interests of the south. This man would have done anything to protect the treasure."

Jean broke in. "This man has left more in his words. The poem speaks of the sun on the knoll of Golden City. There is only one knoll in the town, and it is in the exact location of the Beacon."

"Yes," Pierre interrupted, "and it is also exactly four furlongs from the cheniere, right in between the place where the two battles were held.

Ken broke in, "but if that's true, then isn't that right over the Court of Admirals, in the heart of the consortium?"

"Yes," Jean smiled. "And Catherine's clue in the watch also speaks of it. It said, *What time reveals within the heart can be pieced together only with true intent.* Her clue speaks of the heart... the heart of the consortium."

"All of these clues point to the same place," Johnny said, "but we're still missing a clue."

Dominique had been quiet up until this point, but now he joined in. "The map I was given by Captain Edwards is incomplete. He told me that it would only reveal its secrets if used in conjunction with Michael Pithon's clue. It is apparent we must have that last clue."

"I have an idea!" Randy said. "Ratcliffe didn't see us on the *Hotspir* when we were waiting at the Dungeons of Despair. He doesn't know that we're part of the Revolutionaries of the Defiance now. If we pretended to take Johnny to Consortium Hall as a prisoner, we could get in and cause a distraction while the rest of you sneak in and get the clue from Pithon."

"Absolutely not!" Kate said. "I'll not have you taking my son into that den of vipers."

"Wait a minute," said Jim. "Kate, I know Johnny is just a boy in our eyes, but he's proven he's a man. Back at the dungeons, he faced Clayton and all of the Overseers alone in that room and saved our lives. He doesn't need us to hold him back now."

Kate looked at Johnny, then at Jim. "But what if we lose him again?"

Johnny approached his mother. "Mom, if I don't do this, Clayton will win, and everything that really matters will be lost."

Kate shook her head with a frown. "All right then, but you men had better make sure nothing happens."

Jean placed his large paw on Kate's shoulder. "My dear Kate, we are all very concerned for Johnny. But it is he who must solve this curse. Therefore, I promise that everyone will make sure he is well protected."

The group boarded the *Hotspir* and in time came to the wharf at the Golden City's harbor. An uneasy tension filled the air as they made their way along the boardwalk. Ever so often someone would nod at Jean and hold up their hand, as if they were waving, but then they would put their fingers in the shape of the letter "L."

"What are they doing?" Johnny whispered.

Jean leaned down and spoke quietly. "It is the signal for liberation. It's the way the Revolutionaries recognize one another."

The group hustled through the back streets of the town, avoiding the dangerous main routes. Many of the Revolutionaries along the way made the "L" symbol then warned the others of their kind so they could help the group keep from being discovered. With their aid, the group managed to arrive undetected at the center of Golden City where Kate and the girls were then secretly taken through the back alleys to Goldie's place to hide.

Johnny looked across the open park toward the Beacon. Its light pulsated in the distance, beckoning him to investigate its mysteries. But it would have to wait. Now they made their way to McGifford's store to make their final plans.

Once inside, McGifford informed them of the Pahreefs oppressive raids throughout the bayou. The freedoms of the people were being systematically denied. But the devilish plans of the Overseers to oppress the people had turned against their own cause, prompting more to join the ranks of the freedom fighters.

Pierre ordered his men to bring some iron shackles from the ship's brig. They loosely placed them on Johnny's wrists and ankles so he could quickly free himself when the time was right. Then they gagged his mouth and loaded him in the back of an assemblage. Thoughts flooded through Johnny's mind of the vision he'd seen of himself standing in irons before the Overseers. His previous premonition made complete sense now. This last ditch effort, though a long shot, was the only way they could get into the heavily guarded building.

"That should do it!" Jean said. "You look like a true prisoner. Now once you are inside of Consortium Hall, we will be waiting for your signal. When you say the word *Liberty,* the revolutionaries will attack Consortium Hall."

Johnny nodded and raised his eyebrows. Jean supplied the rest of the group with hooded cloaks, like the Overseers wore to disguise them as they rode in the back of the assemblage. Randy and Palmer took a crystal from McGifford and activated it. The assemblage moved down the street on its invisible sparking wheels of energy.

As the assemblage grew closer to its objective, the hooded men of the Defiance dropped off the back and slipped behind fruit carts and buildings to stay hidden until the time of the attack.

Then the assemblage made its way to the steps of Consortium Hall.

The place was heavily guarded. Pahreefs stood everywhere, checking each person's crystal as they came and went.

Randy and Palmer looked at each other and signaled the *L.* "Well, here goes." Randy said, with a wink. He lowered the assemblage, then he and Palmer unloaded their prisoner. Jerking Johnny around a bit, they put on a show for those around them.

"We'll see how cocky you are once the Overseers see you!" Palmer yelled.

"Hey, you Pahreefs, over there," Randy yelled. "We need a hand here. We caught this guy snooping around down at the pier. Do you know who this is? It's Johnny Leavitt! The Overseers have been searching the entire bayou for this guy."

A group of overzealous Pahreefs apprehended Johnny and led him toward the door, leaving the two men behind. Palmer spoke up. "I guess the Overseers will want to question us, too, won't they?" Several of the guards discussed the matter then surrounded the men and pushed them inside as well.

Johnny found himself in the center of the large room. Great marbled columns lined all of the sides with seating below and balconies above. At the front of the room a podium stood suspended from the ceiling, providing a place for the leader to stand. A retractable plank led from the regular seating area to the suspended podium. Johnny was placed in a lower box with a railing that served as a humiliating place for the accused to be tried.

Johnny was completely surrounded by the leaders of this parallel civilization. The robed Overseers stood directly in front of him with Clayton in the speaker's box. The rest of the Masters of the Consortium sat in the balcony along with the dark Defaun. Like a courtroom of judges ready to demand the guilty verdict, they pompously discussed the new development of Johnny's capture among themselves.

Clayton called the group to order and demanded silence. "Who found thissss boy?" he yelled. The Pahreefs quickly escorted Randy and Palmer to the front.

Palmer began to speak. But Clayton yelled, "Sssilence! You will only ssspeak when ssspoken to!" Palmer nodded.

"Who are you?" Clayton demanded.

"My name is Palmer."

Ratcliffe yelled out. "I know this man. He used to work for me."

Then Clayton addressed Randy. "Who are you?"

"My name is Randy Olsen. I also worked for Mr. Ratcliffe. We helped him bring the Leavitt's into the bayou."

"Ahh, yessss, I do sssseem to remember your

namessss," Hissed the gater. "Where did you find the boy?"

"He was snooping around down by the docks," Palmer said. "We questioned him, but he just lied to us. So we thought it was best if we brought him to you."

"Very good," Clayton said with a sinister smile. "You will be greatly rewarded for your allegiance to the Consortium." Clayton wrung his hands as he studied Johnny through slitted eyes. "Let him speak!" Clayton demanded. Two Pahreefs took the gag off Johnny's mouth. "Ssssoooo, we meet again, Mr. Leavitt. I see this time you are not so bold! Have you come to return my watch?"

"No!" Johnny yelled. "It's not your watch, and it never was!"

"Oh, contrair, all of the bayou is my domain. The Masters of the Consortium have the power to confiscate anything they deem to be a threat to our nation's security and peace. Your watch is a very great threat, as are you," hissed Clayton.

Johnny gathered his courage. "My watch isn't a threat to you. You just want to use it so you can find the treasure and keep the curse going forever. You're afraid of me and the old legends. You're afraid of the Laffite's and what we can do to destroy your power." Clayton snarled, but Johnny continued. "Even if you do get the watch and succeed in your plan to rule the world, it'll only bring a bigger curse on you and on the bayou. You're just a loudmouth dictator, and the Revolutionaries are going to destroy you."

The audience murmured in confusion. A man stood up in the balcony and demanded, "What is this treasure and plan you speak of?"

Johnny stood taller. "Clayton knows all about it. The curse started because of him. He killed Captain Edwards and the others in the original Alliance just to get to the treasure. But

549

all it did was bring on the curse. It was Clayton who tried to steal Napoleon's Gold. And that's why he's trying to stop me!"

"But how do you know all of this?" the man questioned.

Johnny scanned the back wall behind the balcony. Jean and the others were all in place as Johnny faced Clayton. "I'd tell you if I could, but I'm not at *Liberty* to say anything."

The revolutionaries sprang to attack, and Johnny yanked his hands and feet free from the shackles. Then he, Randy, and Palmer made a dash toward the Overseers. The entire room was in commotion as fighting broke out on every side.

Pithon and Ratcliffe joined Clayton in the relative protection of the speaker's box.

"Look!" yelled Randy. "Now is our chance." The three revolutionaries made their way through the crowd and climbed to the suspended speaker's box. Johnny slid the sword from the scabbard at his side and drew it up to Pithon's throat. Palmer and Randy held their swords on Clayton and Ratcliffe. Revolutionaries surrounded the podium and kept Clayton's guards at bay.

"What do you want?" Clayton demanded. Johnny smiled nudging the sword closer to Pithon. "You have a clue we need!" Johnny stated. "A traitor's clue, the one you gave to Clayton."

Pithon laughed with a sinister glare. "Ahhhh, haaa, haaa. You have risked all of this for my clue. You are idiots. Here it is. You can have it!" He pulled a rolled up paper out from under his cloak. "I had planned on burning it during this session of the Overseers. It is no more than worthless drivel, the deluded ranting of the original Alliance. I know it's every word, and there is no clue here."

Johnny took the paper from Pithon, then jumped off of the podium and ran for the door. Pierre and Jean led the battle while Randy and Palmer followed Johnny. They ran from the great hall and headed to the waiting assemblage. Bo anxiously protected Johnny's backpack while Jim was waiting in the driver's seat. Jack and Riley stood ready at the back of the assemblage.

"We've got to get out of here!" Randy yelled as they jumped in, and the assemblage pulled away.

"We need to get to the Beacon!" Johnny pointed to the sun dome. Everything around them was in utter turmoil as small skirmishes broke out in the streets. The war was now completely underway.

"We can't just go to the Beacon," Jim shouted over the commotion that had spilled out into the streets. "We'll be killed out here. We've got to get to the tunnels."

Jim drove the assemblage through the streets. Bo swiped his long claws at an attacker who ran alongside the assemblage while Riley bit the arms of a Pahreefs who tried to jump aboard.

The Maroo pulling the assemblage leaped into a full gallop leaving the pursuers standing in the middle of the cobblestone streets. Soon the assemblage arrived at McGifford's store. Everyone rushed inside.

McGifford locked the doors behind them. "You got yourselves a right good party here," he said with a grin.

"Jean and Pierre say they'll be joinin ya in the tunnels shortly. Pierre said he had a bit a business with ol' Clayton. Seems he promised him a new wooden leg!"

55
Casting the Light on Freedom

The rebels found their way to the back room of McGifford's store where they descended into the winding smuggler's tunnels beneath the city. Soon they were on the run, headed to the heart of the Consortium. They heard the rumblings of cannon fire above followed by loose dirt dribbling down on them.

"We've got to hurry," Jim said. "I don't know how long these tunnels will hold up."

The men ran as fast as they could, relieved to finally see a light up ahead that became brighter as they drew closer. Finally they reached the round room directly beneath the beacon where the tunnels intersected. Johnny opened his backpack and laid out the items on the floor. "We've got to figure out what we're missing here to get to the treasure. There's got to be something in Pithon's clue."

"There is!" a deep voice echoed. Dominique Youx emerged from an adjacent tunnel. Jean and Pierre stood right behind him.

"I'm sorry we were delayed," said Pierre. "But I had an appointment with Clayton."

Jean was not humored and went right to work. "Do you have the clue from Pithon?" he asked Johnny. Johnny took the paper from his jacket and handed it to Jean.

Jean, Pierre, and Dominique all stared in disbelief. "We thought this was lost forever!" Jean whispered. "It is the *Alliance for Truth and Liberty*! This is the original document we all signed with our oath to protect the treasure at all costs!"

The great cat held the delicate document like it was the

most precious thing in the world. Then he began to read aloud:

The Alliance for Truth and Liberty

We the Admiralty of the alliance for Truth and Liberty....Do hereby set forth our True Intent and sign our names to this sacred accord in the defense of Justice throughout all the land.

Therefore, let it be known to all men, herein and hereafter, that unto this accord and before the Throne of Almighty God,

We do vow our lives, our liberties, our hopes and our fortunes unto the maintaining and defending the cause of freedom for all men~

Also let it be known that under the strictest solemnity of oath and vow, We do hereby assume the noble cause of maintaining and protecting the heart of Freedom, Which is the highest token of our devotions before God on this the 18th day of February in the year of our Lord, 1821.

Jean Laffite   Pierre Laffite   Dominique Youx

James Campbell   Jean Baptiste   Aresene Lebleu

Renauto Belouche Michael Pithon Charles Edwards

When Jean finished reading, Johnny turned to Dominique. "Did Captain Edwards ever tell you how to use these two clues?"

Dominique shook his head. "I know no more about it except that Captain Edwards said that I must go to Pithon and find his clue for the map to be valid."

Everyone scoured Dominique's map and the Alliance for Truth and Liberty in the hopes of finding something that would correlate the two. Just like the other clues, the new document said True Intent within its passages. Nevertheless the attempt to correlate the two documents seemed hopeless

As Johnny looked at Dominique's map, he noticed that several places on the map were worn through. At first he thought the holes to be caused from wear or insects, but as he looked closer, he realized that they had been placed there deliberately. Johnny took Pithon's document and laid Dominique's map over it.

The two documents were exactly the same size. After Johnny lined up the edges, he examined the holes on Dominique's map. Within each hole was a word from the document beneath. "Look! said Johnny. "The two papers do work together, it says....

Truth.....of..... fortunes.....under.... the heart

"But we're standing in the heart," said Jack. He pulled the precious stone the Defauns had given him out of his pocket and looked at it. "Is the treasure near us?" he asked. The stone glowed a bright white.

Ken took out his stone as well and asked, "Is the real

treasure under our feet?" The stone remained dark. "There must be something wrong with my stone. It won't respond." Jack voiced the same question and his stone dimmed until it was as dark as Ken's.

"What's going on here?" said Ken. "First it leads us to believe that we're near the treasure, but then it gives us nothing."

"Perhaps the stone is not the problem," Jean said. "Perhaps the problem is the question itself. Maybe we are near the treasure, but need to ask which treasure?"

"What do you mean 'which treasure'? There's just one!" said Riley.

Johnny looked at Jean and then at Dominique. He knew exactly what they were thinking. Then he turned to Jean. "I made a promise not to say anything about Captain Edward's heart, and I've kept my promise. But I think we can trust everyone here. Don't they need to know about it?"

Jean looked at Pierre and Dominique. All three nodded in agreement. "Raise your right hands!" Jean demanded. Everyone glanced around at each other, then with hesitation, obeyed. "Now I want you to swear an oath on your lives that you will not take lightly nor reveal the information with which you are about to be entrusted." Everyone nodded in agreement. "Do you swear?" Jean said.

"We swear," they agreed.

Jean sighed deeply and looked around at the group. "We have told you of Captain Edward's heart. It was the secret cargo hold on the *Intent*. Within it was a treasure far greater than Napoleon's gold. It contained three precious items that could make any country that held them indestructible as long as that country honored God."

"What were these three things?" Jim asked.

"They were artifacts that had been jealously guarded by

the old friar in an abbey in France. The first, a scarlet cloak, the one placed upon the Lord's back when he was mocked. It was later gambled for at the foot of the cross. The second was called the Spear of Longinus or the Bleeding Lance which pierced the side of our Lord at his crucifixion, and last a leather parchment with a genealogy upon it. Written by God's own hand it was the historical evidence of Christ's family and blood line.

"Napoleon took these items from the abbey he had raided in France. This is where the grave of our old friar comes into the picture, as well as the Knights of the Golden Challis.

"The old priest came with the artifacts and even gave his life to protect them. We thought he was long dead at the time we brought these things here. None of us knew that he was more than a passenger on our ship. Obviously he had kept a close watch on the treasures, even after Captain Edwards died and the curse began. He must have taken Renauto Belouche into his confidence and thus, the clue on the headstone about the sun on the knoll of Golden City.

"You see, it is not Napoleon's treasure which we have found here, but Captain Edward's heart that must be nearby. That is why your stone malfunctioned when you asked it the vital question."

"But wait," said Jack. "Even if we find Captain Edward's heart that's not the treasure we need. Don't we need Napoleon's treasure to solve the curse?"

Jean smiled. "Perhaps we have been looking for the wrong treasure all along. Maybe it is the truth in Captain Edward's heart that the curse demands. Perhaps now we have found the true treasure!"

"So Clayton's threat to the three artifacts is what really caused the curse," Bo said.

"Yes, that is correct, and Napoleon's gold only amplified all of its effects," Jean replied.

Jack looked at his stone which glowed white again. "Hey!" said Jack. "Maybe we can use our stones to tell us where to look."

"Ask it if Captain Edward's heart is here in the Heart of the Consortium," Bo said."

Jack voiced the question, and the stone turned a bright red.

"Ask if it's beneath us," Randy said. Oddly enough, the rock began flashing both red and white.

"Be more specific," said Palmer. "Ask how to get to it."

"He can't," Ken interrupted. "The stones only tell us 'yes' or 'no.'"

As the others debated, Johnny closed his eyes tightly and thought of the three precious items. As he did he suddenly saw a very bright light in his mind. It was so bright that it almost gave him a headache. Then he heard these words in his mind: *One must be made low in humility before they can rise in strength.* Johnny took out his notebook and jotted down the words.

Jim noticed Johnny. "What is it?" he asked.

Johnny looked up and smiled. "Well, I was just trying to see if I could use the gifts of the Defauns to help me see where Captain Edward's heart is. But all I could see was a really bright light, and I heard the words: *One must be made low in humility before they can rise in strength.* I guess I'm not very good at listening like the other Defauns."

Jean grabbed Johnny's shoulders and looked him in the eye. "Oh, but you are, Johnny! What do you think it means to be made low in humility?"

Johnny thought for a minute. "Well, if a person's humble, they aren't bold. To be low you need to be willing to bend, like get down from being too proud."

Bo cleared his throat then from the middle of the room,

he said. "What if it means more than being just proud? What if you really had to get down on your knees to see it?"

Bo knelt by the gold sun plate in the center of the room and began dusting it off. Within the dust on the golden plaque it said: *In humility the heart of truth resides.* Beneath these words was an indented symbol exactly like the picture on the front of Johnny's watch. But there was one thing more...on the gold plaque was a small keyhole.

Johnny took the watch out of his pocket and placed it in the indentation. Then he took the key from his pocket and put it in the lock. As he turned the key, the room began to shake and tremble as if a great earthquake were shaking it apart. Johnny grabbed the watch and key and returned them to his pocket as the center of the floor began to rise. The great glass ceiling above the room began to open up as if it were the large petals of an enormous flower. The chamber floor began to rise lifting everyone closer and closer to the giant sun sphere above them.

Johnny stood at the center of the raising floor with Bo next to him. He pulled the sword from his side and raised it high in the air. Closer and closer they rose until the heat from the great sun sphere almost burned their flesh. When the tip of Johnny's sword touched the lower portion of the beacon, an explosion of light and sound immediately filled the room. A high pitched ringing from the sun sphere pulsated loudly. Where the sword had pierced the sphere, a great rift opened up.

Johnny looked up directly over his head. There, floating in the center of the great sun sphere, was the *Intent*!

"Look!" yelled Johnny." We've found it! It was here all along."

"It's impossible!" Pierre whispered.

"It was God's way of protecting the sacred relics from Clayton," Jean said. "The force surrounded the ship when it was threatened. Marie said that the *Intent* disappeared in a ball of fire. And when the curse began, the people found the Beacon in the center of Golden city. All the power within the bayou comes from it because of the power within Captain Edwards' heart! The sphere must have been drawn to the heart of the consortium because that was the place prepared by Captain Edwards to protect the hidden cargo!"

"We've got to try and get to it!" said Jack.

Johnny tried to put his hand on the edge of the rift to climb into the sphere. But the pulsating Beacon burned his fingers. "I can't touch it!" Johnny said. "It's too hot." Then he remembered Dominique's crystal in his pocket, the one Tambuka had given him back at the ruins near Vagabond Alley. Dominique said it had special properties that allowed it to harness the energy of the sphere. He took it from his pocket, then reached inside the rift and placed it in the hollow sphere.

The sphere's glowing surface turned a pale blue where the crystal lay. Johnny watched the affect spread farther from the crystal as it cooled the surface of the sphere. He reached inside. The Beacon's surface was now cool to the touch. Then with a boost from Bo, he climbed inside the sphere.

The entire inside of the sphere cool enough to allow Johnny to walk toward the ship. He reached for a rope ladder that hung down from the ship's side and began to climb. Beneath him the others watched through the rift with anticipation.

Johnny climbed up the rope then over the railing to the deck of the ship. Upon the deck everything remained just as it had the moment the curse began. Even the stains of Captain Edward's blood remained on the wooden floor.

Johnny headed below deck. He wandered past barrels of supplies with creates and trunks strewn about. Then he saw the door to the Captain's chamber. The hinges creaked as he opened the door. The bed was covered in silks and cushions.

Suddenly he noticed a trunk at the end of the bed, just like the one in his parent's room back at Maison Rouge.

Slowly he opened it. The inside was just like the one at home, even with a spy glass. As he lifted the spyglass to look at it, a spring-loaded latch gave way and the bottom of the trunk popped open revealing a trap door. Beneath it, stairs led down into a secret cargo hold.

His heart pounded wildly as he slowly climbed down the stairs. There in front of him on the floor was a single metal chest with a large lock. Johnny couldn't believe his eyes. He had found Captain Edward's heart. With trembling fingers he reached for the key in his pocket. He placed it in the lock and turned it. The lock clicked and popped open. Johnny removed the key and opened the chest.

Inside, just as Jean had described, were the three precious items, all cradled in red velvet. Johnny lifted the bundle, his hands trembling as he touched the items one by one. Thoughts and images began flooding his mind. He saw a beautiful young woman with dark hair. She was in a shallow cave, surrounded by animals and had just given birth to a baby which was being wrapped in a white cloth. Then he saw scenes of the baby's life as it grew to manhood. He watched as this man healed the sick, walked on water, and even raised the dead!

Then Johnny touched the purple cloak. Instantly his hand began to burn. The images of a man being whipped and then crucified were seared into his mind. He reached for the spear and the feeling of heat spread rapidly throughout his whole being. Suddenly he felt excruciating pain in his hands, wrists, and feet. Then his heart began to ache as if it would explode. Suddenly he felt what seemed like a great knife stabbing his side and into his heart. Then he saw the images of the same man on a cross and men gambling at his feet. Dark clouds gathered, and a great storm crashed while the whole earth shook. Then the images faded. Everything was very dark and silent.

Then in a pale pink morning light, Johnny saw the images of a woman crying in a garden near a tomb. Slowly the light increased until its brightness illuminated everything. There standing before the woman within the light was the man he had watched die on the cross. This being glowed with an unearthly white light. Johnny had seen pictures of Christ before, but nothing could compare to the glorious being that stood in that garden.

Johnny could hardly breathe. Tears streamed down his face as he realized the true power within these relics. He closed his eyes tight trying hard to squeeze back the tears. Then he heard a voice. It was a loving, powerful voice and spoke softly at first then became louder.

"Jonathan... It is well! The true intent of your heart has justified these things. I give unto you these tokens of my sacrifice that you may remember me. For I am the Truth and the Light, and true freedom comes only through me. Present these tokens before the curse that you may find freedom and be redeemed through my mercy!"

Johnny sobbed as he listened to the voice. And slowly the images in his mind faded. Then he remembered the words he had heard in his dream: *Through mercy alone the curse will be done.*

"Thank you!" he whispered as he gathered the precious tokens and placed them in his pack. He climbed back up the stairs and back out of Captain Edward's heart though the open chest. He pulled the trap door closed and replaced the spyglass. Then he closed the lid and headed up on deck.

He ran to the ship's railing, climbed down the ladder, and headed straight for the rift in the sphere. The others helped him down from the Beacon as he reached for Dominique's crystal and placed it back in his pocket just as the rift closed behind him.

Everyone sat silently looking at Johnny's tear streaked cheeks.

"What happened in there?" Jack questioned. Johnny looked up, his eyes filled with tears.

"He's real," Johnny whispered. "I saw him!"

"Who?" Jim asked. "Was it Captain Edwards?"

Johnny shook his head no. Then looked around at the others with tears streaming down his cheeks. "I touched the artifacts, and when I did, I saw his life, and I felt what he did for me. Jesus really is the Son of God!"

Johnny removed the new artifacts from his pack and showed them to the others. In reverent silence, he described what he had seen as he touched the priceless relics. The group fell silent. Even the boisterous Riley listened as he felt the power within the artifacts and in Johnny's words. Finally Johnny explained that the only way that the curse could be overcome was to face it with the relics. With an oath of loyalty to God and to each other, everyone agreed, just as the original Alliance had, that they would protect the relics and help Johnny accomplish the task. With new determination the group set their plans. They would take the priceless items back to the *Hotspir*, go into the time lock, then find the curse and face it head on. It was a good plan, but getting back to the *Hotspir* could be difficult with the city at war.

56

Restoration

The group headed back through the tunnels to McGifford's store. It would be essential for them to garner the help of the Revolutionaries if they were to succeed. When they arrived beneath the store they could hear crashing noises above.

The store was being searched and ransacked.

"Stop it!' yelled McGifford. "You have no right here. Go back where ya came from." The crashing sounds suddenly stopped.

Everyone sat quiet, listening for any sign of McGifford.

Above in the store they could hear the muffled whispers of the attackers. "We've got to stop them now before they fix that curse."

"Yeah, but we were told to just let Clayton and his men handle it," another voice said.

"They've already failed, and if we don't stop that kid, he's going to destroy the security of the entire U.S."

Johnny looked at Jean. "That's not the Pahreefs!"

"And it's not the Overseers," Jean whispered.

"I'll find out who they are," Dominique offered. His watery form melted and slowly moved up the ladder and through the floorboards. He returned almost immediately. "I've seen these men before. They work with Clayton. But I think they are from beyond the bayou. They come from Johnny's world!"

"What did they look like?" asked Ken.

"They are all dressed in dark clothing, but one wore a hat with the initials B.S.F upon it!"

"B.S.F!" Randy exclaimed. "But I've never heard of any agency like that. Why would our government be involved?"

"I do not know!" said Jean. "But we will soon find out. Open the hatch." Dominique dissolved through the floor boards above and opened the hatch to the back room. The group gathered in the store room as Jean and Pierre watched through a crack in the door. Jean suddenly turned to the others. "On my mark, we will attack."

He watched until the intruders had their backs turned.

"Now!" he yelled. The entire group sprung on the unsuspecting agents. The fight was a short one, and soon the intruders were overcome.

Jean untied McGifford. He stood up and stared at the row of prisoners. "Well now, it seems the tables have turned a bit."

Jean and Pierre firmly nodded to Dominique who took a position behind the lead prisoner. He placed his icy hand on the man's mouth.

"What are you d.......?" The man tried screaming, then his eyes widened in silence. Now Dominique's death grip began drowning him.

Johnny looked at the struggling man. "Stop! Please stop!" Johnny said. Dominique looked up, and took his hand from the man's face. The man was sweating and trembling as he fell to his knees.

Jean grabbed him by the hair. "Tell us who you work for, and why you are here!" The man tightened his jaw.

Suddenly Pierre lunged at the man and put his knife to the man's throat." We know you are from the B.S.F.! Why are you here?"

The man refused to speak. "Leave him alone!" one of the other prisoners said. "I'm the one you want."

Pierre let go of his prisoner and held his knife to the other man's chest. "Answer my questions."

"We were sent here for National Security. We're from the Bayou Security Force. We're here to make sure no one interferes."

"What do you mean?" Jim interrupted.

"U.S. Security has known about the curse since it began. The Defauns came to us. We know who runs the world banks, and we're here to make sure that nobody upsets the financial balance. The American economy is a fragile thing, and if it goes down, so does the rest of the world.

"You and your revolutionaries think that your little war can stop the Overseers, but you can't stop the curse. The Maroo's will go right on being slaves to their own weaknesses, and you, the waterman, will go on being bound down to the depths of the sea. You see we've made sure that no little insurgency is going to stop us or Clayton."

"What are you talking about?" Jean demanded.

The man sneered. "We have your precious treasure. All of Napoleon's gold is now in Clayton's hands. You can never stop that curse now."

Jean looked back at the others and winked then pretended to become angry. "I should have all of you keelhauled for this. You have destroyed us. Your arrogance will curse the bayou forever." Jean turned back to the others and smiled, letting the prisoners believe that Clayton had won.

"Perhaps they would like to see first hand what they have done," Pierre said. "We will take you to see the curse, and you will know for yourselves."

Pierre nodded to McGifford. "Call for the Defiance to gather. We need to get to the *Hotspir*." McGifford went out to the front of his store and hung a sign on the front door that said "Pirate Sale", the signal for the Defiance to gather. Soon the Defiance gathered in small groups at McGifford's store.

"My men are ready now to take your prisoners to the *Hotspir*," McGifford said.

Pierre, Randy, and Palmer accompanied the prisoners while Jean and the others stayed behind. Once the prisoners were out of hearing range, Jim turned to Jean. "With the nation's security involved, everything makes sense now. Back at Maison Rouge the police tried to stop anyone from investigating Ken's disappearance. They closed the case and threatened Officer Morgan. Now we know why."

"Yes," said Jean. "Sometimes it is very hard to understand one's enemies, especially when it is those we have trusted. But remember, they have not truly won, even if Clayton may have Napoleon's gold. They still do not know of our secret."

"Come," said Jean, "We must go and get the women. They must come with us. It is no longer safe in Golden City."

The remainder of the group headed back down the tunnels to Goldie's place. A trap door led up to an area behind the large stage. Dominique turned to the others. "Stay here while I see if it's safe."

Soon he returned with Goldie. Everyone climbed out of the tunnels and entered the large stage.

"The women are ready to go when you are," Goldie whispered. "We've been listening to the locals. Clayton and his men have taken over this part of the bayou. But there are still plenty of Revolutionaries here to get it back. It's too dangerous for you to try to get to the boat now. They'll recognize you. But we have a plan." Goldie ushered the men into a room filled with all kinds of costumes. Already dressed in costumes, Kate, Laurabeth and Matie came in behind them.

Kate ran to Jim and wrapped her arms around him. "We've been working on your costumes all morning since we heard that the Pahreefs had taken over the pier. Miss Honey and her children are watching the streets, waiting to help us get to the boat."

Kate handed Jim a dress. "What's this?" he asked with hesitation, holding it up to his chest.

"I thought it was about time you men see what we go through. Now be quiet and put these dresses on over your clothes," Kate insisted.

The men put on the disguises. "This is stupid," Riley said as he placed a hat with cherries on top of his furry head.

"Couldn't you find another way to get us to the boat?" He looked with disgust at the little girl's dress and pinafore that he was expected to wear as he tried to figure out which side was the front.

Bo had on a dancing bear costume and looked at Riley. "Hey, at least you don't have to look like a performing bear in a circus. Maybe we'll get lucky and die of embarrassment before we get there."

"Now quit your complaining and hold still!" Kate demanded as she smeared some lipstick on the men. Johnny tugged uncomfortably at the dress he was wearing and checked the pantaloons beneath it.

"Look," said Matie with a sly grin. "Johnny really is wearing girl's pants!"

Johnny's face turned bright red, and he frowned at Matie. "You're gonna get it when we get home!"

Kate and Goldie lined everyone up to inspect their work.

"Well, they're not perfect," Goldie said, "but they'll have to do. They're definitely some of the ugliest dance hall girls I've ever seen!"

Jean and Dominique stood laughing at the sight before them.

"What are you laughing at?" Goldie asked.

Jean just laughed again. "They look like the wenches one dreams of in a nightmare after a long night on the town."

"And a few too many drinks!" Dominique added with his blistering laugh.

"So, why aren't you two dressed?" Kate asked firmly.

Jean put his palms out toward Kate. "We will take our chances with Clayton's men."

"Hey, we'll take our chances with Clayton's men, too!" Ken interrupted. I just hope none of them get any ideas or I'll punch 'em right in the nose."

Jean and Dominique headed for the door.

Jim tried balancing in some high heels. "Well, if you guys aren't going to wear a dress then, I'm not going ..."

"Oh, no, you don't," Kate interrupted. "Besides, there's no time to change now. We have to go."

Kate ushered the men out of the room with Matie and Laurabeth following. They all made their way to the front of Goldie's place where an assemblage was waiting. As the men climbed inside, the horse Maroo pulling the assemblage turned around and whistled. "What a lovely bunch a ladies we 'ave 'ere."

Bo growled under his breath and Jack grumbled at the horse as it started out. The unusual entourage was attracting some whistles and unwanted attention. Kate waved and winked at the onlookers, then nudged Jim to do the same. Reluctantly Jim and the others waved at the crowds as Jean and Dominique sat at the front of the wagon covered in the dark cloaks. Pahreefs lined the streets and nodded with smiles and whistles at the wagon full of so-called girls.

Soon Miss Honey and her children flew to the side of the assemblage and warned Jean to take another street. The horse Maroo clipped along at a fast pace till they arrived at the docks. The *Hotspir* was not among the boats in the harbor. Stepping out of the assemblage the group heard a familiar whistle. Off in the distance, Whistling Pete was sending a message. Revolutionaries all along the pier began whistling the same tune and making the 'L' sign. Tobias and Whistling Pete came out from behind a building, carrying rum bottles, pretending to be drunken sailors.

Tobias grabbed Johnny and whirled him around as if in a wild dance. "Come on girls, 'ow about a ride in me boat?" Pete winked at the so-called girls. Soon the two sailors had the costumed men and the real women loaded on their small boat and started out across the harbor. It didn't take long for the little boat to find the *Hotspir* which had been waiting in one of the bayou's rivers, concealed in thick trees. Quickly they all climbed on board, amid whistles and whoops from Pierre's crew.

When Pierre, Randy and Palmer saw the unconventional manner in which the others had made their escape, they instantly burst into laughter. Pierre looked at Tobias and Pete. "Good work!" he said patting them on the shoulders. "I see that you have brought us the most beautiful women in the bayou." Then he winked at Kate and kissed her hand. Kate blushed at Pierre's joke, but the men were not so humored. They pulled off their disguises and wiped the remains of the lipstick from their mouths.

Pierre ordered his crew to get the *Hotspir* ready to set sail. The ship was filled with more men than normal, and they quickly obeyed his orders. Soon the *Hotspir* was traversing the channels of the bayou. Pierre picked up the time modulator sextant and set the indicators. Colorful time clouds formed around the ship.

Pierre ordered his men to stand by with the green mist sail and be ready at any time to hoist it. He stood at the bow of the ship and called all of his men to attention. "Today you will see the hand of God. Together we will face the curse, and by God's mercy we will conquer it!" Cheers went up from the whole crew as a flash of light engulfed the ship, sending it back through the time lock.

Just as before, the ship soon rested on calm glassy waters. The colorful clouds still surrounded it as lightening streaked around the sides. Johnny turned to Jean. "Are we getting close?" he asked.

Jean looked straight forward with his eyes fixed on the

horizon. "Yes, we are very near the curse now."

"Abyss on the port side," a man yelled from the crow's nest. Pierre's first mate steered the ship hard a port to face the gale.

In the distance the dark clouds gathered, and the waters churned beneath the ship. An ominous feeling silenced everyone aboard. Even the prisoners Pierre had brought from McGifford's store remained quiet in the shadow of the menacing curse.

The dark clouds drew closer. The wind whipped and scattered the colorful time clouds. Torrents of water sprayed over the *Hotspirs* bow as great waves heaved higher and higher around the ship.

"Set the Mist sail!" Pierre ordered. The crew hurried to their posts.

Suddenly Johnny saw it! A great evil face began forming within the darkening cloud. The enormous beast grew bigger and bigger. A sickening heavy darkness overcame the entire ship. Jim drew his family near. Kate and Matie clung to his side, and Ken stood close by protecting Johnny. Miss Honey and her children flew to Pierre and Jean at the ship's wheel. Bo, Laurabeth and Riley stood together below the helm. They had never before seen anything so frightening in their lives.

"It's time!" Johnny whispered as the great cloud undulated fiercely in front of the ship. He drew the three relics from his pack and unwrapped them. With determination he walked to the front of the ship and stood on the bow. "My name is Johnny Leavitt!" he yelled. The storm angrily turned its attention to him as it billowed and blew even harder. Johnny stood fearlessly in the pounding wind. He thought of the power of God's love and mercy. Then he spoke to the curse.

"You, the curse, you exist because of nine men who made an oath. It was a promise they made before God.

Someone else broke their oath, and you've had power all these years because of it. Well, you're not going to have that power any more because we've found something more powerful.

"You change us to Maroo's, and Watermen, and even Defauns. You try to destroy people by breaking up families. But there's one thing you can never have, and you can never take. It's the love God has for our family and the love we have for each other. You can make us all different, but you can never take that love out of our hearts.

"I said my name was Johnny Leavitt, but deep down inside of me runs the true blood of a Laffite. As long as we stand together in the power of God's Love, you will never have power over this family again."

Jean, Pierre and Dominique moved to Johnny's side, then Jim and Ken followed. Then as families, everyone joined arms in a stance of power against the groaning abyss. Angrily the storm screamed and blew in uncontrolled fury. Undulating, the cloud reached toward Johnny as if to consume him. Johnny held up the three relics. As he did, the storm began writhing and groaning as if it were in great pain. Johnny yelled out, "God's Love is what created this family, and it is the greatest power on this earth!"

Great streaks of light burst forth from the spear, the cloak and the scroll. The piercing rays of light shot through the dark cloud before them. Suddenly the great storm burst into a furious tirade and pushed toward the small ship to destroy it. Just as it did, an explosion of light filled the air. More rays of light exploded from the artifacts, piercing the dark cloud like great swords cutting through the darkness. Jean turned and yelled to Johnny. "Darkness cannot exist in the presence of God's Light!"

At these words a deafening sound of thunder shook everything as the great storm cloud burst into a million whirlwinds and quickly disappeared. Rays of light burst forth through the leftover clouds, then a blinding light exploded upon everything. As it did, a great pulsating hum vibrated through everything in the bayou and the time lock. Then in a great flash of light, the *Hotspir* disappeared.

Johnny awoke on the deck of the ship, his head was pounding. As he gradually came to his senses, he remembered the encounter. He jumped to his feet and looked around. Everyone on board lay stricken on the decks of the *Hotspir*. The boat rested in the still waters of the pier at Golden city. Behind him Johnny heard someone stir. Little Matie lay by her mother's side. Johnny's eyes filled with tears as he stared at his sister. She was a perfect little girl again. Johnny looked for Bo and Riley. They too, were normal. He looked over at Jean. The great black cat that had once been this powerful pirate was now a tall, dark-haired man. There next to him, lying on the deck was Dominique Youx. The curse that had once given him and his men a second chance at life had now been compelled to relinquish its hold on the water men. All over the ship they were waking up. Though soaking wet, they were all normal again.

"It worked!" Johnny exclaimed. He ran to his little sister and hugged her. Then he noticed a beautiful woman standing next to Pierre. She wore a brightly colored ball gown and had three small children by her side. It was Miss Honey. As Johnny smiled at her, she curtseyed to him and her children did the same. "Tag, you're it," one child said before darting across the deck.

Jim neared Johnny's side and pointed to the front of the boat. Jean, Pierre and Dominique had moved to the bow. There in front of them was a tall bearded man with a woman by his side. These two individuals were different than everyone else on board. They could be seen clearly, but were made of pure energy. Jean, Pierre and Dominique were weeping as they spoke to Captain Edwards and Catherine Laffite. As Johnny approached, he heard Catherine say, "We love you. We will see you soon." Then they disappeared.

The commotion on board grew, but it was nothing like what was going on in Golden city. Everywhere the good Maroos had been changed back into their former selves. The odd thing was the bad ones hadn't changed. Revolutionaries ran toward the ship. "The curse is ended!" they yelled. "But only for the Defiance. Clayton and the Overseers remain cursed!"

Johnny looked at the B.S.F. prisoners tied up on the deck of the ship. Their leader had received the full brunt of the curse, and had been turned into a skunk. His good men, however, had been freed from their ropes and sat in awe over what they had just witnessed.

Matie ran to Johnny and gave him a big hug. "You did it! You promised you would make us better and you did."

Soon all of his friends and family gathered around to thank him.

Johnny looked at the deck as his eyes filled with tears. "We all did it," he whispered. "But the true power came from the artifacts. They had God's power in them! It was His mercy that really fixed the curse!"

Riley turned to Jean. "What about Napoleon's treasure? What if Clayton does have it?"

Jean smiled. "We will make sure that does not happen."

"What are you going to do?" asked Johnny.

"We will form a new Alliance right here in the bayou and lead the revolutionaries to victory until all of the bayou is free forever. I have an idea where Napoleon's treasure might be, and now that we have conquered the curse, I think we can find it!"

"Can we help, too?" Matie asked enthusiastically.

Jim smiled and looked at Kate.

"Oh, no, you don't!" Kate said. "I'll not be having any of my children becoming pirates. You kids are going right back to Maison Rouge so you can go to school.

Matie scrunched up her nose as Pierre's three children ran past and tagged her shoulder. "Tag, you're it!" one yelled, with Riley in hot pursuit.

Bo put his arm around Johnny's shoulder. "Don't worry. School's not so bad. Me and Jack will show ya the ropes. B'sides there's some really cute girls I wanna introduce ya to!"

Laurabeth slugged Bo's shoulder. "Like you would know! Why do ya think Bo had ta bring me ta the ball. He couldn't get a date!"

Johnny laughed. "Well, I guess it's everything back to normal now."

"Not quite!" said Randy. "Palmer and I have decided to stay on with Pierre if it's all right with him."

Pierre nodded with a broad grin. "Sandy backbones are no problem. And we will need your skills as lawyers. You are almost as good at pirating as we are!" he laughed.

Hundreds of people now approached from the docks, cheering and crying. Then they began to sing one of Whistling Pete's songs.

These transformed Maroos were now freed from the devastating grip of the curse. But only those who had fought in the cause for freedom and had faced their inner weakness had been blessed to receive their proper form. For those who had fought to keep the curse alive, the curse remained, and they received exactly what they desired.

The light of God's mercy and love now filled the entire bayou with the hope and promise in every heart of a new life, of liberation, and freedom for all. The promise of the original Alliance had finally been fulfilled, and the clutches of the curse had given rise to the dawning of new hope within the bayou.

Johnny reached down to pick up his backpack. The sacred relics tucked within its folds. Johnny swung the bag over his shoulder as the driftwood piece fell to the ship's deck. Johnny reached to pick it up when he noticed it had cracked open. "Not again," he thought, "I've broken it." Picking up the delicate pieces he realized it was a carefully crafted wooden puzzle. In his hands the pieces fell apart, revealing two sheets of parchment inside. Slowly the others gathered around as he began to read the first letter.

Monsieur Sauvinet,

The Blue Bloods have killed my dear frère. He alone knew the secret I hold. His last dying wish was that I should conceal his letters in the place you agreed upon within the Golden Bayou. For my oath's sake, I will do so, yet I must remain hidden in silence lest I bring greater sorrow to the bayou and this people.

May the Light of God's influence guide you to what you seek.

J.L.

576

Johnny handed the letter to Jean. "Did you write this?"

Jean looked perplexed. "I have never seen these letters. Captain Edwards must have hidden them here right before he was killed."

Johnny picked up the second letter and began to read:

Dear Captain Edwards,

Concerning the <u>Vigenere'</u> matter before us,

I have concealed your secrets within the "<u>Golden Bayou</u>."

I am greatly concerned since the Friars letters of instruction have not yet arrieved. It is urgent that you give me further instructions.

Your brother in the Alliance,

B. Sauvinet

Jim looked at Jean. "What are the letters they're speaking of?"

"I do not know," replied Jean. "But I think that Savinet could give us some answers."

"What does "vigenere" mean?" Matie asked.

"I don't know." said Johnny. "Why don't you look it up on the Internet when we get home?"

9006876R0

Made in the USA
Charleston, SC
02 August 2011